D0297450

Felaheen

The Third Arabesk

Other books by Jon Courtenay Grimwood

neoAddix

Lucifer's Dragon

reMix

redRobe

Pashazade
The First Arabesk

Effendi
The Second Arabesk

Felaheen

The Third Arabesk

Jon Courtenay Grimwood

EARTHLIGHT

LONDON • SYDNEY • NEW YORK • TOKYO • SINGAPORE • TORONTO

www.earthlight.co.uk

First published in Great Britain by Earthlight, 2003
An imprint of Simon & Schuster UK Ltd
A Viacom Company

Copyright © Jon Courtenay Grimwood, 2003

This book is copyright under the Berne Convention
No reproduction without permission
® and © 1997 Simon & Schuster Inc. All rights reserved
Earthlight & Design is a registered trademark of Simon & Schuster Inc

The right of Jon Courtenay Grimwood to be identified as
author of this work has been asserted by him in accordance with
sections 77 and 78 of the Copyright, Designs and Patents Act, 1988.

1 3 5 7 9 10 8 6 4 2

Simon & Schuster UK Ltd
Africa House
64–78 Kingsway
London WC2B 6AH

Simon & Schuster Australia
Sydney

A CIP catalogue record for this book is available from the British Library

ISBN 0–7434–6117–7

This book is a work of fiction. Names, characters, places
and incidents are either a product of the author's imagination
or are used fictitiously. Any resemblance to actual people
living or dead, events or locales is entirely coincidental.

Typeset by Palimpsest Book Production Limited,
Polmont, Stirlingshire
Printed and bound in Great Britain by
The Bath Press, Bath

For Jamie CG, Sam B and for my father, who has lived many of the things I only write about. I owe you all, as ever . . .

'Since the prince needs to play the animal he chooses among the beasts the fox and the lion, because the lion cannot protect itself from snares and the fox cannot protect itself from wolves. Therefore the prince must be a fox to recognize traps and a lion to frighten the wolves.'

Machiavelli

'If a lion could speak, we could not understand him . . .'

Ludwig Wittgenstein

'Unlike foxes.'

Tiri

Part One

Prologue

Monday 14th March

'Dig,' said the fox.

So Ashraf Bey dug. Fingers bleeding and grit compacted beneath his broken nails. With only their sticky rawness to persuade him that he was still in the world of the living.

'Dig harder.'

So he did that too. Handful after handful of coarse salt tumbling into his face, blinding his eyes and filling his mouth, half open to drag oxygen from dead, fetid air. The voice in his head had promised to help Raf reach the surface but only if he obeyed every order without argument. Foxes were good at digging their way out of traps apparently.

Raf's biggest problem before he got buried alive was that no one had told him how far his authority went as the new Chief of Police for Tunis, so he'd decided to assume it went as far as he wanted; which was how he'd ended up . . .

'Like this, really.'

Raf wasn't too worried about talking to an animal that didn't exist. For a start he had a number of hallucinogens infecting his bloodstream, from an acid/ketamine mix to a particularly virulent grade of skunk. And besides he knew Tiri was just an illusion.

They'd been through this. It was sorted out.

According to Tiri a thousand camels once fell through the crust of Ifriqiya's great salt lake, lashed to each other in a baggage train. With the beasts went their cargo of dates, the master of the caravanserai and those who led the animals. Only one man survived, a slave who was driven into the desert for lying. His untrustworthy testimony had been that nothing existed below the ground over which they'd walked but void. What he'd thought was endlessly real was no more solid than the skin of a drum or the shell of an egg sucked dry by a snake.

'So you see,' said the fox, 'Things are . . .'

'. . . Never what they seem.' Raf punched one fist through earth to reach air. 'So you keep telling me.'

Later, when he had dry vomited fear from his belly, wiped dirt and tears from his face and come to terms with the fact that a surprisingly small hole in the ground near his feet represented victory over death, Ashraf Bey came to a deeper realisation.

He stank.

There was no doubt about it. Rancid sweat and the smell of excrement rose like heat from his body. And with it came the stink of the grave. A sour lingering foulness that varnished his nakedness, clogging the inside of his nostrils and infesting even the shafts of his blond hair.

Maybe it was this smell that drew the ghosts or perhaps the drugs in his blood cleared Raf's eyes to let him glimpse inside the egg. Whatever, when he set out across Chott el Jerrid the ghosts went with him. Strangers who looked vaguely familiar. Some man he'd seen in a queue. A Chinese boy, both too vague and strange to coalesce. Lady Jalila he recognised. Elegant in her sand-coloured silk jacket stretched across ample breasts. Eyes made up, lips perfect, neck broken . . . She started to say something, then went, her words and ghost ripped apart in a gust of night wind.

Then the fat man came.

Which was, Raf realised, probably inevitable. Of all the people he'd killed it was Felix Abrinsky who mattered the most.

'You okay, blondie?'

Raf put one step doggedly in front of the other. Shaded his eyes from the sight and tried to pretend he wasn't crying. 'What do you think?' he said.

'You know how it goes,' said Felix. 'These days I don't have much of a brain for thinking.' And with that he limped away, dragging the foot which had been shattered half a year before, along with most of his skull, in a bomb blast meant for the man he'd just been walking beside.

Chapter One

Tuesday 1st February

'Out of my way.' Major Jalal jabbed his elbow into the kidney of one photographer and shouldered another into the gutter, watching as frozen slush filled the man's scruffy shoes. Ten paces at most separated the limo from the door of the casino but five photographers barred the way. Well, three now.

'Chill,' his boss said with a broad smile. The major wasn't sure if that was an order or if His Excellency was commenting on New York's weather. So Jalal kept his reply to a nod, which covered both bases.

'*Prince . . .*'

'*Over here . . .*'

His Excellency Kashif Pasha was used to catcalls and noise from *nasrani* paparazzi, who whistled at him like he was someone's dog. It was the only thing he hated about coming to New York.

'*Look this way.*'

Kashif Pasha made the mistake of doing just that and found himself staring into the smirking face of Charlie Vanhie, a WASP reporter he'd had the misfortune to meet at least three times before.

'Tell us about your plan to throw a dinner to celebrate your parents' fiftieth wedding anniversary . . .'

Having made the mistake of looking at Charlie Vanhie the pasha then compounded his error by actually speaking to the man. 'Forty-fifth,' he corrected, 'it will be their forty-fifth.'

'What makes you think the Emir will turn up?'

Kashif Pasha stared at the man.

'Given that he won't even be in the same room as your mother. What was it he called her . . . ?'

Major Jalal began to move towards the speaker but His Excellency held up one hand. 'Leave it,' he told the major. 'Let me handle this.'

Around the time Kashif Pasha stood on a snow-covered sidewalk in Manhattan, bathed in the light of a flashgun, a small girl sat at a cheap plastic laptop. She was preparing to answer a long list of EQ questions, most of them multiple choice.

Draped around the girl's neck was a grey kitten worn like a collar. Actually, Ifritah was almost six months old but she still behaved like a kitten so that was how the girl thought of her.

Lady Hana al-Mansur, wrote the girl in a box marked name. Then she deleted it and typed *Hani* instead. There was also a box for her age but this was more problematic since no one was quite sure. She chose *10*, because either she was about to become ten, or she was ten already, in which case she'd be eleven in less than a week.

In the box marked nationality Hani wrote *Ottoman* and when the software rejected this she wrote it again. So then the computer offered her a long list of alternatives which she rejected, finally compromising on *Other*.

The room where Hani sat was in a house five thousand five hundred and seven miles from New York. In El Iskandryia. A city on the left-hand edge of the Nile Delta. Right at the top where the delta jutted out into the Mediterranean.

The madersa looked in on itself in that way many North African houses do. It was old and near decrepit in places. With a grand entrance onto Rue Sherrif at the front and an unmarked door that led out to an alley at the rear.

Guarding this door was a porter named Khartoum, because the city of Khartoum was where he came from and he'd refused to reveal any other. He smoked cigars backwards, with the lit end inside his mouth and had given Hani a tiny silver hand on a thread of cotton to help her do well in the tests.

This impressed Hani greatly and it went, almost without

saying, that Hani would rather have had Khartoum with her than the cat but her uncle, the bey, had forbidden it. Not crossly. Just firmly. Because the box containing the test stated that all computers were to be off-line and no other people were to be in the room when the test was taken.

First off was an easy question about being caught in a plane crash. With her plane going down would she: 1) scribble her will on the back of an envelope; 2) offer her help to the pilot; 3) continue to read a magazine?

The answer was obviously continue to read since, a) she'd never learned to fly and so offering help was pointless and, b) she was unlikely to be carrying an envelope, had she had anything to leave anybody which she didn't . . .

Next question was about her *father/step-father/legal other*. Since Hani had never met the first, lacked the second and was uncertain if her Uncle Ashraf counted as the third she ignored it, as she did two more questions about her family.

Then there was a section on *school friends* which Hani didn't even bother to read. The final bit was the simplest . . . Five hundred faces on a flat screen, each expressing anger or joy, happiness, boredom, sadness or pain.

Her job was to name that emotion. The section started at a crawl and for the first twenty or so faces Hani thought this was as fast as the software could go, but as impatience set in and Hani started hammering at the keys, her screen became a blur and soon the small girl was selecting answers so fast her computer had all its fans running.

She got every expression right except for five bench-mark indicators where the picture was of her. Even so, according to the EQ software, Hani's was the highest score ever recorded for that section, certainly within the time.

The IQ test which followed was infinitely more difficult. So difficult in fact that Hani ran out of time on her very first question. Which was the odd animal out − a sheep, a hen, a dog or a shark? Above each choice was the small photograph, just in case she'd forgotten what the animals looked like.

As answers went, the shark seemed much too obvious.

Especially given this was an intelligence test and identifying the first three as air breathing and the shark as a cartilaginous water dweller took no intelligence at all.

So what else could it be? Sheep were actually domesticated goats. At least Hani was pretty sure they were. Hens had also been domesticated, as had dogs, which were really domesticated wolves. So the answer could be shark but for a less obvious reasons, because humanity had no history of domesticating sharks.

But what if that was still too obvious?

In the end she chose the sheep over the hen, dog and shark because it was a herbivore and all the others ate meat. Although, in the case of the hen, Hani suspected that the bird was actually omnivorous. This seemed the mostly likely of the nineteen possible answers she jotted onto a piece of scrap paper.

'So what went wrong?' her uncle asked later, when he finally tracked Hani down to the madersa's roof where the girl sat oblivious to a cold glowering sky.

'With what?'

'Your second test. You only did one question and even then . . .' His voice trailed away.

'It wasn't the sheep?'

The thin man with the shades, goatee beard and drop-pearl earring shook his head.

'Which one was it?' Hani demanded.

'The shark.'

'Because it's not domesticated?'

Ashraf al-Mansur, known also as Ashraf Bey put his face in his hands and for a moment looked almost ill. He had a niece half the city thought was retarded. A mistress who wasn't his mistress because they'd never actually fucked. And his own life . . . Raf stopped, considering that point.

He'd recently resigned his job, the madersa cost more to run than he had coming in and yet, between them, Hani and Zara were worth millions. He was being chased for debts while living in a house with two of North Africa's wealthiest people, either of whom would give him the money, if only he'd stop refusing to consider it. As Zara said, getting that to make sense was like trying to fasten jeans with a zip one side and buttonholes the other.

Hani sat her test again next morning. This time on the flat roof of the al-Mansur madersa. And she did exactly what her uncle suggested, which was give the most obvious answer to everything. It took her less than fifteen minutes to achieve a score higher than the software could handle.

Chapter Two

Tuesday 1st February

Everything about Manhattan was white, from the sidewalk beneath Major Jalal's boots to the static in his Sony earbead which told the major his boss was off-line again. White streets, white cars, white noise – one way or another snow was responsible for the lot. Well, maybe not the white noise.

Five hours earlier, the wind chill along Fifth Avenue had been enough to make grown men cry but now the wind was gone, snow fluttered down between the Knox building and Lane Bryant like feathers from a ruptured pillow and the avenue ahead of him was as empty as the major's crocodile-skin wallet.

While his boss sat snug in Casino 30/54 losing sums of money the major could barely imagine, Major Jalal had been down to Mount Olive trying to bribe his way into the private room of Charlie Vanhie, the Boston photographer currently being wired for a broken jaw.

The contents of his wallet had gone to the pocket of a porter who took the lot and never came back. And then, when the major gave up in disgust, six sour-faced paparazzi appeared out of nowhere to grab frantic shots of him leaving the hospital, in the mistaken belief that the quietly-dressed, moustachioed *aide-de-camp* was his Armani-clad, elegantly bearded boss. The major just hoped His Excellency was having a better night of it.

Unfortunately, Kashif Pasha wasn't.

Although the casino was in New York and His Excellency came from Ifriqiya, the roulette wheel at which he played originated in Paris. This ensured it had only one non-paying number rather than the zero *and* double zero found on US tables. It was French because Kashif Pasha placed bets so high he could dictate the choice of wheel, thus limiting the edge allowed to the house. But for all this Kashif Pasha was still losing. A situation drearily familiar to his aged mother, the Lady Maryam, his father and his bankers.

'Excellency . . .'

Looking up, Kashif Pasha was in time to see an apologetic croupier lean forward and rake ten scarlet chips from the grid. So busy had he been listening to the dying clatter of the ivory ball that he'd forgotten to check on which number it landed. To Kashif's ear that unmistakable, addictive clicking was pitched somewhere between an old-man's death rattle and the tapping of an infestation of wood beetle.

Both of which reminded him of home.

'You there.' Kashif Pasha tried to snap his fingers and winced, making do with a quick wave of his injured hand. The effect was identical. A young black woman in a short deerskin skirt hurried forward, a box of cigars open on her silver tray. Her legs were bare, her breasts laced into a tan waistcoat that otherwise gaped down the front. A badge shaped like a feather announced her as Michelle.

'Sir . . .' The waitress waited for the well-dressed foreigner to select a Monte Cristo and take the matches she offered. Something Kashif Pasha did without appearing to notice the bitten nails of his own hands which spoke of long nights and too little sleep.

Embossed on the matchbox was a tomahawk. The casino's designer had no idea if Mohawk Indians actually fought with hand axes or, indeed, if any Native Americans had ever used such weapons, but tomahawk sounded like Mohawk and 30 West 54th Street was Mohawk land.

Before it became such, the land on which Casino 30/54 sat belonged to Clack Associates, owners of a small hotel much loved by rich European tourists. Augustus Clack III sold the hotel for an undisclosed sum to the billionaire financier Benjamin Agadir who promptly swapped it with the Mohawks for seven glass necklaces and a blanket. Since federal regulations specifically allowed casinos to be opened on reservations or any Indian land held in trust, this neatly circumvented state law which banned the establishment of casinos in New York City.

'*Faites vos jeux,*' announced the croupier, as if inviting a whole table of high rollers to place their bets rather than just the one.

Kashif Pasha ignored the man.

Striking a match, the eldest son and current heir to the Emir of Tunis lifted the match to the tip of his cigar and sucked. His mother disapproved of smoking, gambling, whores and alcohol but since cigars were not expressly mentioned in the Holy Qur'an, she sometimes kept her peace. Besides Kashif Pasha was in New York City and she was not.

Quite what Lady Maryam would have made of the striking murals in the gentlemen's lavatory it was best not to imagine. Kashif Pasha's favourite by far featured Pochahontas undergoing what Americans called double entry. For what were undoubtedly good cultural reasons, her lovers both sported tails, the back legs of a goat and small horns.

At home there were no paintings in Lady Maryam's wing of the Bardo and no statues. Even his great-grandfather's famous *neue sachlichkeit* collection of oils had been banished, saved only by the Emir's flat refusal to have them destroyed.

Representative art was abhorrent to his mother for usurping the rights of God. But then this was a woman who found even calligraphy suspect. Which undoubtedly went some way to explaining why she'd burnt the present his father sent her at Kashif's birth. (An Osmanli miniature from the sixteenth century showing the Prophet's wet nurse Hamina breastfeeding.) And this, in turn, maybe helped explain why Emir Moncef had refused to see his wife since.

Kashif Pasha smiled darkly, his favourite expression, and pushed five ivory chips onto the number thirteen.

'*Rien ne va plus,*' announced the croupier, as if he hadn't been waiting. No more bets were to be made. There was a ritual to go through, even though the room was almost empty and the roulette table reserved for Kashif Pasha. The wheel spun one way and the ivory ball was sent tumbling another and when a number other than thirteen came up, Kashif Pasha just shrugged, carelessly he hoped.

Over the course of the next hour the rampart of counters in front of him became a single turret, then little more than ruined foundations and finally almost disappeared, leaving Kashif Pasha with only six ivory chips.

The casino would keep the table open for him while Kashif Pasha ordered more counters, that much was given. High rollers like His Excellency got what they wanted. Their own suites, complimentary meals, limousines to and from the airport. Even use of the casino's own plane if necessary. And what he wanted now was a break.

'Okay,' said Kashif Pasha. 'I'll be back here at . . .' He glanced at his Rolex and added two hours to the time it was. 'At seven,' he said, 'Have the table reset. New wheel, new ball, new grid, new stack of counters.' Which was what his croupier seemed to call those $100,000 red chips.

Sliding his six remaining counters across the table, His Excellency smiled. 'For you,' he said and watched the croupier blink. It was a good tip, more so since Kashif Pasha was sometimes known not to tip at all. The croupier would give half to the house, but that still left more than he earned in six months.

'Thank you, Excellency,' said the man, moving aside to make room for a crop-haired woman who'd been watching the game from a discreet distance.

'Your Highness.' This was a title Kashif Pasha didn't warrant but Georgian van Broglie used it anyway. So far she'd acted as facilitator on every visit Kashif Pasha made to Casino 30/54 and he had yet to complain about the social upgrade. 'Shall I have the kitchen organise some supper?'

She took his silence as assent.

'Chicken breast,' she suggested, 'on focaccia, with honey and mustard sauce. A litre of Evian and maybe some more ginger ale?' She nodded to a line of small and empty bottles of Canada Dry, the plastic screw-top kind.

Kashif Pasha's usual order. A glorified chicken sandwich washed down with three plastic flasks of champagne. Quite why a forty-four-year-old North African playboy would want to drink Veuve Cliquot from an empty Canada Dry bottle Georgian van Broglie didn't know, but then she'd never met Lady Maryam.

'Does Your Highness require anything else?'

She saw the man glance across the room to the deer-skinned waitress who'd brought him his cigar. 'No possible,' she muttered apologetically. 'House rules. I'd love to make an exception but . . .'

Kashif Pasha sighed, 'Send up something similar,' he said crossly. 'After you've found me the house doctor.' He checked his knuckles, which were looking more lop-sided than ever. 'And get room service to bring me a bucket of ice.'

Chapter Three

Wednesday 2nd February

'Nicolai . . .' Emir Moncef's call was for his bodyguard. A small and intense Uzbek whose name was probably something completely different. The Uzbek and a Tajik called Alex took it turns to protect the Emir. They were a recent birthday present from the Soviet ambassador. One Moncef had not known how to refuse.

He called again. Just in case either guard was within hearing and then turned his attention back to the snake. Death was always going to come. That it chose to manifest as a slithering viper was unexpected but not impossible. Although, if the elderly Emir had been forced to bet (a vice he deplored), he'd have selected a fat-tailed scorpion as being more likely.

Scorpions got carried into camp on the flatbeds of trucks or in date baskets. Once, if he remembered correctly, a fat-tail had hitched a lift in the turn-ups of an NCO's dress trousers. The man had succumbed within hours and the Emir had banned turn-ups on all uniform from then on.

He would die as he had lived his last forty years, in the simplicity of Ifriqiya's southern desert. A place where privation reduced leaves to water-protecting spikes and insects hid within thickly-waxed bodies to conserve what little water they contained; where beetles survived on one meal in two years, if the habitat so demanded and glass wort displayed a near-suicidal tolerance for salt.

Tossing back his a'aban, a heavy cloak still worn by Berber men of a certain age, Emir Moncef raised a silver-topped stick. Ready to defend himself.

'Get behind me . . .' His order was aimed at a boy in camouflage who still gripped a Nintendo games pad with frozen
fingers.

The Emir's younger son shook his head.

'Murad.'

That the Emir used his real name scared the boy almost as
much as the viper now crawling its way across a carpet. Mostly
his father called him SP, which stood for *small pasha*, a name
he'd been given by his mother before she was killed. His mother
had been one of the Emir's guard, an American convert from Los
Angeles.

Her Jeep had gone off the side of a cliff. An accident.

'Do as I say.'

Looking from his father to the horned viper, the twelve-
year-old again shook his head. Snakes were rare in the camp,
dangerous or otherwise, because intricate webs of woven copper wire lay buried beneath the perimeter. The webs created
an electric field that upset snakes, scorpions and spiders. That
was what Eugenie de la Croix said anyway. And it was her job
to know these things.

'Don't be afraid. Just back away.'

Afraid? Several options presented themselves to Murad and
none involved fear or retreat. His duty was to defend his father,
His Highness Moncef al-Mansur, better known as the Emir of
Tunis and ruler of Ifriqiya (father of his people, loved by all).
This Murad knew from reading it each morning in the cheap,
Arab-language red tops the Emir insisted on having delivered
by helicopter.

Kashif Pasha punches American paparazzi . . .

Today's *Es Sabah* lay on a leather and oak table, one so
ancient its iron nails had gone dark as the wood and quite
as shiny. Under the paper rested a photograph album almost
as old. No one was allowed to look inside. Which was why
Murad had never been able to ask why it contained postcard
after postcard of bare-breasted women ranging from girls his
own age to those as old as his mother would have been.

Berber said some, others *Taurag*. Most were simply described as *Mauresque*, sometimes *Belle Mauresque*, occasionally *Jeune Femme Arabe* . . . Once as *Tuenisch-orientalische Typen*. Almost all stared flat-eyed at the camera. As if trying to withdraw from a world where colonial officers scribbled, '*c'est trés intéressant*' across the back, stuck a five centimes stamp over the breast of a twelve-year-old and posted it to a cousin in Marseilles.

'*Murad.*'

Outside, speakers blared *male habtl madjatch*, a rai track even older than his father whose favourite song it was. The rhythms and repetitions, drum and weird whistle as familiar to the boy as any *adhan*, the call to prayer, though Murad would never admit as much and even thinking so worried him.

So be it. His choice was made. As God wills.

Murad added *inshá allá* without even noticing. The way his mother used to say *bless you* every time he sneezed.

He was twelve, after all. Old enough for what came next.

Fires had been lit for the midday meal and someone nearby was roasting goat over branches ripped from a thorn bush, both wood and goat having been brought in by truck. There was no kindling this far south. He would miss the meal and the camp and his father . . .

Their previous camp had been better, more to do and less sand. The goat-hair tents carried on camels only when photographers were around. The rest of the time a pony-tailed Texan called Pigpen bundled the tents into trucks and broke them down and set them up wherever the Emir wanted.

Few outsiders understood why the Emir allowed a *nasrani* such freedom. Those who did had seen the speed at which the Texan could break down a camp when the old man wanted it done really fast.

'*Pull yourself together* . . .' The Emir was cross now.

'I'm not frightened,' Murad shot back with all the indignation he could muster. 'I'm planning.' His father was always telling him to think ahead.

Dropping his Nintendo, Murad reached for a silver coffee jug and flipped back its lid. The jug was inlaid with copper and bronze. Even its ivory handle was hot. Out of the corner of his eye he saw the Emir shake his head but it was too late, Murad had already hurled coffee into the face of the horned viper.

Most of it missed.

'Guards.'

Ignoring the old man's demand and the sudden hammering of fear in his own ears, Murad threw the silver pot after the coffee, just managing to hit the viper's tail. So much for his first plan.

On a side wall of the tent hung the sword his great-grandfather took from a dying colonel after a skirmish outside Neffatia, the year the French were driven from Tunisia, as Ifriqiya was then called.

The boy was lunging for this when Emir Moncef stepped forward, grabbed Murad by the shoulder and threw him towards the entrance with more force than the old man knew he possessed. He understood when a viper was about to attack, even if his youngest son didn't.

'Alex, Nicolai . . .'

Part of the Emir still hoped that fate might allow him to step back from danger; because courage was one thing and stupidity another and to grow old in this world one needed to be able to tell the difference. But the viper was ready to strike. Something the old man realised, he suspected, even before the reptilian, pea-sized brain that was his death's whole being.

Moncef al-Mansur looked death in the eyes, heard its hiss and felt time slow as the viper froze on the edge of movement.

The Emir was too old and too exhausted by his argument with Murad to be able to avoid a strike completely, so he made do with twisting matador-style in the hope that the bite might be less than total. In this alone he was lucky. One fang buried itself deep into his calf, the other tore the cloth of a robe that time and washing had reduced to the consistency of rotten sack.

'Papa . . .'

The last thing Emir Moncef heard before he fell to the floor and found himself face to face with the carpet was his son begin to scream. A noise loud enough to drown out the music of Cheb

Khaled and the running feet of his absent guards. The last of which, had the Emir been able to hear it, would merely have confirmed his opinion that panic and fury had no place in a well-run camp.

Chapter Four

Wednesday 2nd February

Kashif al-Mansur liked snow and always had done. Mostly he liked it in cities such as New York, where flakes fluttered down between canyons to bury the sidewalks and cars. Everything turning white and picture postcard.

At home when snow fell, which was not often, white sprinkled the mountains of the High Tell and oak valleys towards the northern coast, dusting the red roofs of farmhouses built and later deserted by French settlers. He'd been impressed by that as a child, until he discovered what winter really looked like.

The snow Kashif Pasha really liked, however, fell on carefully-selected ski resorts. St Mortiz in Switzerland, Geilo in Norway, America's own Aspen. Playgrounds that featured mountain lodges, black runs and a large, interchangeable and ever-fluid collection of people who wanted to be his friend.

Thickset industrialists with salt and pepper hair, fake tans and astute eyes readily offered him use of their chalets, snowcats and daughters. Not to mention unsecured loans and bribes disguised as business opportunities.

His father might be a pariah but Kashif Pasha was a different proposition, loved by those who hated every value for which Emir Moncef stood. And Kashif worked hard on his reputation. His loans were always repaid and he was politeness itself to the Western girls who, drunk or drugged, fell against him in the ritzy bars as if champagne or charlie had taken away their balance.

From time to time, there would be a flash that lit the darkness of some bar and another photograph would appear, apparently showing him snuggled up with the daughter of a German industrialist or American banker.

The inevitable result of this was a letter from his mother. Handwritten, sealed with wax and sent through diplomatic channels. Lady Maryam's lament was always the same. At her age and in her state of health, how could he . . . The woman, needless to say, had the nerves of a trained killer and the physical constitution of a battle-hardened commando. Only her age was against her.

Kashif Pasha's replies were as ritual as his mother's complaints. The whey-faced teenager in the photograph was the daughter/niece/lover of some man he barely knew and had certainly never shared his bed. It was doubtful if Lady Maryam believed this, but then she knew far less about her son than she imagined.

His preferences had been formed early, one Saturday in early January while his mother was away, sometime between the calls to prayer at dawn and noon. That was when he'd first noticed Sophia, a barefoot Sudanese maid maybe two years older than him. He wasn't even aware of having seen her before until she came into his room to sweep up and found him still half-asleep in a *bateau lit*.

Her hurried apology got lost beneath his demand that she open his curtains, which were both long and heavy. And the reason Kashif's bedroom had red velvet curtains rather than shutters was that he'd just been moved into a new suite of rooms, one fitted out in the English style. So he would not disgrace himself by exhibiting unfamiliarity on arrival at his new school outside London, a city chosen largely because his father had wanted Paris.

'Open them all,' Kashif's twelve-year-old self had demanded. 'That's an order.'

With reluctance, the girl (whose name Kashif was only to ask a week later) left the safety of her doorway and yanked back the nearest curtain, though it was embarrassment not anger that made her movements so abrupt.

'And the next window and the one after that.'

Sophia went along the wall as instructed, pulling back curtains originally sewn by the venerable Paris textile house of Nobilis Fontan until Kashif had an uninterrupted view of a courtyard outside. One so large that a regiment could have assembled there.

'Excellency . . .' Sophia's curtsy was made clumsy by her dash for the door.

'All the curtains,' Kashif demanded, nodding to the only window that mattered, a small one set high in the wall over his head. To get there Sophia would have to step onto his *bateau lit* and reach up. Kashif watched her face darken as she realised that. She had keloid scars on her cheeks, the way Berber women in the south had tattoos beneath their eyes. Scars, a face far finer than his and huge doubtful eyes.

'That window too please,' Kashif was suddenly polite. As for the first time he understood that she might refuse. If that happened, Kashif wasn't sure he knew what to do.

'Excellency.' Sophia gave something that was half nod and half shrug, accepting the inevitable. Three steps took her to the bed and then, as Kashif watched from the corner of his eye she stepped up onto his mattress, revealing a dark flash of calf. For a moment she fought for her balance, then did what he'd only half believed she might, stepped clean over him and reached up, her fingers tugging the curtain.

He expected her to step down immediately and run from the room but she remained where she was, staring up as if at some vision. And although she wore no pants there was little for Kashif to see. A dark gash for her sex, a curve of bare buttock, more shadow than flesh. Heavy legs. An ankle showing some kind of insect bite.

He was still considering this when Sophia stepped down and gestured towards the bigger windows behind her. All of them revealing the same miracle. For the first time in Kashif's life and, for all he knew, the first time in history, fat flakes of snow had begun to fall on the city of Tunis.

Kashif Pasha smiled.

'Here you go,' he slipped a red chip into the hand of the girl who'd earlier brought him a cigar and dropped another two into the waiting fingers of the croupier. Tipping so much to Michelle was an extravagance and, from the hastily-controlled expression on the face of his facilitor Georgian van Broglie, not quite how 30/54 liked its patrons to behave.

Kashif Pasha's smile grew broader. Next time the cigar girl would come to his suite of her own accord, never realising she'd been bought, in advance, for far less than he would have paid.

'And this belongs to you . . .'

Georgian van Broglie prepared to bristle at the indignity of being tipped, something she'd stopped needing the moment she got put on a cut of the house percentage. And found herself instead holding a business card. The card was just that, a rectangle of thick paper made from wood pulp, its china-clay surface embossed with a small logo. Below the logo, which managed to combine a torque wreath with an old-fashioned propeller was the address of a private airport, one of Long Island's finest.

'Any time you're bored, feel free to call that number. One of my pilots will take you, plus family or friends, anywhere you want and bring you back again, when you want. Caracas, Bombay, Hong Kong . . .'

Her stunned expression was worth the gesture. Besides, Kashif gave good odds she'd never take up his offer. That card would remain in her wallet and get shown to friends, both social and business; while his jet would remain on the ground, fuel unused. So far no one had ever taken him up on a flight. Something about the very extravagance of his gesture prevented them.

Georgian van Broglie was still stuttering her thanks when someone knocked at the door. 'Excellency, I'm sorry . . .'

Outside, in the panelled expanse of lobby stood an officer from the NYPD and beside him, looking flustered, the casino's head of security, all cropped hair and diamond ear stud. Accompanying them was a small man with the smell of a lawyer.

'Kashif al-Mansur?'

No sooner had the uniformed officer spoken than the small man put up a hand. 'Not in here,' he said firmly and glanced at the head of security as if expecting the man to toss the officer onto the street. 'This casino is on tribal land. You know the rules.'

'What's the problem?' Kashif's voice was calm, with an easy familiarity that didn't reach his eyes.

'There's been a complaint . . .'

'Outside,' insisted the small man, managing to look apologetic and determined at the same time. The officer got the determination, Kashif got the apology.

'A photographer alleges . . .'

Before the small lawyer had even relaunched his protest Kashif Pasha was holding up a white booklet. He put it half an inch from the officer's face. 'Do you know what this is?'

The man shook his head. They both knew that was a lie.

'It's a *carte blanche*,' said Kashif Pasha, flicking to the first page. The photograph showed a man younger by four years, a little less worn, his cheeks less full; the beard was the same though. 'Total diplomatic immunity,' Kashif explained, though this was unnecessary. The words were written in several languages across the top of each page. 'You have a problem, take it up with the embassy.'

'The embassy is in Washington.'

'So take a plane. Or even better don't bother. I'm leaving New York in about . . .' Kashif Pasha checked his Rolex, which looked silver but was actually platinum. 'Thirty minutes. Everything I need to do here I've done.' Rubbing his fist absent-mindedly, Kashif rechecked the time and smiled past the NYPD officer at where snow kept falling onto 54th Street outside.

Chapter Five

Saturday 5th February

Once in a time when animals still talked and djin walked the earth quite openly, the Sultan of Bokhara sent for a mullah living in a distant village. His message was simple.

'Come at once. I need advice.' For the Sultan expected the arrival of an Indian ambassador and the Mullah was . . .

A rumble in her tummy made Hani suck her teeth in sudden irritation. Now someone was bound to offer her food.

'Hungry?' Ashraf Bey's question came from across the *qaa*, a reception room which occupied almost all of the first floor of the al-Mansur madersa. The mansion His Excellency shared with his young niece, his Portuguese cook, a Sufi porter and the woman Iskandryian gossip still assumed was his mistress, wrongly as it happened.

In summer the *qaa* was open to the elements along one side but now was winter and the arches overlooking the central courtyard were closed off with specially-cut sheets of glass. A small fountain played in the middle of the *qaa* floor, carved, five hundred years before, from a single block of horse-hair marble.

Silver balloons floated from this because today was Hani's tenth birthday. Although Khartoum who was friends with the cook but tended to disagree with her on almost everything as a matter of principle insisted it was Hani's eleventh. Largely, Hani suspected, because Donna insisted it wasn't.

And as no one could actually find a birth certificate for the child and Hani had been born elsewhere the question remained open. Lady Nafisa might have been able to provide an answer but Hani's aunt was dead. Something else for Hani to feel guilty about.

'Hungry?' Raf repeated.

'No,' said Hani. 'Not really.'

*The mullah's reply to the Sultan was equally simple. 'I am
unable to attend, O King, as I rely for life upon the sweet air
of Qasr al Arifin and have no way to bring this with me in
storage jars.'*

Hani paused, her small fingers hovering in mid air. A matrix
of fine wires across the back of her hands ended in finger
thimbles. Every time her hands flicked across the invisible
keys of her imaginary keyboard, words got added to a processing
package installed on her laptop one floor up in the *haremlek.*
Very clever but not madly practical because Hani relied on
seeing a screen to write.

All the same, it was kind of Hamzah Effendi to send her a
present. Hamzah Effendi was Zara's father and Zara was the
girl her Uncle Ashraf should have married, the one everyone
thought . . .

If only.

Hani kicked her heels against the legs of a silver chair and
sighed. Another four paragraphs and she'd let herself go down
to the kitchen to make coffee.

*At first the Sultan was perplexed by this answer. And then,
after consideration of the mullah's open disrespect, he determined to remonstrate with the man when they next met, famous
sage or not. At about this time the visit from the Indian
ambassador was cancelled and so the Sultan needed no advice
from anyone after all.*

*Many months later, as fig leaves began dropping and the
stars grew cold the Sultan sat down to supper and no sooner
had he picked up his goblet than an assassin leapt upon him.
Immediately, Mullah Bahaudin, having entered the dining
room at this exact moment, jumped upon the assassin and
wrestled him to the ground.*

*'O Mullah,' said the Sultan, 'It seems I am indebted to you
in spite of your earlier rudeness.'*

*Mullah Bahaudin smiled. 'O Sultan,' he said sweetly. 'The
courtesy of those who know is to be available when actually*

needed, not sit waiting for emissaries who will never arrive . . .'

Hani flicked her fingers over a non-existent trackball to shut down her laptop and pulled off her gloves. She would write the rest of Bahaudin's story, particularly the bit where the mullah met a miracle worker who could walk on water – but to get things right she really did need a screen.

'Okay,' Hani said, slipping down from her chair. 'I'm off to make some coffee.' She left her comment hang in the air, a fact that seemed to escape both Uncle Ashraf and Zara. 'Anyone like some?' Hani asked loudly.

'Donna can make it,' Raf replied.

It was the wrong answer.

'Just look at this,' said Donna, waving one heavy hand at her television, as she insisted on describing the kitchen newsfeed. 'Disgraceful. You could get twice the zest out of that.'

On screen a plump boy in a chef's hat was discarding half a lemon.

'Now he's adding *cream*,' Donna said with a disgusted shake of her head. '*Cream*.' The old woman loved watching the German channels for their sheer outrage.

When Hani said nothing Donna switched her attention from the recipe for *Schwetche Kutchen* to Hani's face and then jerked her head upwards, through the ceiling. 'Still arguing?'

The child nodded.

'About you?'

Hani looked at her. 'What do you think?' Everyone in the house knew what Hani thought. She refused to go to school in New York and she didn't want a tutor at home. Hani was beginning to wish she'd never taken those tests.

'Zara just wants to get rid of me,' Hani said. 'They both do.'

'That's not . . .' Donna sighed. 'Sit down,' she said in a voice that allowed for no argument.

Frying last season's almonds in a drizzle of olive oil and grating rock salt over the top, Donna tipped the result onto a single sheet of kitchen paper which she screwed into a ball to remove most of the oil. 'Eat,' she told Hani, when the tapas was ready.

Hani did what she was told. Sipping at a glass of red wine Donna had placed beside the plate of almonds.

'Now you listen to me,' said Donna. 'It's your birthday. You mustn't be upset on your birthday because it makes for bad luck. And this isn't really about you . . .'

'Yes it is.'

'No,' Donna said firmly. 'It's not . . .' She sighed and took her own gulp of Hani's wine. 'It's about something else. Something grown up. You know what I'd like to do with those two?'

'What?' asked Hani, suddenly interested.

'Ahh,' the elderly Portuguese woman shrugged in irritation. 'No matter. You're too young to know about these things . . .'

Although if Donna's solution was anything like that of the madersa's porter, then Hani had a pretty good idea already. Khartoum's suggestion involved bricking Uncle Ashraf and Zara into a room with a bed and not letting them out until they made sheets.

Hani wasn't sure where the bricks or sheets came into it, but she got the general point.

'You want more birthday cake?'

'Not really.' Hani shook her head. 'I came to get coffee.'

'Caffeine darkens the skin,' said Donna crossly. Her own face as brown as the inside membrane of a walnut and almost as crumpled.

'It's for His Excellency.'

The Portuguese woman looked doubtful.

'Papers,' Hani announced before she was even through the marble arch into the *qaa*. Zara and Uncle Ashraf would have had to be deaf not to hear Hani coming, she'd stamped so hard on her way up.

On Hani's tray were a collection of afternoon papers, three tiny mugs of mud-thick coffee and the plate of baklava Donna had insisted she take. Most of the papers blamed *Thiergarten* for the attack on Emir Moncef. Only one chose Washington over Berlin. And that one was more concerned with the miracle of the Emir's survival.

'The Enquirer,' she told her uncle, dropping it onto his table and using it as a mat for his coffee.

Pope To Make Boy Saint?

The Emir of Tunis had been saved from death by a child's power of prayer, the *Enquirer* was quite categoric about that. An unnamed source close to Emir Moncef had confirmed how, in the absence of serum the Emir's youngest son had prayed over the unconscious body of his father, refusing to leave Moncef's bedside until the Emir finally awoke.

Missing from the story was the obvious fact that Pope Leo VII was unlikely to beatify, never mind canonise, a minor Islamic princeling (even assuming the mufti in Stambul was willing). Also missing was the fact that, far from being a hero, Murad Pasha had found himself in deep disgrace. In fact the beating he received for not obeying an order from the Emir left the boy unable to sit for three days.

Raf skim-read the story, shifted his cup to reach the end and then tossed the lies to the floor, narrowly missing Ifritah, Hani's grey cat.

'Uncle Ashraf!'

'It was an accident,' Raf said firmly, and went back to work.

A fine-toothed comb, plus instructions on the correct way to lift potential evidence from pubic hair.

A miranda card, one side listing *inalienable rights*, the other *rules of plain view*.

Two dozen unused post-mortem fingerprint cards, both left and right.

Vacuum-packed latex gloves, eight pairs.

A booklet in Spanish on Vucetich's system of fingerprint classification, stamped *LAPD not to be removed*.

A fold-out chart of poisons, arranged by the time in which they begin to react. Starting with *ammonia*, reaction time zero, and ending with *stibine*, three days to three weeks . . .

One single sheet of 80gsm A4 paper of the kind used in police stations across North Africa. On it the translation of an Ottoman wedding certificate typed on a manual typewriter, which suggested a fear of leaving electronic footprints. The names had been filled in but the dates left blank.

Polaroids, two, of a young man standing by a Jeep.

A jewellery roll made from chamois leather that turned out to contain three scalpels and a collection of surgical steel blades.

A small .22 derringer, two shot, with an over/under configuration and mother-of-pearl grips, badly scratched. A handful of postcards . . .

Set out in front of Raf on an oval dining table, amid the debris of breakfast and the coffee Hani had just brought were fragments from two lives now gone. The polaroids, both faded, had arrived in that morning's post; everything else belonged to Felix Abrinsky, Chief of Detectives in El Iskandryia and briefly a friend.

Because it was a long time since Raf had been this upset the feeling was unfamiliar to him. And what he felt as a tightness in the back of his throat he took to be side-effects from dust thrown up by workmen in a garden beyond the courtyard outside.

Me having a good time, read a card. Flipping it over, Raf paused, eyes sweeping between two women in their early twenties, both bare breasted and joined by a silver chain between nipple rings.

One had a bottle of beer clasped against her button-flied groin in crude imitation of an erect penis and both looked as tired and hot as the old man in the tutu behind them, the one bending bare-arsed over an open grill.

'How very American.'

Raf looked up to find Zara stood by his shoulder. Hollow eyed, full breasted and infinitely fragile since the night a month back she'd come unasked to his room and been sent away. She was younger by three or four years than the women in the photograph and wore significantly more clothes.

'Trudi and Barbara,' Raf said, in answer to a question not asked.

'Friends of yours?' There was enough of an edge to Zara's question to make Hani look up, though all the child did was sigh and return to her chess computer. So far she'd won seventeen games straight. She reckoned Uncle Ashraf could be persuaded to let her buy a smarter model if she managed to get the total up to fifty.

'Felix's daughter and her partner . . . That one's Trudi,' Raf added, indicating the taller woman.

It had fallen to Raf to write to Trudi with news of her father's death. A job Raf took in an attempt to assuage his own guilt. No one had suggested prosecuting Raf over the shooting of Felix because by then he'd already been offered the fat man's job. And arresting El Iskandryia's new Chief of Detectives was widely recognised as being a bad career move.

Of course, that was over too. Raf had lasted about two months as Chief, rather longer than he intended. The gun and the badge had gone back, the only thing Raf kept was the fat man's silver Cadillac and that still sat in a parking slot under the police HQ at Champollion.

'She looks that good?'

Raf blinked, realised he was still staring at Felix's daughter and put the card down, face to the table, one item among many. 'I was thinking,' he said simply. 'About what happened.'

Zara opened her mouth and then changed her mind. She was running out of fingers to count the number of times she'd screwed up in the last six months by opening her mouth before thinking. And bizarre as it seemed, probably her worst mistake was not marrying the man she was so busy insulting.

Zara had no objection to arranged marriages. She just hadn't enjoyed being a piece in her mother's game of social advancement. Other recent screw-ups involved finding herself semi-naked in a local paper and appearing in court, supposedly defending her father.

Which one of the rest was actually the worst was a toss up between . . . Well, that changed. If forced to choose, she'd say her current number one, her all-time recent fuck up was moving in with Raf, though that wasn't how she'd put it to her father. It was the al-Mansur madersa she was moving into, at Hani's suggestion. Raf was just coincidental.

Only he'd never been coincidental, at least not since that evening back in the summer on a boat in the Aegean, when she'd let him slip the shirt from her shoulders and watched it fall. Months later she went to his bed twice in three days; where she did more than she intended and less than he wanted. That was how she'd put it to him later or maybe that was how he put it to her.

Zara found it too cruel to remember.

'You okay?'

'Why shouldn't I be?' Zara's voice sounded mean, even to her, and somewhere across the other side of the *qaa*, Hani sighed.

Raf and Zara sulking wasn't what Hani had in mind for her birthday, but it was still infinitely better than last year. That had fallen on a Friday which meant no presents. From the first call to prayer to the moment Donna put Hani to bed, her day had been spent in silence, sewing and reading. Aunt Nafisa had firm opinions on keeping Friday holy.

Now Lady Nafisa was dead and Hani had balloons, the *qaa*'s small fountain frothed with environmentally-safe pink bubbles and Donna had spent yesterday baking a huge chocolate . . .

'I'm going to get some cake,' said Hani, moving her queen. 'Who wants some?' She stared at her uncle and kept staring until he finally raised his head to look at her.

'Cake?'

Raf nodded.

'Excellent,' said Hani as she recorded another win. 'You can help me get it.' Leaving her computer to shuffle through an ancient algorithm that would return every piece to its rightful place, she pushed back her chair. 'Unless you're too busy . . . ?

'No,' he said. 'Not too busy.' Raf snapped shut the scrapbook he'd been examining as Hani reached his table. Most of the subjects were naked and all were dead, everyone of them showed a wound of some kind or another. Near the beginning some of the crime shots were old enough to be in black or white and towards the end a few used the new Kodak tri-D format which gave the wounds a disconcerting depth. Felix had annotated the lot, his handwriting hardly changing over the years.

'Not good,' said Hani.

Raf looked at her.

'Glue is much better than tape for sticking pictures. It does less damage.' Hani's smile was bright, only her dark eyes betraying her as they flicked from Raf to the album and then across the *qaa* to where Zara sat listlessly reading a novel.

Chapter Six

Monday 7th February

Monday morning brought cloud. Relative humidity stood at 71 per cent, projected to drop ten points by early afternoon. And there was, according to Raf's watch, near certainty that it would rain – hardly shocking news for February in El Iskandryia.

Longer-term predictions featured a severe depression beginning March. One that would, if the forecasts lived up to their current accuracy ratings, pull hot air from the Sahara and wrap parts of North Africa in a *khamsin* wind, but for now temperatures remained around 10°C and the sky was slate grey.

'*Wrong,*' said the voice inside Raf's head, '*it's molten lead.*'

He ignored this and concentrated on ripping apart his breakfast. Peeling back oily flakes to reveal sticky almond paste within.

The next voice came from the world outside.

'Excellency.' Le Trianon's very own maître d' scooped Raf's empty cup onto a silver tray and replaced it with a fresh cappuccino. 'Is something wrong with your croissant?'

'No, it's fine.'

Le Trianon was Iskandryia's most famous café. A statement both Pastroudis and Café Athinos would probably dispute. Occupying the corner site where Rue Missala met Place Sa'ag Zaghloul, with a terrace on Rue Missala and exits on both, Le Trianon offered an aquarium darkness of spotless linen and Napoleon III chairs. Discreet wooden screens managed to combine Art Deco with Moorish fantasia, while a series of Art Deco murals displayed pert breasted, half naked dancing girls in jewelled slippers and diaphanous trousers.

'*You love it really,*' said the fox, who hated Orientalist kitsch.

But then Tiri refused to buy into a rule that defined everything over a century as classic by default.

The table Raf used was on the terrace and he sat facing the street, because this allowed him to ignore a bank of elevators inside. There were three elevators, framed in brass, with Deco moulding and coloured enamel around their doors. Only directors of the Third Circle were allowed to use these, which was fine with Raf because, as the son of a pasha, he automatically qualified for a C3 corner office with magnificent views of Iskandryia's Eastern Harbour.

(Raf had his own opinion about his parentage but as no one else seemed bothered he was attempting to keep this to himself.)

Between the harbour wall and Raf's office stood Place Zaghloul, so Raf's windows also overlooked palm trees, a busy bus station and a stark plinth on which rested General Zaghloul Pasha, nationalist leader and the man who drove the British from Egypt in 1916.

As befitted his rank as a bey, Raf's office featured a Bokhara rug, a white leather sofa, a filing cabinet made from mahogany and edged with brass and a large, predominantly blue and pink Naghi of the square outside, painted in 1943 and borrowed from the Khedival institute in Al Qahirah. What the room lacked was a computer or telephone, files to put in the elegant cabinet and any documents of real importance.

No one expected directors to work, least of all Madame Nordstrom, who in her twenty-fourth year as office manager of C3 regarded all directorships as entirely token, much like the salary. So he spent his mornings in the café downstairs; which was an arrangement that satisfied both Ingrid Nordstrom and Le Trianon's maître d' but was beginning to irritate Raf, not because he disliked drinking cappuccino or reading the papers but because, every morning as Raf was shown to his table on the terrace, Tiri popped up to mutter *emotional institutionalisation*. It was a phrase with which they were both far too familiar.

Most of the visitors to the famous café drank espresso or

sticky, mud-thick shots of Turkish mocha; but then, what with it being February, everyone else ate their breakfast indoors.

Only Raf insisted on a pavement table.

For a while, a matter of weeks only, he'd had bodyguards to hold the tourists at bay and protect him from fundamentalists, crazies, German agents of the *Thiergarten* and anyone else who might be likely to attack the Governor of El Iskandryia; but that was before he resigned, when he had a different job.

'*Wrong,*' said the fox. '*That was when you had a job. Working at the Third Circle doesn't really . . .*'

'. . . count,' said someone, sitting herself down.

Raf blinked.

She was dressed entirely in grey, with a grey plait and minimal make-up. Her beauty had the fragility of old skin over fine bones, worn for so long she took it for granted. 'No magic,' she said. 'You were talking to yourself. One of the many traits you share with your father.'

There was no real reply to that so instead Raf concentrated on his visitor. And even without his acute sense of smell he'd have noticed a stink of camphor rising from her elegant skirt and jacket, spotted the dust under the buckles on her black shoes.

'Mostly I wear uniform,' said the woman, settling back into a chair. 'These were what I could find . . . Your nostrils flared,' she added by way of explanation. 'Anyway I have a file on you. Augmented reflexes, heightened vision, hearing and smell . . . Ever since Khedive Tewfik sent me a copy I've been wanting to ask you if that also went for taste . . .'

'*Obviously,*' replied the fox.

Raf took longer to think about it, studying the woman as he did so. She wore no jewellery, not even earrings. Her blusher was so immaculate as to be invisible. Her jacket well cut, with double stitching to the buttonholes. Although the most noticeable feature was a discreet bulge to one side where she wore a small holster clipped to the back of her hip.

Something small but effective, like a .32 loaded with hollow point.

'Impossible to judge,' said Raf, returning to the question of taste. 'Because, in the end, how do I know how things taste to you?'

'How very Cartesian,' said the woman and raised a finger. 'Espresso,' she told her waiter, 'make it a double and keep them coming.' The man actually bowed. The first time Raf had ever seen one of Le Trianon's waiters do that.

'He's Ifriqiyan,' she told Raf, pulling a cigarette case from a small crocodile-skin handbag as if this explained everything. Flipping open the case, she tapped out a Gauloise, one of the old-fashioned kind without filter. 'You don't mind if I smoke.' Her question was very much an afterthought, if it was a question. It sounded much more like a statement of fact.

'Ashraf Bey,' she said. 'Colonel Ashraf al-Mansur, ex-Chief of Detectives, ex-Governor of El Iskandryia . . . You don't keep any of your jobs very long, do you?'

'I have a very low boredom threshhold.' Raf's voice was deadpan.

The woman laughed. 'Good,' she said. Dragging deep, she settled back in her chair and sighed, smoke softening her thin face and making her appear suddenly younger. She wore no bra beneath her pale blouse, her breasts so small they barely provided a framework for the heavy nipples visible through white silk. Her age was indeterminate, somewhere over sixty but after that difficult to say.

Expats and settlers, Raf had seen other women like her. Bodies kept lean by the heat and a diet of cigarettes and alcohol. Usually they were bottle blonde with faces leathered by hard living and too much sun. Whoever she was, this woman was different. She'd let her hair go grey for a start.

'Who are you?' Raf demanded.

Eugenie de la Croix shrugged. 'Ask the waiter when he arrives.' She nodded to the man bringing her coffee, so Raf asked. And what impressed Raf most was that the waiter looked to the woman, seeking her permission before answering. It took a lot to outrank a director of the Third Circle in a café directly below C3's head office. But it was becoming rapidly obvious to Raf that this person did.

'You've heard about the attack on the Emir?'

'Only what was on the news.'

'Half truths and guesses,' said Eugenie. 'All of it.' She gazed at Raf, face intent. 'What do you know about the Revolt of the Naked?'

Raf's answer was honest, *less than zero*.

'They took over Baghdad,' said Eugenie. 'After the death of Harun al-Rashid. An uprising of the poor made poorer by a dispute between Harun's sons over the succession. I don't approve of chaos,' the woman said, 'but sometimes it is deserved.'

'When was this?'

'About 1200 years ago.'

Behind his shades Raf raised his eyebrows.

'Quite,' said Eugenie. 'So why do I have your half-brother Kashif swearing that something called the NR is behind the attack on your father?'

'Because he's lying?' said Raf. 'Always assuming he is my half-brother . . .'

Eugenie smiled. 'So cynical,' she said, 'and you haven't even met him.'

'Nor do I intend to,' said Raf. 'And if I were you, I'd start with the *Thiergarten*. Berlin usually seems to be behind most problems.'

Eugenie shook her head firmly. 'Not in Tunis,' she said. 'We have an agreement . . .'

'Are you sure?' Raf took a sip of luke-warm coffee. 'I thought the *Thiergarten* were a law unto themselves . . .' Popular rumour had Berlin's agents able to scale sheer walls and pass unseen through double locked doors. A belief that sold papers and did Berlin no harm at all.

'Believe me,' said Eugenie. 'I'm sure.' She spoke like someone who had the negatives, which she did, or at least some duplicates. They were very old and very embarrassing. And the fact the man in question was long dead did nothing to make them less deadly. The Kaiser was very protective of his late father. Understandably, in the circumstances.

'Then start with Kashif's suspects,' Raf suggested. 'See if they really could mount such an assassination attempt.'

'That's why I'm here.'

Raf looked at Eugenie.

'I thought you might do it.'

'No way.' He shook his head.

'I suppose I could appeal to your sense of family duty,' Eugenie said. 'Or mention the fact your aunt's debts seem to have swallowed what little money she left, while your salary from the Third Circle is worth less than nothing. Then there's your boredom . . . Which one would work?'

'None,' Raf said.

'He *is* your father.'

'My father was a backpacker from Sweden.' Raf's voice was firm. 'I'd give you more details but my mother forgot to get his name.'

'Ah yes,' said the woman, 'Per Lindstrom. I've heard that version . . .' She looked at him. 'Some people,' she said, 'would be proud to call the Emir of Tunis their father.'

'A lunatic,' said the fox. *'Ruler of the only country not to sign the 2005 UN accord on biotechnology . . .'*

'Some people aren't me,' said Raf, which sounded either too smug or more bitter than he intended, but Raf let the words hang anyway.

It seemed that Eugenie was not looking for someone to guard the Emir, which had been Raf's first thought. Although Raf only understood why Eugenie was so offended by this idea when he realised she'd already taken that job for herself, along with her job as his head of security, not to mention his longest-serving aide.

'Just as well,' said Raf. 'My reputation is overrated.'

For the first time since they'd met Eugenie smiled. 'I've read your files,' she said. 'Explosives, counter-intelligence, close quarter combat . . .'

'And if I said it was all lies?'

'I wouldn't believe you. But those aren't the skills I need anyway. It's your other talents . . .'

Raf looked blank.

'You solved your aunt's murder,' said Eugenie. 'Faced down the *Thiergarten*. Got Zara's half-brother aboard the Khedive's liner and had him take a war criminal into custody, in the face of Moscow, Paris and Berlin.'

'Yeah, right,' said the fox, sotto voce. *'You want to tell her how it really happened?'*

Raf shook his head.

'What?' asked Eugenie.

'I'm not doing it,' Raf said.

And somewhere inside his skull the fox grinned and kept grinning while Eugenie told Raf what she wanted and Raf explained exactly why it wasn't going to happen.

'Wow,' said the fox as they both watched Eugenie stalk away, slight heels clicking on the damp sidewalk. *'That went well.'*

Chapter Seven

Flashback

'You'll need shoes.'

Somehow that wasn't quite what Sally had expected the Chinese man to say. Of course, at first, she didn't realise Wu Yung was Chinese. She had that English ignorance of Far Eastern looks and took it for granted that as Wu Yung was wearing a blue checked sarong he had to be local, probably Malay and a fisherman. The fact his PhD was in X-linked mutation and he'd been fired from Bayer Rochelle for releasing details of his research on 'GTPases and their influence on brain structure and cognitive ability,' Sally didn't find out until later.

'Why shoes?'

'Because otherwise the coral will rip your feet to shreds.' He nodded to a point a stone's throw out from the beach where the water switched from a medium to a pale blue. 'The reef starts there,' Wu Yung said. 'You'll be safe as long as you swim in shoes.'

The man spoke with a Californian drawl, interspersed with occasional words that sounded unbelievably English, as if he'd once worked for the Home Service. His wispy white beard could be found on bamboo scrolls in hotel shops across Singapore, which was where she'd landed.

A taxi to Semberwang dropped her at the causeway, the stink of durian fruit and raw rubber thickening the air as she approached the Malay side of the straits and the jumbled buildings of Jahore Baru. A better smell altogether than the stink of hydrocarbons that had clung to her clothes in Singapore, that island of tigers where all the tigers were now dead.

As Sally wondered whether to explain she'd thrown away her shoes the better to get in touch with her instincts, she saw Wu Yung's eyes refocus.

'They with you?' he asked, glancing over her shoulder.

Sally shook her head, not even bothering to turn. No one was with her and she was with no one. And that was how she intended to remain. All three of her guide books dealt with how to keep at bay unwelcome attention from local men. Only the Rough Guide had thought to mention that her real problem was likely to be other backpackers.

'Hi . . .'

Rehab is for Quitters read the blond boy's tee-shirt and his shorts were the kind with long pockets and tabs with buckles. Slivers of doubt flecked his blue eyes.

'How you doing?'

The black guy with him stared through aviator shades so cheap they had to be given away with some magazine. His silence could have been intentional but more likely resulted from a battered Walkman he wore clipped to the waistband of his cut-down Fat Boys.

'I'm Atal,' said the blond boy and stuck out his hand. 'Okay if we crash here too? We're out of dosh,' he added by way of explanation.

Wu Yung shook hands, then Sally. If the Chinese man noticed the Oyster Perpetual on Atal's skinny wrist he didn't mention it, Sally, however, made her glance obvious.

'Fake,' said Atal quickly, 'from a market in Bangkok.'

It wasn't.

'Pretty good copy,' said Wu Yung and Atal blushed.

'I suppose the trainers are fake too,' Sally said. They were airPower, the ones with scarlet kangaroo-skin inserts down both sides.

'This is Bozo,' said Atal, ignoring the question. 'He doesn't say much.'

Bozo smiled, a slow and lazy smile that revealed his teeth, which were mostly gold with a hole in one canine where a diamond had worked loose.

'Sally,' said Sally and turned towards the old man, realising for the first time that he'd hadn't given his name.

'Wu Yung III.'

'As in . . .' Atal stopped and did a double-take, eyes widening. His next look at Sally was an attempt to work out their relationship.

'We've just met,' said Sally.

Wu Yung smiled. 'And you're all welcome,' he said smoothly. 'Please stay for as long as you like . . . This island is mine,' he added when Atal stared blankly. 'I take it none of you read Chinese or Malay?' Wu Yung nodded to a peeling sign nailed a nearby palm tree, half-buried behind a tumble of deep green.

The three backpackers looked at each other.

It seemed not.

'You asleep?'

'Not any longer . . .' Sally smiled to take the sting from her words and watched the elderly man duck his head under the low doorway and shut the door behind him. In one hand Wu Yung carried a bottle of white wine and in the other two glasses. A leather camera case hung from a strap about his neck and stuck into the rolled waistband of his sarong nestled a smaller bottle, unlabelled.

This was the point that modesty demanded Sally drag her bed's thin cotton cover up to cover small breasts or at the very least cross her arms.

She did neither.

Instead she sat up straighter. Focusing her eyes in the darkness.

'Like the hut?'

Sally nodded. The shack was old, raised off the rough ground on wooden stilts and leant slightly in one direction, its collapse stopped by a convenient casuarina tree. She had no doubt that the palm roof leaked and that wind entered at will in winter but none of that mattered. It was the most perfect building she'd ever seen. Simple, cheap to build and easily sustainable.

'I came to ask you a question,' said Wu Yung.

Sat half-naked on an old canvas bed with her tits bare to his gaze, Sally was under the impression she'd already answered it. Everything in life had a price and she had no problems with paying.

'Ask,' Sally said.

'Why are you here?' said Wu Yung. 'I mean, what exactly are you looking for?'

Sally blinked. 'I'm not looking for anything.'

The elderly Chinese man smiled, his face lit by the moon through a glassless window. 'If you're not searching,' he said, 'then why come?'

More waves broke on the beach than Sally could number. Waves, breeze and the night chatter of a troop of wak-wak, the scream of long-tailed parakeet. A busy backdrop that did nothing to hide her own silence.

'I don't believe in looking,' she said finally. 'I believe in finding. There's a difference.'

'Yes,' Wu Yung said. 'There is. So let's drink to that difference.' He held up his bottle and Sally suddenly realised there was condensation running down its sides. 'There's a fridge at the house,' Wu Yung explained seeing her look.

'House?'

Wu Yung grinned. 'You think I sleep on the beach? I've got a freshwater pool, air-conditioning, satellite TV . . . I come here to escape the pressures of Hong Kong, not become a monk.' He handed her the wine, waiting until Sally noticed it was already opened. 'Why don't you pour?' he suggested.

When the bottle was finally empty, Wu Yung sat back with a smile and let the minutes drift by in a symphony of insect rhythms and overlapping waves.

'Hear it?'

Sally nodded sleepily. Music was something else at which she wasn't very good. Her fingers never quite found the chords and her one attempt to write a song of her own had been total failure.

'What do you hear?'

'Waves,' said Sally. 'And insects,' she added when he seemed to expect more.

'Nothing else?'

Sally shook her head.

'Go to the window,' Wu Yung suggested.

Sally went. The sea breeze flowing over her bare skin.

'What do you see?' Wu Yung asked her.

'Stars,' said Sally. 'Points of light. How about you?'

Wu Yung climbed to his feet and walked to the window. Stood so close behind her that Sally could feel his breath on the back of her neck. 'I see distance,' said Wu Yung. When he turned Sally round it was to ask her something else.

'Are you worried by the thought of death?'

'No more than anybody else,' Sally said, wondering if his question was sinister. 'I'm one of life's fighters,' she added firmly. 'I work on instinct. It takes a lot to frighten me.'

'I didn't ask if you were afraid of it.' Wu Yung's voice was dry. 'I asked if death worried you . . .'

'You're saying there's a difference?'

'Oh yes,' Wu Yung smiled. 'All the difference in the world.'

Chapter Eight

Monday 7th February

Gulls shrieked, the way gulls mostly do when circling against a wet and dirty sky. Somewhere beyond the drizzling rain the sun's last rays withdrew, unnoticed by everyone except Raf who lifted his shades and flipped frequencies to watch that day's little death, its final flicker lost among chimney flare from the Midas refinery.

At the back of Raf's throat was the burn of cheap speed. Crystals of methamphetamine so filthy he'd picked out the blackest of the misshapen lumps and discarded them into a puddle. The wrap was one of a dozen left over from his brief and glorious stint as Chief of Detectives, evidence signed out from the precinct and never returned. It was, if he recalled correctly, the second to last of those left.

There were several ways Raf could restock his supply. The most obvious was to ask Hamzah Effendi but somehow Raf couldn't bring himself to do that. Another alternative was hit up Hakim and Ahmed, his old bodyguards, but that didn't appeal either; which left buying his own and that brought its own problems, like making contacts and the fact he'd need to find some money.

He was a notable, living if not sleeping with the daughter of North Africa's richest man, he had a title, contacts and a reputation for ruthless efficiency entirely at odds with the facts. His niece was a certified genius. A woman he'd never met had just asked him to investigate an assassination attempt in which the only thing to die had been a snake. Short of not enough sleep and using too much speed it was hard to work out why he was quite so depressed.

Unless it was the rain.

'Figure it out,' said the fox. *'Before we both drown.'*

As North Africa's only remaining freeport, El Iskandryia shipped tobacco, rice and oil as legal cargoes; while illegal cargoes included most of the hashish destined for Northern Europe, commercial information, prostitutes, political intelligence and people in search of new identities.

At the back of Misr Station was an alley that did nothing but fake passports, identity cards, driving licences and new birth certificates; novelties all, apparently, but novelties good enough to pass the brief glance of a harried customs officer. Quality fakes came from the old Turko-Arabic district of El Anfushi, between Rue El Nokrashi and the chemical stink of the western docks.

Only, in El Anfushi were no shop windows full of fake ID cards, no posters advertising *driving licences, any country* . . . Here you needed to be introduced, and even that took money. Zara's father ran this, the high end of identity laundering, just as he controlled the refinery, tobacco shipments and illegal runs that carried hashish to Heraklion and returned with crates of fake Intel chips and memory boards, few of them labelled accurately.

This was where Zara's fortune came from and where Hani acquired her dowry. From the trade in underage Sudanese whores, processed opium and scum on the run as much as from the vast petro-chemical complex that squatted on El Iskandryia's western edge, where slums ended and just before the desert began.

Raf knew this.

His garden was being rebuilt with dirty money. It was dirty money Zara had in Hong Kong Suisse, millions of dollars worth. And it would be Zara's dirty money that sent Hani to school in New York, were he to allow that to happen.

The kind Bayer Rochelle paid to his mother.

Of course, Raf had needed no introductions to acquire his new identity. This had been handed to him, five months back, outside Seattle's SeaTac airport, not so much on a plate as in an

Allesi briefcase, empty but for a passport, a strip of photographs and a plane ticket.

The ticket had been to El Iskandryia, the passport a white leather affair stamped with the Ottoman crest and the cheap fotobooth pictures had been of a younger Zara, happy and smiling, words Raf wouldn't associate with her now. His aunt had been responsible. The dead one.

Just after Rue L'Eglise Copte and a couple of minutes from where he would cut south across the six lanes of Boulevard Cherif Pacha, Raf tripped over what should have been a good memory while splashing through a darkened alley, so recently repaved its glistening cobbles were still unbroken.

Waves.

Opposite a new Starbucks, beside the shell of an empty shop, which was all plaster-skim walls and discarded, half-unravelled coils of wire, he came up with another memory.

Salt.

The final memory dripped from his lip as he crossed the wet expanse of Cherif Pasha and cut round a forlorn man standing in the rain selling roast quail on wooden skewers from a handcart.

Blood.

The summer before, on a smuggling VSV which operated at half stealth, giving it the radar profile of a small fishing boat, she'd bitten his lip, drawing salt. Zara's kisses tasted of olives and red wine, her breasts beneath his hands were fire. If he was honest he'd wanted her beyond thinking.

With the harbour lights in sight she'd undone pearl buttons on her shirt, pulling his head against her until his mouth found her breasts. And later still, as the boat slid into the Western Harbour past the headland of Ras el Tin they'd knelt together in darkness, with Hani safely asleep on the seat behind them and she'd locked both knees around Raf's leg to lose herself inside ragged breath and a spew of words that moved her lips but made no sound.

Somewhere between blood and salt and winter rain his

new life had gone sour, seeding itself with ghosts and the expectation of failure. He'd like to blame the fox but it was working perfectly for the first time Raf could remember. And since his memory was eidetic, stone cold perfect, that probably meant for the first time ever.

Blaming it on the fox had become Raf's default position. They both knew that.

Emotional institutionalisation.

'Deal with it,' Raf told himself and lifted a bunch of red flowers from a bucket in front of a store near the corner of al-Atarinne and Rue Faud Premier.

'*Amaryllis,*' said the fox. '*Originally from the Andes. Discovered in 1828 by Dr Eduard Poeppig from Leipzig.*'

Raf ignored the animal.

'How much?'

'To Your Excellency, fifteen dollars.' The young woman smiled from under a head scarf, mouth wide. They both knew she'd trebled the price and was daring him to argue. Just as they both knew she was in the process of closing up for the night.

Raf waved away the change from his remaining $20 bill. A stupid and empty gesture even by the standards of stupid empty gestures. 'Keep it.'

Gripping the flowers in his left hand Raf headed down al-Attarin, walking with a half twist, holding the amaryllis to his side to protect the blooms from the rain; a minute or two later and the bunch was practically hidden under his coat; by the time he finally stopped under the awning of a suq he was actively looking for a waste bin.

Raf was still hunting for a bin when he passed through revolving doors, planning to cross the fish market's emptying floor and use its exit onto a narrow and nameless side street that led south to Rue Cif. It was one of his less useful decisions.

'*Not your fight,*' said the fox.

But it was. All fights were his fight. Or so it sometimes seemed.

The man with a knife was shorter than Raf, fairly normal for Iskandryia where the average height barely reached five feet eight. His arms were corded with muscle and his back beneath a dirty string vest was broad with years of dragging nets from the sea. Only a tangle of grey across his bare shoulders put his age at, maybe, twice Raf's own.

In his hand was a thin curve of steel, the remains of a blade honed over the years to a fraction of the original thickness. All this, the man's age and occupation, fitness and the fact he carried a filleting knife the fox took in with a single glance. While Raf wasted time staring at the face of a small boy being dragged across the floor.

'Forget it,' the fox said.

'No one ever forgets,' said Raf, 'that's the problem.'

Tiri sighed.

Between Raf and the nearest wall huddled a handful of market traders and a young Japanese couple who stood open mouthed, their attention torn between what was happening to the boy and an old woman beside a stall who was slopping down its white tiled surface, oblivious to the fuss around her.

'Do something,' the Japanese girl said.

Her partner shook his head. 'We don't know there's a problem.'

Out of the corner of his eye Raf saw both become aware that he understood them and then all Raf's attention was on the fisherman, his knife and the grip he kept on the boy's thin wrist.

'Let the kid go,' said Raf, blocking the man's path. He wasn't sure which language he used. Raf had a nasty feeling it might have been Japanese.

In reply he got a growl of dialect and a wave of the knife. And as Raf stepped sideways, easily dodging the half-hearted thrust he saw in the man's face a darkness he recognised. One that stared back at him on the days he dared face a mirror.

'The kid . . .' Raf said, in Arabic this time.

Again came a thrust of blade and again Raf twisted away.

'Increase the circle,' said a voice in his head. The fox was big on rules of combat, though having learnt the rules Raf was apparently meant to forget them.

'Let go your shoulders . . .'

'I know,' said Raf, dropping to a fighter's stance. Shoulders relaxed, knees slightly bent, ragged flowers now hanging loose from one hand. Most of that stuff occurred below the level of conscious control. Now was the time for his heart rate to dip to half that of an ordinary man at rest.

Still wondering if this had yet to happen, Raf watched the blade race towards him with significantly more meaning behind it and, as he blocked, the fisherman finally released his grip on the child, it was the only way he could throw a punch.

Raf had time to notice an inscription on one of the rings and then he was fluid, his right hand sweeping aside the blow. And while the fisherman was still looking dazed at the speed with which his enemy moved, Raf sank two fingers into a nerve on the man's shoulder and watched pain transform his face.

Raf was showing off, he knew that; but he was doing something worse in breaking a rule so old and incorrect that humanity liked to think it had moved on: until it blinked and found this untrue, which was often.

Raf could still remember the words of an old Rasta he'd met on remand, one time in Seattle when they were both sharing a cell. The Jamaican had murdered fourteen people, all of them strangers. It was his job.

Never kill a man in front of his wife. Don't hit a man in front of his child. Walk away if those options aren't available. Anything else is allowed.

Raf blocked the next thrust easily and stepped back to widen his circle, a quick snarl shifting the slower members of the crowd.

The small boy, his tears now dry, was hugging a young woman almost lost inside a vast *hijab* that swathed her face in anonymity but didn't quite hide a bruise below one eye. The backs of both her hands were hennaed, a cheap bracelet ringed her right wrist and the thumb on her other hand was dislocated.

It wasn't a new story.

'*Enough,*' said the fox. '*End it.*'

Stepping in, Raf whipped his flowers across the fisherman's face. A move guaranteed to inflame the man's fury, not finish the dance.

'Pig,' Raf hissed the insult.

'*You fight like a girl,*' added the fox, although the voice it used was Raf's own.

The fisherman looked as if he couldn't quite believe what he'd heard.

'*You heard me,*' the fox said.

With a snarl the man hurled himself at Raf, knife ready.

'*See,*' said the fox smugly, '*punch the right buttons . . .*'

One second the fisherman was feinting to the left, the next his right arm was whipping up as he went for a spike shot, the blade driving for the underside of Raf's chin. And then Raf was inside the movement, no time to spare for fear or thought as he brushed the flicker aside with his left and stepped through the gap, the palm of his right hand slamming shut the fishermen's jaw, so that the man's head snapped back with an audible click.

The rest was almost too easy. A twist of the hips to put one elbow into the side of the older man's head and then, as counter balance, a fist under the ribs, carried there on recoil. As ever, Raf punched through his target, going for that invisible point behind his enemy's spine. Four other moves promptly offered themselves to complete the sequence, but Raf didn't bother . . .

'Knife,' Raf said.

The fisherman clambered to his knees, blood splashing onto the tiles from his torn mouth. Some of his teeth had shattered.

'Drop the knife,' ordered Raf.

Something was said to the fisherman by the girl with the headscarf and, eyes half focused, the man glanced from Raf to the blade he still held. For a second all anyone in the market could hear was the clatter of steel on ceramic tiles and then the Japanese couple started clapping.

'Out of here,' said Raf and stepped over his broken bunch of amaryllis.

'Ashraf Bey is leaving the building.'

'How did you know?' Hani fired off her question the moment Raf walked into the *qaa*, rain dripping from his jacket. She was very carefully not standing anywhere near the marble table, which was enough to make Raf glanced at the collection of objects he'd left there that morning. At least three of Felix's possessions had been replaced incorrectly, including his notebook.

'If you're going to examine things that don't belong to you,' said Raf, 'then at least memorise the position so you can put them back in the right place.'

'I didn't . . .' Hani raised her chin.

'Yes you did,' said Raf. 'And lying's worse than touching. Anyhow, that was just a suggestion . . .'

Zara put down her book.

'What?' Raf asked.

'If you don't know,' said Zara, 'I can't tell you.' Anything else she might have said was lost when Hani yanked hard on Raf's sleeve.

'Come on,' Hani said. 'Tell me how you knew the bad man was stealing Umar . . .'

'Who's Umar?' said Raf.

Hani sighed. 'You were in the fish market . . .'

Raf nodded.

'You had a fight . . .'

It had been on Isk3N apparently, courtesy of newsfeed supplied by a Japanese tourist. And Hani knew infinitely more about the background than Raf did. The small boy's name was Umar, his father had died two years before at Medinat al-Fayoum, ambushed by fundamentalists. Medinat al-Fayoum was known to the ancient Greeks as Crocodilopolis. This last snippet was added by Hani, who believed context was everything.

'So who was the fisherman?' Raf asked.

'You didn't stop to find out . . .' Zara's voice was icy. *'He pulled a knife on Uncle Ashraf.'*

Zara smiled sadly. 'So,' she said to Raf as she pushed back her chair, 'You want to tell me who you were really fighting out there?'

'You want to tell me what's made you so angry?'

'You,' she said. 'Nothing else.'

'Got it in one,' Raf said.

'He was her father-in-law,' Hani announced loudly. 'And kept the boy out of school to work a boat,' she added more gently, once she realised she had Raf's attention. 'But he kept hitting Umar, so Umar's mother took him away . . . You're a hero.'

Raf frowned.

'Ex-Governor stops kidnap . . . It said so on the news.'

Chapter Nine

Flashback

Was it – Sally wondered – immoral to steal a sunrise muffin before smashing up Starbucks or should she trash all the food along with the glass counter? Which was worse, wasting food in a world where hunger killed 24,000 people a day or eating corporate crap, which quite possibly contained GM flour?

Tough call.

Pressing the mute button on her Sony minidisc (an impromptu gift from Bozo, who'd liberated it from near the Exxon Building on Sixth) Sally consigned New York Freeze to silence and pointed to a tray.

'One of those, please.'

'Which kind?'

There were two types, Sally realised. Both looked pretty identical to her and probably came out of the same machine, but maybe the dough mix was different.

'What's the . . .' Sally began to ask and got a mouthful of fluff from her ski mask. So she yanked up the front edge. 'Whatever,' she said. And when the boy still looked blank Sally chose one at random. 'One of those on the right . . . Your right,' she added, when the boy reached in the wrong direction.

'Would you like a drink with that?'

'Skinny latte, grande,' said Sally.

Behind the chrome counter a Hispanic kid who looked about twelve took a sneak at the baseball bat Sally held.

'Easton Z,' said Sally. 'C500 alloy, high-strain graphite core.'

The kid nodded to himself. 'You want that muffin and coffee to go?'

'Yeah,' said Sally. 'Definitely.'

They both waited while another kid made a quick espresso, slopped in milk from a plastic carton and jammed the mixture under a chrome nozzle that blew hot air through it. From the metal jug to a cardboard cup took another practised slop and then the kid drizzled a streak of cocoa across the top.

'I asked for a latte, skinny,' Sally said, then shrugged. 'Doesn't matter.'

'Have a nice day . . .'

Sally nodded. 'And you.' Behind her Atal and Bozo stood in silence, waiting patiently. They were on guard duty and Sally was the person they guarded. That was because, after this, Sally had another job to do, although this was the job she had to be seen to be doing, it had all been worked out.

'Go now,' she said to the two Hispanics. 'You don't get paid enough to get hurt protecting this place.' Sally looked back, to check that Atal and Bozo felt the same and they both nodded.

'She means it,' added Bozo, his voice dark as chocolate, the 70 per cent cocoa-solids kind. 'Get while you can.'

The kid who'd asked Sally which muffin she wanted looked from Sally's alloy bat to the link cutters that hung from Bozo's huge hand, and then took in a neoprene-handled claw hammer stuck in Atal's woven belt. Something gluey was stuck round the claws.

Discarding their silly hats at the door, the counter staff left. Today wasn't a good day to be wandering Manhattan south of Canal St in corporate camouflage. Anyone with a brain knew not to blame the McKids stuck behind counters, who were as fucked over as the coffee growers, beef farmers and dairy men; but not every protestor currently wandering the streets of Manhattan had a brain.

'Do the clock,' ordered Sally and Atal frowned. It was true he outranked Bozo being a vidhead, in as much as anyone outranked anyone, but Sally didn't trust Bozo not to break the clock while he was trying to adjust it.

Climbing onto a chrome stool, Atal yanked the clock off the wall. It was battery operated with hollow wood-effect surround which surprised no one. Twisting a plastic knob on the back, Atal ran the minute hand forward exactly three-quarters of an hour and then wiped down the knob and casing to remove his fingerprints.

'Okay,' Atal said. 'How do you want to do this?'

'The way we agreed.' Sally lifted her baseball bat over her head and then paused while Atal found the angle. There was always an angle, apparently.

'Take it from the start,' said Atal, signalling to Sally that she should put down her bat. 'Okay,' he said, 'now move in from the door and take out the counter top . . .'

She did as he instructed. Going out of the door and coming back so Atal could start running the camera at the point when the door began to shut behind her. Three steps took her to the counter, up went her chrome baseball bat and then down it came, fracturing twenty-feet of hardened glass.

'Now smash the front . . .'

That took two swings, because the angle of attack was awkward. Of course, the whole sequence would have been better with sound, but Atal was scared he'd pick up some interference from outside, like a passing cherry-top and the police would be able to get them from that.

'Tables . . .'

These were chrome topped, but cheap chrome glued over fibreboard circles and edged with silvery plastic that splintered at the first blow. Ten blows, ten tables, that bit was simplicity itself.

'Now the clock . . .'

Swirling round, Atal's camera panning as she spun from the last of the tables to where the clock had been returned to its place high on a wall, Sally did something fiddly with her baseball bat which involved skimming it in a figure of eight, then rolled it three times in a row backwards over her hand. A trick which looked more impressive than it was and the only thing of value she'd picked up from Drew, a nanchuku freak briefly her boyfriend. Since this turned out to be the only skill Drew had, Sally was loath to let it go to waste.

'Do it,' Atal said.

So Sally did.

Snapping the handle into the palm of her hand, she reached up and smashed the clock into fragments and then destroyed every framed poster in the place. She didn't want New York's finest thinking the clock had been given undue attention.

'Okay,' said Sally, flipping her bat in another circle, 'Out of here. We're done.'

Starbucks wasn't the first place they trashed. At Sally's insistence they'd already hit an antique emporium on the corner of 19th and Broadway. The kind of store where narrow people bought expensive things during the week and wide people went window shopping on Saturdays.

Only there were no tourists to gawp as Sally took her bat to the biggest window of the emporium and showered a wooden Buddha with diamonds. Everybody had decided to stay home – except the fashion crowd who were watching from roofs right across Tribeca.

Atal liked the Buddha, needless to say, and so did Sally (if she was honest). What she hated was the fact that it cost more than the person who crafted or found it made in one year, quite possibly more than that person made in one life-time.

So she did the window and liberated the statue, leaving it on the roof of an empty cherry top as a present for the cops when they came back.

After ditching their ski masks and cycling gloves in a bin, Sally, Bozo and Atal swapped jackets, put on shades and hailed a cab on Madison. Apparently the NYPD were waving licensed cabs through a road block near Grand Central. Something that made no more sense to Sally than it did to Singh, the driver with limited English and advanced negotiating skills who finally took a risk and stopped for them.

Two blocks south of 42nd Street, Sally had Singh hang a right just before the Hill Building and shoot over into Park.

'Outside the church,' she said.

They all caught the point at which Singh flicked his gaze from

Bozo's red tarboosh to the stone Messiah above the door of Our Saviour.

'Showing him the sights,' said Sally as she flicked the catch on a Balenciaga bag and over-tipped horrendously. The bag came courtesy of a poorly guarded boutique next to the Thai café on Thompson, between Bleeker and West 3rd. The cash was liberated from Starbucks.

Chapter Ten

Wednesday 9th February

'What doesn't?' Eugenie de la Croix said, stopping opposite Raf. There were plently of chairs vacant but she stood, slightly impatiently, until a waiter slid from the gloom of Le Trianon's interior to pull one back for her, apologising profusely.

'What doesn't what?' Raf demanded.

'Make any sense . . . ?'

He looked at the elderly woman in front of him.

'You said, *It's impossible to work out.*'

'I did?'

Eugenie nodded. 'Then you said, *No it's not. It just doesn't make sense* . . . So my question is, What doesn't make sense?'

'To eat so many almond croissants.'

Eugenie raised her eyebrows.

'Eighty-seven,' said Raf blandly, 'since I arrived in El Iskandryia.'

'I'm surprised you can afford them,' said Eugenie, 'given how little you currently earn. Have you paid off your overdraft yet?'

They both knew the answer to that.

'So how *do* you afford to do this every day?' Eugenie indicated the table and its litter of dirty plates, a half-drunk cup of cappucchino and discarded papers, one or two of which were still running comment pieces about the ex-Governor's *heroic rescue* of Umar.

'It's on tick.'

'Tick?'

'Credit,' said Raf. 'They keep note of what I owe.'

'Which is how much?'

Raf shrugged. 'They're the ones keeping track,' he said lightly and ignored the fox who grinned inside his head, anxious to give him the exact figure.

'You're broke . . .' Eugenie said.

'And you're repeating yourself.'

Eugenie sighed. 'I can pay you.' She opened her bag and extracted a manilla envelope. 'Very well indeed.'

When Raf raised his eyebrows it was in imitation of her earlier expression. Although his shades ruined most of the effect. 'You said nothing about paying me.'

'Nothing . . . ?' For a split second Eugenie looked triumphant but her face fell as she caught Raf's twisted smile and realised he was mocking her.

But she threw out the hook all the same.

'Your father's rich.'

'If he is my father . . .'

Eugenie sighed. 'Believe me,' she said heavily and pushed the envelope across the table. 'He is and you *are* an al-Mansur.'

'Just suppose,' said Raf, pushing it back, 'that really were true. Why would I be interested?'

'What if I told you he wants to disinherit *His Excellency* Kashif Pasha?' Eugenie said, her words curdling around the honorific. 'And that his favourite son is too young to command support of the army. And that without the support of the army Murad can't be appointed the Emir's new heir?'

Raf looked blank.

'That leaves you,' she said. 'Doesn't that make you feel like coming to his aid?'

At the shake of Raf's head, Eugenie shrugged. 'I told him this wouldn't work,' she said but Eugenie was talking to herself.

'I've got a question for you,' said Raf. 'Ignore whether or not they were actually married. Did my mother really sleep with the Emir?'

Eugenie nodded.

'Can you prove it?'

They met again the next morning, Raf already one newspaper

down with two to go by the time Eugenie stepped over the silk rope that separated the terrace of Le Trianon from Rue Missala.

The weather was warmer, almost humid, but Raf wore his black silk suit all the same and she wore the grey skirt and jacket she'd been wearing when the two of them first met, only now they no longer stank of camphor. A discreet holster still sat at the back of her hip. Her make-up remained so immaculate that Raf wasn't quite sure it was there.

As ever, Raf wore his trademark shades and nursed a headache that was three parts caffeine to one part ennui. He'd been waiting for Eugenie's arrival. Which was not to say he'd been looking forward to it.

'Cappuccino,' Raf told his waiter. 'And whatever Lady Eugenie is having.'

'Madame de la Croix,' Eugenie said firmly. 'And I'll have my usual espresso . . . I turned down your father's kind offer of an upgrade before you were born,' she added, once the waiter had gone. 'Around the time I turned down his offer of a bed to share. My chance for immortality was how he described it.' The woman's smile was so wintry that Raf looked at her then, really looked.

The way the fox did when searching for stillness within life's scribble. It was said, at least it was by Tiri, that a full-grown seal was able to sense the wake of a single fish ten minutes after that area of water had become empty. So too could people sense the ghost echo of long-gone events.

If only they knew how.

Looking at Eugenie, really looking, Raf saw a courage unusual for the world in which they lived. Not in the small holster casually clipped to her belt or in the steadiness of her gaze and her refusal to be the first to look away. Her courage showed most in the way she wore her hair, which was long and unashamedly grey.

The woman was old. And made no pretence to be anything other.

A strength that gave her a crueller kind of beauty.

'Your mother . . .' Eugenie said once the waiter had brought the coffee.

'What about her?'

'Can you still recall what she was like?

Raf lifted his shades, though to do so hurt because even with clouds to filter out the sun his pupils were reduced to tiny, steel-hard dots. 'Total recall,' he told Eugenie coldly. 'That's what I've got.'

'About her?'

'About everything . . .'

Eugenie nodded, like that made sense and she didn't feel it necessary to challenge what he said or have him justify the statement. 'Yeah,' she said, 'I suppose you do.'

They sat in silence after that. Raf hidden again behind his shades and Eugenie openly watching the occasional tourist couple stroll hand in hand down Rue Missala. It was too early for the Easter crowd, too late for those who'd come over New Year. The hotels were cheap, the cafés mostly empty. Out of the dozens of horse-drawn calèches that usually plied the Corniche, that great sweep of seafront stretching from Fort Qaitbey down to where the fat sea wall of the Silsileh sat in the shadow of Iskandryia's *bibliotheka*, only a handful were working and those had their leather roofs up, their drivers wrapped in coats against the chance of rain.

'Do you like it here?'

'Yes,' Raf answered immediately, leaving himself wondering if he actually meant it. In many ways Seattle had been better and Huntsville had a certain charm, even though it had been a prison. 'Mostly,' he said, amending his answer.

'And you intend to stay?' Eugenie's smile was part knowing but mostly sad, as if she had reasons for doubting it, reasons she wasn't entirely sure Raf was yet ready to hear. Her attitude irritated the fuck out of him.

'What do you actually want?' Raf demanded.

'Help,' said Eugenie, 'pure and simple. Your help protecting the Emir.'

'I thought that was your job?'

For a split second Eugenie's face glazed, the way faces do when people retreat inside their head. 'I'm getting old,' was all she said. 'The Emir doesn't listen to me like he did and I know he would listen to you.'

Reaching across the table she took Raf's hand, oblivious to the waiters hovering and German tourists on the far side of the rope that separated Le Trianon's terrace from the street. She had a surprisingly hard grip for a woman her age.

'I knew her, you know . . .' said Eugenie. 'Right back at the beginning.' She was talking about his mother.

'What was she like?' Raf's question came unbidden, sliding its way into being before Raf had time to snatch it back.

'Beautiful,' Eugenie said simply. 'Fractured even then. Wild as an animal and as dangerous. She was wanted, you know . . .'

'Wanted?'

'By the FBI and Interpol. I think even the Japanese had a warrant out. Something about a bomb in a research vessel.'

'What kind of research?'

'The kind that turned minke whales into sushi.'

Despite himself Raf smiled. 'How did the two of you meet?'

'Oh,' Eugenie's mouth twisted. 'I was there when she first arrived at the labs. Stupid bitch came trawling out of the desert in a battered Jeep, I almost shot her . . . Should have done,' she added softly. 'Might have made life a whole lot easier for the rest of us.'

Raf wasn't sure he was meant to hear that bit.

Chapter Eleven

Flashback

'What you thinking?' Atal asked, slamming the door on Singh's yellow taxi.

'About our friend Wu Yung,' said Sally. 'About the islands.'

Atal blushed and they both knew why.

As light began fingering the palms that edged the beach, Sally had splashed her way onto the sand and stopped to retrieve her sarong, wrapping red and white dragons loosely round her narrow hips, then padded her way along a winding path between rampant bushes of sea almond and wild orchids until she reached the kampong.

At the entrance of her hut Sally stopped again to kick white sand from her heels and, glancing across the kampong saw Wu Yung leave a house on stilts that Atal had chosen. An empty wine bottle in his hand, the camera around his neck.

She ate breakfast alone that day but at lunchtime she joined the others by the jetty, sitting topless while Atal swam and Bozo chilled under a palm, spliff growing cold between his fingers as he stared in wonder at a cluster of coconuts above, any one of which could have killed him.

On the jetty itself Wu Yung worked a barbecue made from an oil drum cut open end to end and welded to the old frame of a metal table. He had two fish the length of Sally's arm crisping on its griddle, fat spitting on the glowing coals, their eyes gone opalescent with heat . . .

'You okay?' Atal asked.

'Sure,' said Sally as she watched Singh's cab roar away. 'Just remembering how we got here.'

Bozo grinned. He knew exactly how he got there, by Boeing

747 from KL to Idlewild, paid for by the weird Chinese guy and with $1,000 spending money in his pocket. 'We going to do this, or what?' he said, putting on a fresh pair of gloves.

Almost opposite the Church of Our Saviour stood the Hotel Kitano. A lovingly restored fifteen-storey redbrick hotel that majored in roll-out futons and sunken hot tubs for its mainly Japanese clientele, or so Atal said, then got embarrassed when Bozo asked how he knew. And that was where Sally, Atal and Bozo went – across the four lane, cop-car howl of Park Avenue. Although they detoured round the block to let them approach the hotel from a different direction.

Getting in meant staying confident, what with the riots and everything.

'I need to use your bathroom,' said Sally before the uniformed doorman even had time to speak. Whatever the man had been about to say got lost inside her smile.

'It's on the right, down some stairs.' He'd been about to call her lady but the kid's accent was just too upscale for that.

'Wait in the bar,' she told her companions. Shuffling the Balenciaga bag so it sat higher on her shoulder, Sally headed for a dark wood door without looking back.

The woman who exited the chrome, glass and slate bathroom wore Dior lipstick the colour of dry blood, a small pillbox hat and a dress of tissue-thin black silk that rustled over her small breasts and made obvious her lack of a bra. The bag was gone, tossed into a chrome gash can and with the bag her shades and Atal's jacket, all three spoof bombed against DNA tests with crud hoovered up from the back seat of a bus.

It looked on first glance as if she wore no knickers at all. It looked that way on second glance too.

'Champagne,' she told the barman, 'chilled not frozen.' He didn't get the reference. That was the problem with using English tag lines, few Americans ever did. 'And some olives,' Sally added. 'Preferably in brine.'

Over at his table, Atal smirked.

'You both know what to do?' Sally asked, grabbing a chair and leaning forward, so that her dress gaped at the neck. On cue, the eyes of her two companions flicked from their beers to the swell at the top of her breasts.

That worked then.

'Well?'

'We know,' insisted Atal, his eyes still fixed on her front.

'Glad to hear it.' Sally sat back, picked up her drink and smiled. In ten minutes' time she'd be meeting a fiftyish WASP, probably done up in dress-down Fridays twenty years too young for him so he didn't get coshed by protesters. And the man wasn't going to listen to a word she said, which suited Sally fine since she was planning to busk that bit of the routine.

'Finish up,' she said. 'We're on.'

The Bayer Rochelle office was two blocks from Hotel Kitano. Stuck between the Sterling Building and Doctors Mutual International. There were uniformed guards on the door, four of them and they'd taken the mayor at his word and armed themselves with something more deadly than nightsticks.

Although their Glocks were still holstered, not drawn or combat held like guards outside one of the banks they'd driven past earlier.

'Annie Savoy,' announced Sally, flicking on her smile and one of the uniforms unbent enough to check his clipboard.

'Not on the list,' he said and turned away, conversation over.

'Could you check with Charlie?' Sally's voice was saccharine sweet.

Despite himself, the guard turned back, question already forming on his lips.

Got you, thought Sally. 'Charlie Savoy, my godfather . . .'

The man looked at Sally, whose sun-bleached hair was now swept back in an Alice band, black to match her dress. Comparing and contrasting the rugged, well-known looks of billionaire Dr Charles Savoy (son of HR Savoia, a cheese maker from Basilica) with the very English girl stood on the sidewalk, waiting to be invited inside.

He'd had jobs in Lower Midtown long enough to recognise

expensive clothes and he knew, as you were meant to know, that only the very rich got away with wearing so little with so much elegance.

'Your name's not on today's approved list,' he said apologetically. 'But I'll call his PA.' The nod he gave the other three was perfunctory, more a reminder to stay alert than any apology for leaving them.

'Your boss?' Sally asked.

One of them nodded.

'Doesn't like doing door duty, right?'

Another nod, more emphatic this time.

'All hands to the pump I guess. What with anarchists trashing everything of value . . .'

Behind Sally, Bozo turned a snort of laughter into a hasty cough and swallowed his smile inside a hastily-grabbed silk handkerchief. The handkerchief was blue. It matched his stolen suit.

'There's a problem . . .' The returning guard sounded more apologetic than ever. 'Your grandfather's not here at the moment.'

'Godfather,' Sally corrected. 'My godfather. What about Mike Pierpoint?' That was the fifties WASP she actually needed to meet, the one with receding hair and a weight problem. She knew this because she'd seen a shot of him in the back of Harpers, *a moon-faced academic in rimmed glasses out of his depth at some black tie do for ethical genome research . . .*

'He's on the phone,' the guard recited from memory. 'He sends his apologies and asks you to wait.'

'No problem,' said Sally. Sliding past the guard, she strolled towards a bank of lifts and punched the correct button without needing to look at the list displayed in a brass frame on the wall. A puff piece in the local business press had already revealed the right floor.

Gazing down from his 22nd floor office, billionaire Charlie Savoy can almost see the tiny corner shop where his father . . .

'He meant wait down here.' The guard's voice faltered as Sally turned, her face suddenly worried.

'If we must,' she said, sounding less than happy. 'Although I'd feel safer waiting in his office.'

They rode an Otis to the twenty-second floor, thanked the lift politely when it wished them a profitable day and had to wait for Atal to get over his attack of giggles. As the doors shut Atal was still grinning. The man who came out to greet them wore Gap chinos, canvas deck shoes and a striped sweatshirt with an anchor on the pocket.

'Annie . . .'

Sally shook his hand warmly, holding her grip for a second longer than strictly necessary and the man smiled politely, but only after noticing her nipples.

'Beautiful dress.' Mike Pierpoint blushed as he said this.

'Dior,' Sally agreed. 'A present from my father.' And the bald man nodded as if he knew who she meant.

'I don't think we've met?' he said, his question just the wrong side of anxious.

'We did,' said Sally. 'But you won't remember. I was much younger. More of a kid really.'

Mike Pierpoint wanted to say she was still a kid, Sally could see it in his eyes but he resisted the urge, helped probably by the half-glances he kept throwing at her tits.

'At a baseball match or company barbecue,' Sally added, busking it.

'Barbecue,' Mike said with certainty. 'It must have been a barbecue. Your godfather hates baseball with a passion.'

Sally smiled.

'I don't want to keep you,' she said. 'If you can just show me the way.'

The room was everything Wu Yung had led Sally to expect. A huge corner office full of heavy furniture and carpeted in burgundy, with blue washed-silk wallpaper between faux marble half-pillars which supported a panelled ceiling probably made from embossed card, although a century's worth of paint would need to be cut away before anyone could be sure. In the six-foot drop between the ceiling's ornate coving and a slightly-less ornate picture rail, bare-breasted nymphs hit stucco tambourines and flicked their hair in a static wind.

Charlie Savoy's desk was equally imposing. Solid not veneer, made from some wood so ox blood it was undoubtedly endangered.

Atal nodded. 'Meranti,' he said, 'from the shorea tree.' He looked at the wood, considering it carefully. 'Probably thought they were buying teak.'

On top of the desk stood an old-fashioned PC, a stand-alone Dell, lacking even a modem connection. Beside the PC a newish laptop slotted into a docking bay that bled wires in a waterfall to the floor. Atal switched on both machines without Sally having to say a thing.

'Too worried about being phreaked to go infrared,' said Atal, pointing to the wires, his dismissive grin that of someone who'd once read a complete stranger's dear john e-mail across a crowded railway carriage, using a basic Van Eck box.

'The fire door's out there,' Sally told Bozo as she tossed him a pack of Marlboro. 'Check it's not alarmed and then go have a cigarette. Warn me if that creep comes back.'

'I don't use tobacco.'

'That's right,' said Atal, snapping on a wrist band and letting its anti-static wire hang free while he struggled into new surgical gloves. 'Don't you know his body is a temple?'

'Yeah,' said Sally, 'and yours is Disney World.'

With Bozo standing guard by the fire door and Atal busy unscrewing grey boxes, Sally made a slow circuit of Charlie Savoy's office and let her instincts run free. She was big on instinct because instinct was what steered an albatross through storm-torn skies and let salmon do feats of navigation only long-dead Polynesians could imitate, it was what let Aboriginal kids remember routes they'd travelled only once, years back. Instinct was survival hardwired and way more important than most people allowed.

In fact, Sally was pretty certain that even human belief in free will was hardwired and she didn't have a problem with *that contradiction, she had a problem with what it allowed humanity to do to the rest of the planet.*

So if she was Charlie Savoy, local boy made extremely good courtesy of a PhD in microbiology and a couple of lucky guesses, where would she stash all those valuables she couldn't risk taking home?

Assuming she could intuit what valuables such a man might want to stash . . .

Dirty money, maybe. Negatives featuring random acts of senseless sex? Quite possibly from what she'd heard, but she doubted he'd mind having his prowess exposed to the world. It would be something technically brilliant but deeply illegal. Sally was counting on it.

Wu Yung was already in line for whatever Dr Savoy kept on the hard disk of his stand alone which, for all she knew was kiddie porn, but Sally intended to take spoils for herself because Charlie Savoy was one of the bad guys and somewhere there'd be leverage, something to make him stop.

There always was. Look at her father.

In the corner of Savoy's office stood a filing cabinet made from mahogany with solid brass handles. And when Sally opened the top drawer she half expected it to be lined with padded silk like a coffin. Instead she got bundles of yellowing papers in hanging files gone brittle with age. Accounts mostly, a few ancient tax returns. He'd been rich for longer than she'd been alive.

'Story of my life,' said Sally.

'What?' Atal glanced up, the cross-blade screwdriver in his hand a fetching shade of orange. He'd shoplifted it from The Wiz along with his anti-static band the day before. 'What's the story of your life?'

'All of this.' Sally gestured to a row of bronze figures that lined a long ebony sideboard near the filing cabinet. A Roman slave with a rope round his neck lay dying on a poorly-carved patch of earth. A half-naked bronze dancer, wearing a wisp of tin over her pudenda pirouetted on one leg, both arms raised above her head.

'Collectable,' said Atal.

Sally looked at him.

'Late Victorian,' he said. And Sally realised there was a lot she didn't know about his background, but then everything he knew about hers was a lie which probably made them even.

'Got it,' Atal said suddenly, lifting free a Southgate hard drive.

'Good. Now do the laptop . . .'

'Did most of it already,' he said, 'while you were mooning about.'

Sally sighed.

After he'd replaced the PC's casing, so that everything looked normal from the outside, Atal flipped up the screen on the laptop and sat back, feeling blindly in his pockets for a disc. The anti-static wire still hung from his wrist but its crocodile clip no longer clasped anything because Atal didn't need it for what came next.

Extracting a CD from his pocket, he slipped the disc into the slot.

'Got a knife?' Sally demanded suddenly.

Atal had and he watched as Sally slid the blade between the doors of the sideboard, cracking it open. Twenty-five-year-old McClellan, VSOP Hine, two kinds of Bombay Sapphire, Armagnac XS, a bottle of Pussers Rum so dark it could have been treacle . . . The man had something for everyone, complete with matching sets of glasses.

'Okay,' asked Sally, holding up a frosted tumbler. 'What's this?'

'Bohemian,' Atal barely raised his head from the laptop. 'Art Deco, possibly Lalique. Smashing it would be a crime.'

Atal's virus was a kiddie script, captured from a zombie and modified slightly then signed with someone else's tag. Attached to it was what mattered, a hack he'd written from scratch.

As hacks went it wasn't bad.

A quick skim of the network showed a six-car rats' tail exiting through a router, most of those cerberus functions had been disabled, with the machines instructed to look to an IcePort

X2, which doubled as a mail server and did a reasonably neat job with network address translation, meaning everyone was effectively invisible from outside.

More or less what Atal had expected. Solid but not flashy, functional rather than bleeding edge and a good eighteen months out of date. As for the network itself. Well, that still used cable.

'Okay?' he asked Sally.

She nodded.

'Right we are then.' Atal switched off the laptop, counted to thirty and switched it on again. Extracting his disc, he slipped it back into his pocket.

'It's done,' he said and Sally smiled.

Come midnight when the system prepared itself to backup, a sliver of script would lock out anyone still connected, which would be nobody and fuck over the central server. First thing tomorrow, when the network came up all the keyboards would freeze and every local disk would reformat itself, several times.

Of course, it was possible to stop this by switching off individual machines at the wall, but experience proved that few people ever did that until it was too late. And the joy of the whole hack was, what with the trashed server, failed network and general panic, it might be as much as twenty-four hours before anyone thought to check inside Charlie Savoy's stand-alone to discover exactly why its hard disk kept failing to boot.

'Shit,' Sally said.

Atal turned at the heart-felt expletive and found her staring down at the splintered front of a small drawer.

'Georgian card table,' said Atal. 'Extremely valuable . . . Well, it was.'

Only Sally wasn't listening. She was gazing at a transparent plastic folder and Atal had to agree, for that amount of damage it wasn't much of a haul.

'The drawer can be mended,' he said soothingly. 'So only an expert will be able to tell.'

'Really?' said Sally but her attention was on the folder. It showed handwritten specifications for a genetics lab recently built in North Africa by Bayer Rochelle in conjunction with the Emir of Tunis. A joint project was mentioned, provisionally named *Eight Score & Ten*.

'You okay?'

'Sure.' Sally nodded. 'How about you?'

'Me?' said Atal. 'I'm good.' They'd been lovers briefly at the kampong. For the week or two it took them to admit they both preferred Wu Yung. After that, their time sharing a bed was limited to those rare occasions their host summoned them both.

From his other pocket Atal produced wet wipes and started to clean down the stand alone's grey case and keyboard, then did the same for the laptop, finishing the laptop's TFT screen for good measure.

Just to muddle forensics still further (given he'd messed over both machines wearing gloves and the wipe down was a put on), Atal upended a small plastic envelope of the kind banks use for loose change and dribbled the desk with crud hoovered from a bus stop in Tribeca.

It was fair to say, Atal felt, that the obvious advantages of spoof bombing every crime scene with a random collection of dead skin, broken hairs and artificial fibre had given a whole new lease of life to those little hand-held vacuum cleaners that Radio Shack sold for extracting dust from computer vents. 'You done?' he asked Sally.

She smiled.

Chapter Twelve

Thursday 10th February

'So you see,' said Eugenie, 'it went like this . . .'

Before Arabic was reintroduced as the court language of Tunis all laws were issued in Turkish, legacy code from the city having been ruled by an Ottoman *beylerley*, which translated as some kind of pasha.

The return to Arabic took place around two centuries ago, at least, it did according to Eugenie. She kept her grip on Raf's wrist while she talked.

Already prosperous, Tunis had grown fat on the rewards of slaving, piracy and trade. And when the *moriscos* were finally expelled from al Andalus in 1609, many settled in Tunis, adding their skills in cookery, ceramics and metalwork to the city's existing richness. It was a city of pragmatic compromise, where Jewish merchants flourished alongside those princely pirates the corsairs, who built ornate dars to house their families and influenced Ifriqiya's foreign policy. Renegade Europeans mostly, converts to Islam from Spain and Italy, sometimes excused the requirement to undergo circumcision.

As for the wives of Ifriqiya's rulers, these were either Turkish or captured Christian, rarely indigenous. And the solid foundation of the state, those who worked the fields, led caravans or bartered in the markets were often Berber, a people given to mixing magic and mysticism with their Islam.

Quite why Eugenie felt it necessary to tell him all this Raf wasn't sure; until she got to the bit about captured foreigners giving birth to ruling beys. And then the grip on his wrist was as sharp as the steel in her grey eyes.

'Think about it,' she said.

Bizarrely, Eugenie stood to say her goodbyes, first shaking Raf by the hand and then dipping forward to kiss him on the cheek.

'I'm sorry,' she said.

'For what?'

Eugenie paused, briefly considering her answer. 'I could say,' she said, 'that I'm sorry I couldn't convince you. That I failed to persuade you to help the Emir. But it's more than that . . .'

'If you can fake sincerity,' said the fox and got shushed into silence. If Eugenie was counterfeiting then she was a better actor than him. Raf could almost feel her regret punctuate each word.

'I'm not faking anything,' Eugenie said flatly. 'You're not doing yourself any good behaving like this and you're not helping Zara or Hani. I've read your file,' she said. 'I know when someone's got *issues*.'

'I . . . don't . . . have . . . issues . . .' Raf said.

'No,' said Eugenie. 'Of course you don't. You have the fox instead.'

Breakfast slid into elevenses, a very English meal that seemed to exist nowhere but in Raf's memory, the way elevenses would eventually slide into lunch. At which point, he'd have read *The Alexandrian* at least twice, and be sick of the sight of the waiter who hovered on the edge of his vision, anxious to provide anything the Excellency might need.

'Which would be what?'

Raf thought about it.

'Well?'

To give the fox its due, Tiri waited ten minutes for Raf's answer and only re-entered Raf's mind when it realised the man had no intention of replying.

'How can I reply,' thought Raf, 'when I have no idea of what the right answer is?'

'Can I ask a question?'

Raf nodded to himself.

'Why didn't you just fuck her?' said the fox.

'Because I didn't.'

'You want to tell me why?
'The time wasn't right.'
'And is it right now?'
'No,' Raf shook his head. 'Now it's too late.'

Whether that was strictly true Raf had no idea but it was becoming, almost by default, an article of faith for him. What might have been with Zara was fractured, smashed into fragments too many to identify, never mind glue back together again . . .

'Excellency . . .'

Glossy and elegant, wrapped round an old photograph and placed in an envelope from El Iskandryia's most famous hotel, the snake skin was soft enough to be finest leather. The only flaw Raf could see was a ragged hole where the reptile's head should have been.

The envelope was delivered at lunchtime by a man on a scooter. A Vespa with a Sterling engine conversion. The man wore a black biker jacket, one that looked scuffed until you got close enough to see that the damage was imprinted on the surface.

The lining was spider silk impregnated with steel and could stop a blade, no matter how narrow. It also spiralled around a slug (should anyone fire one), enabling paramedics to extract most handgun bullets with the minimum of tissue damage. High velocity bullets, of course, were a different matter. They did their own extracting, mostly of soft tissue that got caught in the vacuum on pass through.

Eduardo was very proud of his jacket. And in the list of his prized possessions it came a close second to his scooter, which was Italian and nearly original, apart from its engine and the new seat.

'Sorry to trouble you . . .'

The man at the table looked up and frowned.

Once, several months before, Eduardo had made another delivery. That time the envelope had been much bigger, the contents more obviously dangerous.

In the first package had been a chocolate box from Charbonel & Walker, empty apart from a slab of high-brisance explosive. The man now at the table had been the target, Felix Abrinsky took the blast and the *plastique* had been stolen from the offices of the Minister of Police.

Now Eduardo worked for Raf. Although Eduardo used the term loosely. He didn't exactly work *for* His Excellency, more helped him out occasionally in return for a small monthly retainer and the use of office space behind the tram station at Place Arabi.

Both the office and retainer came out of El Iskandryia's police budget, from an account reserved for high-level informers. Raf had never thought to mention this to Eduardo. Nor had he thought to cancel the arrangement when he resigned.

'This was delivered to my office.' *His office*, Eduardo still liked the sound of that.

'When?' asked Raf.

Eduardo examined his rather impressive silver Seiko. 'Twenty-eight minutes ago,' he said firmly, then watched the big hand click forward and amended his answer to twenty-nine.

'Who delivered it?'

'A woman,' said Eduardo, 'very neat. Looked old, behaved young . . .' He paused, shuffling his thoughts into a logical order, the way he imagined an ex-detective like His Excellency might do. 'She had a grey jacket, neat skirt, dark shoes. A watch . . .' Eduardo smiled at his own powers of observation. 'Which was silver like this one.'

It had been platinum and matched Eugenie's cigarette case. Made long enough ago that the metal was grey and slightly matt, having been manufactured in the early 1920s before jewellers discovered how platinum might be polished as brightly as white gold. A fact Raf didn't bother to mention.

'And her hair?' he asked, already knowing the answer.

'Long,' said Eduardo, 'and grey.' He stopped to look at the bey. 'You recognise her?'

Taking the envelope, Raf noticed that its flap was folded inside, the way his mother insisted he do. The snake skin he wasn't expecting; the photograph Raf was. He shook the skin from its envelope the way Felix once taught him, dropping it onto an open napkin without once touching it, so that he left no DNA traces of his own. To handle it this way was ridiculous, because Raf knew who'd sent it, as one simple call to her hotel would confirm.

In fact, one simple call was what he would make. Toggling his watch, Raf chose voice only and told his Omega to connect him to the Hotel Cavafy.

'I'd like to speak to Madame de la Croix.'

'When?'

'You're certain?'

'What flight?'

Madame de la Croix had checked out. Her limousine had been booked the previous night. And the clerk on the desk didn't know which flight she'd been catching. Not one to Tunis, certainly. A UN resolution, bolstered by edicts from the IMF, had closed down commercial flights to Ifriqiya more than forty years before. To get the ban lifted, all the Emir had to do was sign the UN Biodiversity (Germline Limitation) Treaty and allow entry to an international team of inspectors, the make-up of which was to be chosen by Washington, Paris and Berlin.

Until then, flights to Tunis remained banned.

All this meant, of course, was that she'd catch a flight to Tripoli and join the bullet train for Tangiers, changing at the border before the *turbani de luxe* was sealed for its journey through Ifriqiya. A variety of local diesels ran from just over the border to Tunis itself.

Raf knew this because in the week following his arrival in El Iskandryia he'd checked the trans-Megreb timetable and in so doing had memorised it.

'Is Your Excellency all right?'

Raf looked up to find Eduardo standing rather too close. 'Sit,' Raf said and Eduardo did, suddenly self-conscious to find himself on view in the city's most famous café.

'Have you had lunch?'

Eduardo shook his head. In the top pocket of his coat he

had a pair of Armani sunglasses, like the ones Raf wore. Only Eduardo didn't quite dare wear his, what with the grey sky and Place Zaghloul being a patchwork of slowly drying puddles.

His Excellency on the other hand always wore shades, even after dark.

'Omelette,' Raf told the waiter. 'And for you?'

'The same,' said Eduardo. 'And a coke with ice,' he added, keen to show his independence. 'Make it diet.'

'As Your Excellency wishes.'

Eduardo grinned.

While Eduardo ate most of the bread basket, Raf extracted the brittle photograph from its wrapping and flipped it over. Then spent the rest of lunch trying to make sense of the picture. He'd expected to find himself in the face of his father as he'd done once before. And in that, at least, Raf was right. A young man with a goatee beard and drop-pearl earring did stare into the camera, shading his eyes from sunlight. It was the two people with him who were wrong.

Behind the Emir stood a huge patchwork tent sewn from strips of striped carpet, old prayer rugs and squares of black felt, its flap held open with ropes. And in the entrance, smiling and topless was a blonde girl wearing a smile and baggy shorts. A leather choker with a fat amber bead was around her neck and her breasts had been made prominent by a trick of the sun. She was unquestionably beautiful.

She was also, Raf realised, undoubtedly his mother.

A bare-chested boy in ripped jeans and open-toed sandals sat at her feet, his blond hair pulled up into a samurai top-knot and tied with red ribbon. One of his legs was in plaster, his arm firmly around Sally Welham's legs. He was glowering.

On the back, in one corner, Raf found two dates in black ink, one under the other and beneath these a question mark. The second of those dates Raf knew. It was the death of his mother. While the first, presumably the death of Per, was long before Raf had even been born. Which made no sense at all.

'Suppose the Emir dies,' Eugenie had written, 'who will you ask then . . . ?'

'*Yeah right,*' said the fox.

'What?' Eduardo glanced up from his omelette, realised he might have been rude and amended his question. 'Did Your Excellency say something?'

Chapter Thirteen

Flashback

Four nuns sat by one window, two pairs facing each other across the carriage like sour-faced crows. They had black habits and whatever those white hats were which went straight down, giving them cheekbones they didn't deserve.

They all wore sensible shoes for the journey, flat soles and laces. And they carried sandwiches wrapped in grease-proof paper and a salami in its own cotton case, like a fat cloth condom. Sally was pretty sure she'd seen sisters in New York wearing pale blue jumpsuits, God Loves baseball caps and trainers; but maybe convents were tougher in North Africa or perhaps this kind were just a different genera – or should that be species?

Whatever, they didn't approve of Sally's bare legs and tee-shirt and that struck her as unfair. Particularly as she'd been on her best behaviour ever since tumbling into the carriage at Banghazi in a clatter of rucksack and carrier bags, with her ancient Leica still safe in its pigskin case. And it wasn't her fault the boy opposite her had decided to practise his English, which was adequate, or his seduction techniques, which stank . . .

Sally, however, had to admit that whipping up his white shirt to show her a stab wound was a new one. Clever too, since it let the boy show off his six pack and slim hips without being obvious. Unless, of course, it really was his stab wound she was meant to be admiring.

The scar was bigger than Sally expected. An ugly strip speckled with pigment-dark dots where both edges had been stitched. A night club was involved somewhere and a Danish girl, blonde like her but not as beautiful, the last said hastily as if Sally might suddenly take offence . . .

'Seven litres,' he told her proudly, 'that's what I lost.'

Sally considered pointing out that the human body couldn't hold seven litres of blood but restrained herself. Maybe the red stuff had been pouring out one side while being pumped in the other.

He'd told Sally his name, she was sure of that. And unfortunately they were several hours too far into a conversation for her to ask it again. Particularly since her name peppered his every sentence, Sally this and Sally that . . .

If every compartment hadn't already been full and the corridor outside locked solid with people standing she could have moved; but the very thought of pushing her way from carriage to carriage past hundreds of grinning men was enough to make Sally stay where she was.

So what if the nuns stank of garlic sausage cut in fat slices from that salami? She didn't smell so hot herself. A stink was on her own fingers from using a station loo at Tripoli and she needed a bath. It was five days since she'd stayed at a tiny pensione outside Catania airport, where a fat Sicilian customs inspector had stopped mid-search when he reached the box containing her contraceptive cap.

'What's in here?' he'd demanded.

Dropping to a squat, Sally had spread her knees and mimed shoving a finger into her vagina. He'd let her go after that although his scowl followed her all the way through the air-conditioned hell of Arrivals and out into the sweet heat that told her she was back in Sicily.

The pensione was the first one she'd come across. A drab little house with peeling yellow paint that turned out to be immaculate once she stepped through the door. Clean sheets in her attic room, a double bed charged as a single as there was only one of her and the little hotel was hardly over-busy. A dining room that they opened especially, so that the English student didn't have to eat alone in her room.

And then a bath to wash away the dirt of New York. The

pensione had plenty of hot water the owner told her proudly, little knowing that Sally would take hers shallow and almost cold. A habit she traced back to school.

She was tired from the flight and a twelve-hour stopover in London. Most of her spare money gone on a ticket that agreeing to the stopover made just about affordable. Although breaking at London meant she spent one night camped at Heathrow fighting off bad pick-up lines and assuring the security staff that yes, she did have a valid ticket for onward travel. Of course, Sally could have afforded to fly more or less direct, with a simple change of planes in Frankfurt but then she wouldn't have had enough money left for what she needed to do.

Later, as she dried, Sally tried to see herself as Atal had seen her, as Wu Yung and the boy before the man that Wu Yung was. Staring in the looking glass of the pensione's attic. Wondering what had they seen, the three men she'd bedded in the two years since she first let herself seduce Drew, the nanchuku nut, from boredom . . . She'd told Wu Yung fifteen lovers, to stop him thinking she might take him seriously; which Sally had, though common sense made her keep that private.

A thin face. Good bones her grandmother would have said. Pale blue eyes. Narrow shoulders and small breasts. A flat stomach and no hips. That was her most obvious flaw. She had, an early gym mistress once told her, the figure of a natural athlete. That was shortly before the woman tried to massage knots from the cramped muscles of Sally's inner thigh.

Examined coldly in the flecked mirror of a cheap pensione within spitting distance of the airport's razor wire, Sally still looked good; a fact which made life easier but did nothing to make her proud. She kept herself fit, she didn't take drugs, not even the pharmaceutical kind and she avoided meat. All the same, her looks and intelligence were the product of good genes which were, whether she liked it or not, the result of careful breeding on the part of her grandparents and parents. Though her grandmother referred to it, rather sweetly, as making a good marriage.

Something Sally had no intention of doing.

After rough bread and rougher wine for which she was not charged, Sally relinquished her room, the bed unused and took a bus south to Siracusa. She'd been planning to hitch but the owner's wife told Sally that good girls didn't do that in Sicily and when Sally discovered how little a ticket would cost, she decided to be good after all. Staying with the bus until it reached its destination, the port.

So white in the sunlight that it almost burnt Sally's eyes, the SS Gattopardo was anything but inside. Stairs scabbed with chewing gum, heat-mottled lifeboats, walkways and rusting steps painted an institutional green and rough unshaded benches bolted in rows on the upper deck. Made worse by a stink of oil from the engine room and a sour tang of static that clung to every surface.

To top it all the Gattopardo *broke down six hours out from Malta, its first stop, and, having sat out a blazing afternoon, decided to limp back at dusk, arriving just as Valletta's cathedral rang midnight. Invited to go ashore and return at daybreak, Sally refused and ended up sleeping on a floor in a women's loo, having first made safe the door by tying a short length of climbing rope between its handle and the nearest tap. Just one of the survival tips she'd picked on her travels.*

Noon next day found Sally arguing with a steward who refused to accept she'd been aboard the previous day and was thus entitled to the complimentary lunch recently announced over the ship's tannoy. Eventually the man gave up and watched in disgust as Sally stuffed her rucksack with oranges and figs, pocketed a fat shard of hard cheese that wanted to be Parmesan but wasn't and took a dozen slices of prosciutto just because she was pissed at him. The fruit and cheese she kept, the meat went frisbee-style over the side to feed the gulls.

All that remained after that was to negotiate customs at Banghazi and she was running for a carriage, filthy clothes, rucksack and all.

'Sally . . .'

The Arab boy with the scar was tapping her bare knee, which was a new one, except that it seemed he really did want to get her attention.

'What?'

Looking round, Sally realised their train had halted in the middle of nowhere. At least nowhere that looked like anywhere. All she could see from her dusty window was an wide expanse of red earth dotted with bushes of some kind.

'We've stopped,' she said.

The boy nodded and one of the nuns suddenly started to fire short, frightened sentences at her in a language Sally definitely didn't understand. When Sally shrugged, the woman repeated herself louder.

'Any idea what she's saying?'

He nodded.

'Well,' said Sally. 'Are you going to tell me?'

'Sure,' shrugged the boy. 'Why not . . . ? She's says this train's been hijacked by bandits who will kill her because of her faith and rape you because you're not wearing enough clothes.'

'Is that true?'

He shrugged. 'Anything's possible,' he told her. 'Not likely, but possible.' The boy looked from Sally to the nuns and back again. 'Do you have anything with longer sleeves?'

She did, in her rucksack.

'And anything other than shorts?'

Jeans, if those were any good.

'It's probably unnecessary,' said the boy, sounding apologetic, 'but you might want to change just in case.'

Peeling off her top while simultaneously popping the plastic buckle on her rucksack to extract Atal's favourite shirt, Sally shook out a Paul Smith she'd borrowed on the Islands and never returned.

Needless to say, Atal had insisted it was a fake.

The shirt was white with thin stripes, made from cotton and had tails old-fashioned enough to cover her modesty as she wriggled out of her shorts and slid into jeans. At school, most Friday nights she used to change back into her uniform in the rear seat of a taxi that would drop her fifty yards from the small gate.

With her rucksack safely shut and back in an overhead rack, Sally turned to find the entire contingent of nuns glaring, not at her this time but at the boy who'd been watching with obvious interest.

'Thank you,' Sally told him.

'My pleasure.' His smile revealed the kind of teeth that travelled third class on a slow train between Tripoli and Tangiers. As ruined as Sally's own were perfect.

And although her father, ever the unthinking traditionalist openly admitted to choosing Sally's mother on looks alone (just as Sally's mother admitted marrying for security), her mouth's perfection was down to more than genes. It was the product of three years of night braces, nylon train tracks and restrainers. Every kiss had tasted synthetic. Which maybe explained why there'd been so few.

'You think it's bandits?' she asked the boy.

'Probably not,' he said, 'but better to be safe.' For a moment he looked serious. 'Your clothes . . . Long sleeves are better. And only small girls have bare legs here. Very small,' he added in case she hadn't understood.

Chapter Fourteen

Friday 11th February

'He'll be back from his mission soon,' said the note. *'Look after yourself, Tiri.'*

That was it, nothing more.

And Uncle Ashraf hadn't even bothered to disguise his handwriting. As for it being a real mission . . . That seemed unlikely because then he'd have left a better note under her pillow, one that bothered to lie properly. He was running away, from her crossness and Zara's anger, the noise of the builders and breakfast at Le Trianon and Hani wasn't at all sure he'd ever come back.

Keying the note into her diary, Hani recorded the time – 19.58 – and shut down her screen. She was trying fairly hard not to cry and even harder not to mind that Zara was still sat in the *qaa* with some stupid book while Hani was banished upstairs and Donna had rattled round the kitchen all day, so put out by His Excellency's unexplained absence that she'd shouted at Hani for bothering her.

Pushing open a box of matches, the long kitchen ones, Hani put flame to her uncle's message and watched curls of ash crumble into her basin.

Hani kept her diary inside a lion. When the words got too tangled she hacked off whole threads and hid those in other animals. Uncle Ashraf's arrival in Iskandryia occupied a hippopotamus. Anything to do with Zara got a gazelle, which was being generous. The murder of Hani's Aunt Nafisa filled a vulture, Egyptian obviously. And since *neophron percnopterus* had a scrawny neck and nasty little eyes this was entirely appropriate.

(What had happened to her other aunt occupied no space at all, since the General had decreed Lady Jalila's death a secret, back when General Koenig Pasha was still Governor and Hani wasn't confident her idea of scrambling text inside picture code was entirely original.)

The day-to-day details of life at the al-Mansur madersa got a Barbary lion, one that stared myopically from her screen with an awareness in its pale blue eyes of approaching extinction.

'I thought of you as my mountain top,
I thought of you as my peak.'

The words were Uncle Ashraf's own. Well, Hani strongly suspected they weren't, but he'd been the one to say them on first seeing her lion and no amount of web searching had pulled up their real owner. Hani wasn't too sure what they meant but the sentiment sounded sad. And sometimes Hani liked sad but at the moment she was just plain furious. That was why she'd refused to go to noon prayers. She'd have gone with Khartoum to his little mosque, only she was a girl and he was a Sufi, wasn't he?

So she'd been sent to her room by Zara, which was novel. A waterfall of raw emotion tumbling across the older girl's face, as sudden fear that Hani might refuse turned to shock that she'd just scolded someone else's child and ended with anger at being put in that position. Hani was good at reading faces. Growing up with Aunt Nafisa one had to be . . .

And Hani had been tempted to refuse and probably would have done if it had been her uncle, but that was silly because if Uncle Ashraf had been there Hani wouldn't have refused to go to prayers and Zara wouldn't have been upset. So Hani went to keep Zara happy, if that made sense.

The problem with being eleven or ten (or whatever she was actually meant to be) and having a dead mother and two dead aunts was that Zara now felt the need to look after her. Hani had a dead father too, of course, but since she'd never met him that was different.

'Weird . . .' She tossed the comment over her shoulder. Ifritah glancing up just long enough to make certain that nothing important had been said.

On her way out of the *qaa*, Hani had stopped at the lift, turning back. 'He loves you,' she'd shouted louder than she intended. 'Even if you don't love him.' And as she slammed the grille she knew absolutely/for certain that tears already blinded Zara's eyes.

Highlighting the code for some sad-eyed bushbaby, Hani opened the picture with a word-processing package so cheap it failed to correct her grammar. Page after page of scribble filled the buffer and right towards the end, round about where anyone normal would begin hitting page-down out of sheer boredom, Hani found her list of clues.

1) Suits still in cupboard.

Ascertaining this was less hard than it sounded given that her uncle's total collection came to three suits, two pairs of shoes, five shirts and a red tie.

2) Missing jellaba. One of Hamzah's men working on the garden had complained his jellaba was gone.

That was it . . .

Chapter Fifteen

Monday 14th February

'Isaac and Son?' The street sweeper repeated Raf's question slowly. Unaware of its exact meaning. The Isaac he got, this was a foreign version of Isacq which was a common enough name, the rest of it . . .

He shrugged.

'Máa Saláma.' Raf said polite goodbye to the man with the broom and stepped back from the pavement, running his eyes along a row of shop fronts. He was looking for a sign. Something hand-painted onto board to judge from the other signs that hung above darkened windows. Actually he was looking for far more than that.

Ali bin Malik watched the beggar limp away. The stranger's shoes were those of the very poor. A slab of rubber cut from a tractor tyre and punctured with two loops of twine to fit the whole foot and the largest toe. But even these shoes were better than the striped jellaba he wore. This was torn beneath one arm and stained around the ankles with mud or dried concrete.

'Wait,' Ali called after the beggar and the man stopped. 'Ask Ahmed, my uncle.' Pointing along the street he indicated a shadow crouched by a dustcart . . .

'El-salám aláykum.'

Ahmed looked up from his spoils.

'Ahmed?'

A brief nod. And then the man remembered his manners and returned the peace. *'Waláykum es-salám.'*

'Máhaba,' Raf said. Hello.

That earned him another nod, less abrupt this time.

'I'm looking for an office,' said Raf, 'that's meant to be on

Rue Ali bel Houane.' With a shrug he glanced both ways along the almost deserted street. As if the office might be hiding somewhere in the half-dawn. It was maybe six in the morning and Raf could see everything as clearly as if it had been high noon with the sun direct overhead; a lot clearer than most people in Kairouan could have seen even then.

Raf's eyes liked early morning. When the world came into complete focus. There were times when Raf felt sure his circadian rhythms were reversed. That what his body expected from him was to sleep in the day and wake at night.

Baudelairian delusions of Bohemia, Zara had called it in one of her crosser moments. Maybe the only moment he'd ever really seen her cross. After she'd come to his room in the haremlek at night and found him dressed, sat by an open window in the dressing gown of a dead man. He'd tried to explain to her then who he thought he really was. It was an unwise move. After she'd gone, he looked up Baudelaire and Bohemia to confirm what she'd been saying. A verdict he would dispute but understood how she got to where she got. But then that was negative capability all over, an over-developed talent for seeing both sides of everything and agreeing with neither.

Putting the time at six was a guess as Raf had left his watch in El Iskandryia. The *fajr* call to prayer had been twenty minutes before, however, and the sun was somewhere on the horizon, although buildings prevented Raf from knowing exactly where.

'This office . . . You know the number?' Ahmed had a smoker's voice and nicotine stains on the sides of his fingers to match.

'Its number . . . ?' Casually Raf pulled a packet of *bidi* from the ripped pocket of his jellaba and lit one, dragging deep. As an after-thought he passed the packet to Ahmed and then offered Ahmed his cigarette so the street cleaner could light his own.

'Afraid not.' Raf shook his head.

It was a lie, of course. That number became fixed in Raf's head the first moment he stood in the *qaa*, with steps leading from the courtyard to the madersa's first floor behind him and

Lady Nafisa ahead, angrily pushing a letter in front of his face only to withdraw it and read him extracts, her tone furious and disdainful.

'On the 30th April, Pashazade Zari Moncef al-Mansur, only son of the Emir of Tunis, married Sally Welham at a private ceremony in an annexe of the Great al-Zaytuna Mosque. She was his third wife. He divorced her five days later.'

He'd had to take her word on that because the only bit he'd been able to read was the letter head. Isaac & Son: Commissioner for Oaths, 132 Rue Ali bel Houane, Kairouan, Ifriqiya. The rest was in Arabic, a language he now spoke but was still unable to write or read in anything but the Western alphabet.

(A fact Raf justified by telling himself that Arabic script had a minimum of six styles, codified in Baghdad by Vizir Ibn Muqla at the beginning of the 10th Century. Three used for the Holy Qur'an and three for official work, administration and correspondence. And out of these had developed other styles, at least one, *shikaste*, decipherable only to a practised reader. Added to which, letters changed shape according to their position in a word.)

'But you know the owner's name?'

Raf nodded. 'It's a law firm,' he said. 'With offices in Kairouan. Isaac and Son.'

The old man thought about it, shook his head and sat back down on the pavement where a pile of rubbish waited to be sorted into heaps. There were cola cans, empty and sticky, discarded paper, mainly oiled wrappers from the pastry shops lining Rue Ali bel Houane, empty packets of cigarettes, local mostly but one of them, the one with a broken cigarette still inside, an Italian brand of which Raf had never heard.

Ahmed tucked the foreign cigarette behind his ear and went back to sorting out rubbish. All the cans went in one bag, the paper in another. Rags got tied to each other until they looked like a string of drab bunting. 'It doesn't bring much,' Ahmed said, 'but it brings a little.'

'Inshá allá,' Raf said.

'Inshá,' the street cleaner agreed.

Around them Kairouan was beginning to stir. A small woman with arms as thin as twigs and a bird-like strut bustled onto the pavement from a nearby shop and scowled as soon as she saw Raf. Then she noticed Ahmed sitting the other side and promptly relaxed. Everyone offered the peace, then said good morning and finally said hello. By the time that was done another shop had begun to open. Metal grille being pulled back from the doorway and an awning being wound down in a screech of rusty metal.

'Ishaq and Son?' Ahmed said to the woman who twisted her thin neck to one side, making her seem more bird-like than ever.

'Ishaq?'

'This man's looking for their office.'

And not finding it, Raf thought to himself. Most of the shops did without numbers but even counting forwards from some that did and back from others he'd failed to work out where number 132 should be.

With one hand on a tarnished metal pole she'd been about to use to wind down her own awning and her other on a bony hip, the woman considered Ahmed's question, head still cocked to one side in thought. 'Ishaq and Son . . .' Slowly she straightened up, small eyes turning to gaze at Raf.

'Perhaps this was a notario?' she suggested.

Raf nodded.

'Ibrahim ibn Ishaq,' she told the street cleaner, jerking her head backwards to signify somewhere behind her. 'He used to be above the French bookseller.'

'Used to be?' Raf said.

'He died,' said the bird-like woman. 'Years ago. Pneumonia. After that really bad spring.'

'His son took over?'

'Ibrahim was the son. That was it. The place is empty.'

Surprise should have been the first thing Raf felt. Or maybe shock, disbelief and blind refusal to accept the impossible. All of those would have been normal. But what Raf actually felt was sick. A cold nausea at the centre of his gut spreading out through his veins, his skin growing pale as blood withdrew from his capillaries and shivers syncopated the length of his spine. It felt like static playing across his body, twitching muscles and burning like ice along the branching pathways of his nerves.

The fox coughed, its bark close to laughter.

Just because something is chaotic doesn't make it random. Raf remembered a man in a white coat telling him that. Years before. The term *phase space* keep cropping up but the surgeon had been talking about his brain.

'Are you all right?'

'Ibrahim was family?'

Two questions asked together, voices male and female but both worried, though the man at least glanced away from the tears that had sprung into Raf's eyes. Wiping them clumsily with the back of his hand, Raf laughed. The small embarrassed laugh of a man who has let emotion get the better of him.

'My mother's cousin,' he said with a small shrug. 'I'm fine but I know she will be upset.'

To make up for Raf's disappointment the woman insisted on showing him where the office had been, walking slowly so that he could keep up with her in his crude shoes. Kairouan was Ifriqiya's most important city, she told him on the way. A place of real learning, unlike Tunis with its crowds of *nasrani* and unsavoury way of life. If he was lucky he might find a job at the market.

From Kairouan to Tunis was maybe 150 kilometres by road, perhaps less; although, as no railway reached the city and Raf had been forced to leave at M'aaken to catch a bus, the distance would be more than this by the time he returned to M'aaken and rejoined one of the local services for Gare de Tunis.

'There you go,' she said, pointing to a window above a dusty shop front. 'That was where your cousin used to work. We had to reach his office from the back . . .'

Raf thanked her, then did so again. Leaving her stood on the pavement a hundred paces from her own shop as the first customers of the day came out to buy pastries and fruit for breakfast.

On his way to catch the return bus to M'aaken, Raf detoured into an alley that ran parallel to that side of Rue Ali bel Houane and walked slowly along the narrow street, counting openings and looking at signs painted directly onto the peeling length of wall. He found the one he wanted halfway down, faded and partly lost under a smear of concrete that someone had used to patch a hole in the plaster.

Isaac & Son: Commissioners for Oaths. The only words he'd been able to read from the letter in Lady Nafisa's hand. The door to the office was bolted from the inside and had an extra padlock hooked through a rusting clasp at waist height, as if locking an empty office from within might not be enough. Next to the door was an odd cast-iron blade set into a small arch at ground level; which Raf eventually worked out was for scraping mud from boots during the winter months.

'Talk to me,' said the fox.

All Raf gave him was an angry shake of the head. He knew how absurdly easy it always was to give in. To welcome Tiri back and make it speak to him or, rather, make Tiri speak *for* him, because that's what the fox did, they both understood that now.

And Raf wanted the cold deep in his bones to go away and the memories that flooded his veins like iced water to vanish. Most of all he wanted to spend the rest of his life, however long that was, knowing that when he woke each morning the room in which he slept would not have changed colour, that no hedges would have grown to maturity from seedlings outside his window, that the season when he awoke would be the same as when he shut his eyes.

If banishing the fox from his head was the price Raf had to pay to achieve this then the fox would have to go. And it had been a stupid idea of Tiri's anyway to go ask advice of a lawyer who was already dead.

Chapter Sixteen

Flashback

Sometime around noon, with the sun burning down on the outside of Sally's airless carriage, three men wearing combat trousers, khaki tee-shirts and checked kufiyyeh *came by to throw passengers off the stalled train. At least that's what Sally assumed was happening given that the nuns suddenly stood up and began to collect together their baskets, wrapping what was left of the salami inside its white cloth and burying the package at the bottom of the biggest basket, as if bandits might have stopped the train to steal their food.*

'I find out what's happening,' said the boy and nodded to Sally, pointedly ignoring the nuns as he jumped down onto the track. Sally watched him walk away, dodging between exiting passengers until he disappeared from sight. After a while she realised he probably wasn't coming back.

Everyone waited in the sun for two hours beside the train. And then its diesel engine fired up and the abandoned carriages began to reverse slowly away from where the passengers still sat, picking up speed as they went. True to type, the nuns immediately formed a small circle with their baskets in the middle, as if they were the wagons and their luggage the settlers waiting for an Indian attack. Occasionally one or other would glance over to where Sally stood, too nervous to sit, but that was all.

As dusk arrived so did the soldiers. Teenage conscripts with hard haircuts and soft eyes, the clash between appearance and their friendliness not yet kicked out of them. They carried stubby sub-machine guns stamped out of cheap metal which they played with endlessly, flicking the safety catches and snapping out quarter-curve magazines only to snap them back again. The conscripts seemed to have no more idea of why they were there than Sally did.

Night never really came. The moon was too bright and, though air convected and a warm wind blew from the distant sea and a whole orchestra of insects finally fell silent, darkness stayed away. Sometime after midnight a new train rolled up. It looked much like the old train but dirtier, with carriages that were separate, unlinked by any corridor. The man driving wore combat fatigues, with an AK49 slung across his back.

'Great,' said Sally. No corridor meant no loos. And that meant six hours locked in a carriage with an uncertain stomach.

'Need help?'

Sally turned to find a bare-foot boy wearing a samurai top knot, the baggiest Fat Boys she'd ever seen and a leather choker with a plum-sized amber bead tied round his neck. The orange lettering across his tee-shirt proclaimed, 'Rock and Ruin'. And underneath in much smaller letters was a line that read 'archaeologists do it in spades'.

Sally sighed. 'Help with what?'

'Getting on the train.' The blond boy pointed at her rucksack, then nodded to the nearest carriage which stood empty with its door still shut. It was, Sally suddenly realised, going to be hard enough clambering up without having to drag her luggage after her.

'Yeah,' she said, 'that would be good.'

Still smiling, the boy pushed out his hand and announced, 'I'm Per.'

'Sally,' said Sally without thinking about it and remembered too late that she'd meant to travel as someone else.

Together they clambered up into a dusty-smelling carriage and Per yanked down the blinds on the side where everyone stood, blocking out moonlight and the shuffling crowd beyond. For about five minutes it looked like this might work, as compartments either side filled with noise but no one tried their door.

And then, with the train shuddering as its diesel fired up, the door was jerked open and a close-cropped skull gazed up at them. Whatever doubts the conscript felt about being faced with two nasrani lost out to his need for a seat. Pulling himself up, he was about to shut the door when someone shouted his name.

Five conscripts tumbled in after him, pushing and swearing until they saw Sally by the far window with Per opposite.

'Hi,' said Sally and six faces blinked as one. They were kids she realised, only a few years younger in age but a dozen in experience, uncertain how to react to some foreign girl in men's clothes. Their problem, Sally decided, not mine and nodded to one of them to shut the door.

'Sleep tight,' said Per, settling into his seat.

Sally wasn't sure if that was the Swedish boy's idea of a joke.

Along with everyone else in the carriage Sally found herself slipping down in her seat as the minutes turned into hours, until her head rested on her arm and her legs were supported by the seat opposite. She had Per's bare toes almost in her face, clean but dirty (if that made sense). And her own sandalled feet were being used by Per as a cushion. Without even thinking about it he'd wrapped his arms round her knees, pulled her feet in close and fallen asleep, so that now his breath came slow and regular as waves against a summer beach.

'Sleep tight,' she said but he was already.

Headed for sleep herself, Sally hardly noticed Per shift onto his side and brush one hand along her calf. For a second she imagined it an accident but then the touch came again, so softly she could have been dreaming if not for the rattle of rails and dark sky scudding past outside.

Shutting her eyes, Sally decided to be asleep; remaining asleep as Per's fingers crept up from her ankle to knee before smoothing down towards her ankle again. He moved his fingers in time to the lurch of the wheels. As if that somehow made it coincidental, merely part of the journey. And she kept feigning sleep as Per's stroking became heavier and his hand moved higher, until the top of every stroke almost reached her buttocks.

Part of Sally, the part to which she usually refused to listen, regretted changing out of her shorts, because those were baggy and, well, short really.

'You awake?' His voice was soft, concerned.

Sally almost shook her head.

Shifting in her seat, she moved lower so she was almost balanced between the seats. At the same time she kept her eyes shut and her breathing regular, even when his fingers found the back of her thighs and slipped between them, smoothing along a seam.

That was where Per's fingers stayed, their movement so slight Sally could barely sense it though the effect was like water rising behind a flood wall. The warmth between her legs more than mere body heat, the dampness not just sweat.

'Per . . .'

The Swedish boy stopped. One bare arm still hooked round her leg and his hand crushed between her thighs. A barrier was formed by his half-turned body, screening them from the others, those sleeping children with their cruel haircuts and faces made soft by rest and dreams.

'Too much?'

Sally wondered what he'd do if she said yes. Not that she would.

'Wait,' she told him and sat up in her seat. Switching sides quickly, Sally snuggled down facing Per. Only this time round she was the barrier between the woken world and the snoring conscripts.

'Better,' she said.

'Much,' Per agreed.

They kissed or rather Sally kissed Per. And when his hand reached for her Sally didn't move away but put her own fingers over his and snuggled closer, holding it there.

Per skipped several of the stages she'd come to expect from boys her own age, stages that Wu Yung had also ignored. And when Per removed his hand it was to reach between the buttons of Atal's shirt and expose one breast.

'Small,' she told him.

'Perfect,' he replied, dipping his head.

When Sally eventually opened her eyes, it was to see one of the conscripts watching her in the window, his distance doubled by reflection. The boy said nothing but neither did he look away.

'Okay?' Per asked, his head still buried between her small breasts, licking salt and a distant echo of cheap soap from a bath she'd taken in Catania; so distant as to be almost lost under the dirt of five days' travelling without a break.

'Sure,' said Sally, 'everything's fine.'

Per's back was to the window and his head was bent, his arms tight around Sally and little doubt could exist as to what his reflection tasted. On the other hand, for two strangers making out in a railway carriage they were being unusually discreet. So Sally shrugged and shut her eyes again.

Somewhere between barest dawn and reaching the Italianate Gothic monstrosity of Tarabulus station Per dropped his fingers to the waist of Sally's jeans and discovered she'd already freed the top button. As she wouldn't let him ease the jeans past her hips, he made do with sliding his hand inside.

She bit his shoulder so hard when she came that Per was the one who cried out. A muffled yelp, hastily swallowed. Although had Per turned round he'd have discovered how redundant that was. Every conscript in the carriage was already awake, wide eyed and envious.

Discreetly, so that her move wasn't too obvious Sally put her hand down and held Per, watching him tense. She waited until he shut his eyes at the intensity of her grip and then let go.

'Your turn after Tantabulus,' she said. 'That is, if you're not getting off at this stop.'

Per hesitated.

'I'm going on to Gabes,' Sally added.

'Take a break,' he suggested. 'Spend a few days in Tripoli.'

'No time.' Sally shook her head. 'I've got stuff to do.'

'What stuff?'

Sally dropped her hand into his lap making it look casual. 'I'm on a quest,' she said.

'For what?'

'The Libyan striped weasel,' said Sally and gave his trousers a squeeze.

As they pulled out of Tantabulus less than an hour later, sat in a carriage that was once again theirs alone, Per asked what had been troubling him from the first moment they met beside the stopped train.

'How old are you?'

Without even stopping to think Sally lopped three years off her age. And tried not to grin when the Swedish boy looked suddenly appalled.

Chapter Seventeen

Monday 14th February

'Yeah,' said Raf, 'I already know . . .'

A life of brain-rotting boredom awaited Tunisia's last bey, who took with him into exile his wife, his German mistress (standard *Thiergarten* issue, one), a dozen French-educated ministers, most of his children and a 392 piece set of china made in the Husseinite colours by Naritaki.

And while the brave speech made from the door of his departing train was enough to make some doubt the probity of supporting Colonel al-Mansur's plot to overthrow the government, the convenient discovery two days later of an empty beyical treasury was enough to make those same people realise how right Colonel al-Mansur had been to propose himself for the new position of Emir.

'You done now?' Raf asked.

Inside his head, Tiri nodded and smiled, glad to be back. Raf's refusal to talk had lasted a whole bus trip and half a train journey. So now the fox was sticking to easy thoughts and simple facts. Which was why it didn't mention what was happening up ahead.

The secret police were waiting for Raf on platform three of Gare de Tunis. It was nothing personal. They were waiting for everyone. Although, to be honest, Raf didn't care. He was being someone else for the day, maybe longer.

Maybe forever.

Slung under the arms of each *mubahith* was a new-model H&K7, the complete works right down to Zeiss laser scope and double-length magazine. Since Ifriqiya was on the UN embargo list for weapons sales and the ministry in Berlin responsible for overseeing H&K shipments obeyed the ruling when it suited them, shipping must have been via false end-user certificates. Presumably the same applied to the military-issue BMW bikes parked on the concourse behind.

Their black uniform wasn't one Raf recognised but whatever force they represented it seemed to require them to wear steel-capped 18-rivet boots cut from shiny leather. Always a bad sign. For his part, Raf still wore sandals cut from an old tractor tyre and a filthy jellaba. His skull was hidden under a cheap Dynamo's cap and three-day stubble accentuated rather than hid the scar on his jaw; he looked rough, made worse by the fact that seventy-six hours of not eating had hollowed his cheeks and put dark circles round his naked eyes.

The smile on his face was that of an idiot savant. Or maybe just an idiot.

That the *mubahith* wore aviator shades went without saying, since mirror shades and big boots went together across most of North Africa like midsummer riots and fear gas. Raf's own dark glasses were missing and in their place he wore cheap contacts that turned his eyes brown and overlaid the world with a haze of ghostly smoke.

'You.' A hand clipped his shoulder, sending him stumbling. 'Can't you read?' A soldier with corporal's stripes was pointing to a sign. A dozen soldiers and an officer in khaki were there to do the actual work. The *mubahith* just stood around in black uniform looking bored.

Raf shook his head mutely and the corporal sucked his teeth.

'Into line,' he ordered and indicated a row of barriers set up to funnel passengers through one of two metal arches. Men, who made up the bulk of the crowd, jostled and pushed their way towards one arch, where a bored soldier sat off to the side, chain smoking in front of a bank of screens.

The few women alighting from Raf's train had their own arch with no screens visible. All results of their strip scans were hidden within the walls of a tall black tent and seen only by trained nurses. *Sécurité's* gesture to common decency.

'Come on.'

Most of those who passed through the arches raised little interest. Although a few of the men were pulled out of line and made to turn out their pockets just for show.

'*Your turn*,' said the fox and Raf nodded, dropping his *bidi* to the platform and grinding it under heel. Raf had no real idea why he did that. Unless it was meant to be polite.

Shuffling forward with the *felaheen* gait of those too poor to own correctly-sized shoes Raf passed under the arch. And all might have been well if he hadn't looked up and stared straight into the eyes of Sergeant Belhaouane, recently promoted to the *mubahith*.

'You,' the man jerked his heavy chin. 'Come here.'

Raf did what he was told.

'Look at me.'

Reluctantly Raf raised his head then looked away. He stank of sweat and his jellaba was rotten beneath the arms from lack of washing.

'Your papers.' The order was barked out. It didn't take the fox to tell Raf that the security man was enjoying himself, which didn't stop the fox from telling him anyway.

'What did you say?'

'Nothing.' Raf shook his head. 'Nothing, Captain.'

Sergeant Belhaouane looked almost mollified by his sudden promotion. Although that didn't stop him from clicking his fingers loudly to hurry Raf along.

'Come on . . .'

Raf hurried. Scrabbling in his jellaba pocket, then in all the pockets of the tattered trousers he wore beneath. Finally, when the sergeant's patience was almost gone he found his wallet.

'Your Excellency,' said Raf, producing it.

The *mubahith* flipped open the battered square of leather and looked inside. Then he checked the pocket behind the empty slots where credit cards would have been were this *felah* the kind of man to have credit cards.

A hundred US dollars hid there, in tatty green $10 notes. One month's wages to the sergeant, three months' wages to someone like Raf. About as much as a family might scrabble together to send one of them to the city to find work.

'These your identity papers?'

Raf shuffled his feet.

'Thought so.' The man pocketed the notes with a twist of the wrist as deft as any magician making cards disappear. 'Right,' he said when that was done. 'What's your business in Tunis?'

'Work,' said Raf. 'I came to find a job.'

'Doing what?'

'Unloading ships . . . There's a strike.'

Sergeant Belhaouane snorted. Work at the docks passed from father to son, strike or no strike. The only way an outsider like Raf could ever get dock work was to marry the daughter of a stevedore and hope that, when the time came, the jetty bosses were open to bribes and the man about to retire didn't already have a son.

'What's your village?'

Raf named a place so small it didn't occur on most maps.

'Where?'

In reply he named a town nearby not much larger. Although the sergeant appeared to have heard of it this time, probably because Segui was known as a place of annual pilgrimage for Soviet *nasrani* who spurned UN sanctions and raced the salt lakes with sail boards on wheels.

It was obvious from the sergeant's dismissive gaze that he held out little hope of Raf finding work enough to send money back to his village. The concrete-stained sandals and filthy jellaba identified Raf as a man mostly used to casual graft. And construction in Tunis was run by one family. If you didn't pay for an introduction you didn't work. Life was that simple. And since the last thing Tunis needed was another itinerant from the south Sergeant Belhaouane decided his best course of action would be send the idiot back to Segui on the next train.

Unfortunately the fox disagreed.

So they stood, not yet shouting. A security policeman in black uniform with a sub-machine gun and an unarmed, newly arrived itinerant worker. A man little removed from a beggar.

The kind Zara called salt-of-the-earth without understanding the irony of what her father had done to leave such poverty behind.

Already there were others watching. Suits with briefcases, pimps and pickpockets. Other members of the *mubahith*. A French hooker so elegant her steely perfection deflected even the scowl of a *hijab*-wearing boutique owner. A rat-faced rent boy and half-a-dozen whores, mostly Bosnian, given de facto freedom to work by the Emir's refusal to admit that prostitution or homosexuality might exist.

'Run,' suggested the fox. But Raf was already running through a crowd that didn't so much move out of his way, as trip over their own feet in their haste to let him get to the exit on Rue Ibn Kozman. A woman screamed, Raf noticed, freezing an image of the chaos around him. An old man burst into tears and a boy put a hand to his mouth like he was about to vomit.

'Ditch that gun.'

'What gun?'

'Heckler & Koch, 52-shot magazine. Laser targeting. Night sights . . .'

The one with blood on its stock.

'Fuck.'

'Yeah,' said the fox. *'Something like that.'*

Jinking round a fat man wearing white robes that marked him out as from the Trucial States, Raf sprinted for the black Zil from which the man had just alighted, only to have it pull away in a squeal of tyres, back door flapping.

The driver behind took one look at the gun in Raf's hand and reversed hard, straight into a taxi. Headlights shattered, fenders tore and then it too was gone, followed by the cab trailing diesel fumes and fear.

When Raf next bothered to look he was running down a slip road with a shunting yard to his right and overlooked on his left by red-brick tenements. Dark windows, mostly shuttered. A car without wheels raised on breezeblocks. It could have the wrong side of the tracks anywhere. Although the air smelt different to

that of El Iskandryia. Fresher somehow, less owing its taste to
the sea. Fewer cars. Not so heavy on the hydrocarbons.

'This way . . .'

Raf ignored the voice. Only to freeze when a hand grabbed
his sleeve and swung him round, pushing him towards a
metal fence.

'Through here,' insisted the voice. It wore an old uniform
with a peaked cap and fat leather belt, black tie and pale
blue shirt. The belt was new and the uniform slate grey, with
silver-piped epaulettes on a narrow jacket and a cheap metal
monogram adorning each lapel, letters intertwined so tightly
that it took Raf a second to make out SBCF.

'Société Beyical des Chemins de Fer,' said the fox.

Raf shrugged. 'Whatever.'

'Come on,' hissed the small man, still gripping Raf by the
sleeve. 'Do you want them to catch you?'

'Who?'

'Kashif Pasha's *sécurité*, of course . . . He's taking control,'
added the man as he bustled Raf through a mesh door in an
inner fence and simultaneously pulled a key from his pocket
to lock it behind them. 'Everyone knows his father is dying.'

Raf frozed.

'You must know,' said the man. 'A week ago in Tozeur the
Emir was bitten by a poisonous snake. They're keeping the
seriousness a secret.'

Raf knew all about *them* and *they*. Most of his childhood
had been spent in *their* hospitals and special schools. Suits,
smoked-glass windows, pretty little mobile phones. And endless lies, half of them his.

'I thought the Emir was unharmed?'

'That's what they want you to believe.'

'What proof do you have?' Raf demanded, regretting it
immediately.

'What proof . . . ?' Key still in the lock the man halted
and then started to scrape the key in the opposite direction,
infinitely slowly. This time round the man was worrying about
his own escape route. Raf's tone had been wrong. Not just

his question but the position from which that question was asked . . . One that posited a right to make such demands and an expectation that these would be met; assumptions totally at odds with Raf's ragged jellaba and home-made sandals.

Of course the small man didn't think of it like that, he just felt tricked, his closing down into sullen imbecility the defence of the weak against someone who might represent those who were strong.

Raf took a deep breath. 'Forgive me,' he said and shrugged, then shrugged again and switched into Arabic. 'My French is not good. Only what I learnt as houseboy at a hotel when I was young. I was just asking if the illness of the Emir was true . . .'

Between being a houseboy at a hotel and an itinerant labourer lay a whole life's worth of wrong choice that the old railway worker was much too polite to investigate. So he smiled instead and shrugged in his turn. 'That explains your accent,' he said. 'It's very elegant. And yes, it's true about the Emir.'

He hustled a silent Raf towards a shed that stood dark and near derelict at the foot of an abandoned signal box, pushing his new friend inside.

'Wear this,' he ordered as he ripped an orange boiler suit from a locker. 'And carry that.' The bag he offered was long and made from oiled canvas. On both ends the SBCF logo could just be seen inside a faded circle. 'It's for the gun,' he said with a sigh when Raf just stared at the thing.

'Sorry.' Raf ripped the magazine from the H&K, wiped it with a rag taken from the floor and then did the same for the weapon, dropping both into the bag before zipping it shut. The rag he returned to the floor.

'Who are you?' he asked the man.

'Someone whose eyes are open,' the man replied and grinned, exposing a row of crooked teeth. 'You can call me Sajjad. I work the Gare de Tunis. How about you?'

'Me?' Raf glanced round the tiny hut and spotted a two-ring Belling in the corner, plates thick with grease. A stack of take-out trays next to it said the old-fashioned cooker didn't get much use. 'I'm a chef,' said Raf. 'One who's looking for a job. Name's Ashraf. My mother was Berber.'

Which wasn't exactly true. It was his father who'd been Berber according to everyone from Eugenie de la Croix and the Khedive to Raf's Aunt Nafisa, but she was dead and most of what she'd told Raf had turned out to be lies anyway.

'And your father?'

'I never knew my father,' Raf said and was shocked to realise that he probably never would. And even more shocked by how much he minded.

Sajjad shrugged. 'These things,' he said as he clicked on a kettle and reached for a tin, 'they happen.' Such unhappy beginnings went altogether better with the torn jellaba than did Raf's earlier question, abrupt and barked as it had been.

'Lose the jellaba in a locker,' said Sajjad a minute or two later, pouring water onto coffee grounds. 'We'll find you another,' he added when Raf looked doubtful.

Any residual doubt Sajjad had about Raf got forgotten the moment he saw the scar tissue mapped onto the young man's back. A veritable landscape of pain, with ridges of scarring that fed between a star-shaped city on Raf's shoulder to ribbon developments of raised tissue around his ribs and abdomen.

To Raf the only thing remarkable about it all was how little of the pain he'd actually felt, mostly that had been the fox's job.

Sajjad whistled.

'They did this to you?'

'They certainly did,' said Raf.

Chapter Eighteen

Friday 18th February

The lift in the al-Mansur madersa was an old-fashioned Otis which worked on counterweights, great slabs of lead that rose between two greased poles as the Otis descended and went down when the lift rose. Apparently the lift was now so ancient it was valuable.

For the bulk of her short life Hani would no more have dared visit the men's floor than she'd expect a man to visit the haremlek, where her own room was situated. Uncle Ashraf's arrival from America had changed all that. Along with other things such as eating breakfast in the kitchen, to the intense disapproval of Aunt Nafisa's elderly Portuguese cook.

Uncle Ashraf's cook now, she supposed.

Donna was afraid of Hani's uncle. That much was obvious from the way she always tapped her forehead, tummy and one breast after another every morning when Uncle Ashraf first came into the kitchen. For herself, Hani relied for safety on a silver hand of Fatima worn under her vest on a length of black cotton. Not that Hani believed her uncle possessed the evil eye.

His power was baraka, the sanctity that clung to those who walked the difficult path. Hani had discussed with Khartoum her idea that baraka might have required her uncle to vanish and the fact the old Sudanese porter hadn't dismissed her idea out of hand was beginning to convince Hani that she was right.

Easing open the brass grille Hani slipped into the Otis and pushed herself into a corner; all of which was unnecesary because Hani had only just seen Zara cross the darkened courtyard below the *qaa* and disappear under a marble arch that led to the covered garden. Gone to see how far her father's workmen had got, probably . . .

Hani checked her watch. Four hours since lunch. Well, if the tray of pastries Donna had left discreetly outside Hani's door passed for lunch. And two hours before their visitor was due to arrive.

His Highness Mohammed Tewfik Pasha, Khedive of El Iskandryia and ruler of all Egypt . . . One time puppy prince to Koenig Pasha's mastiff. Hani reeled off her cousin's titles, adding a few choice ones of her own.

These days of course the General was fighting US attempts to extradite him for kidnapping a psychotic battle computer that answered to the name of Colonel Abad. Since Washington simultaneously insisted that Abad was merely a machine, Hani was puzzled as to how General Koenig Pasha could be charged with kidnapping particularly in an American court; always assuming Washington managed to extradite him, which was unlikely because the General was many things (including her godfather), but what he wasn't was without friends.

The day before the day before yesterday, which was a Tuesday. (Hani checked that fact in her head and discovered she'd got it right.) The day before, etc an invitation had arrived for her uncle and in his absence Hani had felt obliged to open it, watched unfortunately by Donna who'd also heard the knock at the door onto Rue Sherif. And Donna had been less than happy when, having skim-read the Khedive's note Hani promptly vanished up to her room to feed it through a pink-plastic scanner.

Having saved the file, Hani typed an answer on her uncle's behalf, folded it neatly and took it down to the kitchen for Donna to post. The reply, brief to the point of rudeness regretted that Ashraf Bey was unable to attend the Khedive as invited and suggested that instead the Khedive might visit the al-Mansur madersa at 7pm on Friday 18th Jumaada al-awal, 1472 AH . . .

'Stay there,' Hani told her cat and lost Ifritah's reply in

a crunch of lift wheels. Until Zara took Hani shopping at Marshall and Snellgrove, Hani had assumed that all lifts were like this one; but then, until eight months back when Uncle Ashraf first arrived, Hani hadn't been outside the madersa, ever . . . So what did she know?

Hani shrugged.

She had work to do.

Two facts were insufficient. Hani had stopped calling them *clues*, because they revealed so little. Her uncle was gone. A workman's jellaba was missing. *Not clues*, Hani told herself crossly, *isolated facts*. A situation she was about to change by finding others.

The room her uncle used was dark, silent and damp so Hani folded back his shutters to let in air and with it sodium haze from the surrounding city. Directly below was the courtyard, its fountain silent, and beyond the courtyard a flat-roofed store used by Hamzah's builders. In the old days the open-sided store had been a room for entertaining visitors not quite grand enough to be invited up to the *qaa*. Now it was full of sacks of cement, endless sheets of glass sorted into piles and machines for sand-blasting metal.

On the far side of the store began the garden. Only most of its roof was gone, each glass pane carefully removed so that the supporting framework of Victorian girders could be stripped back to metal, treated against rust and repainted. In the middle of the garden, staring blindly into a muddy pit that would become a carp pond stood Zara, unaware of being watched. Unaware, it seemed to Hani, of anything very much since Uncle Ashraf's disappearance.

In one corner of her uncle's room was a *bateau lit*, sheets folded down neatly. A silver chair stood next to it made from walnut overlaid with beaten metal. Apart from that there was only a double-fronted wardrobe against one wall, doors inset with matching oval mirrors which reflected Hani back to herself, a silhouette watching a silhouette, and a bow-fronted walnut chest against another wall. A tatty rug occupied the floor in between.

Having confirmed that there were no loose tiles beneath the rug Hani debated her next move and decided on the wardrobe. In a shoe box underneath it she found a revolver and picked this up by the handle, only then remembering to consult the notebook she'd borrowed, her tiny magnalite playing over the fat man's spidery writing. It took Hani longer than she liked to find the right page.

Never touch evidence with bare hands . . .

Well, that was a good start.

Doing something clever like hook her torch through the revolver's trigger guard was out because Hani needed that to see what she was doing. And it was true there were wire clothes hangers, any one of which would have done, dozens of the things on an otherwise empty rack in the wardrobe, but just looking at those stung the back of Hani's legs. So instead Hani transferred her grip from handle to trigger guard and brought the barrel up to her nose. It stank of old fireworks.

Other than this the wardrobe was bare. Nothing on top or in either drawer beneath.

Search systematically, said the notebook.

For all its dusty elegance and probable value, Raf's chest of drawers was equally devoid of clues, lined with crinkled white paper and filled mostly with dust and dead spiders. Just to be thorough Hani yanked out one drawer after another to check that no one had taped anything important to the back.

She knew for a fact Donna had tidied no clues away because the old woman was far too terrified of her uncle to enter his room. It was Khartoum who cleaned this floor and Khartoum had been nowhere near the main house for . . .

Now that was interesting.

Hani thought about it and grinned.

Once she was done here, she'd wander over to the porter's room next to the back entrance of the madersa and have a serious talk with Khartoum, assuming she still had time. The arrival of her cousin the Khedive obviously took precedence.

Make notes, the book said somewhere. So Hani wrote *bedroom* in pencil on a blank page towards the end and put a tick next to it. On the line below she wrote *bathroom*.

Her uncle's cast-iron bath was full of dust, its enamel yellow with age. One of the claws at the tap-end showed black metal where an old accident had chipped the surface away. Maybe his shower cubicle would hold more clues.

Make that any clues, Hani thought to herself.

Coal tar soap. A dry flannel. Camomile shampoo. The shampoo was half full and the flannel as stiff as peeled skin. It was the soap that was interesting. Tiny splinters of hair porcupined its surface. Not washed-out strands as one might expect but clippings. Dropping to a crouch, Hani ran one finger across the bottom of the shower tray and came up with a whole criss-cross of clues.

He'd cut his hair then. No, Hani crossed that out and pencilled in *cropped* instead. Uncle Ashraf had cropped his hair. And that meant he *was* in disguise. Something she should have known from the missing jellaba. Disguise meant Uncle Ashraf *was* on a mission. Hani nodded to herself, heading for the lift. There was work to do. Khartoum would have to wait.

'His Highness the Khedive . . .' A lifetime of cigars gave the old Sufi's words gravitas to go with their edge.

The slim boy in the dark suit nodded to Khartoum, then glared around the almost deserted *qaa*. Etiquette demanded he be met at the door to the al-Mansur madersa but the only person to be found at the entrance on Boulevard Sherif had been polishing its door knocker.

And it didn't help Tewfik Pasha's self-esteem that Khartoum still had his cleaning cloth dangling from one hand like a dead hare. In fact, thinking about it, Tewfik Pasha decided he should have insisted on bringing his bodyguards with him rather than leaving them on the sidewalk by the Bentley.

'*Your Highness.*'

Very slowly Zara put down her needlepoint and climbed to her feet. She was working on a circle of canvas stretched over a large hoop, onto which she'd sketched a map of the world. Zara hoped the Khedive appreciated her artistry. Particularly the fact she'd chosen to edge his domains in the exact blue used to outline Prussia.

'This is a pleasure,' said Zara, her tone indicating that it was anything but . . .

If Tewfik Pasha noticed the cheap silver band on Zara's finger he didn't let it show. Wedding rings were gold and what Zara wore signified, as it was intended to signify, that whatever she had it wasn't a marriage.

Actually it wasn't anything at all. A quick grope on a boat and two nights heavy petting at the gubernatorial palace, while Raf stood in as Governor and her father was on trial.

'Are you all right?'

'Why shouldn't I be?'

'No reason . . .' The faltering in the Khedive's voice revealed him for what he was. An anxious seventeen-year-old stood in front of a girl both older and out of his reach.

'Well, I'm here,' Tewfik Pasha said.

'So you are,' said Zara.

Glancing round anxiously, the Khedive almost flinched when he met Khartoum's sardonic gaze. 'Perhaps Your Highness would like coffee?' The old Sufi's voice was slightly gentler than before.

'Coffee . . . ?' Tewfik Pasha wanted to be peremptory. To have grown men falter at his gaze and women wait on his slightest word – or was it the other way round? Whichever, the General could manage both without even noticing. While the most Tewfik could manage was to hold a room for a few tense minutes, provided one of his audience didn't answer to the name of Zara Quitramala.

'That would be good,' he told Khartoum. 'And perhaps some biscuits . . . ?'

'At the very least Ashraf Bey should have been here as well,' said Tewfik Pasha as he put down his tiny brass cup to suck mud-like coffee grounds from between his teeth. He sounded peeved and not at all princely. Somehow the thought of Zara with Ashraf Bey always had that effect on him.

'Yes,' said Zara. 'Then the three of us could have had a cosy chat.'

Hani snorted. She couldn't help herself. And having given away her position she jumped down from the top of the lift, which was an excellent place for seeing everything without being seen, and landed in an untidy jumble of arms and legs.

The Otis had been unused for the last half an hour; which was twice as long as Zara had been sitting in the *qaa* wondering exactly why His Highness the Khedive of El Iskandryia might suddenly decide to pay an impromptu visit. Now she knew.

'*Hani . . .*'

'Your Highness.' If the child's greeting skirted the edge of mockery her curtsy on standing was right over the edge. Its flamboyance made more absurd by oil blackening her palms and streaking one leg of her jeans with a dark tiger stripe.

'That's . . .'

'Risky?' Hani grinned at her cousin. 'Everything interesting always is,' she said, adding. 'Someone once told me that.'

Zara blushed.

Switching her attention back to the Khedive, Hani's small face becoming serious. 'This is for you,' she said and untucked her tee-shirt to pull a long white envelope from her waistband. 'Well, not for you exactly, but you'll see . . .'

The envelope she gave the Khedive came complete with oily thumbprint. And it was only when Tewfik Pasha held the envelope that he realised it was made from bleached chamois.

He looked at Hani.

'It arrived a week ago,' she said. 'Special messenger. At night.' She had intended to say that the messenger came disguised as a motor cycle courier but decided this might be too much. 'Uncle Ashraf didn't say who brought it.'

The Khedive lifted the flap carefully and extracted a sheet of foolscap that was surprisingly ordinary given its sublime wrapping. He skimmed the letter. 'You've seen this?'

The small girl nodded apologetically.

Without a word, Tewfik Pasha handed the letter to Zara.

Raf was to undertake a mission of the utmost danger and secrecy. No goodbyes were to be said. No one was to be told. At the top of the page were the Sublime Porte's personal arms. At the foot a scribble in purple ink.

'Raf showed you this letter?' Zara asked, her voice flat.

'Yes, he did.' Hani blinked at the misery on the face of the woman opposite. 'The Sultan's my cousin,' she said lamely. 'Ashraf Bey is my uncle. It's just family stuff . . . Everyone's my cousin,' Hani added. 'Even him.' She jerked her chin at the Khedive who stood shuffling from foot to foot, embarrassed to see tears threatening to brim from Zara's eyes.

'I'm not,' Zara said and stalked from the room. Slamming the *qaa* door behind her.

Chapter Nineteen

Saturday 19th February

'In here.'

The bar was narrow and smoky. Little more than a low vault hidden behind bead curtains at the rear of a café in one of the poorer suqs. The brick walls were windowless and the effect was to make those inside feel they were below ground. A sensation heightened by the fact that the street outside was also roofed over.

'Sit,' someone said.

Raf sat.

From above, the roof of this part of the medina looked like sand dunes frozen solid and painted white, or giant worm casts under which hidden streets ran into each other or branched off only to meet again. Scrawny weeds forced their way between cracked plaster, scrabbling an existence amid bird droppings, feral cats and rubbish that shop owners had carried up three flights of stairs to dump onto this bizarrely beautiful moonscape.

Mostly the rubbish included bicycles and broken electric heaters, rusting cans of Celtica (a cheap beer allowed on sale by the Emir because it upset the mullahs) and cardboard boxes gone soggy in the rain and dried into improbable angles.

There were other things. Stranger things.

None of this Raf yet knew.

'Why bring him here?' The boy speaking wore a charcoal-stripe suit cut from Italian silk, the only person in the whole cafe not wearing a jellaba. His upper lip hid behind a new moustache while a Balkan Sobranie dragged at his lower lip. Raf disliked Hassan on sight.

Sajjad shuffled his feet. 'It seemed like . . .'

'It was,' said a dark man sat by the far wall. 'In fact, in the circumstances, this is the ideal place.' And it seemed to Raf that levels of significance resonated within the words; but then Raf was tired and filthy, unshaven and ravenous from surviving on what little food Sajjad had been able to bring to the hut by the signal box, so stripping meaning from obscurity was probably low on his list of talents.

There were no tables in the narrow room, only stone benches that ran down both sides and a shorter bench against the far wall, where the dark man was sitting.

He was bald and musclebound, with the face of a street brawler and five gold hoops in one ear. Someone had smashed his nose years back and although it had mended well there was a tell-tale scar at the top of the bridge where flesh had ripped. He wore a rough woollen robe.

'How long have you had him?'

'Five days,' Sajjad shrugged. 'Maybe a week.'

'And no one saw you leave?'

Sajjad shook his head.

'Good,' said the man. Pushing himself up off the bench he threaded his way between people's feet and stopped in front of Raf, dropping to a crouch so he could look straight into the newcomer's eyes.

It was all Raf could do to stare back.

'We live, we die, we live again,' said the man. 'Always remember this.'

There didn't seem to be much of an answer.

'And you are welcome,' the man added, bowing slightly. 'My name is Shibli. I've been looking forward to meeting you.'

'*Right,*' said the fox.

Shibli nodded. 'Right,' he agreed and went back to his seat.

When a boy tapped Raf's shoulder, Raf thought he was being offered a plastic mouthpiece for the glass and silver *sheesa* currently doing a circuit but what the boy in the check shirt actually held was a spliff, plump as a cockroach and already sticky with tar.

'I don't . . .'

'Then start,' said the boy, 'you look like you need it.'

Watched by Sajjad, the kid with the check shirt and the fat boy in the Italian suit, Raf slotted the spliff between his first and second finger, cupped his hand and sucked at the gap between first finger and thumb. Paper flared and transmuted to ash as half the roach vanished in one massive hit. He had their attention now, Raf knew that.

All it ever took was simple and childish tricks.

He held the smoke in his lungs as he counted himself into darkness. On remand in Seattle where everything was freely available and widely used, most of the dopeheads held down their swirl for a minute or so but Raf could double that, which had to do with possessing more red blood cells or maybe just better ones.

Three minutes after he'd taken the toke, with all eyes now on him, he tossed out the dregs of his breath in one whale-like blow . . .

There was little Raf didn't know about *cetacea*. Not that he ever got to travel on the observation ships with his mother. Although she never forgot to mention in interviews that she always took with her a photograph of her young son, or that the picture was by some photographer better known for naked models and ageing rock stars.

The other thing she never forgot to mention was the time Norwegian commandos boarded *SS Valhalla* outside Spitzbergen and she'd had to hide two rolls of Kodachrome in her vagina and follow it with a tampon. This, she reminded everyone, was the point she converted to digital photography.

'You done with that?'

Raf looked at the olive-skinned woman sat opposite. Given that every single café he'd seen on his short walk through Souk El Katcherine had been filled only with men her sex made her a rarity.

'It's obvious,' she said, plucking the roach from his fingers. 'I'm allowed in because Jean-Marie, my uncle owns the café. Besides, I'm half French so I don't know any better.'

Isabeau Boulart had one of those ambiguous faces, the kind that are angelically innocent from the front but slightly dissolute in profile. A gap separated her front teeth and she had a gold nose stud. Her chin was strong, her lower lip narrower than the upper as if top and bottom didn't quite meet or match. Her figure looked good, though, neat breasts pushing at a cotton top slightly too short to cover the soft curve of her tummy.

'Finished staring?'

Raf smiled blissfully and across the room Sajjad laughed. 'Prime kif,' he said. 'Idries imports it himself. Guaranteed to take away your senses . . .'

'Yeah,' said the woman, 'if you have any to start with.'

Idries was the boy in check shirt and jeans who'd handed Raf the roach. Somehow, in a way Raf hadn't yet worked out, Sajjad was waiting for Idries' agreement on something. And Raf was still just about awake enough to know it concerned him.

'Where are you originally from?' Idries' voice was casual, unthreatening. Which was enough to make Raf try to clear his thoughts.

'I'm, well . . .'

'You can tell us,' said Isabeau. It was hard to work out whether or not she was being sarcastic.

'I don't know,' Raf admitted finally. 'I've never known the answer to that question,' he added, when Isabeau raised her eyebrows. 'People ask and my mind goes empty.' It would have been easier to give them the name of the village he'd told the soldier but that had gone out of his head.

'What was your father's name?' Idries demanded.

'He doesn't know his father,' said Sajjad flatly. 'And I saw him half kill a member of the *mubahith*. He's one of us.'

The fat boy in the Italian suit kept hogging the *sheesa* and Shibli went on quietly sipping his hot mint tea from a small glass but the others were listening and watching, weighing up his words.

Waiting.

The kif had done its job if that was to flood Raf's brain with delta-9-tetrhydrocannabinol and make him reveal the

truth. Something he'd be happy to do if only he could recognise it.

'Where did your train come from?' asked Isabeau.

This Raf could handle.

'Ben Guerdane.' He named a two-horse town on the Jeffara
plain in the shadow of Jebal Dahar, maybe twenty klicks from
the border with Tripolitana. Originally the fox's plan, such as
it was, had been to bus the distance from Ben Guerdane to
Kairouan, then take another to Tunis, but the night bus had
already gone so Raf caught a local train instead, buying his
ticket at one window, booking his cracked wooden seat at a
second and confirming the ticket he'd just bought at a third.
The entire cost of his ticket and seat reservation was less than
a cappuccino at Le Trianon.

'That's true,' Sajjad nodded. 'I saw it come in.'

'Where were you standing?' Hassan demanded.

'In the café overlooking the concourse. The one with the
balcony.'

A place with a façade that could have been lifted straight
from the Marais in Paris and probably was. All green tiles
and glass. As well as a whole sprawl of red-roofed suburbs,
the French had managed to build a cathedral, an Art Nouveau
theatre, an opera house and the Gare de Tunis by the time the
Emir's great-grandfather threw them out of his city.

Raf was glad he could remember that.

'No other way onto the platform?' Shibli asked.

Sajjad shook his head firmly.

'Okay,' said Shibli, 'so we assume he got off that train. Let's
deal with the next point.' He nodded to Idries and told the boy
to pass Raf the leather bag Sajjad had lent to him.

'Open it,' he said. So Raf did and pulled out the sub-machine
gun. Someone, probably Sajjad, had slotted the magazine back
into place and without thinking Raf broke it down again.
Separating clip from chassis.

'How did you get this?'

Raf told his story for a third time. Sajjad having been the
second time and the first.

'Didn't you realise there would be *mubahith* and soldiers?' Shibli looked more puzzled than anything else.

No, Raf could honestly say the thought never occurred to him. Police yes, in North Africa the police were everywhere, but soldiers questioning every *felah, khamme* and Berber clansman to climb from a local train . . . ? That was something else again.

'Okay,' said Shibli, putting down his tea glass. 'Let's take this from the top . . .' He smiled and for a split second it was possible to see the man he'd been. Someone whose hunger for meaning had taken him through all life had to offer and out into a stark stillness beyond.

'Do you want to keep the gun?'

Raf shook his head.

'Good . . .' The Shibli held out his hand, looking puzzled when Raf made no attempt to hand over the H&K.

'Fingerprints,' Raf explained apologetically. Without really thinking about it, Raf freed a catch on the side and dropped to his knees, field-stripping the H&K on the dirty floor in front of him. When the weapon was reduced to barrel, breech, stock and chassis, Raf reached behind him and took a tiny bowl of olive oil from Isabeau's plate without even asking.

Ripping a strip from the leg of his borrowed SBCF jumpsuit he soaked it in oil and wiped over the parts in front of him. As an afterthought Raf flipped the bullets from their magazine and reloaded them, having first made sure each was clean.

Thirty seconds later the gun was whole and the room was in silence. Most of the expressions when Raf looked up were unreadable.

'You originally travelled from Egypt?'

Raf looked surprised.

'The jellaba you wore,' said Shibli, 'Sajjad said the pattern was Egyptian.'

'Not mine,' Raf said.

'Meaning what?'

'I needed some clothes so I stole them.'

'And what were you wearing when you stole someone else's jellaba?'

Raf thought back to his black Italian suit, white cotton shirt and red tie, the shades, his black shoes and the gold cufflinks Hamzah Effendi gave him for something he once did.

'Uniform,' said Raf finally. 'I was wearing uniform.'

In Tunis, as in many cities along the North African littoral, *salafi*, those who followed al-Salaf al-Salih, the venerable fore-fathers talked about war as if it were always within or between religions, but those with eyes open knew it was between poverty and wealth. Yet Shibli found it hard to blame them. Soviet kids in particular came to the city on holiday, UN sanctions or not, bringing their currency and worse behaviour. Object lessons in the fact that despite the words of the saints, humility and virtue did not automatically bring material reward.

And it was hard to explain to those with nothing, that compared to the rest of Europe the 'packers and Soviet kids with their jeans and weird jackets were as poor as most Ifriqiyans were in relation to the Soviets.

Only those whose eyes were open could see these things.

'Who has *marc*?' Shibli's question was so blunt that Idries mis-timed his draw on the *sheesha* and collapsed into a fit of coughing; one that lasted longer than strictly necessary as he tried to work out the right answer. In the end, Idries did what he usually did when faced with one of the Sufi's questions. Told the truth without knowing if that was the right thing to do or not.

'I have a small flask . . .'

Shibli held out his hand.

Spirits were prohibited in Tunis by tradition not law. Those who wanted to drink marc or armagnac could go to a café or visit the bar of a big hotel. The Emir's reasoning was simple. Those who wanted to drink could while those who knew spirits to be evil didn't need his law to tell them this. Besides, the Soviets all drank heavily. In his own way the Emir was a very pragmatic man.

This was the cause of his wife's discontent. Or so it was said. Shibli didn't know if her son, Kashif Pasha, also believed what the old mullahs told his mother or if His Excellency was just using them as they used him. It was, as he'd once heard Isabeau say, a bitch of a call. What was unquestionably true, was that most of the army believed, but then uniforms and absolutes seemed to go together, whether God willed or not.

Flipping open Idries' flask, Shibli took a long swallow and felt cheap brandy burn his throat on its way down. Seconds later it ignited his stomach which served him right for forgetting, once again, to eat before leaving his madersa.

He drank to make a point. Whether any of the others had eyes open enough to understand his point was their business. Offering the flask to Raf, he watched the man drain what was left and wipe his mouth with the back of his hand. He did it without hesitation. Without the slightest thought of refusal.

An officer, Shibli decided, noticing soft fingers and unbroken nails. An officer who broke down a gun like any grunt. One who drank. An officer on the run. Or an infiltrator, an *agent provocateur* willing to break sharia law in the course of his job? A man who would need to be watched while he watched them . . .

'Who are you really?' Shibli's question was aimed at Raf but Sajjad got in his reply first.

'A conscript, he said so.'

Which wasn't what the soldier had said at all though Shibli let that pass. Taking another glance at the drunken man in the orange jumpsuit, Shibli tried again. 'What are you running from?' he asked.

'What have you got,' said Raf.

And fell sideways off his stool.

Chapter Twenty

Flashback

Per gutted supper with a swift cut, turning his knife sideways to hook out the rat's intestines which tumbled onto the coals at his feet. Without pause, he sliced a ring around the neck of his catch and tossed the blade aside to ease his fingers beneath the animal's skin, peeling it back like a man turning a glove inside out. Only then did he answer the blonde girl sat in the dusk opposite.

'Sure I'm sure . . .'

'It's safe to eat?'

Per nodded. 'You'd be surprised what's safe if you cook it properly. You certain this isn't a rare species?'

Sally was.

When Per first returned with supper wriggling in his hand he'd asked Sally if his catch was rare. Since the rat was obviously still alive at this point Sally had assumed Per was trying to avoid killing something endangered. Now she was beginning to wonder. The small stuff she knew, his hatred of shoes, the fact the first thing he did each morning was re-tie his hair, and the raw tramlines across his back were definitely hers: but she still had little idea as yet of what was inside his head. But then it was fair to say that Per had less than no idea of what was in her own.

'Rosemary,' Per said, crumbling leaves under her nose. 'And this one's fresh thyme.'

Sally had watched the snake-hipped Swede build a fire from brushwood, doing everything the way Sally felt it should be done. First he dug a small pit and ringed it with stones collected from the outcrop under which they camped. Raked a wide area around the pit with his fingers as a second move, brushing aside anything that might flare like tinder. And filled the pit with twigs, arranged by thickness as his third move. Spaghetti thin in the middle, pencil fat around that and fatter still around the outside and over the top.

The flame came from an old lighter; so old she hadn't seen that kind before.

'Just petrol,' said Per, noticing her interest. 'Works even in a high wind.' He did something vaguely obscene with the chrome circle at the top of the lighter and Sally realised he was jacking it up and down like a metal foreskin. 'Belonged to my grandfather,' he said proudly.

'And you still use it?'

'Why not?' said Per. 'It still works.'

Sally smiled. He was an odd mix. A carnivorous technopagan who thought modern war inherently immoral but happily believed killing to be a hard-wired human reaction, if only on a personal level. As for global politics, genetics and the other stuff that really interested Sally, they hadn't even begun to go there. The only thing that really fired Per was history and old ruins.

'What are you thinking?' His voice studiedly casual, borderline curious. Something about her obviously fascinated him and Sally had yet to work out what. Leaving aside the obvious.

'That you're a good fuck . . .'

Per grinned. 'And you're a good judge of these things?'

'You're not?'

Still grinning the boy put his lighter to the kindling and they both watched flame catch. An immediate helix of twisted vision rupturing the air between them. There was no smoke to disturb the summer sky, only a spiral of heat haze. Sally was impressed by that.

They could have got off at Gabes but Sally wanted a bank and knew, because she'd already checked, that Coutts & Co. (Tunis) kept a branch where Avenue de Carthage intersected with Avenue de Paris.

So she made Per look after her luggage in a café across the road while she sauntered into one of those grey-stoned colonial mansions with sash windows, bay trees at the door and industrial-strength air-conditioning and banged her cheque book on the counter, which was Italian horse-hair marble, obviously enough.

The florid young man who glanced up looked first at Sally's tatty cheque book and only then at the blonde foreigner and Sally was glad it was that way round. The five minutes she'd spent cleaning up in the thin trickle of water extracted from an ablutions hose in the café loo had done little but smear dust across her sun-burnt face. Dirt still grimed her arms and Sally's hair was a mess under her scarf. Although Sally had to admit that tying back her hair helped make her look local.

'Madame?'

'Mademoiselle,' Sally corrected without thinking. Mademoiselle it was and mademoiselle was the way it was going to stay. She'd seen the price her mother had to pay for security and that was just too high.

'I'd like to check my account.'

Sally pushed her book to Kaysar Aziz and watched him flick back its cover and discreetly check the laser-stamped photograph embossed on the inside. Equally discreetly, Aziz fanned a dozen of the most recent stubs. The amounts scrawled in a variety of cheap pens got smaller each time.

'If you could just wait here.' He vanished through an oak door to check her balance, something he could have done quicker by flicking alive a flatscreen angled into the counter-top. This was discretion apparently.

She knew the answer the moment Kaysar reappeared, long before he had time or need to frame his reply.

'Empty?'

'I'm sorry . . .'

Sally shrugged. 'Not your problem if my father's a prick.'

His blink was lightning fast.

'Cancelled,' Sally explained. 'Until I come home. He's been

threatening it for months. Now he has . . . You got a loo round here?'

Aziz looked blank.

'Toilet,' Sally said. 'Which way?'

Rinsing her hands to wash off the soap, Sally started on her face and realised, too late, that she was splashing water down her front. The decision made itself. Unwrapping her scarf she shoved it into the pocket of her jeans and pulled her damp tee-shirt over her head, revealing bite marks below one breast and a barbed-wire tattoo round her upper left arm. The tattoo was a mistake, an old one. The jury was still out on the navel stud and the gold dumbbell through her left nipple.

The body of an animal, Wu Yung had said and that was when Sally knew she'd finally outgrown him. The old man meant lean and muscled like a predator but he'd missed the essential truth. What he thought was a compliment was merely a statement of the obvious. And the fact Wu Yung never realised this disappointed her. She was an animal as was he, as was Bozo and Atal, that over-privileged, under-challenged little idiot with his kangaroo-skin shoes.

Homo sapiens. One point three per cent off being a chimpanzee. A species outside evolution and seriously in need of an over-haul.

Sally sighed.

When she'd wrung out as much water from her hair as she could Sally wrapped it still damp in her scarf, splashed cologne onto her breasts from a bottle on a glass shelf above the basin, struggled back into her tee-shirt and turned to go. That was when she noticed an elderly Arab woman sitting in an alcove.

Gazes met and held, pale blue and darkest brown and Sally nodded, shrugging off the lack of a nod in return.

To make a point she left her last US dollar in the saucer by the door.

'Well, that went perfectly,' Sally announced as she slumped into the chair opposite Per and reached for her Leica.

'You got your money?'

'Yeah.' Sally picked up the dregs of Per's espresso and downed it in a single gulp. 'Every last penny in my account.'

'What now?' Per asked.

'We go our separate ways I guess.'

'And your way is where?'

'Into the desert.'

Per smiled. 'You've been practising that,' he said.

'Practising what?' Sally demanded, her puzzlement real.

'That line,' said Per, brushing aside his floppy hair. He put one hand to his pale eyes to shade out a sun already kept at bay by a café umbrella and pretended to peer into the far distance. 'Searching for your famous weasel?'

Sally nodded and Per laughed.

'I don't believe you,' he said. 'Not even an English woman chases into the desert after a weasel.'

'I do,' said Sally. 'Chasing things is how you find them.'

'But they're not even rare,' Per protested. 'I know, I looked them up.' He pulled a battered Nokia from his rucksack and flipped up the number pad to reveal a foldout keyboard and pop up screen. 'So what are you really after?'

'Really?'

Per nodded.

'Lions,' said Sally, smiling at his expression. 'Barbary lions. The kind that ate Christians in the Roman circus.'

'What do they look like?'

'Much like this,' Sally said and she pulled a tatty newspaper clipping from the back of her wallet. It showed a lion cub so pale it almost looked grey. 'The last known Barbary lion was shot in Morocco eighty years ago.'

'So how are you going to find one?

'By looking,' Sally said flatly. 'There've been rumours for years that a pair exist in captivity at a private zoo.'

'Whose?'

Sally smiled. 'The Emir's own,' she said. 'Apparently he sees nobody, but I think he might see me. He's partial to single blondes . . .' She tapped quote marks either side of the words, stressing the irony.

'You want company?'

Sally was about to point out the contradiction between what she'd just said and his question when she noticed the local newspaper tucked into the side pocket of Per's rucksack. It was folded open towards the back and she could just about see the small-ad headings from where she sat, not that she needed to. The boxed-out advertisement for Hertz told her all she needed to know.

'You're going to hire a car?'

'Too expensive,' said Per. 'I'll buy one.'

'This works out cheaper?'

'Depends what I buy. Get a mahari and it'll run like clockwork, Soviet clockwork . . . Four cylinder, two stroke, made in Portugal,' he added, seeing Sally's blank look.

'And that runs like . . .'

'It was a joke,' he said patiently. 'Maharis break down daily but even a child can mend them. What I actually want is a jeep.' Tossing the paper across, Per said, 'Take a look.' He'd ringed three possibles and put lines through two of those. 'Too old,' he said, jerking his head towards the first one. 'And the other's too expensive. The last one looks okay though.'

As she expected the price was substantially more than Sally had. 'You off to see it now?' she asked hopefully.

'I wish.' Per shook his head. 'I called and the first time they can do is ten o'clock tomorrow. Which means finding somewhere for the night.'

'Not a problem,' said Sally. 'There were a dozen guest houses near Gare de Tunis. We can try there.' And so they did, although they ended up with separate rooms because the woman behind the desk refused to rent them a double. She did this by the simple expedient of refusing to understand what Sally and Per were asking for.

One room was under the roof of a narrow four-storey guesthouse that advertised itself as L'Hotel Carthage, the other on the second floor, up a flight of stairs from the reception area. Both looked onto a narrow side street parked with cars but only the lower one had a shower and loo. Sally chose the roof *because her window had a better view. That was what she told Per anyway, in fact the main thing her room had going for it was being a third cheaper than the room Per took.*

'You want to go eat?'

'Not really hungry,' said Sally. 'Although you could always pick up a bottle of red if you go out.' She watched Per nod and smiled to herself. Now she had a reason to drop by his room later if that was the route she decided to take; which it would be, but Sally was planning to spend an hour or two fooling herself first.

Chapter Twenty-one

Tuesday 22nd February

Empirical evidence proved that sitting quietly in front of a half-eaten croissant could keep a waiter from Le Trianon at bay for half an hour. The secret was not to run over thirty minutes. Doing so resulted in someone coming to ask if there was a problem with the food.

Opening her laptop, Hani called up a photograph and stripped off yesterday's additions, starting again. The foreigner's strange shirt was replaced with a new scoop-neck top, her hair made presentable courtesy of digiGloss, which billed itself as the software make-up experts used. Hani had downloaded a fourteen-day trial version of this and a freeware version of Wardrobe v3.1 from a teen site in Kansas City.

Her uncle was missing, check.

Khartoum knew why but wouldn't say, check.

And check Zara moping about in the *qaa* like some consumptive. *Merde* and *merde* again, as Zara herself would say. Hani took a large bite from her croissant and chewed hard. Yesterday she'd come across the woman sitting by the small fountain in the *qaa* reading Runi. If this was a side effect of love then . . .

Hani sucked her teeth.

'Is everything all right?' The waiter who materialised beside her table looked worried, his eyes flicking from the child's face to her plate.

'The croissant is delicious,' Hani said firmly, 'and I don't need another coffee. But actually I do need to see the maître d' . . . to borrow a pen,' Hani added, when the man looked worried. Slipping down from her chair, she strolled through the terrace door into Le Trianon and headed for the elderly person stood at a small lectern, leafing through a reservations book.

'Problems?' Hani asked politely.

'Nothing serious.' The thin Italian smiled at her. 'A double booking for the same cover . . .' He nodded to a table for six beneath a mural, the one decorated with a dancing girl in jewelled slippers and a wisp of cloth. 'Sometimes I just think it would be easier to do everything myself.'

'It is,' said Hani, raising the lip on her notebook and hitting a hot key. It would have been obvious even to someone less versed in the ways of Lady Hana al-Mansur that the child was hovering on the edge of a question.

'What is it?' the maître d' said and kept his smile in place to stop the girl from being anxious. 'You can ask . . .'

Hani held up her pink plastic notebook. 'My uncle's on a mission,' she said seriously. A flick of her eyes around the almost-empty café found it safe to talk. Her look swift, instinctive and enough to convince the man that Hani believed what she said. And why not . . . ? Everyone had heard the rumours that her uncle Ashraf Bey was in the direct employ of the sultan in 'Stambul.

'A mission?'

'Secret,' said Hani. 'Very secret.'

Not being too sure how else to proceed, Hani thrust the screen at the man. 'I have to find this woman,' she said and watched his eyes. Glad that he didn't like the look of her either. 'To deliver a message.'

'This message is from His Excellency?'

Hani shook her head and left it at that.

'I see,' said the thin Italian, visions of the Khedive using his young cousin to pass secret messages to unsuitable foreigners flicking through his head. Or maybe it was Hamzah Effendi, because rumours had the industrialist quietly financing a return to power for Saiid Koenig Pasha.

'The thing is,' Hani began. 'I was wondering if she'd ever eaten here?'

*   *   *

'I forgot to give you this . . .' Hani held out the pen.

'Thank you.' The maître d' smiled. It was only after she'd slipped away the previous afternoon that he realised Lady Hana had taken his silver Mont Blanc with her. He should have known she'd return it just as soon as she realised.

'A parcel came for your uncle.'

'I know,' said Hani, 'I'm here to collect it.'

The maître d' looked doubtful.

'It's wrapped in brown paper,' said Hani. 'Madame Ingrid brought it down this morning. Gave it to you herself.'

At least Hani imagined that was what had happened. She'd been very specific in her instructions to the bank. His Excellency needed the money wrapped in paper and delivered to his office. The parcel was to be given only to Madame Ingrid. The note Hani sent to Madame Ingrid on her uncle's behalf was actually a postcard taken from a box in her dead aunt's old room. The card's surface was waxy, ivory rather than white. Across one side, at the top, ran the words, *al-Mansur Madersa, Rue Sherif, El Iskandryia*. That alone must be enough to make the card an antique, since the door onto Rue Sherif had been walled up for . . .

Hani wasn't sure, but ages anyway. And it had only been unbricked after Aunt Nafisa died. She'd risked using her printer to fake Uncle Asraf's signature on this, because she was pretty certain Madame Ingrid wouldn't be feeding the card through any machine. All the woman would do was what she was told, which was deliver any parcel left at C3 straight to the maître d' at Le Trianon.

It was a smooth-flowing, perfect circle of transferred responsibility.

Hani held out her hand.

'The parcel's in my office,' said the maître d' and Hani nodded wisely, although she hadn't even known the Italian had an office. 'Why don't I have someone bring you a cappuccino while I fetch it?'

Hani did her best not to sigh.

Chapter Twenty-two

Wednesday 23rd February

Mubahith came looking for Raf. At least they did according to Isabeau. But this Raf only found out later and first there was another shift to get through. His seventh in three days. Two scraping dishes, one sud diving, three prepping vegetables and now this.

'More fire . . .' Chef Antonio skimmed the hot chicken breasts across his kitchen, one after the other and a commis chef ducked.

It was inevitable the new broiler man should fumble the catch. If only because he had two hands and there were five flying breasts of chicken. But he caught three and won $20 for Idries who'd bet Raf would catch more than he dropped.

'Owe you,' Idries told him.

The kitchens at Café Antonio were thick with steam. The floor slippery. A radio spat raiPunk and the only thing louder than the fury of Cheb Dread was the chef's voice.

'Burn it,' Antonio snarled. 'Blackened chicken needs to be fucking *blackened.*' With a scowl he swung round, gearing up to persecute somebody else.

Out of the fat chef's sight Raf grabbed a hand towel and began to wipe off his fumbled catches.

'Run them under a tap,' Idries said over his shoulder.

So Raf did, then tossed the five chicken breasts back into oil and smoking butter. Sixty seconds later, having seared both sides to charcoal against the pan's heavy bottom he scooped them out, rolled them on cheap kitchen paper and dumped them back on a plate.

'Ready,' he shouted and discovered the plate was already gone.

'Swordfish two,' came the cry from a teller, 'and let's hustle, tagine three.'

The tagine would be lamb because that was the only kind Café Antonio served. Lamb tagine, blackened chicken and pan-seared swordfish, those were Antonio's bows to ethnic cookery; and if the Soviet kids with their rucksacks and cheap condoms didn't know that tagine came via Morocco, the chicken courtesy of the Caribbean and the swordfish recipe from Malta then Antonio wasn't about to tell them. His ingredients were local, mostly . . . The fish caught by boats from Odessa and frozen on site. When the Soviet crews docked at Tunis, which was rarely, Antonio would be waiting, ready to come to an agreement.

The captain would eat free for his entire stay, much vodka would be drunk and one or maybe two sides of frozen swordfish would go missing.

Other than these dishes Café Antonio served pizza and that was all. Antonio pushed the pizza because he was from Naples after all and his staff also pushed pizza, whatever their nationality, because that's what they were told to do. Pizza was good to eat, quick to cook and the mark-up was excellent; the other dishes took more time, cost more to make and irritated Antonio with their inauthenticity.

'So why serve them?'

Idries shrugged. 'Have you seen the real thing?'

Apparently Antonio needed the ethnic dishes for the kind of tourists who thought they wanted to eat local food but never did when actually presented with lumps of goat heart, fatty lamb still on the bone or fish that scowled back from the plate.

'Swordfish three.'

'Got it,' said Raf and reached for a dish, realising suddenly that it was empty. 'I'm . . .'

'Fucking amateur,' said a dark boy, dumping a pile of swordfish by Raf's station. He was wearing check trousers and clogs, a white jacket and a scarf to keep curling hair out of his eyes; only his grin removed sting from the words. 'Next time, call me before you get eighty-six.' They both knew the boy should have got there first.

A quick flick with a blade to free a steak from the frozen stack and Raf rattled it, still hard, onto the griddle following it with a second and a third. Ninety seconds later the fish was seared.

'Chicken, fire five.' Antonio grabbed a ticket from a teller he felt was working too slowly and shouted out the orders, hanging each yellow slip from a peg when the list was done.

'Come on,' he howled at Raf. 'What are you waiting for?'

Fallout from the oil that hissed in his pan worried Raf not at all. He'd assigned the pain to colours, running the rainbow according to intensity and length. Most of his double shifts sped by in a low level intensity of blue with the occasional flashes of purple.

Already his wrists were freckled with tiny burns and his first finger raw from pressing down on a knife. There would be real calluses later Isabeau had explained to Raf the day before, turning over her own hands. Somehow he'd felt the need to check and then, holding her hands, had not known how to give them back.

Which, obviously enough, was the point Hassan slammed into the cold locker. And the sudden snatch of her fingers had looked like guilt to all of them.

'Chicken,' Raf shouted and scooped blackened breasts onto kitchen paper, rolled them over, then dumped them into a heated dish. Someone else would dress the plates. Glancing over to the hatch to see what other orders were headed his way Raf found the teller leant against the wall, a cigarette ready for lighting.

A red-headed Australian waitress with a flour handprint on her behind was scowling as she dusted the ghostly fingers from black jeans. Raf looked round for anybody with an answering print on their face but all he got was Hassan looking smug.

The last order had just been served. Wind-down could begin.

Café Antonio had a shower room in the basement. This saved the staff from having to climb five flights to their dorm in the attic. Unfortunately there was only one shower and both sexes worked the kitchen, so it alternated as to who got to use it first.

But today that didn't matter because Isabeau was doing a morning shift at Maison Hafsid, the Australian waitress refused to wash at all, something about natural oils and the Bosnian dishwasher, the one who wore tights but no knickers had resigned yesterday, shortly after Raf was promoted to work the broiler instead of her.

'Call for you,' said a pearl diver, soap suds still gloved down both wrists. He held the dripping phone in one hand, a plate in the other and was looking at Idries.

'Tell them to fuck off,' Antonio ordered. 'We're going drinking.'

'I think you should take it,' the boy said to Idries. Very carefully not looking at the chef.

'It won't take a minute,' Idries promised as Antonio scowled.

Afternoon sessions were banned unless the chef suggested them. In the three days he'd been working double shifts Raf had discovered a dozen such rules. Spoken and unspoken. Along with a web of loyalties, pragmatic friendships and alliances, feuds that simmered below the surface and a few that didn't. All institutions were the same and few places came more institutional than a restaurant kitchen.

Small wonder Raf felt at home.

Over at the vidphone Idries was talking intently. His body hunched around the phone in his hand.

'Time's up,' said Antonio. His voice hard. A tumbler of cooking brandy away from developing a dangerous edge.

'It's Isabeau,' Idries said over his shoulder. 'She needs to talk to Raf.'

* * *

'You like snakes?' Isabeau's voice was neutral. All the same Raf knew it was a loaded question because he'd sensed her distance grow as he went from one dirty window to the next, matching labels to the reptiles inside. By the time they'd reached the third row she barely bothered to glance into the cases at all.

She was lost somewhere inside herself. Arms folded across her front. Shoulders hunched as she walked beside him. Dressed in what looked like new jeans and a pink tee-shirt with three-quarter length sleeves. A blue scarf hid her face. If Raf hadn't known better he'd have said she was afraid.

Maybe he was meant to have reacted more to her news. That strange men were searching for him. At least, they were searching for someone. A soldier on the run. Only, Raf knew there was no soldier, was there . . .

Or if there was it wasn't him.

'Put it this way,' said Raf. 'Snakes remind me of my childhood.' Absent-mindedly sliding his hand into the pocket of his own jeans to touch the memento Eugenie had given him, Raf added, 'You could call it a family interest.'

His mother had once shot a series in the Amazon with the working title *Good Snakes Gone Bad*, probably for the Discovery Channel. It became *Renegade Reptiles* and paid less than zilch and took eight months out of her life. She came back with dysentery, ringworm, different colour hair and a brooding Brazilian boy who lasted two months in New York before demanding a ticket home.

Before this was footage for Channel5 involving a python and a naked baby, taken using a table-mounted Sanyo with remote control, so she could also be in shot. A thin woman in her early twenties, bare-breasted and with hennaed toes on a Berber rug beside the snake and child. Because she showed no fear of the reptile, the infant showed no fear and because the infant lacked fear it yanked happily at the sleepy phython, digging small fingers into snake flesh and pushing the python around like a toy.

When this didn't elicit a response, the child dragged a heavy coil to its mouth and tried to chew its leather-like skin. Finally the infant got bored and crawled out of shot, leaving the woman smiling into the camera.

A fifteen-second snip later got used for a campaign selling life insurance.

It was years before Raf realised the child was him.

'But do you like them?' Isabeau insisted.

Raf shook his head.

'Then why suggest we meet here?'

'You wanted to talk . . .'

She would age, Raf realised as he watched her frown. Her compact body fill out and her face acquire lines. That residual puppy fat on her arms would become less puppyish, more obvious, her looks would go and breasts lose their battle with gravity. She would put on weight and grow old, something the fox once promised would never happen to him.

'Sometimes,' said Raf. 'I get voices that tell me what to do . . .'

Or maybe that was *invent*? Raf was uncertain. For as long as he could remember there had been a fracture between mind and body, observed and observer. A rupture of identity that kept him distanced from himself, often thinking of himself as *he*. What if the fox was right and it didn't exist . . . If his memory wasn't as perfect as he pretended?

What if he was just running away?

Isabeau stared back. Worried but not frightened, not yet.

'And these voices told you to look at snakes?'

'Actually,' Raf's smile was rueful, 'I think that was my idea.'

'Your . . .' And after a second Isabeau almost smiled back. It was a nervous smile but it lifted her face and bled some of the anxiety from her eyes.

'These voices?'

'Once there was a fox,' said Raf, staring into a darkened case. 'A dangerous and deadly ghost. Always waiting, always there.' On the other side of the filthy glass a boot-lace tasted the air with a sullen tongue. Around its nostrils splashed colours that no human eye could see. Knowledge Raf could tell Isabeau or keep to himself. 'And then it wasn't.'

'What happened?'

Raf looked at her. There were no colours hidden in her face. Nothing Isabeau couldn't see in her own reflection.

'To the fox?'

She nodded.

'Someone repaired the bloody thing . . .'

Hammered into a grassy bank between the ring road and the main fence surrounding the zoo were enamel signs every hundred paces or so, to warn visitors not to climb over. A crude silhouette of a wolf reinforced that message.

At the bottom of the track stood metal gates and on the far side of those, just before a main road, was a neat ornamental lake crowded with wading birds and waterfowl. Around the edge strolled what looked like smart Tunis. Girls walking hand in hand and young men with their arms around each other's shoulders in expressions of friendship that could only have been political back in Seattle.

A small wading bird with clockwork legs and blue bottom raced across damp concrete and plopped into the lake, bobbing beneath the spray of a fountain on its way towards a tiny island in the middle. The concrete was damp because the fountain plumed straight out of the water and every gust of wind carried fine droplets towards the shore.

The scene was sickeningly normal.

'Let me buy you a coffee.' Raf nodded to a low café across the lake, its tables almost as crowded as the paths. 'Then you can tell me about Maison Hafsid and who these men were who came looking for me . . .'

In reply, Isabeau glanced at her wrist.

'You need to be somewhere else?'

Isabeau looked suddenly embarrassed, even slightly panicked; a blush suffusing her face. 'No,' she said hastily, 'being here is good.' They finished the stroll in silence. Only this time it was a quieter, less strained silence and could almost pass for friendship if not for the anxious glances she kept throwing in Raf's direction.

All that changed when Raf saw a child feeding bread to a

duck. No one he'd ever seen before. Just a girl of about nine wearing a head scarf and feeding crusts to a duck so full it could barely waddle. She had long hair, tied back. White sneakers and cheap dark glasses that kept sliding down her nose. So wrapped up was she in watching the duck that the rest of the world might as well have not existed . . .

'Raf,' said Isabeau. She was pulling at his arm.

'What?'

'What are the voices saying?' Worried eyes watched him. 'And why are you staring at that child?'

'No reason,' said Raf. And was shocked to discover he was crying.

'You miss your kid?' Isabeau demanded when the waiter had gone.

Raf put down his coffee, thought about it . . . 'Yes,' he admitted finally.

'Because he lives with his mother?'

'She,' Raf corrected, 'and I think her mother's dead.'

'You think . . .' Isabeau tried hard not to be shocked. Divorce was more common in Ifriqiya than in other North African countries. But not in the way it was in the West. All the same, Isabeau figured she'd know if a person she'd married was alive or not.

'You *were* married to her mother?'

'I've never been married,' Raf said. 'Although I was engaged once but that was to someone else.' He caught Isabeau's expression and smiled. 'It's a messy story,' he said.

'They usually are.' Glancing round the café terrace with its noisy children and couples relaxing after a stroll in Jardin Belvedere, she shrugged. 'You don't have to tell me that.' When Isabeau spoke again it was to ask a question that had been troubling her. Her voice was hesitant, as if Isabeau was uncertain of the wisdom of asking.

'You're not really who you say you are, are you? If you know what I mean . . .'

Inside Raf's head the other Raf grinned, all teeth and

no smile. '*Okay,*' it said smoothly, '*answer that and stay human.*'

Raf couldn't. Which he guessed was Tiri's point.

The *capuchin* was milky, came in glass mugs and had a scum of thin froth across the top. Raf promptly embarrassed himself by mishearing the price and blithely handing the waiter a note roughly equivalent to U$5, a good portion of Raf's wages for that week.

'Does Your Excellency have anything smaller?' It was obvious the old man thought Raf was trying to impress Isabeau.

Raf shook his head. 'Wednesday's pay day,' he said. 'That's how I was given it.'

'Must be a good job.'

'Kitchen work, seven shifts in a row,' Raf said wryly and saw rather than heard the old man suck his teeth.

'No so good . . . I'll get you change.'

A dozen grubby notes and a fistful of change, some of it old enough to be real arrived on a chipped saucer, while Raf and Isabeau sat at their table and watched two toddlers, an old man wearing a red felt *chechia* and a young woman cross the wooden bridge leading from the gates of Jardin Belvedere over a narrow strip of lake to where Isabeau and Raf sat nursing warm coffees.

At Raf's end stood a camera crew trying to film two laughing girls in red headscarves, arms tight around each other's waists as they strolled across the same bridge, but every time the girls got halfway some toddler would run into shot or a passing family would halt and stare. Once, an old woman halted the two girls just as they reached the café end of the bridge. She wanted to ask them the time.

'Who are they?'

Isabeau snorted. 'Now I *know* you don't come from around here,' she said and named a famous Tunisian soap that had been running for eighteen years. 'They've been friends since before kindergarten,' Isabeau explained. 'But their fathers have hated each other ever since Jasmine's father had Natasha's mother's kiosk at Gare de Tunis torn down because she hadn't applied for a tobacco-sellers permit. So now they have to meet in secret.'

'Are they lovers?'

Isabeau's eyes went wide. 'Such things don't happen in Ifriqiya. Especially on television.'

'Don't happen or aren't talked about?'

'Both,' said Isabeau. And for a moment Raf was looking through a broken window into the darkened basement of her soul.

'So why the fear?' Raf asked.

Part of Isabeau wanted to ask *what fear?* The rest needed to get up and walk away. Instead she sipped at cold coffee and watched two twenty-three-year-old actresses pretend to be fifteen.

'In America,' Raf said, 'they'd close this café, hire extras to drink coloured water and have police tape off the road both sides of the gate. Everything would be done in one shot . . . The only people allowed near that bridge would be the actresses and the crew. And if the actresses decided to fuck each other it would be out of boredom.'

'You've been to America?' Isabeau sounded disbelieving.

'Once,' said Raf. 'Years back. When I thought I was some-body else.'

'Why tell me this?

'Because I can?'

'And I can't tell anybody.' Isabeau nodded, as if that was obvious. 'Without you telling them about me . . .' Her voice was thoughtful.

'So Hassan doesn't know?'

'Hassan!' Raf could almost taste her irritation. 'Oh, Hassan wants to marry me, all right. So he can get his hands on my quarter of the café.' It took a second for Raf to work out that Isabeau meant the smoky tunnel in Souk El Katherine where he'd first met Idries. 'That won't be happening . . .'

'You already have a lover?'

The broken window was instantly back. The room inside darker than ever. As black as those places where the fox hid. In the days before Raf finally accepted that the fox was him.

'Okay,' Raf said. 'No lover.'

'No,' Isabeau agreed. On the far side of the bridge the camera crew began packing equipment into a white van, faces relieved and both the actresses now sat in an old green Lincoln that waited to pull out into traffic, watched by a crowd of schoolchildren.

'What about you?' Isabeau asked, her eyes never leaving the car.

What indeed. Any answer Raf might be prepared to give was aborted by a sudden buzz from Isabeau's bag.

'It's me,' she said, having reached for a cheap mobile. 'What?'

The answer froze Isabeau's expression. One second, she was watching a distant schoolgirl with bare legs and checked dress the next blood drained from Isabeau's cheeks and her mouth went slack. Spiralling adrenergic hormones. Textbook shock.

She turned off the Nokia without saying another word.

'I have to go.' Eyes unfocused.

'Go where?' said Raf. And when Isabeau didn't answer he reached forward to take the mobile from unresisting fingers and put it back in her bag. Without thinking he also wiped a fingertip of sweat from her forehead and absent-mindedly licked it. Shocked and scared, the Raf inside Raf decided, been there/done that/probably about to do it again.

'You in trouble?' Stupid question really.

'I have to go.' Metal scraped on concrete as Isabeau pushed back her chair and three tables away people winced. 'My brother, Pascal . . .'

'I'll come with you,' said Raf.

She shook her head.

Raf sighed. 'Whatever it is,' he said. 'I can help. And if you're really in trouble then a couple is less easy to spot than a single girl in a city like this.' His nod took in the café crowd and the busy sidewalk on the other side of the bridge.

'How can I trust you?' Isabeau demanded. 'And how do I know you are who you say you are?'

'You don't,' said Raf. 'And I'm not.' He tossed some change onto their table for the waiter and gripped Isabeau's hand, refusing to let her pull free. 'Smile as you walk away,' Raf ordered, and Isabeau's face twisted in misery.

Halfway across the little bridge he made her stop to watch a waterbird swim beneath their feet, take a last look round the lake and then stroll arm in arm with him towards the gates. On the way out, Raf bought a loose bag of biscuits from a stall. They were sweet to the point of sickness and warm from being on display.

Chapter Twenty-three

Wednesday 23rd February

'I wonder if you could help . . .' Hani's voice was polite but firm. As if she regularly wandered alone as evening fell, trawling expensive Italian boutiques on Rue Faransa, a street once rather more famous for its Victorian brothels and opium dens.

'A dress?' Returning Hani's demand with a question was all the stick-like owner could manage. Backed up inside Madame Fitmah's head were a dozen other, infinitely more important questions, starting with how was this child planning to pay and ending with what should she, Madame Fitmah, call the small girl since *madame* was obviously out of the question?

'I've got cash,' said Hani, yanking a roll of dollars from her fleece pocket. 'And you can call me *mademoiselle*.' She grinned at Madame Fitmah's blossoming shock and nodded towards an antique brass till inlaid with silver and bronze, although the mechanism was strictly electronic. 'You glanced at that,' Hani explained, 'then you looked at me and seemed puzzled.'

'*Mademoiselle?*'

Hani nodded. 'And I've got cash,' she stressed, holding out the roll of US dollars but still the woman looked doubtful.

El Isk was, by the standards of North Africa, surprisingly liberal in its approach to life. In part this was down to its status as a freeport and, in part, to the fact that liberalism had been General Koenig Pasha's only defence against creeping fundamentalism. True, a woman still couldn't inherit property, hold a job without the consent of her father or husband, drive alone on Fridays or initiate a divorce; but she could own a credit card and was liable for any debt she incurred. Unlike, say, Riyadh or Algiers, where all a man had to do was repudiate his wife's right to incur debt and no court would enforce an order.

Children were different, obviously enough. In Iskandryia, boys were considered responsible from the age of fourteen; for girls the age was twenty-one. Although where marriage was concerned the differential reversed. Then the legal age was fourteen for the girl and sixteen for a boy.

Even if Hani had possessed a credit card, Madame Fitmah would have been unwilling to sell her anything without an adult present to countersign the slip. Cash on the other hand . . .

'What kind of dress?'

'Gold,' said Hani. 'Thin as the wings of a Great Admiral butterfly, with pearls around the neck and sleeves seeded with emeralds.'

'I'm not sure we've . . .' The Italian woman looked round at steel shelves lining her *haut minimaliste* boutique. A shop space taller than it was wide. And when she shrugged apologetically her scarlet Versace dress creased at the shoulders. 'I doubt if anyone's ever . . .'

Hani sighed and the gown that Sheherazade wore on the last of her one thousand and one nights crumbled in her imagination and was gone.

'Show me what you've got,' said Hani and sounded so like Zara that she tagged on a hurried *please*, before climbing onto a chrome and glass chair to position herself so that she stared at a red flower painted on the far wall, her spine rigid and legs bent at the knee. A move which did more than ever cash could to convince Madame Fitmah the child belonged in her boutique.

'You've been measured before.'

'Oh,' Hani smiled sweetly. 'I'm always being measured.' And so she was, against the edge of a door in the kitchen by Donna, who took a fresh measurement every month and wrote the date against it. Although obviously this wasn't what the woman meant.

'But you don't have your card . . . ?'

'I've grown,' Hani told the woman. She sounded ridiculously smug about this, as if the growth spurt had been down to her and not to nature. That wasn't the real reason Hani had left her card behind, of course. The one she'd had done with Zara featured Hani's name and address encoded on the chip.

The scanner was silent as it passed through the small girl's fleece, tee-shirt and jeans to map the skin beneath, then looked through skin to the bones and measured those as well. Any clothes cut to measure would fit perfectly but Hani was too impatient to wait so Madame Fitmah matched her measurements to an inventory of stock.

'I'm sorry,' the owner began to say and stopped as the face of the child in front of her immediately dissolved into tears. Half a second later and the grief was gone, pulled back into glistening eyes and a trembling mouth. A second after that and Hani's face was neatly composed.

'I'm sorry to have troubled you,' Hani said as she slipped from the chair. Pushing her bundle of dollars back into a fleece pocket, she headed for the door.

'Wait.' Madame Fitmah stood beside a screen, scrolling down the list. 'I'm sure we can adapt something. Is this for a special occasion?'

'Oh yes,' said Hani. 'One of my cousins is having a party for his parents.'

Chapter Twenty-four

Wednesday 23rd February

'Next time,' Chef Antonio's voice was flat, 'I sell your ass to my Nephew Hassan, who likes that kind of thing.' He took back his high-carbon Wusthof and threw the recipient of his scorn a cheap Sabatier kept for casual labour.

The Australian boy in question looked from Antonio to the blade that quivered in the door beside him and his shock, outrage and (let's be honest) unconcealed admiration went a tiny way towards restoring the chef's good humour. There were basic rules in life and first up was touch someone else's knife at your peril.

Antonio pointed to a half-full bucket of tomatoes. 'You don't stop until you've skinned the lot. You understand?'

The Australian did.

With a sigh the chef turned back to his radio. 'Sources close to the police say the man just arrested has known links to fundamentalist terror groups.' The newsreader spoke with an accent so impossibly Parisian it had to be fake.

Antonio twisted the dial and watched a needle judder its way across a thin strip of glass inscribed with stations that, like as not, no longer existed. The radio was Soviet, the size of a breeze block only three times as heavy. Someone, probably a prisoner in a gulag workshop, had painted individual swirls of grain across its metal casing.

'. . . more news for you on the hour.'

'Try another station,' demanded Hassan

Antonio took time out to stare at his wife's nephew but he still did what the fat boy suggested, stopping as the hiss of static thinned into Arabic.

'No further news on the murder at Maison Hafsid . . .'

Running the length of the dial twice, Antonio checking out as many of the local stations as he could find. It was easy to tell an approved station because those were the ones carrying identical versions of the same story. The pirates were more interesting but nothing they suggested sounded remotely like the truth.

'Any news on Isabeau?' Chef Antonio demanded.

'She hasn't phoned back.'

'Okay,' Antonio told Idries. 'Let me know if she does . . .' But when a call finally came it wasn't from Isabeau.

'For you,' Hassan said.

'Who?'

Hassan returned the stare he'd been given earlier. 'For you,' he said and dropped the receiver to let it spin vine-like, tipped by a matt-grey plastic fruit.

Sometime or other Antonio was going to have to talk to his wife. It was all very well having her nephew on board, but the deal was that the boy was here to learn, not behave like he was already part owner.

'Yes,' Antonio barked, voice harsher than he intended. 'What?' Whoever answered had presence enough to fill the chef's voice with something very close to respect. 'I'll be there.' The chef listened again. 'We'll be there,' he agreed, amending his words.

'Scrap the tomatoes,' he told the Australian boy. 'We're closing for tonight.' He nodded at Idries. 'Turn off the ovens and put everything back in the cooler . . .'

'You know,' said Raf, the nouvelle ville rattling by behind his head in a succession of dusty shops and pavement tables. 'There's something I still don't quite get.' Tapping his last Cleopatra from its packet the way Hamzah's builders did, Raf crumpled the empty box and dropped it. A flick of a cheap lighter and he passed the cigarette to Isabeau, who dug deep and handed it back.

'What's to get?' Isabeau asked flatly.

'Who are you running from?'

Jagged glass/broken bulbs. Raf was going to have to get over matching images to emotions, his own and other people's. Shock of some kind had finally swallowed Isabeau; shaking her hands and dragging her thumb repetitively across her finger tips, grinding her heels into the floor.

One 30c ticket each had bought them an hour in which Isabeau shipped her growing panic out towards Tunis Maritime, back towards Place de Barcelone and up to Place Halfaouine. Parc du Belvedere. Place Bardo. Crossing the rails for a different line, switching directions. Two stops this way, one stop that, change lines every third move. Regular as clockwork and about as useful. It was like watching chess played by a child who lacked the rules but had one set of winning moves written on the back of someone else's envelope.

'Welcome,' said Shibli as he climbed to his feet and touched his hand to his heart. Chef Antonio made do with returning a slight bow, not quite confident enough to return formal greetings to a Sufi master; particularly as the man still looked more like a bouncer than a mystic, what with his freshly shaved head, bare arms and pirate earrings. Although, admittedly, this time round Shibli wore a pale kaftan rather than his usual striped jellaba.

'Discard your knife.' Shibli pointed to a brass tray by the café door. It contained a handful of cheap switchblades and one ancient revolver.

'My knives remain in the kitchen.'

Shibli smiled. 'Then find a space,' he said, 'and make yourself comfortable.'

Antonio and his staff had reached Bab Souika in two taxis, passing through the gate into the medina on foot with a five minute gap between each taxi. Partly this was caution, but mostly it was because the majority of taxis stuck to nouvelle ville, leaving the suburbs to buses and illegal cabs. And Idries said calling cabs out to Café Antonio would be a risk.

By the time the chef ducked under the low doorway to greet Shibli, his sous-chef was already settled on a bench at the far end of the room, apple-scented smoke filling the crowded vault from a *sheesha* on the floor in front of him. Chef and sous-chef looked at each other and Idries stood.

'Take my seat,' he suggested.

Antonio shook his head and pointed to a space on one of the longer benches. 'I'll be fine there,' he said. The embarrassment between them was palpable. Made obvious by this very public reversal of roles. In his kitchen Antonio was god, though he'd never claim so in the presence of his staff, most of whom were believers. Here it was Shibli and, to a far lesser extent, Idries who commanded the room. A dozen races and twice that many languages survived within the walls of the medina and there were very few penalties to being born *nasrani*.

Except now, except here. In the presence of those whose eyes were open, the wool wearers and those who went naked.

Every café, shop, restaurant and brothel in the city paid protection to Kashif Pasha's police. A few, no one knew how many, chose to pay again, a different kind of insurance. Chef Antonio was one of those. How much he paid was up to him and depended on how good a week he'd had. Sometimes, at the height of the 'packer season, a week could be very good indeed and then Antonio would stuff an envelope with enough notes to make it fat and give this to Idries, who passed the envelope to Shibli. Where the money went after that neither Antonio nor Idries asked.

'Drink and eat,' ordered Shibli, nodding to a trayful of painted glasses filled with sweet mint tea and half a dozen yellow bowls rimmed around the top with white metal that wanted to be silver. The tray hung on a strap from around the neck of a small, one-armed man wearing *shalwar kameez* and a three-fist beard so wispy it hung like unspooled cotton. He was the only person in the room to whom Shibli was unfailingly polite and rumour had it that he was one whose eyes had been so completely opened that he was now near blind.

When everyone had eaten baklava and drunk tea Shibli clapped his hands once and the room fell silent. 'Where's Isabeau?' he demanded.

'With the soldier.'

'And where's the soldier?'

'Here,' said a voice from the curtained doorway. Pushing his way through dangling beads, Raf blinked at the thickness of smoke. Behind him, wearing a new coat, minus her scarf and with her hair tied back, came Isabeau. She was still shaking.

'We've been hiding.' Raf said.

'Who from?' Shibli looked interested.

Raf shrugged. 'Ask her,' he suggested, but his voice was gentle and his hand on Isabeau's arm was light as he guided her towards a space at one end of a bench.

'Take a seat,' Shibli told Raf. 'I'll ask when the time comes.' And with that, he reached into his kaftan and extracted a book-sized block of hashish, stamped on both sides with Arabic lettering. Pulling a clasp knife from his pocket, the Sufi prised it open and shaved a dark sliver from one corner.

'A fresh *sheesha*,' Shibli demanded and Idries disappeared through the bead curtain, returning with a waterpipe into which the Sufi crumbled both honey tobacco and fragments from the block. He took the first puff himself and then passed the waterpipe to Isabeau.

'I'm sorry about Pascal,' he said gently and Isabeau nodded. 'Such things happen,' he added. 'Sometimes they're unavoidable.' Shibli sighed. 'If you know who might have wanted him dead then you must tell me . . .'

'I don't.' Isabeau's voice was small. Already distant.

'Then who were you running from?' The question was Hassan's, from the far corner of the room.

Isabeau glanced from Shibli to Raf and then back at Hassan. 'From myself,' she said and both Raf and Shibli nodded.

The story was complicated the way such stories usually are. But it seemed Isabeau's brother had been found murdered in an alley behind Maison Hafsid, a restaurant at which some of Café Antonio's staff regularly worked and where her brother was pastry chef.

Ahmed, a cousin to Idries, had been arrested for the crime. Shock mixed with outrage in Idries' voice as he admitted this, but his predominant tone was worry. Despite their apparent closeness Idries admitted his cousin was not eminently likeable. Ahmed's habit of using his fists was mentioned. His inability to walk away from a brawl. His use of alcohol.

'But Pascal was stabbed?' Raf asked.

'Yes,' said Idries, 'that was what it said on the news.'

'Did Ahmed carry a knife?'

Raf's question earned him an amused glance from Shibli.

'We all carry knives,' Idries said gently.

'But Ahmed was the kind of man to use his fists?'

'That's true,' Shibli admitted, eyes suddenly shrewd.

'So, what about witnesses?' Raf asked gently. It was a dangerous game he was playing. Giving them more of himself than was safe to give. But one that was worth the risk. Maison Hafsid was a step closer than Café Antonio. And Shibli had Isabeau under his wing. A wing Raf imagined to be vast and black, bat-like, spreading its spines across the city and hiding wonders in its shadow.

'Did anyone see what happened?'

'God . . .' Hassan's voice was harsh. 'You talk like a policeman.'

'That's because I was a policeman,' said Raf flatly. 'I've been many things. Not all of them good.' He stared round the windowless room and when his gaze stopped it was on Idries. 'So, were there any witnesses?'

'We don't know,' admitted Idries. His voice tired. 'And we can't ask Ahmed,' he added, 'because the police won't let anyone see him until he's pleaded guilty.'

Raf nodded, as if this was to be expected. 'Okay,' he said, 'you'll need to show me the site.'

Chapter Twenty-five

Thursday 24th February

'You be good,' Hani told Ifritah, placing the cat firmly on her bed. No sooner done than Ifritah jumped for the suitcase Hani was trying to buckle, claws ripping into old leather as she scrabbled for a hold.

Hani sucked her teeth. 'Try,' she told Ifritah. 'At the very least, try . . .'

Hong Kong Suisse had delivered her cash. Late, admittedly, but Hani was no longer cross about that. She had a party dress made from red silk, green velvet and real gold embroidery. It was designed for someone several years older than Hani and on Zara would have been indecently short. On Hani it fell to her ankles like a ball gown. Added to which Madame Fitmah had even given her discount on a pair of matching shoes.

Mortgaging her uncle's madersa to finance the trip had been wrong, Hani realised that. And if she'd been allowed access to her own money it wouldn't have been necessary. But to get that would involve asking Hamzah or the Khedive, and then they'd want to know why she needed money. Hani shook her head. Sometimes simplicity was everything.

So she'd written to Uncle Ashraf's bank instead, using headed paper and quoting his account number, which had been ridiculously easy to find since it featured on various statements kept in a desk outside his bedroom. Marked *confidential*, her letter inquired delicately about the opportunities for mortgaging a famous seventeenth-century madersa in a prime position. An equally circumspect (Hani liked that word) reply from HKS suggested that, unless His Excellency really wanted a mortgage of the kind that needed repaying over a number of years, the best option might be a straight loan, at no interest, since usury was obviously forbidden, but with a settlement fee to be paid as the final part of the reckoning, please see sample contract enclosed.

The bank had used longer words than that – because banks always use complicated words – but that was what Hong Kong Suisse meant.

Hani's reply ended with a flamboyant impression of her uncle's initials and the only thing that stopped her from scanning an original into her laptop and using that was a slight worry that HKS might use some kind of fluorescing system to distinguish fountain pen from printer ink.

As a final touch, Hani found her uncle's spare comb, removed a single hair and dropped it into the envelope, which might be one touch too many but by then she'd stuck the envelope and used her only stamp.

Next morning and the morning after found Hani waiting for the postman, cat in hand. Swapping Ifritah for his fat bundle of letters she chatted about the weather while sorting through the pile. The letter she wanted was one of five. Four of these were bills, three of them red reminders . . .

The loan was agreed and the fact Ashraf Bey had initialled rather than signed his contract as requested was nowhere mentioned: but then Hani remembered reading that the Empire State Building had once been mortgaged against an unsigned deed and she was no longer surprised. All that remained, those were the words HKS used, all that remained was for His Excellency to nominate a receiving account.

Hani took this to mean she should tell the bank where to send the money. So she wrote again on a sheet of the paper taken three days earlier from her uncle's office at the Third Circle.

Stealing it was easy. All Hani had to do was buy a chocolate sundae at Le Trianon, leave most of it and use the café's internal lift to go straight to C3's reception on the floor above. The story she'd prepared about wanting to collect a toy dog from her uncle's office went unused. Madame Ingrid was giving evidence to a tribunal investigating the crimes of Colonel Abad and, with their office manager gone, most of her junior staff had left for lunch early, while the rest just nodded at Hani or ignored her.

Taking a single sheet of headed paper from its holder on Uncle Ashraf's desk, Hani promptly changed her mind and slipped a thick wad of the stuff into her rucksack. One never knew when it might become useful. As an afterthought, she added a rubber stamp that sat on the desk beside the wooden box holding the paper. It was a very ornate rubber stamp with brass claws to hold the block of rubber and an ivory handle, but it was still a rubber stamp.

From the desk of Colonel Pashazade Ashraf al-Mansur, Ashraf Bey. Looking at the faint script left by the stamp on the inside of her wrist Hani raised her eyebrows. She hadn't realised her uncle was a colonel; at least, she didn't remember knowing that but the fact didn't surprise her. Secret agents and assassins were bound to have military ranks, it was obvious really. Everyone in North Africa had a rank of some kind or other.

Hani was just letting herself out of the office when she finally realised what she'd missed. A briefcase, with a gun-metal grey combination lock, below a black coat hanging from a rack topped by an Astrakhan hat she'd never seen Uncle Ashraf wear, tight curls of baby fur soft enough to make Hani cringe.

Hat, coat, briefcase.

Hide in plain sight.

Since Madame Ingrid might notice if the case disappeared, Hani resolved to examine it in situ. Would it be very conceited . . . ? Assuming she really was eleven, not ten, Hani fed her own birthdate into the combination lock and Uncle Ashraf's case opened first try. Which was just as well, because there was serious potential for stalemate if it had been his own birthday and it was bound to be the birthday of someone or other.

Statistically most combination locks used a birth date within the owner's immediate family, 73 per cent of them in fact. And Hani knew just how hard her uncle worked at appearing normal. Being a son of Lilith required one to hide in plain sight, normal being interchangeable with invisible. Hani knew all about it. And if she ever forgot, all she had to do was stare in a mirror.

Hani paused to think that last thought through, which was slightly recursive but necessary. She had no doubt she could become exactly like her uncle if she tried. Actually, Hani suspected she'd become like him whatever. Flipping open his case, she spread her catch on the tiles. Another gun. No, she corrected herself, a Colt *revolver*. Specifics were always important. A *carte blanche* which was – Hani flipped it open – less than a month out of date. And inside it something else.

Folded within the *carte blanche* was a letter from a lawyer in Tunis adressed to her Aunt Nafisa. Skimming the script as it flowed, elegant and fluid, from right to left across a perfectly ordinary piece of office paper, Hani began to memorise the contents word for word. It seemed that Zari Moncef al-Mansur, eldest son of the old Emir of Tunis had married Sally Welham, an English photographer on the . . .

The date was so wrong that Hani brushed it aside, stumbling over the fact that he'd divorced her five days later and halting altogether when she got to the date of her uncle's birth. Had the letter been printed out on some computer she'd have dismissed the year as a simple typing error but the note was handwritten, which made the date either beyond careless or very odd indeed.

Pocketing the letter, Hani turned to a strip of Zaras, the photobooth kind. Younger, somewhat fatter, her eyes less troubled than now, despite the scowl with which she faced the mechanical camera. And then a photograph of Uncle Raf, staring into the sun with the *Jammaa ez Zitouna* in the background.

Okay, so whatever he'd told Aunt Nafisa before she died, Uncle Raf *had* been to Tunis because la Grande Mosquée, built by the Emir Ibrahim Ibn Ahmed in 856CE was not only the second largest mosque in Ifriqiya (the largest was in Kairouan) but also one of North Africa's most instantly recognisable heritage sites.

In the photograph he looked older. That was, Uncle Ashraf looked as he did now, not as he should have done back when this was obviously taken. There was one final photograph.

'Oh . . .' Hani placed it face down on the tiles and carefully packed the Zaras and Uncle Ashraf outside la Grande Mosquée into her rucksack, sliding them between sheets of headed paper. The Colt she put back into her uncle's case. That left his final photograph.

The girl didn't look poor because on her wrist was an Omega and an empty camera case hung around her neck. But the Fat Boys were definitely frayed and her feet were both bare and dirty. Her hair also looked like it needed a wash, being matted into rat tails around her thin face.

What shocked Hani was not the dirty hair or bare feet. Not even the half-open shirt she wore, washed so fine that what couldn't be seen of the woman's breasts through the gap was revealed by the translucence of the cloth. It was the way she leered into the lens, her mouth half open, her eyes obviously fixed on the person holding her camera.

This Hani hadn't considered and she doubted if Zara had either. Men went to brothels and, if they were sensible, women ignored this fact. So Hani had learnt from listening at the door to her late aunts, Nafisa and Jalila. As for mistresses, if a man could afford to run more than one house this too was acceptable. Not least, Aunt Nafisa had sighed, because it did so help to lighten the load.

But a *nasrani* girlfriend . . . One who was thin, dirty and badly dressed?

Hani took another squint at the photograph. What with her rat's nest of fair hair and narrow face, washed-out eyes and tight lips the bare-foot woman was unlikely to be anything but *nasrani* . . . If this was the real reason her uncle refused to marry Zara then that changed everything. For the first time since he'd stamped up the stairs into the *qaa* all those months ago, Hani came close to deciding that maybe she didn't like her uncle after all.

Chapter Twenty-six

Flashback

'Too fucking hot.' Even at thirty mph, which was way too fast for the ruts in the track, the wind roared in Sally's ears and swept words from her mouth. So she said it again, just in case Per hadn't heard her the first time.

'Yeah,' said Per tightly, 'I know.' Swinging the wheel of his black Jeep to avoid a missing bit of road he bounced Sally hard into her door, setting off a new round of swearing. The Jeep was eighteen years old, cigarette burns pocked the top of its plastic dash and he'd been forced to buy a petrol rather than diesel version. Black was also, in Sally's opinion, just about as stupid a colour as it was possible to find for skirting a desert; since it positively lapped up direct sunlight and made the interior too hot to touch.

The Jeep's air-conditioning – and there'd been air-conditioning when they started – had lasted for all of three days. Per blamed Sally's habit of hanging out of her side window for burning out the unit. Sally's view was that if he'd bought an open top model as she originally suggested, he wouldn't have needed air-conditioning and she wouldn't have had to keep opening the window to take photographs.

She now knew about his interest in mythology, bush meat and oral sex. His plans to open a restaurant and the age he first smoked blow. He knew she liked cameras.

Having first dwindled into tight-lipped sentences, their con- versation had since shrunk into near silence. They still fucked like animals but no longer had anything to say to each other afterwards. There were a lot of relationships like that, Sally realised. And she did enjoy fucking Per far more than talking to him. And they were animals. So . . .

Opening the Leica with one hand, Sally removed a completed roll of film and dropped it into the foil packet she'd already ripped from its replacement.

'What the fuck is there to photograph?'

The whole absurd and cruel beauty of Ifriqiya's Chott el Jerrid. Shrubs so hardy they came back from the dead, Lazarus like; grasses able to tolerate saline levels that killed other plants; the distant pinks and yellows of minerals blooming across a flatbed of salt.

'Nothing,' Sally said, snapping shut her camera. 'Absolutely nothing.' Beside the road stretched the largest salt lake in North Africa. Rock hard in summer and partly flooded in winter, drying in early spring to brine pools and a treacherous skim of crust. Mysterious and wonderful. Utterly at odds with the olive groves and ubiquitous hedges of prickly pear which made up yesterday's trip south. Those could have be found in southern Spain, Sicily or Greece.

This was different.

How different the pale-skinned Swede could not even begin to realise. Here life was leaner, sharper and better able to deal with exotic levels of deprivation. At the edges of existence, life was forced to make a compromise. One that the world would soon find itself forced to make if the canker of global interests could not be cured.

In that at least Wu Yung was right. Although his way was not her way. Something the old Chinese man had still to realise. Anymore than her way was Atal's way or even Per's . . .

Sally Welham shook her head. Per had the soft liberal reflexes of his class, race and age. He would no more understand what she wanted from the chott than accept how she intended to achieve it. He was a mindless fuck and a zipless one at that; defined by over-privilege, education, a simplistic rejection of Calvinism and a carpet bag of beliefs strip-mined from other cultures.

Whereas she . . .

At least Sally had the grace to grin. Grin, shrug and discard the comparison. She was the same, the difference was that she knew this fact.

'Ruin,' said Per, seconds ahead of slamming on his brakes. Sand slid down a bank like snow and when the Jeep stopped it was half on the track and half off, one rear wheel hanging over the side of a ditch.

'How about giving me some warning?' Sally snapped.

'I just did,' Per said and pushing open his door he was gone, all stiff backed and straight shouldered.

Sally sighed.

Piss ran across sand after she casually dropped her jeans, then stayed to watch the warm stream run mercury-like over the sand's crust, hardly touching its surface. That was the problem, rainfall raced across the desert's surface like piss, filling oueds and flooding chotts and wadis. Grasses grew, flowers happened, insects bred; life blossomed and died in the time it took the sky to squat.

Still grinning ruefully, Sally stepped out of her jeans, yanked her tee-shirt inside out and went to find Per. He'd be looking for mosaics in the ruins of some hovel he'd insist was Roman.

'Don't walk on it,' Per said, not looking round. He was on his hands and knees sweeping rubbish from a floor with his fingers. Sally was willing to bet it was made from stamped-down dirt and that she had better chance of becoming pope than Per did of finding a priceless mosaic beneath the crap that carpeted his goat hut.

Still, she let him brush away ring pulls and screw caps, plastic bottles and disposable nappies until his enthusiasm faded and he looked round to see Sally behind him, naked and with filthy feet. An equally dirty grin written across her face.

'Lie flat,' she told him, so Per did and Sally stepped forward and squatted again. His face was hot between her thighs, his tongue frantic. He licked and (later) fucked with the hunger of someone still drunk on her body. And Sally might have found such innocence endearing if she wasn't already waving Per goodbye in her head.

She found the Swedish kroner at the bottom of his sleeping bag, along with a passport that revealed Per to be three years older than he'd admitted. For a second Sally was tempted to take the money but Ottoman banks liked dollars, marks and francs; even sterling gave them trouble, so God alone knew what they'd have made of kroner.

Besides, her quest was almost over. And what Sally already had, sewn into the lining of her rucksack, was worth more than Per's cash or passport could ever be. Still smiling, she put his money back.

Sally woke Per with a hand job, something of a speciality for her. Then rolled him onto his back and unzipped his bag before Per had time to notice its bottom end had been slashed open. He fucked with his eyes closed, even in daylight, spasming beneath her.

Little death they used to call it. They being almost every culture at some time or other. And so it was, in its way. Sex was the point at which individuality became unimportant. Life's purpose over in everything but name the first time one fucked and was fertile; or would have been, but for contraception, medical advances and falling levels of fertility introducing design flaws into Darwin.

When the deed was done the torch was passed, to flame or die, except that now science kept even the weakest flames alight. Mutations happened for a reason, Sally accepted that utterly. And benevolent or not, Galton was right. This was not a statement Sally would have dared say in front of anyone she knew. Only to herself did she dare say it and only recently, once she realised that if the planet could not be saved then humanity itself would have to be changed.

What the world needed was fewer farmers and more hunter-gatherers. Fewer cities and more wilderness . . .

'Sally?'

'What?'

'I need a pee,' Per said suddenly. He looked apologetic.

Sally stopped trying to rock the Swede back into action. 'No problem,' she said, shrugging as she clambered off him, watching Per watch the darkness between her legs.

'I'll see you in a second,' he said, blushing.

The moment he was gone, she rolled up his sleeping bag, with the money and passport still in the foot and stashed the roll in his Jeep alongside her own. And by the time Per came back Sally was dressed and in the passenger seat, ready to go.

'What about . . . ?'

'Later,' said Sally. 'First let's get breakfast.' Glancing at their map, she pointed to a gap between two red hills. 'There's a town on the other side with a government hostel. It's got showers.'

For the first time in days Per looked almost happy.

The hills turned out to be sand dunes and the road which had been worn when they set out quickly became little more than a path. Per's fleeting happiness vanishing with the blacktop. Tyre marks were few and mostly softened to shadow with a drifting sand somewhere between grit and dust. The only fresh tracks were donkey or camel.

'It's an oasis town,' Sally promised. 'Probably ancient.'

Per kept his doubts hidden behind a pair of shades.

'Another mile,' said Per, when ten minutes had turned into half an hour and the hills were behind them, 'then we turn back.'

'Sure thing.' Sally lifted the Leica off her lap and tucked it inside its leather case, stuffing the case under her seat. The rolls of film she pushed through a crease between the upright of her seat and the seat itself, casually reaching behind her to do so. If another mile came and went without incident then she was in the wrong place and several months of her life had been wasted.

Only Sally was in the right place and it took less than five minutes to run over a screamer. At least Sally assumed that was what alerted Moncef Pasha's guards as Per's Jeep crested a ridge and stopped.

'Shit,' said Per and Sally could only agree.

Spread out below them was a complex of squat buildings, painted a dirty red-yellow to blend in with the earth. A handful of antique-looking trucks was parked in the middle, hidden beneath a hangar's worth of camouflage netting that looked like it had been there forever. Under the cover of another awning two ant-like figures were working on the blades of a helicopter.

Sunlight heliographed from a roof as an officer swung his binoculars and finally caught sight of the Jeep.

'That doesn't look like an oasis town,' Per said, slamming his gears into reverse. Somewhere below a siren was sounding.

'Soldiers,' said Sally but her warning was unnecessary. No one, not even Per at his most stoned, could miss five teenagers strung across the track, squat rifles pointing directly at his windscreen.

'Bad idea,' she said.

In reply Per stamped on his throttle and hung a left, stalling when he hit the base of a dune. Which was how Per, rather than Sally, got shot through the leg by a fourteen-year-old in designer combats, Armani shades, a silk kufiyyah. Everything from tyres to doors got raked in one long burst and all the shots stayed low. Combat training had conditioned the soldier to take her opponents alive if possible.

Opening her door, Sally tossed out her rucksack and then stepped out of the Jeep, her hands already clasped behind her head. She'd been in enough trouble to know the drill. Unasked, Sally assumed the position, face so close to the hood that she could feel heat shimmer from its surface.

Per meanwhile had a white tee-shirt at arm's length and, between sobs, was waving it frantically through his window. Sally almost pointed out that in the desert white wasn't necessarily the colour of surrender (the Mahdi's battle flag had been pure white; until dust, blood and machine gun bullets rendered it into sullied rags), but she decided not to bother. The Emir's guard looked competent enough to recognise an idiot when they met one.

'Prince Moncef?' said Sally, pointing to the complex below. Although no one replied she got the feeling that at least one of them understood. Unless it was just that the word Moncef was familiar.

'He's famous,' Sally added. 'For making plants grow where most plants die.'

The soldier with the highest cheekbones stared at Sally with interest. And since the entire troop was female and any vibes, conscious or otherwise, came in under Sally's school-tuned gaydar she figured the soldier's look was entirely professional.

'He improves on nature,' said Sally and promptly wondered if what she'd just said counted in North Africa as blasphemy. 'Takes the potential God has given it,' she amended, 'and develops that.'

'You think this is good?' Although she obviously understood English, the lieutenant asked her question in French, in an abrupt and very Parisian way that made Sally glance at her, wondering.

'The man's a genius.'

'Whatever that means . . .'

'It means,' said Sally,' that you leave an area of art or science changed from how you found it . . . I learnt that at university,' she added.

'What did you study?'

'Genetics at Selwyn College, Cambridge.' She named a college at random. Although, when she thought about it, that wasn't entirely true. Selwyn was where Drew, the nanchuku nut, went, which was random enough.

The woman nodded and loosened the kufiyyeh that was half-obstructing her mouth. She was not, Sally realised, Arab in origin, her face was European. And now, when she spoke, her amusement came through clear and unobstructed.

'I suppose you want to see Moncef Pasha?'

'Yes,' said Sally, 'if that's possible . . .'

Blonde hair, small breasts, skin like milk . . . Once the questioning was done, then yes. 'Chances are that might prove possible,' said Eugenie de la Croix. The smile on her face turning sour.

Halfway down the track, with the Jeep temporarily abandoned somewhere behind them and the Emir's complex up ahead, Sally clutched at her gut and begged, practically in *tears to be untied. She needed to use a nearby thorn bush and she needed to use it now if she wasn't to soil herself.*

'You leave your bag with me.'

Sally nodded meekly and dumped her rucksack at the feet of the officer, running towards the bush with indecent haste. Only, once there, what Sally actually did was kneel, hook out her contraceptive cap and kick sand over it. Then she counted to sixty and pulled up her shorts.

'Feeling better?'

Sally smiled at the woman. 'Much,' she said. 'Thank you.'

Chapter Twenty-seven

Monday 28th February–1st March

Goats grazed in three rooms at the back, wandering in from a darkened courtyard through a hole in the rear wall. They were white with black faces and stunted horns, too fat, over-fed and pampered to be convincing scavengers. Besides, their leather collars betrayed them. Most goats kept within the medina made do with string, if they had collars at all.

Chef Edvard kept the goats to amuse. And amuse his dinner guests they did. But then Maison Hafsid's evening crowd were usually friends of Kashif Pasha, those with money and those who had actually travelled outside Ifriqiya, the kind of customers cosmopolitan enough to pay for the privilege of eating elegantly prepared retrofusion in the dining room of a draughty, half-wrecked Ifriqiyan palace opposite a mosque still called *new* because it was constructed during a trade boom in the mid-eighteenth century.

Maison Hafsid was owned by a tall and elderly Madagascan called Abdur Rahman, so labelled because this was one of the names specified by the Prophet as beloved by God. And, as his mother had reminded him often, 'Names matter. So will you be called on the day of judgment . . .'

On his arrival in Tunis ten years earlier Abdur Rahman changed his name to Edvard. And under this name he was known to most, even Kashif Pasha and his mother Lady Maryam. But it was as Abdur Rahman he owned Maison Hafsid, because this was the name that mattered. And it was as Abdur Rahman that he had shares in Café Antonio and three other restuarants.

'You done yet?' Chef Edvard shouted.

'Nearly,' said Raf and raised his chopper. Steel bit into flesh, then wood. Slicing the lamb into rough chunks, Raf slid them off his chopping board and into a glass bowl. Some kitchens kept specialist butchers. At Maison Hafsid the work was done by whomever Chef Edvard designated. It kept the cuts from getting too neat.

'I'll take it,' said Isabeau and the bowl was gone.

'Well,' Raf said, entirely to himself. 'We're here.' His voice echoed the fox's growl. That was their compromise. The fox still spoke but now Raf realised the fox was him. So far it seemed to work for both of them.

'Yeah,' said Raf. He tried not to mind that the fox sounded impossibly smug. As if it, rather than chance or Raf, had been responsible for getting Raf to the kitchens of Maison Hafsid, site of one murder and supplier of culinary staff to the notables of Tunis. 'Right where we need to be . . .'

Had the fox been someone else, Raf could have reminded it that its plan of sneaking off to hunt down Ibrihim Ishaq of Isaac & Son, Kairouan, had not been an unmitigated success. As well as mentioning that Those Who Went Naked had not turned out to be the revolutionary masterminds Eugenie seemed to suggest. He could even have admitted that he missed Hani and Zara and was adrift in a city with only an instinct that here was where he was meant to be to keep him from going home.

But he'd only be telling himself. And they both knew that.

There were Turkish baths less hot than the cellar kitchens at Maison Hafsid, so everyone kept telling Raf, who was beginning to believe them. Idries had already taken him to one of the city's poorer public baths, a place of cracked tiles and broken mosaic situated just behind the central market, where he'd sat surrounded by a dozen strangers, sweat dripping from every pore as a robed attendant ladled water onto heated stones.

The cleansing room had stunk of physical effort and butchers who killed most days but sweated themselves clean once or twice a week because that was all they could afford. They were polite to the stranger in their midst. Not friendly but polite. And once, when talk touched on Carthage Dynamo vs Sophia

Crescent, the conversation widened to include him. Other than that, the atmosphere had been restrained, almost elegant in a peeling, impoverished sort of way.

Maison Hafsid was something else. No one was polite. At least not down in the kitchens. And what constituted conversation was a hard-edged banter likely to get you knifed in most bars in Seattle. Ear-bleeding nu/Rai ripped from a corner-mounted wall speaker. In the kitchen Raf didn't speak at all. He screamed into the steaming chaos. And others shouted back. Mostly about his parentage, race, sexual orientation and short life expectancy.

Anyone who took offence at Chef Edvard worked elsewhere. Actually, anyone who took offence, full-stop, left for some other industry: one not driven by impossible hours, heavy attitude and dirt cheap drugs.

'You,' he said to Raf, next time Raf staggered by under the weight of a lamb carcass. 'I want to know where to file you.'

Three kinds of scum ended up in kitchens apparently. Those on the run too stupid to do anything else, brilliant and spoilt artists, and finally mercenaries, those in it for the money, mostly solid and reliable line cooks. Some American years back had given his name to this law, but Chef Edvard didn't mention that, he merely wanted to know which label fitted Raf.

'All of them,' said Raf.

'All?' The elderly Madagascan eyeballed his newest recruit for a long second and then slapped Raf on the shoulder. 'Misfits are good,' he said, his Arabic thicker than coffee grounds, 'they stay longer.'

Everything Raf had learnt at Café Antonio was unlearnt at Maison Hafsid. At Hafsid no one ever served swordfish or blackened chicken, even if customers asked politely. Right now Raf's job was to braise those chunks of lamb (bone and fat and skin and all). The ironically crude chunks reached the table drizzled with a custard-yellow sauce made from cloudberries flown in from Table Mountain. Given the price Maison Hafsid charged for its speciality dishes, Raf could only imagine the berries travelled first class.

'Faster,' Edvard barked.

Raf nodded, but the chef was shouting at someone else.

On a marble slab to Raf's left were a series of bowls filled with herbs and spices, which a kid of about eleven kept topped on a regular basis by ripping handfuls of wilting oregano from fat twigs or grating nutmeg against a tiny grid hung on a string around his neck. Raf used a lot of oregano and nutmeg; also olive oil, anchovies, dried juniper berries and small pods for which Raf didn't yet have a name. The chef seemed to use those in almost every dish.

A great aluminium pot roiled on the edge of 100 degrees at a station behind Raf, creating its own microclimate, waiting to soften whatever pasta was required. Linguine mostly, with a weird locally made thread noodle which came semi-opaque and ended up near invisible; not that much of either got eaten to judge from the quantity scraped from dirty plates into a metal trough that ran the edge of one wall. The noodles and pasta seemed to be something between a base and a garnish.

'A hand to six . . .'

The chef's eyes found Raf, who held up five fingers and nodded. Five minutes to braise the lamb for table six and pass it across for plating. That was the difference between home cooking and doing it for real. Restaurant food got dressed, just like the customers. And an artistic sprig or a near odourless/tasteless swirl of sauce could hide culinary sins as easily as discreet make-up and good clothes could hide sins of the flesh. Warm plates, flamboyant furnishings, elegant garnishes and adequate food, the demands of haute cuisine at Maison Hafsid were less than its devoted clientele imagined.

'Three,' shouted the chef and Raf swirled his pan, smelling oil, seared flesh and oregano. Across the other side of the cellar was a wood oven for which Raf sometimes seared lamb or beef to be roasted, so that no steam from raw meat might dampen the oven's desert-like dryness. It wasn't really Raf's job but Raf was racking up favours, taking shifts he didn't want, helping to hump crates too heavy for one person alone. He'd even rescued a cucumber sauce for wild greyling with a nylon sieve, a splash of Chablis and nerves of steel, decanting it onto a warm plate seconds ahead of the plate heading for the hatch.

Mind you, Raf probably wouldn't be forgiven that one. The sauce came from an Algerian sous-chef and the deputy was less than happy. Particularly now Chef Edvard had decided Isabeau's earlier boast about Raf having been a sous-chef himself in Seattle was true.

To test the claim, Raf had been handed a red fish of a species he'd never seen and told, in front of a watchful kitchen, to find a knife and ordered to fillet the thing

Pulling a Sabatier from the back of his belt, Raf oiled up a sharpening block and set about giving himself an edge. All the while checking the fish, noticing its every curve and the geometric relationship between anus, eyes and upper fin, the way the scales changed near the tail.

When Raf cut it was swift, taking his stance and the looseness of his wrist from a Sushi master who ran a dock-side café his old boss Hu San often frequented. Raf spent one memorable evening there near the beginning of his time with the Five Winds, as Seattle's most influential triad was named. And for a while, with tiny dish after dish reaching their table and Hu San chewing in silence, her eyes closing at particularly impressive slivers of raw fugu, Raf thought he was in disgrace and then, when she looked up and smiled almost without thinking, he realised she intended to sleep with him.

He still hadn't started to shave and she was in her late thirties, maybe more, but her tastes were for the raw and the fresh. Whatever, the moment never arose and as her Lincoln pulled up outside his flat Hu San dismissed him with a polite goodbye and left him stood on a sidewalk in the rain.

Raf cut three times in all. Once to gut the fish and discard its entrails. Once to fillet one side of the fish and once to fillet the other. The skin he'd already removed in a single scoop of his thumb, not using his knife and not damaging the flesh.

'Done?' Chef Edvard had asked. His face impassive.

Raf nodded and waited while the chef told a boy to fetch

a set of scales. First Edvard weighed the entrails, then both fillets and finally bones and skin.

'Not as bad as I expected.'

Behind Raf's eyes he scowled but Raf kept his face impassive, eyeing a strip of skin so clean it could have been sent for tanning. Not a flake of flesh clung to the spine or ribs, the cut at tail and gills was near perfect.

'I'm out of practice,' Raf announced finally and the skeletal chef almost smiled.

Then came three questions.

Where had he cooked before?

Raf named Antonio's pizza place and a five star hotel in Seattle so famous that even the silent and anxious Isabeau recognised its name.

'This true?'

That question was for Isabeau. Asked almost politely. No one had said anything to Raf but he'd caught the glances. There wasn't a single person in the kitchens unaware of her brother's murder. Even Chef Edvard was making allowances.

'He's been working for Antonio,' she said. 'I can't guarantee the other.'

'Why do you want to change jobs?'

'Debts,' said Raf. 'Waiting to be paid.'

'I work my staff harder,' Chef Edvard told Raf flatly. 'Believe me I make you sweat for every extra cent.'

And so the slot became his, at least until Idries' cousin got released from prison, if he did. Two points went unspoken. One, should Raf turn out okay then Edvard might keep him on anyway, and two, if Idries' cousin was not released then Raf had the job until someone better came along.

But first Raf had to do a day's sud diving to show he was serious. And do it for nothing. Those were the rules. So he scraped plates, hosed them down and loaded them into a washer the size of a small truck for as long as it took for some elderly Fhilipino to fry his own fingers in a red-hot wok – which was about four hours. The man wanted to work on but Edvard insisted on wrapping his hand in a towel filled with ice and ordered him home. Only the promise of a full day's pay got the crying man out of the kitchen and into a corridor that ended in steps leading up to an alley at the back. Even then someone had to walk the man up the stairs and shoo him out into the alley.

'Want me to handle his station?'

'Screw up and you're out.'

Raf took that as a *yes* and stripped to the loose cotton trousers he'd borrowed from Antonio's and would one day return, with luck. He took a coat someone handed him.

'Nice scars.'

The chef's smile was mildly mocking, as if his own might prove far more impressive if only he could be persuaded to discard his white jacket with the word *Edvard* embroidered over the pocket in red silk. And to judge by the jagged seams up both wrists and a yellow callus thick as tortoiseshell at the base of one thumb anything was possible.

So Raf cut lamb and braised goat, spatchcocked quail and generally kept the meals coming, on time and done as ordered.

'It's not a skill, you know . . .'

'What isn't?'

'This shit. Being able to do everything. That's just a design function. You telling me you can't recognise an adaptive mechanism when you see one?'

'Hey, white boy . . . You okay?' Raf looked up from wiping out his iron skillet to find the tall Madagascan stood next to him, frowning. A couple of the others were staring across as well.

'Sure,' Raf said. 'Just talking to myself.'

'Well,' said Chef Edvard, 'when you've got a moment.'

They went to the table. An old black thing that looked as if it came from a French farmhouse that had burnt down. Fire damage chewed along one edge but someone, probably years before, had scraped most of it away with the flat of a knife and put that edge to the wall.

'Drink,' Chef Edvard said, pouring Raf a glass of marc. 'And then listen . . . I've got a job if you're interested. You know about Kashif Pasha's party?'

The whole of Tunis knew. At his mother's suggestion, the

Emir's oldest son was holding a dinner to celebrate his parents' forty-fifth wedding anniversary. If both of them turned up it would be the first time they'd met in slightly over forty-four years. The meal was Kashif Pasha's attempt to heal the rift, a peace offering to his father and a sign of the pasha's developing maturity where the Emir was concerned. That was the official version anyway.

'You want me to cook?'

Amusement tinged the old man's eyes. 'You're not that good,' he said. 'You wait tables . . . Still interested?'

'Oh yes,' said Raf, 'it's exactly the kind of opportunity I've been waiting for.'

Juggling a fat cowpat of harissa in her hands, Isabeau tried to stop it from dripping oil onto her jeans. Chef Edvard preferred dry mix that needed oil adding but none Isabeau and Raf had seen in Marché Central looked good enough, so she'd bought freshly made paste.

That was a difference between them, Raf decided. If the old Madagascan had sent him to buy dried harissa then that's what Raf would have bought. The best he could find from the range available. However, he was there to buy lamb. And talk to Isabeau.

Raf sighed.

'What?' Isabeau asked.

'Chef Edvard's worried about you . . .' He shrugged. 'Everyone's worried. So if you need to take time off. Maybe go back to Tarbarka?' Raf named a town on the northern coast. The only town in Ifriqiya where descendents of French colonists still outnumbered residents of Arab and Berber stock.

'That's why we were sent out together? So you can suggest I go home to my grandmother?'

'In a way.'

'Yeah,' said Isabeau, 'I can see everyone liking that. Solves the problem doesn't it? Isabeau's gone off the rails so let's send her somewhere else . . .' Isabeau's voice was loud enough to make a man standing by the shellfish stall stop shovelling cracked ice onto a marble tray and watch them instead, iron trowel poised in his hand.

'I don't think chef meant it like that,' Raf said.

'Really?' said Isabeau. 'How did he mean it?'

'He's trying to help.'

'No one can help,' Isabeau said fiercely. 'What's happened has happened. Pascal is dead. Nothing anyone can do will bring him back. I have to live with that fact.' Tears were rolling down her face, glittering trails of sadness. 'Nothing can make it better.'

Carrying a cape of lamb over one shoulder, Raf watched the crowds part to let him through rather than risk having blood dragged across their clothes. The floor of the indoor market beneath his boots was wet with melted ice and slick with tomatoes dropped and trodden to pulp, the green walls sticky with handprints and streaked with condensation. He walked ahead at Isabeau's insistence. She needed space. Time enough to get a grip on her tears.

They exited near Bab el Bahar, the city's sea gate in the days before the ground between the medina and the Gulf of Tunis was mapped by French engineers for ersatz Parisian boulevards now old enough to be heritage sites in their own right.

The bab still functioned as the main gate into the walled heart of Tunis. By law, no buildings within the medina could be changed from one use to another. Shops remained shops and cafés remained cafés but little money existed to pay for their upkeep so even the famous suq roofs that cast whole alleys into half gloom were pitted and peeling, cracked across their roofs like lightning, sometimes actually dangerous.

There were also alleys where people lived rather than just made or sold things. And the houses that lined these looked in on courtyards just as the walled city looked in on the suqs and the surrounding ville looked in on the walled city. Within the medina were small squares, the result not of planning but of enough narrow alleys meeting to make a passing space necessary. Maison Hafsid looked onto one of these.

The entrance doors to Chef Edvard's restaurant were studded with nails, as was usual, and with hammered strips of black iron that formed crescents, six pointed stars and spirals. This last being reserved for the Medina's grander houses. Both doors were mirror images of the other. Crescent for crescent, spiral for spiral.

These Raf avoided, heaving the lamb carcass around to the rear, where his struggle to lift it off his shoulder without covering himself in slime was watched by Isabeau and a boy sat in a door opposite. Aged about seven, the boy was sorting straw hats into those damaged by winter rains and those still good enough to sell.

Every city was like this. Interlocking circles, poverty and plenty. As was every life. The only difference being that no one bothered to write guides about the picturesque poverty of London or New York, Seattle or Zurich. Or if they did, it was in no language Raf read.

'Has anyone asked him if he saw anything?'

'What?' Isabeau sounded puzzled.

'That boy,' Raf said, nodding to the child who was now watching them. 'Has anyone asked if he saw what . . .' He stopped as soon as he realised Isabeau was no longer listening. She had leant against the wall, near the top of the stairs that lead down to Maison Hafsid's cellar kitchens, hands over her face.

'It's okay,' said Raf, which was about as dumb a thing as anyone could say.

'No, it's not,' Isabeau said.

Raf took the lamb and the large lump of harissa Isabeau held, neatly wrapped in its grease-proof paper and carried them down the steps, along a short corridor and into the kitchens. He spoke to Chef Edvard, got the man's agreement for letting him have time off to take Isabeau back to her flat and then went back to the alley. Isabeau was stood exactly where she'd been when Raf left. The boy with the hats was gone.

Salt on his tongue. Raf woke with Isabeau naked in his arms. Worrying enough. What made it worse was a blinding headache and the packet of condoms by her bed. They were unused, unlike the brandy bottle beside them.

Taking one out, Raf squinted at the small print. American, which he could have guessed from its gold coin wrapper. A quality mark, a use-by date and a warning from the Surgeon General about retro Virus.

'Belonged to my brother . . .' Isabeau said, opening one eye.

Nodding hurt, so Raf just watched the naked girl go back to sleep.

The use-by date was two years ahead.

Very slowly, Raf shifted one arm from under Isabeau's shoulders, twisted until his legs hung over the edge of the cast-iron bed and sat up; regretting it immediately. For the time it took him to stop feeling sick, he played that game where the room spun when he looked at it but stopped if he shut his eyes again. Between spinning and darkness Raf played a second game of remembering what was in the room and wondering, why?

Once expensive but lately fallen into disrepair, its sash window glazed with only a single pane of glass, Isabeau's room was soulless, almost sullen. A small music system sat on a metal table, both chrome. Although the sides of the music system were ersatz, coated plastic. There were no pictures on the walls. No looking glass nor dressing table.

'This isn't her room, is it?'

'No,' said Raf, agreeing with himself. 'It's not.'

The room was emotionally cold and Raf read Isabeau's room as ironic. Littered with mementoes from a recently discarded childhood. A Cheb Rai poster. A row of those kitsch blue Chinese foals, piebald with dust as they rolled across some glass shelf. A vase, bad cut glass. An anorexically thin marble Madonna. The kind sold in St Vincent de Paul . . .

Raf reined in his headache. Ran that thought back.

Someone like him, or rather someone like the *him* he'd become back in El Isk, might wear jade wrist beads while carrying a silver and coral Fatima key ring but neither Hani nor Zara would ever own something forbidden just because they liked the way it looked. Even a rust-eaten antique Buddha that Raf had found in a suq and placed in an alcove in the *qaa* drew odd looks from both of them. Mind you, it drew scowls from Donna and she was Catholic.

Which meant . . .

'Let me get this right,' said Raf. 'You're sitting in a dead man's room beside a naked woman and you're internalising some seminar on comparative religion?'

Yeah, Raf nodded to himself. That was it exactly.

He'd fucked Isabeau. No matter that his memory of the exact act was bricked off with rising doubts, alcohol poisoning and emotional shutdown. The very fact he was having this conversation with himself was proof enough.

Pulling back Isabeau's covers, Raf swallowed what he saw. Flash-freezing her high breasts, soft stomach and hips permanently into memory. Comparing her figure, despite himself with his memory of Zara. They were alike enough to make Raf feel ashamed. The only real difference, apart from the fact he'd fucked one and not the other (and the one he'd fucked was not the one he loved) was that a small crucifix on a gold chain twisted sideways in the crease between Isabeau's breasts.

'Okay,' agreed Raf. That did explain the marble Madonna of his imagining.

There were plane trees beyond the window. Chrome blinds. A crack that ran across the floor where grouting between tiles had snapped along a stress line, then opened up, until the crack changed direction and broke tiles instead.

But the tiles were clean and recently scrubbed. Come to that the whole room was spotless.

'Which says what?'

That Pascal was too poor to afford repairs on the flat he shared with his sister but still liked it kept clean?

'Or wasn't anal enough to worry about internal decoration.'

That too, except the tiny music system, sand-blasted metal bed and chrome table had anal retentive written through them like rock. Walking to the bedroom door, Raf glanced at the area beyond. A living space with Toshiba screen. Black leather sofa. Another chrome and glass table. Doors led to a small kitchen.

A bathroom with shower stall. And finally, a second bedroom, half the size of the one in which he awoke. The other difference was a lock recently fixed to the inside of that door. Ceramic foals sat on a glass shelf but there were no posters or pictures and no slim marble Madonna. Nothing of real interest in the small bedside cabinet.

'Well,' said a voice behind him. 'Find what you were looking for?' The question came from Isabeau. She was leant against the door frame of what he now knew was her own room, wearing a towel, which only made Raf more aware of his own nakedness.

'What I needed?'

'You were going to find out who Pascal was, remember? Get inside his head and work out who might have really killed him. Since everyone believes Idries, who's convinced it wasn't his cousin. And apparently I'm meant to believe Idries too . . .'

Raf put a hand to his aching head. 'I told you I wanted to come here so I could *empathise*?'

Isabeau nodded.

'And the other stuff,' he looked at her towel, 'that just happened?'

'Sure,' said Isabeau, turning away. 'If you must put it like that.' Raf heard her feet on the tiles all the way back to the room they'd shared. There was a slam of door. Two minutes of muted shuffling and then the noise of the door being opened again. He listened to her shoes slap the tiles and then she was gone with a slam of a different door.

Having dressed, Raf let himself out.

Chapter Twenty-eight

Tuesday 1st March

A neatly-bearded man in a tarboosh stared out from a creased page. Below him a caption informed the scruffy girl in black headscarf, jeans and silver trainers that the Emir's eldest son would be dining at the Domus Aurea and, in a return to best Ottoman tradition, his mother had asked that all attendants at the celebratory meal be both deaf and dumb.

Unfortunately, finding staff who fitted this profile while possessing sufficient experience had proved impossible. They had, however, all been carefully screened for suitability.

The rest of the page was equally bland, its headlines subdued and reverential; which was probably why someone had dumped that day's *El Pays* under a chair in the buffet car.

Putting down the paper, the girl swallowed the last of her coffee and returned her plastic cup to the attendant, even though she had to stand on a cat basket to reach his counter. Then, just to be tidy, she collected up half a dozen other discarded cups and returned those too.

'Thank you.' The man at the counter smiled. 'Are you this tidy at home?'

Hani nodded, even though it wasn't strictly true. Donna did all of the kitchen cleaning at the madersa and got cross if Hani tried to help. And although Khartoum had explained that Donna was the kind of person who preferred others not to interfere, this wasn't much help because Hani's Aunt Nafisa had spent her life telling Hani to pick things up, tidy away her toys and generally be busy and industrious, preferably somewhere else.

So now Hani tidied on instinct. It was a hard habit to break.

'Problems?'

'Not really,' said Hani, putting down the last of the cups and nodding towards the next carriage. 'Unless you count blocked loos and messy basins.' She shrugged. 'You know soldiers . . .'

The man looked at her. 'Ifriqiya needs conscripts,' he said, more serious than before.

Hani looked like she wanted to disagree but all she did was shrug her thin shoulders and wrap her *hijab* more tightly around her face. 'You're probably right,' she said, 'but I'm not entirely sure it needs them to vomit in the basins . . .'

Despite himself the man smiled. 'Luckily,' he said. 'I have my own loo.'

Hani looked at him.

'For attendants only,' he explained carefully.

The girl kept looking and it was the man's turn to sigh.

'Through there,' he said and pointed to a blank door. 'Don't take long, I'm closing up in a minute.'

The girl who entered the first class carriage wore dark glasses with drop-pearl earrings and the only thing that detracted from the look, besides the fact Hani's glasses were too big and blood smudged one ear (where an earring had been forced through flesh), was a tatty rattan cat basket so large it scraped against her leg as she walked.

Catching sight of herself in a window Hani wiped away the blood with her finger and thumb and adjusted her shades.

'Is that seat taken?'

The foreigner in the stripy jacket looked so bemused that Hani switched to French and, as she thought, the seat by the door was free. Hani hadn't really expected him to understand Arabic, but Zara insisted its use was politically essential so Hani tried to remember to use it first. Quite why Arabic should be the natural language of North Africa when almost everyone she met spoke French Hani wasn't sure.

'Okay,' said Hani as she scratched a fingernail against rattan. 'We're here.'

Inside Hani's basket, Ifritah scratched back, meowed noisily and then hurled herself against the grille with a thud, leaving the foreigner looking more bemused than ever.

'Wild cat,' Hani said, reaching for its handle. And it was almost true. The one thing Ifritah wasn't was house-trained . . .

Even before she stepped onto the platform Hani knew she was going to like Tunis. It had as much history as El Isk plus pirates, corsairs and freebooters. She really didn't understand why the Germans, in particular, and the Americans hated it so.

'Ready?' Hani asked her basket. Without waiting for Ifritah's answer, Hani pushed herself out of her seat, slammed down the window of her still-moving carriage and swung open the door to a shout of outrage from a porter on the platform.

Jumping down Hani almost tripped over her new shoes. Really she'd wanted to keep her trainers, but dumped them in a bin along with her jeans, tee-shirt and *hijab*. In their place Hani wore a skirt made from red silk with an embroidered green waistcoat over a white shirt. Since the silk, velvet and white cotton were sewn together, the outfit probably counted as a dress even if it didn't look like one.

On the breast of her green waistcoat Hani had pinned a spray of diamond feathers so impossibly extravagant they had to be fake. As the white shirt left more of her neck bare than Hani really liked, she'd borrowed a fat row of amber beads from Aunt Nafisa's old leather jewellery box. She knew the beads weren't of good quality. If they had been her aunt would have sold them.

Stalking past the scowling porter, Hani worked hard on looking like someone who knew exactly where she was going. Grown-ups tended only to notice anxiety. So the secret to being invisible was to be seen. Hani smiled at that, pleased to realise she was finally beginning to think like her Uncle Ashraf.

'Okay,' she told Ifritah, 'first we send Zara a postcard and then we find a taxi . . .'

The postcard bit was easy. Hani had taken a free card from a rack in the transAtlas express and also a free pen; one of those cheap blue ones too short to write with neatly. It was currently pushed under half a dozen rattan strands on Ifritah's basket.

'Table,' Hani told herself, looking round the crowded platform. There were a lot of soldiers at one end, plus a dozen men in black uniforms with guns who might have been police. Whatever they were, they were so busy watching the soldiers separate people by sex and herd them into a tent or under a metal arch that they forgot to glance at Hani as she slid under a barrier and strode towards a café near the entrance to the station's marble concourse.

'Is this seat taken?' This time the man Hani asked understood Arabic and smiled an old man's smile as he told her it was free. He left Hani in peace to scribble her message and no one appeared from inside to take her order, both of which were a blessing. Message written, Hani thanked the old man for part use of his table and headed for a nearby post-box.

Zara was going to be cross, that much was obvious. She'd been coldly furious when she first realised Raf was gone without a word and now she'd be more furious still. And not just with Uncle Ashraf.

'Tough.' By the time her card got delivered Hani intended to have found her uncle, delivered the diamond *chelengk* and given him back his dark glasses. So if Zara did turn up in Tunis she'd never know that Raf wasn't really on a secret mission. Mind you, that would probably just make her more furious still.

In the end Hani decided against trying to get a taxi. All her notes were too big anyway and she wasn't really sure where she needed to go . . .

Lieutenant Aziz liked station duty. It was undemanding, he got to drink endless cups of hot sweet cocoa given free by grateful cafés and there was a long list of brother officers only too happy to share the work. This meant the lieutenant got to go home on time. He wasn't a real lieutenant, of course, just some maths student from Bizerte unable to graduate until he'd done national service. That was the deal. Between passing his finals, which he already had, and actually graduating came a year in the army.

That he'd been commissioned into the National Guard the same month that he got married was his own bad luck. Or bad planning on the part of his mother. Either way, he'd been taking weeks' worth of grief from his colonel about his eagerness to slope off early.

Of course, some of that eagerness really was about getting back to his new bride. The rest of it, well, politics weren't his thing but somehow everyone else in the regiment seemed to feel differently.

'Excuse me . . .'

Lieutenant Aziz looked down to see a girl in ludicrously large dark glasses holding a rattan basket. She wore a dress that might have belonged to a gypsy princess in some German operetta.

'I'm trying to find my cousin.'

The girl looked so serious that Aziz almost laughed. Luckily he had a young sister and enough imagination to know that his sister hated people laughing at her. So instead he dropped to a crouch, aware that his men were watching.

'Are you lost?'

'Not yet.' The girl looked around her. 'But I will be soon if you don't help.'

Aziz smiled. 'When did you lose him?' He took it for granted that her cousin was male.

Hani looked blank.

'Your cousin,' said the lieutenant.

'He's not lost.' Hani said. 'I just haven't found him yet.'

Lieutenant Aziz paused. 'Okay,' he said. 'Your cousin was meeting you from the train . . .'

Hani shook her head.

'He didn't expect you to find your own way home?' Aziz looked so shocked that Hani reached out and patted his shoulder without thinking.

'Of course not,' she said. 'He doesn't know I'm coming yet.'

'He doesn't . . . ?' Runaways were the responsibility of the Ministry of Public Order, which meant he'd be perfectly justified in handing over the child and walking away. Something the lieutenant knew he wouldn't be doing.

Aziz started again.

'Where does your cousin live?'

'In the Bardo Palace. But he's going to be at Domus Aurea tonight.'

Hani wasn't quite certain how to put what happened next but whoever had been smiling out of those eyes was now hidden. All she got was perfect blankness.

'Domus Aurea . . .' Lieutenant Aziz dragged the address out as if uncertain where it should stop.

'That's right,' Hani twirled round to show off her outfit. 'I've come for the party.'

'And your cousin . . .'

'Kashif Pasha,' Hani said. 'Or the Emir, he's also a cousin.' She put her head to one side as she thought about that some more. 'Actually,' she said, 'everyone's a cousin, except Zara . . .'

The lieutenant commandeered a parked taxi by the simple expedient of telling its driver that his passenger was Emir Moncef's cousin. And having handed the child to a flustered officer at the gates of the Golden House, Lieutenant Aziz told the taxi to take him home.

Chapter Twenty-nine

Flashback

'So, tell me . . .' Accompanying the demand came a mild slap. An aide memoire, little more. A warning of what might become real. 'Why are you really here?'

'To see Prince Moncef.' Sally chewed the inside of her lip, hard enough to tear flesh. Then spat the salt taste from her mouth, allowing it to dribble slowly down her chin. 'As I already told you. So why not just fuck off and . . .'

The second slap splashed blood across her cheek, as Sally had known it would. She spat more of the salt onto her chin, readying herself for another blow.

There were rules to this game. Hell, there were whole websites devoted to handling how to be questioned. Not that Sally needed websites for instruction. She'd been through the mill for real in London, Vienna and Florence. She'd got away without questioning in Madrid and never even been picked up in New York.

In Zurich the police had skipped on questioning and turfed her over the border with a warning that to return would result in a long prison sentence or worse. A leer from a fat uniform as he told her this was intended to indicate what might be worse than several years' incarceration in Europe's most boring country.

'Enough,' said a new voice. The light in Sally's face went out. A moment later fingers grabbed her bottom lip and yanked it down.

'Quite the little professional.'

They'd met before on the ridge overlooking the complex. Only this time Eugenie de la Croix wore black trousers and a white shirt, Jimmy Choo slingbacks and a scarf that did *little to hide a waterfall of dark hair. Her beauty was such that Sally almost forgave the fingers pulling at her bleeding lip.*

'Where did you learn that little trick . . . Seattle?'

'I wasn't in Seattle,' Sally replied from instinct and saw Eugenie grin.

'How about New York?' Although her eyes were amused, Eugenie's hold on Sally's lip tightened and there was a realness to her questions lacking until then. Eugenie was not the baby-faced guard she'd replaced. She could, and would, rip apart Sally's mouth. 'Well?'

Sally's answer was just about comprehensible.

'Really,' said Eugenie, suddenly letting go the lip. 'You weren't in New York either? She dropped a handful of papers onto a table and stood back so Sally could see. Photocopies of NYPD reports, mostly. Plus a fat file from a detective agency in Kuala Lumpur. There were also a handful of flimsies but what Sally noticed first was a P10, request for arrest, issued by MediPol, the terrorism clearing group for Southern Europe, the Levant and North Africa.

'Cut off her clothes,' Eugenie ordered the puppy-faced recruit, who blinked. 'What?' said Eugenie. 'You have a problem with that?'

The recruit shook her head. 'No, ma'am.' She glanced between Eugenie and the English girl tied to a camp chair. 'Which end do you want me to start?'

The only remotely painful thing to happen after this involved a caustic lip salve and Eugenie's demand that Sally rinse her mouth out several times with Listerine. What remained of her shorts and the tee-shirt she'd been wearing on arrival were removed, along with the contents of her pockets, never to reappear.

Having been washed and shampooed in a canvas bath, Sally was handed a cotton towel and told to dry herself and then dress. The robe the young recruit offered Sally was white. The shawl was red, with tassels and geometric patterns. It

took Sally a second to realise that she was meant to put it
on her head.

'This is what you wanted, isn't it?' Eugenie said, stepping
through a curtain that separated the bath from a room beyond.
She was holding a gun, but loosely, like some expensive fashion
accessory.

'What is?'

'To have Moncef Pasha's babies . . .'

The two women looked at each other. Their look holding until
it seemed that neither could break the gaze binding them tight.
And then Sally nodded.

'He's been working on . . .'

'Quite probably,' said Eugenie. 'He's always working on some
plan.' Her voice was studiedly dismissive. 'Most of them come
to nothing. Does your friend know what you intend?'

The woman meant Per, Sally realised. 'I doubt it,' she said.
Driving straight at the soldiers had been Per's choice. And if the
Swede wanted to be that stupid then, once again, that was also
his choice. All Sally wanted to do was meet the pasha and make
her offer. Although, looking down at her gown, Sally realised
this wish might be redundant. The man was already one giant
step ahead of her.

Berlin always insisted the al-Mansurs controlled a network
of spies which threaded the cities of the world, corrupting and
turning good to bad. Off-shore oil provided the means and
dogma the driving force. Camps deep in the desert hid training
facilities; shown only as occasional smudges against sand in
satellite photographs released on Heute in Berlin, usually in
the run up to an oil summit.

Sally had always dismissed it as so much propaganda. Now
she was no longer sure.

'What will happen to Per?'

Eugenie stopped twirling her Colt. 'He'll be shot,' she said
lightly. 'Unless Moncef Pasha has a better idea.' Sally found it
hard to work out whether or not the woman was joking.

'Why should humanity change?' Sat next to Sally in the rear

seat of a small Soviet attack helicopter, Eugenie was having trouble making herself heard. 'Especially given we're the ones winning . . .'

'What!'

Eugenie smiled at Sally's outrage and nodded towards the ground. 'Kairouan,' she shouted at the English girl. 'Almost there.' They were on their way to Tunis. To an annexe of the great mosque where Moncef Pasha had an iman waiting.

If the Emir's eldest son wanted this woman, then fine. Equally fine if he wanted access to those precious papers she'd found in New York. But it was as well he'd lacked the time to research her properly. Eugenie had read Sally Welham's files, copies of the originals. Had her boss understood that Sally was a card-carrying atheist he'd never have proposed what was to come next.

Static crackled in Eugenie's headphones. 'I have a message.'

'From Moncef?'

For a second Eugenie looked irritated. 'Who else?' she said. 'His message is this, The smaller the lizard the greater its hopes of becoming a crocodile . . . I hope that means something to you because I doubt it means anything to anyone else.'

Eugenie took a sideways glance at the English girl. Thinner, taller, a little younger than Eugenie had been expecting from the photographs snatched along the way. Trailing Sally had been Eugenie's idea from the moment she came to Moncef Pasha's attention. An intrusive foreigner scouring the net for awkward information.

A blackbird had followed the woman for much of the most recent trip before fading into the background with a change of clothes towards the end.

For a while, early on, Moncef himself had decided that flying a blackbird might work, but even without having met the target Eugenie could have told him otherwise. No one that desperate to become Moncef's lover would risk being foolish. Which was why Eugenie steadfastly refused to believe a single word of Per's story about passionate nights spent with this girl.

'You ready?'

Sally adjusted her headscarf and nodded.

'Wait for the blades to stop,' said Eugenie, 'then follow me.' Ducking under the doorway, she dropped to a crouch, eyes already scanning La Kasbah for the Zil that would drive them to meet Moncef Pasha.

'I'll be your interpreter,' Eugenie added. 'But for the actual marriage you have to make the responses yourself, in Arabic. They're very simple and I've written them out phonetically on a piece of card.'

Chapter Thirty

Tuesday 1st March

'Quiet,' hissed a black-haired boy sat next to Hani. He stared down at his plate, on which a tiny bird sat in the centre of an elaborate matrix of sauce dribbled into the shape of recurring arabesques. So far he had yet to touch his meal.

'Why should I?' Hani demanded, still not bothering to lower her voice. She wanted to know why her Uncle Ashraf was not at Domus Aurea and no one seemed able to tell her. Hani found it hard to believe he hadn't already achieved what he set out to do. Whatever that was.

It also hadn't occurred to Hani that her uncle might miss Kashif's party.

Dressed in a silk kaftan with gold embroidery around the neck and wearing a Rolex several sizes too big, Murad Pasha glanced nervously across to where his half-brother sat watching them. 'My brother doesn't approve of noise.'

'And I don't approve of the pasha,' Hani announced rather too loudly. A grey-haired woman standing with two Soviet guards behind the Emir glanced across to smile. Hani got the feeling she didn't like Kashif either. 'Anyway,' Hani said, 'if he prefers silence why are *they* here?'

A jerk of her chin took in a white-robed group who stood slap-bang in the middle of the cruciform dining room, below an impossibly huge chandelier. Five of them were chanting while a sixth beat time on a goat-skin drum.

'These are the Emir's choice,' Murad Pasha said, as if that should be obvious. 'Those are the artists selected by Kashif.' He pointed behind him to a group of *nasrani* over by a far wall, all dressed in black suits and white shirts with black bow ties, like Kashif, in fact. One of them carried a perspex violin which he swung loosely by its neck.

'Great,' said Hani. 'I can't wait.'

The boy seemed roughly her age but still half a head shorter, which made him rather small for eleven. He had narrow shoulders and girl's wrists and might have been good at running, except he looked far too sensible to run anywhere. Everybody else at the top table was talking, but the only time the boy opened his mouth was to answer one of Hani's questions. The rest of the time his eyes slid past her to watch Kashif, the Emir and Lady Maryam.

'Don't you want that?' Hani pointed at his quail.

Murad shook his head without bothering to look at her.

'Why not?'

Murad Pasha sighed. 'I'm vegetarian,' he said. 'I don't approve of killing animals. And I'm only here under protest.'

'So you don't mind if my cat has it?'

The area in which they sat had once been a *biat bel kabu*, the living quarters for a corsair and his family. Shaped like a fat, crudely drawn cross, with a long down stroke leading to a courtyard, now glassed over, and the shorter up stroke opening onto a smaller, still uncovered courtyard where Chef Edvard had set up his kitchens, the cruciform room had sidebars that led nowhere.

In total there were six archways into the dining room. And in the centre, below the chandelier, three tables had been positioned, one high table at which sat Murad Pasha and Hani, Kashif, the Emir and Lady Maryam and two lesser tables, at right angles to the top table.

The Berber musicians occupied the open space between the three and because they always faced the Emir everyone on the side tables saw the singers only in profile. Behind the Emir stood Eugenie de la Croix, flanked by two guards in jellabas, their striped robes in contrast to the drab uniform of a single major who stood behind Kashif Pasha.

Hani didn't recognise Eugenie or anyone else and was happily unaware that at least one of the men sat at a side table had recognised her.

'So who's the girl?' Senator Malakoff demanded of his elderly neighbour, a Frenchman famous for knowing everything about everyone. His enemies, who were legion, would say this was because St Cloud traded in souls. His friends, of whom there were fewer, limited themselves to describing the Marquis as the kind of man who never let go a favour or forgave a good deed.

'The al-Mansur brat.'

'But I thought . . .' His American neighbour looked puzzled. 'Aren't they all al-Mansur?'

'After a fashion,' St Cloud said heavily, helping himself to oysters flown in from Normandy. Without thought, he held up a glass and felt its weight change as a waiter hurriedly filled it with Krug. St Cloud made a point of not noticing servants unless they were both young and beautiful, and then, man or woman, his charm hit them like prey caught in a hunting light. The sex of his conquests mattered little: as St Cloud readily admitted, he was strictly equal opportunities.

'That's Lady Hana al-Mansur,' he explained, returning to the question. 'She recently came into a rather large sum of money. Courtesy of Hamzah Quitrimala . . .' Having mentioned North Africa's richest man St Cloud watched understanding finally reach the American's face.

'Ahh, yes,' said the Senator. 'Her uncle is Governor of El Iskandryia. Wasn't he implicated in that dreadful . . .'

'Ex-Governor,' St Cloud said firmly. 'He *resigned*.' The way the Marquis said this suggested that Ashraf Bey's resignation had been anything but voluntary.

'Wasn't there also something last year about his niece being kidnapped?'

'Apparently,' said the Marquis, draining his glass. 'Something like that. And I have to admit to being rather surprised to see Lady Hana.' Not to mention furious, St Cloud thought to himself. Quite apart from the fact he was now unable to gossip loudly about Ashraf al-Mansur, and the Marquis had been counting on doing precisely that, St Cloud had paid hard currency for a *complete* list of guests, then paid out again to swap his chair for one two down, less prestigious, obviously, but infinitely more useful.

$5,000 had been the cost of getting to sit on Senator Malakoff's left rather than his right. US dollars well spent because Malakoff's right ear was perforated, a fact known only to its owner, his doctor and the Marquis de St Cloud who'd made a point of acquiring his medical records. Apparently the Senator's partial deafness was the result of a recent diving accident in Baja, California. And since the Senator was forbidden to dive by his wife who believed he'd been revisiting his misspent youth with a prostitute in Tijuana, well . . .

So now the Soviet first secretary was juggling the upside of finding himself in a better seat than expected, with wondering exactly why America's latest roving fact finder consistently ignored every comment the ambassador made.

'I'm having a little party afterwards,' St Cloud said quietly. 'Very select. I was wondering if you'd be interested?'

'A party?'

'Out at Cap Bon. At my house.'

The building in question was actually a palace erected for an exiled prince of Savoy and St Cloud's parties were anything but small. The Marquis was relying on the American to know that.

'You, me, some friends, a few girls . . .'

He'd have mentioned boys but the Senator had voted against repealing legislation outlawing homosexuality and St Cloud was not someone to come between a man and his prejudice. At least not when that someone was retained by some of the biggest oil shippers in the world.

'Mostly Japanese girls,' St Cloud admitted. 'Although I have borrowed a rather lovely Mexican, a bit inexperienced but very beautiful.' The girl in question, who was actually Spanish, had been told to keep that fact to herself.

'Mexican?'

St Cloud nodded. 'Lovely girl,' he said, 'you'll adore her.'

After oysters and champagne, Kashif Pasha's nod to the two terms he'd spent studying at the Sorbonne, came wood pigeon stuffed with dates and wrapped in layers of fine filo pastry, so that each mouthful became an adventure in archaeology.

With the smoked pigeon came a wine St Cloud didn't recognise, tannat and auxerrios, almost prune-flavoured, made from grapes grown in an iron-rich subsoil beneath a sun slightly too hot for real subtlety. One of the Emir's own vineyards probably. Although, if this was the case, then St Cloud wasn't sure why each bottle was carefully wrapped in a linen tablecloth to hide its label.

The very fact Emir Moncef served wine outraged half his visitors, while the fact he justified this by quoting Jalaluddin Rumi, rather than relying on timeworn arguments of modernisation and rationality, worried the other half.

St Cloud looked to where the old man sat silent at the top table, trapped between his son and the wife he hadn't seen for decades. This was, everybody understood, an important moment of reconciliation. Getting father, son and wife into the same room had taken high-level negotiation and no one quite understood why the Emir had finally agreed.

'God he looks miserable,' Senator Malakoff said, noticing St Cloud's gaze.

'Wouldn't you?' said St Cloud. He glanced pointedly at Lady Maryam whose moon face was almost hidden beneath a silk *hijab*. There was no doubting that she was almost as wide as she was tall.

Senator Malakoff nodded. Yes, he could honestly say he'd be miserable if that was his wife. 'How much more of this do we have to endure?' he asked the Frenchman.

'Hours,' said the Marquis. 'We've only just begun.'

Which wasn't strictly true. As well as the guest list, St Cloud had seen the menu and, provided one discounted the palate-cleaning offering of sorbet and the snails, goats cheese and fresh figs which were to be served last, the number of courses was limited to five, since wild trout and rabbit were due to arrive simultaneously as were baklava and baked alaska.

'Hours?' The Senator looked so sick that St Cloud smiled. As well as partial deafness the man suffered from a notoriously weak bladder; a serious flaw in someone charged with establishing contact with the party of Kashif Pasha.

St Cloud knew about that too . . .

Clicking his fingers for a waiter, the Marquis whispered something in the boy's ear, leaning rather closer than was necessary and watched the waiter scurry off, reappearing seconds later with an empty jeroboam of champagne.

'Piss in this,' St Cloud said, placing the bottle beside the Senator's chair. 'That's what most of us do.'

Pigeon was replaced by lamb roasted in charcoal, testicles still hanging from each gutted carcass like fat purses. Each table got two of the animals. Enough to enable every guest to reach forward and pinch fingers of hot meat without having to stretch. Unnoticed by most guests, the Sufi dancers gave way to a shaven-headed young man backed by a trio of *nasrani* jazz musicians dressed in black. Each note that ululated though the dining room had a haunting quality that filled St Cloud with feelings of loss and regret. The Marquis hated it as a matter of principle.

'He's good,' said Hani.

'Who is?' Murad Pasha spoke though a mouthful of roast peppers. He was fastidiously picking slivers of vegetable from the dish on which the lamb sat. His fingers getting so soiled and greasy that he'd abandoned his napkin and taken to using the edge of the table cloth instead.

'The Sufi.'

'Is he?'

Hani looked at her cousin, who shrugged.

'How would I know?' Murad demanded. And there was a sadness to his words at odds with the wry smile that lit his face. No boy should have eyelashes that long, Hani decided before considering his question.

Knowing such things came naturally to Hani and so she'd never stopped to wonder how she knew. Reading was part of the answer. She did a lot of that. And questions. Aunt Nafisa always told her she asked too many of those. But mostly she just made connections. Adding one fact to another to arrive at a third which was obvious in retrospect.

'Our porter,' she said carefully. 'He's a Sufi and this is his kind of music. Also my Uncle Ashraf . . .'

Murad Pasha raised dark eyebrows. He'd heard all about Lady Hana's uncle. 'He's a Sufi too?'

'Possibly,' said Hani with a shrug. 'They like the same music. I was going to say that really he's . . .' She lowered her voice and the boy bent closer, head tilting so that Hani could whisper; but the truth about the sons of Lilith went unspoken as one of the guards behind the Emir suddenly yelled.

Grabbed for his automatic.

'Emir.'

Time slowed and within its slowness Hani watched the Sufi raise a revolver, thumb back the hammer and let go, the trigger being already depressed. His first shot drilled the bodyguard through his still open mouth. Blood and splinters of vertebrae exiting in a vivid splash from the back of Nicolai Dobrynin's neck.

'No . . .'

Murad's scream broke time's crawl and in the acceleration which followed Hani saw the grey woman try to throw herself across Moncef just as his other bodyguard decided to do the same. Flame flared again from the Sufi's muzzle, there was a crack of gunfire and in the after-silence Eugenie and the second Soviet guard tumbled together. As for the man with the gun, a shot from behind dropped the Sufi where he stood.

All this took maybe a second. Perhaps fractionally less.

Murad Pasha was still rising from his chair when Hani grabbed him and tipped hers back, their chairs hitting the floor with an impact that knocked what little was left of the boy's shout from his body.

'Stay down,' said Hani.

Murad shook his head.

'You'll be killed.'

'Look,' Murad said, as he snatched free his wrist, 'No one's shooting at you or me. It's my father they want to murder. Okay?'

The boy's scramble to stand upright ended abruptly, when Hani grabbed one ankle and yanked hard.

She didn't mean to let go, but the moment Murad's other foot raked across her knuckles instinct cut in, and by the time she'd taken her hand from her mouth Murad was on his feet, looking for his father who appeared to be missing.

Hani swore. Bad swearing. The kind Zara used when she thought no-one was there. But Hani clambered to her own feet all the same, trying to stay low so bullets went over her head, if there were any more bullets.

Which was how she came to see a distant waiter, thin and white jacketed with a staff tag that read *Hassan* wrestle a Browning hiPower from a tuxedoed musician.

'Shoot him,' barked the officer who'd stood behind Kashif Pasha. Hani wasn't sure which one he was talking about either. 'Do it,' Major Jalal insisted. When no one moved the major drew his own automatic. Only Major Jalal never got to pull the trigger because one second the waiter and musician were struggling and then they weren't.

For a moment the waiter just stood, watching the other man crumple and then he retreated towards the outside kitchens, Browning hiPower still in his hand and muzzle pointing firmly at Major Jalal's head.

A parting shot over the head of the crowd kept Kashif's guests from rushing after him. The metallic clunk that followed was the waiter ramming a spit between handles on the other side of the courtyard door.

'Shoot out the hinges,' Kashif Pasha ordered.

'No,' said an older voice. 'Not before securing the room.'

Hani knew without looking that she'd just heard the first words Emir Moncef had uttered all evening. It was a grey-haired, steel-eyed kind of voice. One that allowed for little compromise. Although that didn't stop Kashif Pasha from pushing Major Jalal towards the blocked door.

'Do it . . .'

'We said no.' Moncef's words were firm. Far firmer than the steps which carried him back into the room. 'That exit could be booby-trapped. Either wait for a bomb squad or send someone round to check from the other side.' The Emir addressed his remarks to everybody but most guests understood, as did Kashif Pasha, that the rebuke was aimed at him alone.

'But . . .'

'Do what His Highness says.' Flat as a line showing cardiac arrest, the voice came from behind Moncef. The woman to whom it belonged was neat, compact and had skin the colour of ripe aubergine. A single pip on her shoulder gave Fleur Gide's rank as lieutenant. The gun she carried was a Heckler and Koch, capable of 850 rounds a minute. She carried it low so it raked across everyone in sight, even her commander.

'I thought we agreed . . .' Kashif's voice was harsh.

'And we thought you promised to provide adequate security,' said the Emir, his face hollow with grief. 'Nicolai and Alex are dead. And our oldest companion.' He stared down at the grey-haired woman killed with a .45, one that had drilled through her ribs and still held enough velocity to kill the guard stood behind. She lay in a cloak of blood on a white floor, eyes still open.

Leaning heavily on his cane, the Emir knelt to close the woman's eyes himself, muttering a prayer for the dead.

Kashif Pasha was shocked to realise his father was crying, not just in public but openly. Over two Soviet guards and a *nasrani* mercenary. In the circumstances the only thing he could do was ignore the fact. 'Where's my mother gone?' he demanded.

'I took her to safety,' said Lieutenant Gide. 'As I did your father when the shooting started. Those were *madame's* orders, should the need arise.' Her gaze made it clear that the madame to whom she referred was the elderly woman dead on the floor. Kashif Pasha ignored her. 'Arrest everyone in the kitchens,' he told Major Jalal. 'Before they run away.'

'And just why would they do that?' the Emir asked.

'Because they're *nasrani*,' Kashif Pasha said through gritted teeth. 'Because one of them just shot an undercover member of military intelligence.'

'Undercover? *I thought we'd agreed . . .*'

Kashif Pasha scowled at his father's mimicry and the Emir smiled. 'Arrest them if you must,' he said, 'but release them afterwards.' He held up one hand to stop his son from interrupting. 'Understand me. None of them are to disappear.'

Chapter Thirty-one

Wednesday 2nd March

Hani/three seats away from where Eugenie got shot/eyes locking on his/too frightened to be puzzled at not recognising a face so familiar.

Raf re-ran that sequence in his head, letting Alex, Nicolai and Eugenie tumble endlessly in time to his own, real world punches. To turn back like this, to attack an enemy was probably the last thing anyone hopelessly outnumbered was meant to do . . . But then, as he'd spent a lifetime telling himself, Raf wasn't anyone.

He was the guy with an 8000-line guarantee and weird-shit eyes, bat-like hearing and a sense of smell acute enough to revolt a dog. A man with pixel-perfect memory for every last one of those bits of his life he was able to remember. And ice-cold gaps where the rest should be.

Slamming the soldier's head against a wall, Raf lowered a limp body to the ground and began stripping it. The tunic was too tight across Raf's shoulders and the trousers short. The boots were good, though, and the cap fitted. After dressing the conscript in his discarded trousers, shoes and shirt (the waiter's tunic having already been dumped), Raf dragged the unconscious man into position against an alley wall.

'Drunk,' said Raf as he stood over the body. He sounded disgusted but not quite disgusted enough. Pushing his fingers down his own throat, he retched across the other man's chest and down into his lap. Alcohol and scraps of food stolen from serving plates being taken back into the kitchens.

'Who's that?' demanded a voice. An NCO stood behind him

in the entrance to the alley. Ahead of them both was a side door into the Domus Aurea.

'Some filthy drunk,' Raf said and kicked the body.

Originally, way back, the *dar* had been built for some half-Alicantean *taifa*. Isabeau had told Raf its history as they both helped Chef Edvard set up his makeshift kitchen in a small yard off the *bait bel kebu*. The red and white horseshoe arches that provided access to the dining room, the carved capitals in Mudejar style, gilded stucco muqarnas work across the ceiling, the intricate, impossibly complex tiling. All had been purchased with the spoils of piracy. It was like discovering that Dick Turpin held up stagecoaches because he had a passion for snuff boxes and French enamel . . .

'Keep looking,' ordered the NCO.

'Yes sir,' Raf said.

There were days now – whole days, sometimes days that ran into each other – when Ashraf Bey understood that he'd created the fox. What had happened when he was seven was his responsibility alone. He had chosen to walk out across that girder, the soles of his school slippers melting with every step. Just as he'd chosen to steal a fox cub from its cage and hide in the attic. Not knowing that the fire he'd set would reach his hiding place. And certainly not knowing it would burn down his whole school.

He'd wanted to destroy the biology building. An ugly block of cheap polycrete faced with pine slats like some tatty ski lodge. That was where the animal experiments were done. Where frogs were dissected and road kill skinned to reveal underlying muscle structure. Where he'd been made to peg out the pelt of a badger and rub salt into stinking leather, having first scraped it so thin that in places it looked almost translucent. 'What's done is done,' Raf told himself and headed into another alley, stopping at a door to kick it open. 'So why cry?' The question was rhetorical, Raf accepted that. But he answered it all the same.

'No reason.'

He was beginning to see how it worked. Every question he'd

ever asked the fox he answered for himself. Pulling information from memory to provide those clinically precise, unhelpful answers. Sweating the small stuff to make the big stuff go away. His life had been one long refusal to take the real facts and make them add up.

Raf searched the house swiftly, five rooms on three floors, saying nothing to the frightened inhabitants. On his way out he shook his head at a couple of conscripts on their way in. 'Empty,' Raf told them. 'No one hiding.'

Why was he upset? Good question.

Tiri had been kept in a wire cage at the rear of the biology block. Most of the smaller animals lived inside. Hamsters and rats, mice bred for so many generations that generations of biology masters had lost count. A black widow spider permanently catatonic with cold. Sickly stick insects. Guppies in water thicker than fog. And a single, magnificent Siamese fighting fish, all broken fins and ragged tail.

Raf freed the rats and shook the stick insects onto grass at the front of the block. This had seemed like a good idea at the time. Although later, looking down from his burning attic at fire trucks lining up on the lawn he realised he hadn't given them a better life at all. He hadn't known what to do with the fish so he removed most of the water from the guppies because their tank was dirtier than that of the Siamese fighting fish, then tipped one tank into the other. If Raf couldn't free the fighting fish he could at least give it a decent meal.

He'd never liked guppies anyway.

Some soldier had lit the spotlights around Domus Aurea but these only did what they were meant to do, threw walls into relief or picked out aspects of architectural interest.

There were trucks on the road beyond the medina, circling the old city walls with soldiers hanging from their open doors. Kashif Pasha's men. All of them searching for him. A grinding of gears came from a square ahead, more trucks arriving for the hunt. From Raf's left came shouted orders. Further away, to his right, beyond a low line of workshops, more orders, more shouting. Engines racing and truck doors that slammed.

This was no way to track a fugitive. Even without the fox
Raf knew that. Or rather he knew that without needing the fox,
because he *was* the fox. One and the same. Separated not at
birth but stood on that burning girder. What Raf knew (such as
it was), he knew for himself and in himself. Just as Raf knew
that he needed to get out there. To become himself. A man with
responsibilities and a life.

And if not a man then whatever he was.

Part Two

Chapter Thirty-two

Wednesday 2nd March

On the dirt track a group of hunters struggled with a dead boar. They had its carcass lashed to a pole and slung between two of their party. A third man had a Ruger across his back and carried the rifles of the first two, slung one under each arm. Behind those three walked two more men, rifles ported across their broad chests.

Gravel crunched beneath their boots and each wore a loden coat with broad belt, tweed plus fours and long woollen socks.

Every last one of them watched the Bugatti Royale grind past. All their guns had telescopic sights and featured extended magazines that came only as an (expensive) optional extra. The man at the back had two dead rabbits hanging from his belt.

'Season ends in about three weeks,' said Hani. She waved to the hunters who stared back, eyes hard. The Bugatti, one of only seven ever made, had been climbing for the last five minutes towards a distant farmhouse that kept vanishing behind the hill. The track over which it rattled was rough, edged with thorn and a few bare oaks unwilling to accept that spring was due.

'There it is . . .'

Thick walls washed white under a roof of red pantiles. Windows kept small to protect the inside from winter winds. Protecting the glass were oak shutters, their wood stripped bare by winter frost and summer heat. A hunting lodge really, built by a wine shipper from Cahors. It could have been lifted wholesale from the Lot valley and set down amid the pines and oaks of Ifriqiya's rugged north coast.

Its original owner was long dead. His marble tomb decaying in a colonial churchyard where a pubescent angel stood guard over his final resting place, her downcast eyes at odds with the plumpness of her body and the thinness of her robes. Now she waited, rendered wingless by vandals, an atrocity victim waiting for eternity.

Claude Bouteloup began his life as a peasant farmer and ended it a baron, gold having dug deep enough to discover a previously overlooked family title. The walls of his old home remained lined with heads taken from the boar he'd shot in the Northern Tell. An implausible spread of horns over the main door stood memory to his plan to reintroduce aurochs. A few of which still roamed the hills, but fewer by the year.

All this Hani read out to Murad and Raf as her uncle yanked the Bugatti's 14-foot wheel base round a tight bend in the dirt road while trying to ignore a drop that fell away to a white, storm-fed river far below.

'Put the book down,' Raf told her. 'Before you make yourself feel sick.'

'Too late,' said Hani. She flicked backwards for a few pages and then flicked forward. 'This guide doesn't say who owns it now,' she complained, skim-reading the entry again.

'It wouldn't,' said Raf.

The first clue that this wasn't just another hunting lodge came at the gates. These looked normal until Raf got close enough to see otherwise. Tiny cameras tracked his arrival, watching from stone gateposts where they were bolted discreetly between the open claws of granite eagles

Micromesh, fine enough to be virtually invisible, lined the far side of the gate's flowing wrought iron. Its heavy, old-fashioned lock was electronic. Cracking paint covered hinges that Raf was willing to bet conformed to some exacting military standard he didn't even knew existed.

'You step out of the car,' said Murad. 'And then someone opens the gates if they like the look of you . . . I've been here before,' he added, without glancing up from his toy Ninja Nizam. Hani and he had spent from Tunis to Bizerte arguing about whether or not action figures were childish.

Hani kept on saying they were. Until finally Murad announced that as Hani did nothing but play with a stupid cat her opinion didn't count.

'Ifritah's not a toy.'

'Did I say he was?'

After that came blessed silence, from Bizerte to just past Cap Serrat, where Raf turned the Bugatti off the crumbling blacktop onto something that barely qualified as track. The Ettore-Bugatti-built coupé Napoleon had been a present from the Prince Imperial in Paris to the Emir's grandfather and, until Raf claimed it, had been garaged in a mews at the back of the Bardo Palace.

No one had dared to stop Raf commandeering the 275bhp, 12.8 litre monster. But then, from the chamberlain who ran the nearly empty palace to the uniformed sailor who first saw a blond notable in shades and black Armani suit striding towards its main door, no one had known how to treat Ashraf al-Mansur at all.

Finding a new suit had been as easy as kicking in the window of a boutique opposite Ibn Khaldoun's statue in Place de la Victoire, about 300 paces from Bab el Bahar. By then, dawn's call to prayer had come and gone and only isolated trucks still circled the medina like flies disappointed by the quality of their meal. The boutique was very elegant, with a wide range of supposedly embargoed Western goods but it should have spent more on security.

On his way out Raf met a handful of other looters on their way in. They liked his suit too. In fact they liked it so much he went back to point out the appropriate rack. And it was only after he left the second time he put on the shades he'd taken to match, casually ditching his cheap contacts into a storm drain.

An hour's walk from Ibn Khaldoun's statue took him to the edge of the Bardo. A complex of original buildings with rambling faux al Andalus additions, the Bardo featured palaces built on palaces, the bedrooms of one situated over the reception rooms of another until the different parts ran together into one impossible mess.

No one had ever catalogued its contents. Records even differed as to the number of rooms. And each attempt at rationalisation made matters worse. Although it was widely agreed among architectural historians that the rebuilding of 1882, during which medieval mashrabiyas were replaced with sash windows along one whole side was undoubtedly a low point.

All the same, the Bardo complex still counted as the most recognised façade in North Africa. One result of an old etching featuring in the opening credits of *A Thousand Flowers*, a long-running, widely syndicated Turkish soap based in the nineteenth-century harem of Ahmed Bey, where a thousand concubines languished under the guard of five eunuchs, played by bald Sudanese women.

No men were ever seen. And although some flower would occasionally be plucked from her languid divan and sent through *the Door*, she would return an episode later, usually in a state of unspecified bliss, distraught or just more worldly-wise.

Gossip, treachery and friendship, the plot ran regular as celestial tram lines. Its avid following the by-product of the originator's desire to draw her cast from a dozen nationalities. In the way Ifriqiya's beys had filled their harems with a variety of Egyptians, Turks and Southern Europeans, mostly captured slaves.

Various bearded Jesuits were sent, both in reality and in the soap. And indeed, in reality one such missionary spent three years camped in a wing of the Bardo Palace waiting for an audience that never actually came; despite an invitation from a bey devoted to the memory of his *nasrani* mother.

Now the Bardo was home to the world's largest collection of Carthaginian mosaics, an unquantifiable number of bad Victorian paintings and Kashif Pasha, his retinue and his mother. (With only Kashif's direct appeal to the Emir ensuring that Lady Maryam and he were allocated different sections of the crumbling complex.)

No flag flew from the mast over the main gate when Raf

arrived, which meant no adult member of the al-Mansur family was currently at home.

'We're closed.' The young sailor guarding the gate held his rifle slung across his chest, the way those on guard always did. His face was set. And only his eyes revealed uncertainty.

Raf halted, smiled . . . Made a minute adjustment to his maroon Versace tie. 'Good morning,' he said. 'I'd like to see your commander.'

Sailor and notable stared at one another. Although all the sailor saw was himself reflected in the blankness of Raf's new shades.

'Now,' Raf added, his voice polite but firm. He'd once watched his school doctor use just that mixture of courtesy and menace on Raf's Swiss headmaster.

'I don't have a commander.'

Raf sighed. 'Then get whoever you do have,' he suggested.

Leaving his post, the boy vanished through a small door cut into one of two double doors behind him. Endless heavy nails had been hammered into both to form repetitive patterns which, to Raf's eye, looked out of place against the delicacy of the pink marble columns supporting the arch into which the doors were set.

With a shrug, Raf stepped through the arch after him and found himself in a courtyard.

'You left the door open,' Raf pointed out, when the returning guard opened his mouth to complain. Behind the boy Raf saw a grey-haired man in blue uniform raise his eyes to heaven.

'Morning, Chief,' Raf said.

The elderly Petty Officer nodded. And in that nod was everything he felt about using untrained conscripts as guards and about notables who turned up at dawn, expecting to be shown round the Bardo.

'The palace is shut, Excellency.'

'I know.' Raf knew nothing of the sort, but that wasn't really the point. Straightening up, he adjusted his cuffs almost without thinking. 'I'm Ashraf al-Mansur,' he said, 'the Emir's

middle son. I've been asked to investigate last night's attack on
my father.'

'Attack?'

Raf didn't bother to reply.

'So it was . . .' The NCO's voice faltered.

'I think you'd better introduce me to your commander,' Raf
said and stepped further into a courtyard overlooked by fifty
sashed windows and a dozen balconies. The European kind.

He looked around him. 'My father here?'

The old man shook his head.

'Lady Maryam?'

Another shake and a quick suck of yellowing teeth.

'Okay,' said Raf. 'How about Kashif Pasha?'

The NCO opened his mouth and then shut it again. Had the
pasha been in residence then, as well as having the al-Mansur
flag fly over the main gate, that gate would have been guarded
by Kashif's own soldiers instead of raw recruits. As it was,
Kashif's men were rumoured to be busy, making wide-ranging
arrests.

The one person Raf did find was Hani, although he found Ifritah
first, scooping the grey kitten up from a tiled floor and tossing it
over his shoulders like a stole.

'Hey,' shouted a young girl who slid through a door and kick
stopped, leaving a smear of burnt leather on the marble under
her heel. 'That's my . . .'

She took a look at the man facing her.

'Oh,' she said crossly, 'you're back.'

'No,' said Raf, 'I've been here for days. You're the one who's
just arrived.'

'I was here yesterday,' Hani said. 'You can ask him.' She
pointed to a door through which a young boy appeared. He
was dressed in a blazer and had a striped tie quite as smart
as the one Raf wore.

'Murad al-Mansur?' said Raf and watched the boy glance
round before nodding. They both knew what was missing from
the picture. 'Where's your bodyguard?' Raf asked.

'Kashif Pasha doesn't think I need one.'

'Because no assassin would want to kill a child?' Raf's voice made it obvious what he thought of that.

'That wasn't what I said.' Shrewd eyes watched the new-comer. 'Or what he meant.'

'Murad's my cousin,' Hani announced.

'And this is my niece,' said Raf nodding to Hani. 'I do apologise.'

The boy looked between them. 'Then you're . . . ?'

'Ashraf Bey,' said Raf. 'Your half-brother, her uncle and the new Chief of Police.'

At the bey's side the NCO froze. His reflex reptilian. Almost as if stillness could put a wall up around his thoughts. All it did was draw Raf's attention.

'You,' Raf said to the man. 'Tell me what you've heard . . .'

'Heard, Your Excellency?'

'Outside, you said, *So it was* . . . The question is, *so it was what*?'

'The Army of the Naked,' said the man, his voice hesitant. 'My chief said they'd carried out an attack.'

'That's a lie,' Murad Pasha said. And blushed when the NCO gazed at him in surprise. 'I've got a radio,' he explained hurriedly. 'A *Radiotechnika Atlas*. The kind that gets all the stations . . . A birthday present from the Soviet ambassador,' Murad added, as if owning a radio needed explanation. 'The AN absolutely deny having anything to do with the attack.'

'They have a radio station?' Hani asked.

'A pirate station,' Murad stressed. 'Which changes frequency every night. You have to look for it.'

Hani nodded. 'Zara's brother has a pirate station,' she said. 'But Avatar only has to change every week.'

'Whose's Zara?'

'My uncle's mistress,' said Hani, then stared in bewilder-ment at the elderly NCO who suddenly broke into a coughing fit.

'The AN want to overthrow the government,' Murad said. 'But they didn't try to kill my father.' A tremble in his voice was the first sign Raf had sensed that the boy was not nearly as composed as he wanted to appear.

'I thought you said you were in the government?' Hani sounded puzzled.

'Minister for education,' Murad agreed. 'Also for archaeology. Kashif's everything else apart from bio-science and technology. The Emir kept those for himself.'

'Did you see the attack?' Raf demanded.

Murad nodded. 'We were there,' he said. 'I was invited and Hani invited herself. We sat next to Kashif Pasha as it happened.'

'When *what* happened?' Raf asked.

'Someone tried to shoot the Emir,' said Hani. 'Eugenie died saving him. And two guards, a Sufi and a musician. Now everyone's arguing about . . .'

'Who tried?'

Hani paused. She'd got older without him noticing, Raf realised. More confident. A little bit taller. He tried to remember back to that age and couldn't.

'Well,' said Murad. 'There was this waiter.'

'You can't go in there.' The bird-like woman was out of her seat before Raf got halfway to the door of Kashif Pasha's inner office.

'Tell me about it,' Raf said tiredly. People telling him where he couldn't go was getting to be something of a refrain. He kept walking and the woman dropped her hand, as if she'd somehow just scalded her fingers on the cloth of his sleeve.

Used to wielding power but resigned to it always belonging to someone else, the woman fell back on formality. 'Can I ask if you have an appointment?'

'I don't need one,' said Raf. 'Police business.' He pulled a leather cardholder from his pocket and flipped it open, flashing an identity card he'd taken off Kashif's unconscious soldier. It was shut again before her eyes even had time to focus.

'Well, he's not here.' The woman's hair beneath her scarf was thinning and deep lines slashed down both sides of a thin mouth. The world had not been kind to her. 'So you'll still have to come back.'

'Even better,' said Raf, hand already turning an enamel door knob. 'That gives me a chance to search his office.'

'You can't . . .'

'What's your name?' Raf asked her.

'Leila el-Hasan. I'm the pasha's private secretary.'

'Get yourself another job then,' Raf told her, not unkindly, and shut Kashif's door behind him, shooting its bolt.

The décor could go either way. High Arabesque, which got called Moorish in guide books, or ersatz European, which usually meant oak panels, dark furniture and oil paintings. Those were the default options when it came to North African government buildings. There was a third alternative, of course. Seattle Blonde was what you got if you fed old Scandinavian through late period Edo, but pale kelims and steam-shaped ash was never going to be Kashif Pasha's thing.

What Raf found was High Arabesque. An office centred around an alabaster fountain so massive that this bit of the Bardo had to be last century despite the obvious antiquity of the horseshoe arch surrounding its door. No floor underpinned with anything but steel could have supported that weight. Beyond the fountain began carpets, large and probably priceless; obscured by a faded leather ottoman and a couple of wing chairs. And against the furthest wall, beneath a window so vast it needed sandstone pillars down the middle to support it, stood an office desk, notable only for its ordinariness.

Raf read the subtext in a single glance. Look at the magnificence imposed upon me by birth. Notice how modest my own expectations. Contrast the two and be aware of my modernity. And it must work, because half of Europe regarded Kashif Pasha as Ifriqiya's up-and-coming saviour.

The only thing missing from the room was a portrait of the Emir and it didn't take a man of Raf's talents to read that. Although he read the subtext below the subtext, the one which suggested that while Kashif was ambitious he lacked advisers to help him plan his moves with subtlety.

But then lack of subtlety was never a problem when dealing with Paris, Washington or Berlin. Particularly Berlin.

None of Kashif's desk drawers were locked. Which either said look how open I am, or else, so great is my power no locks are needed to protect my privacy. Alternatively it might have been because there was nothing in the desk of the slightest significance.

No state papers or smoking gun. Not even a bottle of Jim Beam or a Hustler imported under diplomatic seal. Mind you, Raf had expected little less. He'd visited Kashif's office for one reason only. To rattle a few bars and see what tried to bite.

And to judge from the hammering at the door he was about to find out.

Opening the door was one option; letting whoever was on the other side smash apart original ninth-century panels was another.

'Wait,' Raf ordered, voice hard.

On the other side of the antique door the hammering ceased.

Raf took his time to walk across the office, but then, given the size of Kashif Pasha's room, this was not unreasonable.

'Right,' said Raf, slipping back the bolt, 'It's open.'

Two men in bottle-green uniforms came tumbling into the room. They had heavy moustaches, light stubble and hard glares. One glance at the glowering pasha behind them showed where that look originated.

'Up against the wall,' the thinner of the two barked. 'Now.'

Raf shook his head. 'You can go,' he told the man. 'Take your fat friend and shut the door. I want to talk to my brother.' That got their attention. Got the attention of Kashif Pasha as well.

Ashraf Bey stepped forward and held out his hand. 'This won't take long,' he told Kashif Pasha, 'I need to ask a few questions about last night's shooting.'

'You need . . .' Despite himself, Kashif Pasha's eyes slid to the *chelengk* recently pinned to Raf's lapel. Such exalted signs of Stambul's favour were rare. Given only to victors in battle and those who had rendered personal service to the Ottoman throne.

'Who are you?'

'Ashraf al-Mansur,' said Raf, letting his hand drop. 'Acting on behalf of the Emir.' Which was almost true. He'd been asked to act by Eugenie who'd led him to believe that this was the Emir's suggestion. Close enough to count. He shrugged. 'I thought you'd like to be first,' said Raf. 'Before I track down your guests.'

'That won't be necessary,' said Kashif Pasha crossly. 'Everyone who should be has already been pulled in for questioning. My men were arresting people all last night.'

'Everyone who should be . . . ?' Raf raised his eyebrows.

Kashif Pasha's nod was abrupt. Furious.

'So you've questioned the Marquis de St Cloud?'

'Don't be ridiculous.' Kashif's fingers were knotted into fists. Although Raf doubted if the man even realised that. 'The Marquis is a personal friend.'

'How about Senator Malakoff? Ambassador Radek?' Raf was enjoying himself. 'Or are you carefully ignoring anyone important . . .'

A crowd had gathered in the outer office and through the door he could see Kashif Pasha's secretary, her face twisting with anxiety as a man in a grey suit attempted to comfort her. Behind them hovered a handful of clerks.

This was exactly what Raf had needed most, an audience.

'So,' said Raf, 'why haven't you questioned the Marquis?'

'*What are you suggesting?*' Kashif Pasha stepped in close, like someone facing down an enemy but Raf knew different. Once, longer ago than he remembered, a Rasta on remand in the same jail as him had explained about clinches. They were where weak fighters hid when seeking protection, nothing more.

'I don't know,' said Raf. 'Why don't you tell me.'

Chapter Thirty-three

Wednesday 2nd March

'Why did Kashif's soldiers walk you to the car?' There was something in Murad's voice that said he'd been mulling over this question for most of the trip. Which he had. He'd been trying to decide if asking it would be rude.

'No idea,' said Raf and pulled the borrowed Bugatti into a parking space in front of the farmhouse and cut the engine.

Behind him Hani snorted but Raf ignored her. He was too busy watching Murad in the rear-view mirror. Everything from eye colour to skin hue was different. The boy had narrower shoulders than Raf. A softer face. And thick dark hair instead of the fine ash blond that made Raf so visible. But there was something lost in his face, the same closed-down expression and the boy even chewed his lip in the same way.

Only Raf's squint was missing. His habitual reaction to trying to see without shades. Those had come later, after the second round of operations in Zurich. Besides, the dark glasses were meant to be a temporary fix, Raf could remember being told that.

'You okay?' he asked the boy.

'Sure.' Murad shrugged. 'Why not?' And in a way Murad was telling the truth. For a twelve-year-old who'd recently seen four people murdered he was doing fine, especially as one of them was a woman he'd known all his life. Opening the Bugatti door, Murad stepped out onto gravel. It was the only way he could avoid more questions . . .

'You know,' Raf told Fleur Gide, stepping through the front door. 'My brother thinks Berlin turned that Sufi.'

'Berlin, Your Highness?' Major Gide looked genuinely shocked. 'I assumed it was Washington or Paris.'

She'd been the one to take the decision to let the Bugatti through the gate. A responsibility that fell to her as Eugenie's temporary replacement. Fleur Gide was as ambitious as the next special forces officer but this was one promotion she would happily have done without.

'Someone turned him, you agree?' said Raf. 'And you don't have to call me Highness. I'm an Excellency at the most. If that . . .'

The newly promoted officer nodded doubtfully.

'Word on the street has the Sufi working for Kashif Pasha,' Raf said. 'Only that's wrong. Well, it is according to my brother.'

Mentioning that the nearest he'd got to checking the word on the street was listening in while Murad Pasha scanned a dozen pirate stations seemed inappropriate. A twelve-year-old princeling lacked something as an information source when dealing with Ifriqiya's new head of intelligence, temporary or not.

Rough flagstones covered a hall which made do without carpets. On the walls, sporting prints showed stags at bay and scenes from a duck shoot. There was a fireplace, carved from granite and featuring an ornate coat of arms with two of the quarterings themselves showing quarterings. Above the mantel hung a simple mirror while flames danced in the hearth below, filling the ground floor of Eugenie's old house with the scent of burning pine cones.

A thick-set, bejewelled woman stood in front of Raf and refused even to glance at the prints on the walls. Only a boar's head mounted onto a mahogany shield with the date 1908 engraved onto an ornate silver label below drew any reaction. Lady Maryam shuddered every time she accidentally turned in that direction.

'I came because duty demanded it,' Lady Maryam said heavily. And Raf knew he was being warned not to judge her by the objects to be found in the house.

'Sometimes,' said Raf, 'that's all you can do.'

He'd heard the other version. The one where Major Gide bundled the Emir into a car to get him to safety. Only to have Lady Maryam clamber in the other side and refuse to budge. What upset Major Gide most was her certain knowledge that Eugenie would have had no hesitation about dragging the sullen over-weight princess from the car and leaving her in the courtyard. And that was before factoring in the Emir's fury that she'd allowed Lady Maryam to travel with them while leaving Murad, his favourite son behind.

'Wait here,' said Lady Maryam. 'While I see if my husband is awake.'

Tracking her footsteps across flagstones, Raf followed them up a flight of stairs and across bare boards. The knock at a distant door was surprisingly gentle.

A creak of hinges died when the door shut, leaving Raf with a waterfall of near silences, none of them significant because they were not what Raf listened for. Below the clatter of dishes on a work surface and the small-arms pop of water pipes stretching hung the rustle of wind through a pine tree beyond the window. The wings of an owl. Slow and methodical. And under this the claws of a rat scurrying across the gravel at the front of the farmhouse where Major Gide's guards patrolled creaking gates. Falling through silences, one at a time. Hyper-real . . .

'Uncle Ashraf!'

Ashraf Bey came awake to find himself watched by Hani, Murad and Lady Maryam. There was one other person present. A thin man with swept-back grey hair and blue eyes above a hawk nose that had once been broken. A day's worth of white stubble only heightened the hollowness of his cheeks. And he leant heavily on a stick. All the same, there was a ferocious intensity to his gaze; as if he burnt with fever or was some celestial body in its final stage of immolation.

'So you're Sally's child . . .' The Emir's smile was sad. 'You know,' he said, 'she told me you died. And then you turn up all those years later in El Iskandryia. I wouldn't have believed it without seeing you.'

The hand that shook Raf's own was hot, dry like paper, the bones beneath the age-bruised skin weak as twigs. Even the slight grip Raf gave was enough to make the old man wince. There'd been a dozen things Raf had always wanted to say to his father and none of them seemed appropriate.

What the man opposite felt, Raf found hard to tell.

'Don't you *want* to talk to each other?' Hani demanded.

'It can wait,' said the Emir. 'What are a few minutes after this long?'

When the old man walked, it was slowly, leaning heavily on his stick. And at every change of level Murad Pasha positioned himself at the Emir's side so the old man could reach out and steady himself. A fact Lady Maryam obviously hated, to judge from the sourness of her expression.

Although that could also have been down to the Emir's refusal to admit she even existed. She might as well have been a trophy mounted on the wall since she obviously created in him the disquiet that the boar's head seemed to inspire in her.

The farmhouse had been built into the hill. With its back only slightly higher than the front. This meant that the room into which they finally passed had earth reaching two-thirds of the way up its outside walls; good for warmth in winter and useful in other ways too.

'Don't tell me,' Raf said, 'the place was like this when Eugenie found it.'

Emir Moncef smiled.

'She made a few adjustments,' he admitted. 'Mostly involving chicken wire and concrete. Well, loosely . . .' Which was true. If chicken wire included military-grade titanium mesh and reinforced polyfoam walls could be described as concrete.

'How much of the farmhouse is actually left?'

'Ask Major Gide,' he said and clapped his hands.

It seemed the answer was virtually nothing. Apart, that was, from the original eagle gateposts, the granite fireplace and the flagstones in the hall. All walls, internal and external, conformed to Moscow's best standards for blast resistance. Steel-cored doors hid beneath veneers of oak. Screamer wire looped the immediate forest at ankle height. A Molniya spysat hovered high over head, streaming live data to combat software stashed in the cellar. The fat pantiles on the roof featured thermal feedback to keep the surface at ground ambient, day and night. Even the glass in the windows, double-glazed and shatterproof, vibrated at a random pitch to confuse anyone hidden outside with a parabolic mic.

All of it was black tek. All of it shipped in contravention of numerous UN resolutions banning the sales to Ifriqiya of weapons' grade technology.

'Those hunters,' said Raf.

'Georgian *Spetsnaz*.'

'What about the boar?' Hani demanded.

'Fake,' interrupted the Emir. 'Eugenie de la Croix's idea.' He nodded to Hani and smiled at Murad who just looked at him, eyes wide, then glanced between the Emir and Raf and scowled.

'You think we look alike,' Moncef said. It wasn't a question.

The small, dark-eyed boy nodded but Hani just shook her head.

'No,' she told the Emir, 'you look way older.'

'It's flu,' Lady Maryam said when Raf finally asked.

'You're sure?'

'Of course, I'm sure.' Lady Maryam's voice was sharp.

'How do you know?' Raf demanded. He'd already seen over the whole farmhouse and apart from two large rooms upstairs, one used by the Emir, with another on the ground floor now claimed by Lady Maryam, meaning Major Gide had to share the dorm with her troops, that was it. Apart from the hall, kitchen and cellar. The *Spetsnaz* slept at a house in the village. One of the major's jumpsuited teenagers did the cooking. There was no one else and nothing that looked like a surgery. As it was, Raf and the others were going to have to make their way back to Tunis that night because anything else presented too much of a risk.

'Major Gide is also his doctor,' Lady Maryam said shortly. 'I'm surprised you didn't know that.'

They were back in the hall by the fire. The darkness outside was such that stars bled diamonds across black velvet through the one window left uncurtained. The longer he stayed the jumpier Lady Maryam became, her politeness becoming ever more brittle by the minute. She'd already added Murad to the list of things at which she was unable to look, banishing Hani and her cousin to the kitchen.

'I should go,' Raf said.

'Yes,' agreed Lady Maryam and as she clapped her hands a wattle of flesh on her wrist quivered. She was old, Raf realised. The way the Emir was old. Made older by bitterness and four decades of marital exile. All she had on her side was that her son had been born first.

'I'll have someone fetch the children,' Lady Maryam said.

Raf nodded. 'That would be kind,' he replied, knowing that kindness had nothing to do with it. 'But first I need to ask the Emir some questions . . . That's why I'm here,' Raf said, when the woman looked at him blankly. Turning for the stairs he was irritated to hear Lady Maryam's heavy steps following behind.

'I need to see him alone.'

'He's my husband,' said Lady Maryam.

And my father, apparently. Raf said. But he said it under his breath.

The huge room was hot and dark. The smell of vomit obvious. A glass of water stood on a table beside a hardly-touched bowl of couscous. Most of what had been eaten splattered the floorboards beside the bed.

Within the round belly of a wood-burning stove flames flickered. On a mattress, leant back against his pillows lay the old man, his pillow cases tallowed with sweat. A window that shouldn't have been open was. So it was just as well that Lady Maryam remained outside. Kept from entering by a shout that reduced her husband to a coughing fit.

'She keeps cooking me food,' the Emir said tiredly when his breath was back. He smiled at Raf's surprise. 'Don't worry,' he added. 'I make her eat a spoonful of everything first. She's only here to look after me because she knows how much I hate it.'

It was Raf's turn to smile.

'So tell me,' said the Emir, 'before we talk about things that matter. What did you do to get her wretched son so upset? I've had Kashif on the line swearing undying loyalty and warning me not to trust you.' The Emir sounded amused. 'What did you do, besides tell him you were now Chief of Police? Which, I have to say, was news to me . . .'

'I didn't say that at all,' said Raf. 'Merely that I was investigating the attack. And I suggested, obliquely, that he might have hired the Sufi.'

'Do you think he did?'

'That depends,' said Raf, glancing round the room until his gaze reached an angular chair made from pine and painted in a brown so deep it looked back, 'on who else would like to see you dead.'

'Paris, Washington, Berlin. Half the mullahs in Kairouan. That woman outside. And then there's you . . . Feel free to sit,' he added as if he thought Raf was angling for permission rather than working out exactly what worried him about the Emir's room.

'Why would I want you dead?'

Moncef's only answer was to glance at a ring resting between a revolver and a copy of the Qu'ran. The ring was gold, set with bloodstone and a swirl of script; the *tughra* engraved into its surface was that found on every 50 dinar coin for more than forty years.

The gun was a Colt .38 with pearl grips.

'There's more to ruling than owning a ring,' Raf said.

'Not much,' said the Emir, his laugh a fox-like bark, carrying more pain than amusement. 'Especially if you have the other two as well. You don't really like me, do you?'

'Probably more than your wife does,' Raf said sourly. 'She tells me this is the first time she's ever visited . . .'

'First and last,' said the Emir. 'This house was bought for Eugenie. Government money but her name on the deeds. She was many things, that woman. Only one of them my chief of intelligence.' Unashamed tears were in his eyes. Or maybe just unnoticed.

'You were lovers?' Raf said. It was barely half a question.

'That's one way of describing it.'

'She said you weren't.'

He smiled sadly. 'Eugenie kept her life in compartments,' he said. 'Jobs that people knew about. Those they didn't. Her personal life was one of the smallest. Maybe the least visited. Sometimes Gene needed to forget what she kept there . . . You see,' he explained, 'sleeping with me was probably the only unprofessional thing Gene ever did in her life. And all I did was get her killed . . .'

The Emir gestured to the table beside his bed where the ring lay between the book and the gun. 'Make your choice,' he said. 'And learn to live with it. That's all any of us can do.'

A glow from the wood-burning stove gave the Emir's face the look of a fallen angel, broken and beautiful; haunting in its promise and cruel beyond imagining. Behind the words was a desolation so deep it went beyond Raf's ability to understand. And in that moment he finally believed something his mother once said, which in itself was unusual.

His father was certifiably insane. She'd been holding a vodka when she said this. Her anger filtered through a freebase crash and the bottom of a Bohemian shot glass. Somehow they'd moved from filming Arabian wildcats as they learned to hunt, her latest project, to Raf's father, the man she refused to talk about. Of course, back then Raf thought she'd been talking about the Swedish hitchhiker.

'Why come now?' the Emir said into Raf's silence. 'When you wouldn't come before?'

'I was busy.'

'Having your garden rebuilt with someone else's money. . . Going to a job you didn't do . . . What changed?' asked the Emir, his eyes watching from within the red shadows of the stove. The very fact he hadn't asked why Raf wore shades in a room that sweltered in near darkness told Raf that

Eugenie's original suggestion was right and he had been wrong. Whatever had been done to Raf, his mother had not made those choices alone.

'What changed . . .' The answer died on Raf's lips. The snide, the furious and the easy comebacks all wiped by the obvious. 'I did,' said Raf.

Chapter Thirty-four

Thursday 3rd March

Dr Pierre smirked from the side of a barn, his mouth supercilious above the fading remains of a silk cravat. A lifetime of rain had worn his luxurious sideburns to a ghost of their former glory. A jagged scar split his chin where a builder had repaired cracked brickwork with no thought for the advertising mural beneath.

He was advertising *pâté dentifrice*. As used in Paris.

'Where are we going now?'

'Cap Bon,' said Raf. 'To question the Marquis de St Cloud.'

It said much for Murad's cool that he didn't ask why his half-brother had the Bugatti's headlights switched off. Recalibrating his eyes, Raf glanced in the mirror and saw Murad lit by screen glare from Hani's pink plastic laptop.

'Can you turn the screen down . . . ?'

'Why?' Her voice was petulant. As if she still hadn't quite forgiven him for one or more of the many things for which he still needed her forgiveness.

'Because too much light makes driving difficult.'

'If I must,' said Hani and flicked off her laptop. Adjusting the screen being much too easy an option.

Raf didn't tell Hani his other reason. That somewhere above them would be a UN spysat capable of tracking their journey from the farmhouse to Cap Bon. If they were lucky, that was. If they were unlucky, then the satellite had probably just captured every one of Hani's keystrokes.

He drove in silence. Letting darkened walls and hedgerows flow around him until the dirt track became a minor road and then something that actually had central lines. Shortly after that came the *périphérique* around Tunis, the city flickering by in a smudge of suburbs as the huge Bugatti burnt up the outside lane, lights out and its three passengers shadows held in darkness, like ghosts going on holiday

One of the cardinal points of the Emir's work creation programme was that everyone in Ifriqiya should have a job. And if that meant more road sweepers, line painters or ditch diggers than there were roads then so be it.

What Ifriqiya needed, of course, at least in the opinion of every visiting dignitary, was fewer donkeys and wider roads. Only the land lost to build the roads would, when added together, shave hectare after hectare off the country's reserve of perfectly good smallholdings. On the Emir's orders, a survey had been carried out after some commissar with mining interests in Gafsa had complained that trucking phosphate was becoming increasingly uneconomic.

In response to a hint from Moscow that the CCCP might help Tunis fund a programme to build new motorways the Emir sent them the address of every family who'd lose land and invited Moscow to write to each, explaining why it was necessary.

To the reply that this would be pointless, since most of those would undoubtedly be unable to read, he pointed out that the literacy rate in Ifriqiya was slightly higher than western Russia as a whole, and at least 25 per cent above that of Georgia, which was where both the commissar and the Soviet president originated.

The roads remained unwidened. Still lined with prickly pear except in the far south, where the ground was too barren to grow even that.

'What are you thinking?' Hani asked, her voice no longer sullen. On her lap the computer balanced on top of Ifritah's cat basket. Now forgotten.

'About prickly pears,' said Raf.

Hani nodded, as if that was to be expected. 'The roads,' she said. 'And Moscow's plan to widen them. It's mentioned in the official guide book.'

'Probably,' said Raf. From what he'd just seen, Emir Moncef

was quite capable of having it included just to signal his independence from the only country still willing to trade openly with Ifriqiya.

'How do you two do that?' Murad demanded, his tone more interested than aggrieved.

'Do what?' Hani and Raf asked together.

And the answer was he didn't know. Raf accepted that he'd no more understood what his own mother was thinking than she'd known what hid inside his head. They had remained, from his birth until her death, two strangers separated by common blood and long silences: every glance between them was embarrassed, each hug brief and gratefully cut short. If ever he took her hand she flinched. Every time she touched him he froze.

It was a relationship safe only when conducted at a distance by e-mail or letter. So maybe Zara was right and he really was the last person to be looking after a troubled, hyper-intelligent, unquestionably lonely small child.

Alternatively, he was ideal.

'You okay?'

Raf glanced in the mirror and saw Hani watching intently.

'Thought not,' she said. One thin hand came up and gripped his neck, small fingers digging into muscle knots on both sides. 'Twist your head,' said Hani.

Raf did and heard bones crunch as something slid back into place. 'Donna does it,' she said. 'Every time I get a headache.'

'You get many headaches?' Murad asked. And Raf realised he had no idea of the answer either.

She looked at Murad. 'Since my uncle arrived,' said Hani, 'life's been one long headache.' She smiled as she said it and neither of the other two quite noticed she'd avoided answering Murad's question.

'Almost there.' Hani's announcement came just before Raf turned right between two houses and edged his way through a tiny village, headlights still unlit. She'd been collecting old advertising murals and so far she had a *Dr Pierre*, two *Fernet-Branca (la digestif miraculeux)*, a faded blue *dubo, dubon, dubonnet* and one for underwear by *Rhouyl*, which, if she understood the faded French correctly, was guaranteed to induce health-giving static.

Staring from his window of the still-moving car, Murad tried to focus on the world outside. Just enough moon was filtering through the clouds to bathe the soft slopes of Cap Bon in a ghostly fuzz which was almost, but not quite, light. 'How do you know that?' he asked.

Hani shrugged. 'I just do.'

Around them were orange groves in blossom, wizened pine trees, the occasional villa set back from the coast and even a wrought-iron bandstand. A spindly confection set down on a promenade overlooking blue-painted fishing boats which bobbed at anchor.

On the wall opposite, another notice, paper this time, reminding everyone that falcons could not be captured for training until the second week of March. The warning was pasted next to an older poster advertising the *festival de l'épervier*, dated from June the previous year. Light from a bakery window lit both and through its glass could be seen an old man in vest and floppy trousers kneading dough . . .

They ate their brioche from the bag. The pastry still warm enough to make the paper turn translucent down one side. The old man had been polite. Totally unsurprised to be disturbed at three am by a man and two children wanting food. And he threw in two tiny tarte tatin for Hani and Murad, smiling and nodding as he shooed the three of them towards the door.

'Work to do,' he explained.

Raf nodded.

What passed for a plan in Raf's mind the fox would undoubtedly have dismissed as cage circling, the dysfunctional repetition of a narrow range of gestures. Have an idea, repeat it endlessly until all value is wrung from the original . . . With a sigh, Raf straightened his shoulders and pulled a bell handle.

Welcome to the Andy Warhol school of detective work.

Somewhere inside Dar St Cloud a Victorian bell tipped

sideways far enough to hit a silver clapper and the faintest tremor of that blow whispered back through the wire to reach Raf's fingers. The bell was an affectation. One made worthless by two small Zeiss cameras that swivelled, crane-like to catch Raf and his companions in their gaze.

Re-tuning his eyes, Raf shifted through the spectrum. Checking out what he already knew; the three of them were blanket-lit by infra-red and targeted at waist height by pinhead lasers. He could see tiny lenses set into the portico walls. Then the door opened and Raf forgot about armaments. Only panic could make the Marquis do something that stupid and this was not a character trait associated with Astophe de St Cloud, recognised *bâtard* of the French Emperor and a man who'd once offered Raf more money than he could even begin to imagine.

Three per cent of the price of North Africa's biggest oil refinery, plus the same cut on oil fields in the Sudan and various off-shore sites. All Raf had needed to do in return was betray Zara's father. Hamzah Effendi would fall. His share of a refinery that flickered ghosts of flame across the night sky on the edge of El Iskandryia would go up for sale. Enabling St Cloud to significantly increase his prestige and personal wealth.

Raf had not forgotten that offer any more, he imagined, than St Cloud had forgiven Raf's refusal to oblige.

'Tell St Cloud that Ashraf Bey needs to ask him some questions.'

'Is His Excellency expecting you?' The man who showed them into the hall was Scottish, though he spoke in an Edinburgh accent so clipped it could have come from an English film, the kind where butlers wore frock coats which, actually, was what he seemed to be wearing.

'What do you think?' Raf replied.

'I'll see if His Excellency is in.' And with that St Cloud's major-domo shuffled off towards an arch outlined in two shades of rose marble, leaving the three of them alone in a hall lit by gas-fired sconces designed to look like candle flame.

'Well, what a pleasant surprise.' The voice was higher than one might have expected given the undoubted gravitas of the man limping his way toward them in gold dressing gown and leather slippers.

'You know why this room is so high?'

'No,' said Raf. 'But no doubt you'll tell me.'

The Marquis laughed. 'I had to make a trip,' he said and something in those words raised hairs on the back of Hani's neck. 'So I left my butler in charge . . . This was years ago,' he added, as if the age of the house wasn't obvious. 'And I told him to tell the *felaheen* when to stop and gave him a height to which to work.'

The old man raised a silver-topped cane and gestured at the nearest wall, where tiny alternating blue and white tiles filled the spaces between evenly-spaced double pillars, each of which was topped by a broad capital. The pillars were pink marble, the capitals sandstone.

'You based it on Cordoba,' Hani said.

St Cloud nodded. 'Only my man got so drunk that when I got back, this had happened.' He pointed to a second tier of double pillars above the first. 'Not those pillars, obviously, just the height of the wall behind. The workmen expected to be told to stop so they kept on building.' The Marquis shrugged. 'Fair enough,' he added, in a tone of voice which made Hani decide on the spot that, where St Cloud was concerned, fairness was unlikely to come into it.

'What happened to your butler?' asked Murad Pasha, his voice thoughtful.

A smile broke across the face of the Marquis and in it Raf saw pure emptiness. 'There was a building accident,' said the Marquis. 'Such things happen. Well, they do in North Africa.' Glancing from Hani to Murad, St Cloud raised his eyebrows. 'You should know,' he told Raf, 'I've been very cross with you – so it was sensible to bring me presents.'

Hani merely blinked, but Murad's eyes widened and he might have stepped backwards if the girl at his side hadn't taken his hand, then hastily let it go. Both Hani and Murad suddenly blushing.

'This isn't a social visit,' Raf said flatly. 'And the children stay with me. We're here so Murad Pasha could meet the man who tried to murder his grandfather.' He turned to the still-flustered boy, almost as if intending to introduce him formally to St Cloud.

'I did no such . . .' Outrage froze words in the old man's throat.

'You are not to leave this house,' announced Raf. 'And you will surrender your carte blanche to me and the keys to all the cars in your garage.'

'And the helicopter,' Hani whispered. Catching Murad's eye, she shrugged and explained, surprisingly gently for her, 'there's a heli-pad on the lawn.'

'Out of the question.' St Cloud had found his voice. One that Raf could only describe as oozing bile. 'I have total diplomatic immunity. God . . .' The old man shook so hard with fury that for the first time since his visitors had entered Dar St Cloud he actually need his silver-topped stick. 'You can't just march in here.'

'Actually,' said Raf, 'I think you'll find I can. Because the alternative is that I place you under arrest and call police HQ in Tunis to have a van come out to collect you.' Raf shrugged. 'Who knows,' he added, 'given your tastes you might enjoy a week in the cells with a child molester. I'm sure you'd have lots to talk about . . .'

'And if I refuse?'

'Refuse what?' Raf asked. 'To be arrested?'

St Cloud's nod was stiff. His scowl that of a man who'd faced worse things than two nervous children and the black-suited son of an Emir. 'What will your officers do,' said St Cloud coldly, 'man-handle me into a car? They wouldn't . . .'

'Dare?' One second Raf was watching St Cloud, the next he had a pearl-handled Colt pressed hard into the side of the old man's neck, at an angle guaranteed to remove most of his skull.

No one could remember seeing him move.

'Other people might be afraid of you,' said Raf. 'I don't have that problem.' Pulling back the hammer the way the Sufi had done, he squeezed the trigger so that only his thumb kept the hammer from falling. 'You really think you can resist arrest?'

Around the Marquis the hall began to darken as the face in front of him changed unexpectedly/impossibly from human to something positively other.

The old man could taste smoke and feel a flat wall of heat that threatened to sear his papery skin. Every tile beneath his feet was burning. Except that there were no tiles because he was walking over a glowing chasm of red ember and flickering flame. While some unseen thing ripped mouthfuls of flesh from his shoulder.

He knew, without needing to be told, that he was stood over the entrance to hell.

'Well?'

St Cloud blinked.

The tearing in his flesh dissolved as the pressure against his throat lessened and then almost disappeared.

'Well what?' he asked in a voice little more than a whisper.

'Still feel like resisting arrest?'

Merely blinking was enough to spill tears down cheeks no amount of laser peel had been able to give back their beautiful youth. 'No.' St Cloud shook his head, the slightest movement. All he wanted to do was check his shoulder for scars and look in a glass to see if that unforgiving heat had seared his face, but didn't quite dare.

'I had nothing to do with that attempt,' he said. 'Nothing at all to do with the death of Eugenie de la Croix. You have my word.'

'And you have mine,' said Raf, 'that I *will* find who tried to kill my father. And when I do that person will be arrested, no matter what.' The very flatness of Raf's words threatened more clearly than any anger could do. 'Feel free to pass that on to anyone you think should know . . .'

Chapter Thirty-five

Thursday 3rd March

As dawn's white thread became visible over the Golfe de Hammamet a call quavered onto the wind from the minaret of Nebeul mosque, *Allahu Akbar* intoned four times, followed by *Ashhadu anna la ilah ill'-Allah*, I testify there is no God besides God. And finally, towards the end, a phrase to distinguish this call from those that came later. *Al-salatu khayr min al-nawn.* Prayer is better than sleep.

Though both of those were a rarity for Raf.

Only now was he beginning to understand, as opposed to know, the difference between various types of Islamic building. A *mosque* was a church, well, it was to Raf. A *marbarat* the tomb of a saint at which believers might pray (a habit discouraged in the Middle East, but popular in North Africa where Berber instincts lightened the stark purity of their conqueror's interpretation).

A *ribat* was a fortified monastery, *medressa* were schools, somewhere between a tiny university and a religious college, *zaouia* were shrines, often Sufi . . .

What Raf didn't understand, or even know, was what value this knowledge had for a man who lacked all belief in God; for whom mosques were works of intricate beauty and calls to prayer haunting echoes of antiquity; but who saw nothing at the centre. Who saw, in fact, no centre at all.

'Can I ask you something?' said Hani, when she'd finished her prayers.

'Of course.' Raf dropped the Bugatti down a gear to overtake an elderly truck loaded with soldiers.

'Who's Tiri?' She hesitated for a second. 'When you left that note. You signed it Tiri.'

'My fox,' Raf said and Hani nodded.

'What fox?' Murad demanded crossly. He was leaning on Ifritah's basket, which rested between Hani and him on the fat leather back seat of the Bugatti. Raf wasn't sure where he'd put his action figure but Ninja Nizam hadn't appeared once since Hani accused Murad of being childish.

'The fox . . .' Raf thought about it. 'The fox is an identity.'

'Ashraf Bey's an assassin,' said Hani. 'So he needs to be lots of different people . . . I didn't know the fox was called Tiri,' she added.

'It's called lots of things,' said Raf. 'And I'm not an assassin.'

'No,' Hani said. 'Of course not.'

Beyond Hammamet was a turning for the A1, south towards Sousse and Kairouan. Glancing in his mirror before overtaking the next truck, Raf saw Murad still staring at him. The moment the boy met Raf's gaze he dropped his own.

They'd had a brief quarrel on the road back from Dar St Cloud. Anger exploding from the boy as he demanded to know why Raf had failed to arrested the Marquis. In that shouted fury had been everything the twelve-year-old felt for his father; mostly love and fear, plus a primal, night-waking panic at the thought of life without certainty or comfort.

'You should have arrested him.'

'St Cloud didn't do it,' Hani had said softly, resting one hand on the boy's arm. Murad shook her off.

'But Ashraf Bey said . . .'

'He was bluffing,' explained Hani as she climbed into the car. Her smile faded the moment new fury twisted Murad's face. This time it was at being excluded from what Raf had known and Hani only suspected. Their visit to Dar St Cloud had been cage rattling, little more. The Marquis paid no taxes, had tastes that were highly dubious and based himself in a country without a single extradition treaty. He had more to lose from Emir Moncef's death than almost anyone.

Since learning this, Murad had been almost translucent with silence. Pointedly ignoring Hani and her endless spray of facts about Khayr el Din, better known as the Barbary pirate

Barbarossa, and the sack of Tunis by Charles V of Spain, in which 70,000 men, women and children were slaughtered.

That he'd asked about the fox at all was significant.

'I'm sorry,' Raf said. 'One problem is I don't always know what I'm going to do or how things are about to work out.' He yanked the Bugatti's thin steering wheel and managed to avoid a cartload of goatskins, untreated ones to judge from the smell. 'That makes it difficult to warn people in advance.'

'It's a children of Lilith thing,' Hani added. Although it was obvious from Murad's blank stare that this didn't make it any clearer.

The boy shrugged with all the weight of coming adolescence on his shoulders. 'I just was wondering,' said Murad. 'You know, back there, what exactly happened?'

Raf opened his mouth to answer but Hani got in first.

'What happened,' she told Murad, 'was that Uncle Ashraf put a curse on the Marquis. Children of Lilith can do that.'

Murad's eyes widened and, without even realising, he made a sign against the evil eye. And then flicked his glance fearfully from the face of his cousin to the dark-suited stranger in the front. The elder brother no one had bothered to tell him he had.

'Do you believe in magic?' Raf asked.

Murad nodded, fiercely.

'You shouldn't,' Raf told him, 'it doesn't exist. There are no djinn. If you hear something go creep in the night and it's not a burglar then it's a cat . . . Everything can be explained,' he added, before Hani had time to protest. 'Even those things that can't.'

'How do you explain things that can't be explained?' Murad demanded doubtfully.

'By admitting we don't yet have an explanation.'

The boy thought about that for as long as it took Raf to drop back a gear and overtake three trucks, leaving soldiers radiating outrage as he roared by in the half-dark, lights still off.

'So what happened with the Marquis?' said Murad. He spoke slowly. Listening to his own words as he said them. Raf could remember another boy like that. A boy who tasted each word as it was said. Who survived in dark places because his words, wielded viciously, could do more damage than the fists of other boys.

Which left Raf wondering whose fists Murad had been avoiding. Or if he'd learnt to think before he spoke for other reasons.

'I put a gun to his throat,' said Raf. 'That's usually enough to make anyone afraid.'

The boy nodded uncertainly. 'But he's St Cloud,' Murad said, obviously unable to think of another way to put it. 'Even my brother Kashif Pasha is scared of him.'

'Kashif is scared of Uncle Ashraf,' Hani pointed out. 'Anyone with any sense is. He works for the Sublime Porte.'

'No, I don't . . .'

'Then why wear the *chelengk*?' Hani asked triumphantly.

He thought about what she'd said before that. 'Are you?' he asked.

'Afraid of you? Of course I am,' Hani said. 'Every time you do whatever you did back then.'

Raf sighed. 'Did you notice a mark left on his neck afterwards from the muzzle of the gun? And my hand on the back of his neck?'

Hani nodded.

'I cut off his blood supply. Oxygen starvation combined with panic. It made an ancient part of St Cloud's brain kick in, nothing else.'

'That was it?' said Murad.

'Sure,' Raf said. 'Simple oxygen starvation.' He avoided mentioning the flames still dancing djinn-like across the inside of his eyes or the rawness that tightened his face like the after effects of searing heat.

Chapter Thirty-six

Thursday 3rd March

'Wait in the car,' Raf told them when they finally reached Kairouan. 'I'll get some breakfast.'

'Crêpe,' suggested Murad. 'With jam and cream cheese.'

'I don't think so,' Hani said. 'Does it look like that kind of place?' She wound down her window and sniffed, inhaling the cafés, street stalls and rotisseries. 'Get some *briek*,' she told Raf. 'And Coke, if you can find any.'

A dozen signs for local colas swung in the breeze. All variations on a theme of red and blue. None had names Hani recognised. This whole country was less like El Iskandryia than she'd first imagined.

'I'll see what I can do,' Raf promised.

Watching her uncle stride away, Hani waited until he was lost in the crowd. His black coat swallowed by the burnous and jellabas of those around him. 'Okay,' she said, turning to Murad, 'I'm going shopping. You wait in the car.'

Murad Pasha stared at her.

Hani eased open her door and checked that the road was clear before beginning to slide herself out.

'I'm coming with you.'

'No,' Hani said hastily. 'Someone has to stay with the car,' she insisted, 'and you're the boy . . .'

'So?'

Wide eyes watched him, apparently shocked. 'I'm a girl,' said Hani. 'Surely you don't expect me to stand guard over the car all by myself in a strange city?'

Murad settled back. His eyes already scanning the shop fronts. 'Don't be long,' he said.

The first chemist Hani entered was full of old men who stared as if she'd walked in from another planet. So, muttering an apology, she gave an elegant bow, which she hoped would muddle them even further. The second catered for Soviet tourists. Hani knew this because a poster in the window had pack-shots of painkillers and cough mixture above simple descriptions written in five languages, three of which Hani could read.

Catering for Soviet tourists was entirely different to there being any. Hani realised this as soon as she pushed her way through the shop's bead curtain and found the place empty, apart, that was, from an old man with what looked like the inward stare of a mystic or kif smoker. Although, it turned out to be neither because when Hani got closer, she realised his eyes were milky with cataracts.

'*Saháh de-kháyr,*' she said politely.

'*Saháh de-kháyr,*' he replied, then added, '*Es-salám aláykum.*'

So Hani had to start all over, replying *and to you peace*, before re-wishing him good day. Formalities complete, she stopped, unsure how to continue. She could see what she thought she needed on a shelf behind the counter, low down and almost out of sight.

The man waited while Hani opened and shut her mouth so often she was in danger of turning into one of Zara's promised carp.

'*Telephone?*' she muttered finally.

Absolute silence greeted this request.

Pulling a note from her pocket, Hani held it out to the old man. The note was American, a $5 bill.

The man called something over his shoulder and a young woman appeared, hastily wrapping her scarf around her head. Only to relax slightly when she discovered her customer was a child.

'Telephone?' Hani repeated.

Taking the bill from the man's hands she held it up to the light and then slipped it quickly into her dress pocket. Man and woman had a hasty conversation, so fast and so low that overhearing was impossible. Whatever the content, they seemed to reach a conclusion.

'No telephone,' said the woman. 'Not here. But I take you . . .' She gestured towards the rear and Hani realised that she was meant to follow. For about fifty paces she fought her way down a busy back alley and then the woman steered her towards a small door set in a crumbling wall.

'Through here,' she said, as she pushed Hani ahead of her, shouting, *'Hamid,'* as they came out into a small courtyard.

A second yell produced a head peering from an upstairs window. Another burst of conversation followed in what Hani finally realised was *chelha*, the original dialect of Kairouan's Berber inhabitants.

'Where do you want to call?' asked the woman, tossing Hani's answer up to the boy, then stopping for his reply.

'El Iskandryia we can do,' she agreed, 'but it will cost more than five dollars . . .'

Reluctantly Hani peeled another note from the roll in her dress pocket and palmed it into a small square before making a pretence of searching her remaining pockets, muttering crossly all the while.

'My last one,' she said.

The mobile was a Siemens. Unquestionably illegal in a country where all cell phones had to be registered with the police.

'Two minutes,' said the woman, 'call me when you're done.' And she vanished into the house to give the foreign girl some privacy. Although the boy remained, sat on a stone bench next to the courtyard entrance just to make sure Hani didn't suddenly disappear with his phone.

Hani could just imagine it. Donna stood in the kitchen surrounded by pans, trying to ignore the buzz of the coms screen, Zara out shopping and Khartoum lost in thought or re-reading tales of the Ineffable Mullah Nasrudin, all of which he already knew by heart.

She sighed.

The message Hani left was simple. She was in Kairouan

with her uncle. On her way to Tozeur. There was nothing to worry about.

'Where have you been?' Murad demanded when Hani finally got back.

'Getting these,' said Hani, handing him a cardboard dish of *makrouth*, lozenge-shaped sweetmeats filled with date paste. She dropped a cheap paper napkin next to his knee and clambered up into the huge Bugatti. The rest of the napkins she stuffed into a side pocket. She let Murad eat the sweetmeats because, unfortunately, even after her walk her tummy still had cramp.

Chapter Thirty-seven

Thursday 3rd March

Second coffee. That was how Eduardo counted his days. First coffee, second coffee, third coffee . . .

The first always found Eduardo listening to IskTV. While others watched the newsfeed avid for every close-up, Eduardo listened carefully as he doodled hats and moustaches onto pictures in *Iskandryia Today* or filled in the Os in every headline.

The Emir of Tunis had been taken into protective custody following the declaration of martial law in Ifriqiya. The story was in his paper as well as on screen. *Iskandryia Today* treated this as news while IskTV assumed it was background, leading with a different story. One that had His Excellency Kashif Pasha, the Emir's eldest son, swearing that his father was alive, safe and would remain that way. Apparently Kashif Pasha swore this on his life.

What IskTV found interesting was the fact that this promise was relayed on Kashif's behalf by a half-brother, Ashraf al-Mansur who personally visited the *Mosque de trois ports* in Kairouan to pass the message to the head of the Assiou Brotherhood.

The head of the brotherhood had, as requested, released Kashif Pasha's promise to the world.

So Eduardo wasn't surprised to receive a scrambled call just after second coffee. Although it took him a moment to remember that he needed to connect an optic from the silver Seiko he wore to the computer on his desk. That was what the man had told him to do, plug in as soon as Eduardo heard the hiss and never try to make a connection using infrared.

Which was fine, because Eduardo wouldn't have known where to start.

A doctor at the Imperial Free once suggested Eduardo reduce his coffee intake to one cup a day but Eduardo had barely paused to consider this. The man was a foreigner, newly arrived in the city and would learn. No one who actually lived in El Isk for longer than a week could have made that suggestion.

Instead, Eduardo had agreed with himself to cut his intake to eight cups a day. This wasn't always possible, given the nature of his job: but his success or failure gave Eduardo something to talk about to Rose, a mild-natured whore he'd met a few months earlier, when the man sent him to do a job at Maison 52, Pascal Coste.

Rose claimed to be English and, although she had the hips and buttocks of an Egyptian, the smallness of her breasts convinced Eduardo that this might be the truth. As did the half-smoked Ziganov forever hanging from her fingers, its gold band stained with lipstick. In Iskandryia, even licensed whores didn't smoke in public.

But then women tended not to visit cafés either. Unless it was one of those expensive places around Place Saad Zagloul like Le Trianon, where ordinary rules seemed not to apply. Money did that, Eduardo had decided. It rewrote the rules. Or perhaps it just remade them into something so complex and discreet that ordinary people like him no longer understood what they were. The man was like that, governed by rules Eduardo took on trust.

Eduardo's office was above a haberdashers at the back of a bus station on Place Zagloul. The place was a walk-up with winding stairs and a toilet on the half landing which Eduardo had to share with the shop below. It had a melamine desk, a cheap chair in black plastic that looked almost like leather and a grey metal filing cabinet. Plus a state-of-the-art computer, quite out of keeping with the rest of the furniture.

The computer lived on a side table. Well, it would have been a side table if it hadn't actually been an old door supported at either end by plinths of crudely mortared bricks. Eduardo, whose work it was, had tried to apologise for its ugliness but the man had waved away Eduardo's explanation. It seemed Ashraf Bey liked the door/table combination more than he liked anything else in the office.

Sharing Eduardo's office space were two cockroaches and a colony of ants who dwindled come autumn and, Eduardo imagined, would be back with the spring. He wasn't sure, not having had the place long enough to find out. The cockroaches remained however, sharing his desk and living off a diet of sugar that fell from Eduardo's morning doughnut.

With his first coffee, which he drank just after dawn, Eduardo ordered almond croissant. He'd adopted the habit after having breakfast one morning with the bey because this was what the bey ate.

'Eduardo?' The voice came hollow with static and thin from being bounced off a satellite too far above El Iskandryia for Eduardo to really comprehend. All the same, he would have known it anywhere.

'Excellency . . .'

The voice sighed.

Eduardo was meant to call him *boss* on the phone. Even when answering his watch in the office out of sight of everyone else.

'I'm here, boss,' the small man said hurriedly.

'You listening?' The voice on the other end wasn't cross, just careful.

'Sure, boss. Always . . . No, I mean it.' Eduardo tried to sound hurt but the man was right, Eduardo hardly ever listened. And when Eduardo did he always had to concentrate extra hard to make sense of what the other person said.

'Yeah, I got it,' Eduardo said finally, when the voice had finished explaining what Eduardo was expected to do. 'Well, except for that bit about becoming a policeman . . .'

Life was a series of comings and goings . . .

Some philosopher said that, or it might have been Cheb Rai; every time the thought popped into Eduardo's head he got a tune just out of reach. Three chords leading to a fourth that

Eduardo knew would, should he ever remember it, give him the whole.

All the same, whoever said or sang them, the words rang true. People came and went. They walked into one's life and then walked out again with no reason that Eduardo could see, but then he wasn't very clever. Lots of people had told him that. Smarter people could see the threads that tied together events. And none were smarter than the bey. Eduardo really believed that.

In the cafés people talked of how the trial of the warlord Colonel Abad was tied to a dock strike rolling out across the North African littoral. And how Ashraf al-Mansur, now in Tunis had gone there to kill the father who'd abandoned him. Others insisting he was there to save the old man's life. And a few, mostly Bolsheviks, were of the opinion that the Emir was already dead and all al-Mansur wanted was to make sure he got his share of the inheritence.

Eduardo knew different.

Ashraf Bey was trying to find his mother's original wedding certificate . . . Sometimes politics were way more complicated than Eduardo could understand.

Chapter Thirty-eight

Friday 4th March

An elegant young woman outside Arrivals was waving for a taxi. Something Eduardo didn't need to do since he had a car already waiting. At least, he had a uniformed driver clutching a board with Eduardo's name on it so Eduardo assumed he had a car as well.

Eduardo almost offered the woman a lift into the centre but when he nodded to her she just scowled. So Eduardo went back to helping Rose navigate her way through a crowd of C3N cameramen waiting for taxis at the front of Tunis Arrivals.

This was what happened if one suddenly lifted the embargo on flights to facilitate the departure of non-essential diplomatic staff. More people turned up than left. He was pretty sure that wasn't what the UN had in mind.

'We're here, sir.'

Eduardo liked that last word. It suggested that the driver thought he and Rose looked properly Western, which they were more or less. Soviet tourists would have got *commissar*, not meant obviously but always good for increasing *baksheesh* as tourists called tips, getting wrong both country and language. Anyone local wearing a suit like Eduardo's would have merited *effendi*, just to be on the safe side.

So that *sir* meant the young driver realised Eduardo was not local and not a Soviet tourist. Unless, of course, the boy called everybody that.

Originally Eduardo had been planning to fly alone and travel first class, the man having said buy any ticket he liked as long as the flight left that afternoon. But when Eduardo realised that premium cost half the price of first he decided Rose should come with him.

So that was what they did. And though Eduardo got the feeling Rose had never flown before, she insisted she'd flown dozens of times to numerous destinations. But then he'd told her exactly the same.

What's more, she'd enjoyed the flight. Eduardo knew, because he'd been careful to ask. And she looked great. He'd been careful to tell her that too.

The Benz waiting outside Tunis Arrivals was big and black, smarter than Eduardo could ever have expected, with metal pipes coming out of the engine and running down either side of the bonnet. The pipes had been silver to start with but now they were grey with wide bands of kingfisher blue, like petrol floating on top of a fresh puddle.

Alexandre, who was young and wore the uniform of a Tunis detective (something he suspected his visitors might not yet have realised), walked round to the back door of the Emir's second-favourite car and held it open.

At a nod from the small man, the woman clambered in and smoothed a black dress covered with red roses down over her pink knees. Leaving her partner still anxiously eyeing their luggage, such as it was.

'My case . . .'

Ashraf Bey's original call had told Eduardo to buy a new suit, new shoes, several shirts and a tie. The man had even specified the colour of each: dark blue for the suit, white for the shirts and red for the tie (no stripes). He'd said nothing about buying a case in which to put these things.

'Of course, sir.' Alexandre was apologetic. 'I should have realised you'd need your case with you.' He picked up the cardboard box with its cheap handle, wondering at its lightness and waited for Eduardo to join the woman. Only then did Alexandre put the case in the well of the borrowed car, beside Eduardo's feet.

'Where to, sir?'

Eduardo thought about it. 'What are my options?'

Alexandre tried not to sigh.

Accelerated entry to officer level and descent from an ex-colon family which had owned dairy farms in the High Tell guaranteed he got given the shitty jobs by sergeants who grew up in the medina or the nouvelle ville, people he'd outrank within the year and who knew that fact, but could never forgive it.

All the same, the fact Alexandre had been warned to handle this job with discretion meant the anxious-looking man in the rear seat had to be somebody important. Exactly why that might be became clear when Alexandre opened his mouth to answer, only to discover that the man sat behind him was already talking, mostly to himself.

'We could start with the Police HQ, I suppose.'

Alexandre nodded.

'Or we could go find the boss . . .'

To Alexandre that meant his colonel. He got the feeling this man had someone else in mind. 'The boss?' Alexandre asked, in a tone he hoped was politely casual.

'Ashraf al-Mansur . . .'

'You know the bey?'

'He's my boss.' Eduardo sounded as proud of the fact as he felt, which was very proud indeed.

'And my boss too,' Alexandre said. 'Apparently Ashraf Bey is the new Chief of Police.' That was what he'd been told anyway. It was all change at HQ.

'Actually. . .' Eduardo glanced at Rose and looked embarrassed. 'The thing is, you see . . . I'm the new Chief.' Eduardo tasted the words as he said them and sat up a little straighter in his seat.

And, like a good detective, he noticed the way Alexandre immediately did the same, straightening his shoulders and quickly adjusting his cap. That was when he realised Alexandre was one of his men.

'I'm sorry, Your Excellency. I didn't know.'

'Why should you?' Eduardo said, feeling expansive. 'And you don't need to call me Excellency, sir is fine . . . All the same, I have a question for you. An important question.'

Alexandre froze.

'What do you know . . . ?' Eduardo whipped out a leather notebook he'd bought at Iskandryia airport, flipped it open and watched the opening page come alight. 'Let me see, what do you know about a pâtissier called Pascal Boulart? Other than the fact he was stabbed in an alley behind Maison Hafsid and a sous-chef was arrested . . .'

It turned out Alexandre knew even less than that. He knew the killing all right, he just had no memory of anyone having been arrested by the police. As Alexandre tried to point out, as circumspectly as possible, this might just mean the murderer had been picked up by Kashif Pasha's men.

Although the military wing of the police was meant to liaise with the civilian branches, this sometimes failed to happen very occasionally, obviously.

'Find out if they did,' said Eduardo. 'And get me files on everyone killed in the massacre at the Domus Aurea.'

'There were only four.' Alexandre regretted the remark as soon as he made it. 'I mean, the fifth one got away.'

'Four is enough,' Eduardo said firmly. 'Now take me to the hotel.' He needed a shower, as did Rose. And with luck, if the shower was big enough, they could share.

'Hotel . . . ?

Eduardo nodded.

'You are not staying at a hotel, sir. My orders were to take you wherever you wanted and deliver your luggage to the Dar Ben Abdallah.'

'*Dar, maison, hôtel,*' said Eduardo, 'it's all the same, you know.' He turned to Rose. 'In French,' he explained, '*hôtel* means big house, like in *Hôtel de Ville*. Isn't that right?'

Alexandre nodded, not taking his eyes off the road.

On their way into the city all the other traffic moved out of the way. Eduardo was wondering about this until he remembered the flag. He wasn't sure what the flag on the bonnet stood for but it looked very official.

Chapter Thirty-nine

Sunday 6th March

Palms shaded yellow earth, so that sunlight sketched patterns across the banks of a narrow stream, highlighting twigs and dead fronds. The water in the *seguia* was dirty, the grass edging the ditch and the undersides of the palms less bright than Zara expected. Only ungrown dates, tiny and green and still vulnerable to the sand winds, seemed created from a brighter scheme altogether. This was a world of ochres and earth hues. An Impressionist umbrella restricted to the palette of a Klee.

Further along, half in/half out of the stream lay a fallen palm with its trunk ringed like an endlessly extruded pine cone. The crown was gone but, since fronds extended finger-like from beneath the sand that covered a newly repaired foot bridge, the reason was not hard to find.

The coolness of the gardens was in welcome contrast to the last fifty miles across the chott, when the air had been salt and hot, unseasonably so the taxi driver had told her, several times.

'I'm here to collect Lady Hana al-Mansur.'

Zara stood on the edge of Tozeur's famous grove, home of the translucent *deglet nur* and site of a quarter of a million palms fed by two hundred springs which carried water to the date trees. The only thing to stop her reaching a small palace on the other side of the stream was a single soldier guarding a narrow bridge. The palace had been built by one of the old beys or emirs. It must have been, because only a notable could get away with building a palace on land historically reserved for growing dates.

Over the centuries, gold and slaves had passed through this

area, carpets and priceless manuscripts, swords and spices. None of them creating the wealth of the date palms. At its height, a millennia before, a thousand dromedaries a day were said to have left Tozeur, laden with dates and even now many of the town's inhabitants were *khammes*, sharecroppers who maintained the groves and in return took one fifth of the harvest as their pay.

Behind Zara in an airport taxi sat a driver, looking in disbelief at a pile of notes on his lap. She'd paid him what was on the meter, Tunis to Tozeur, having brushed away his offer to negotiate.

In fact, the man could honestly say she'd hardly glanced at the meter their entire trip, most of which she'd spent watching distant green fields turn to sahal before becoming moon-like around the phosphate town of Gafsa. A place of which a wise man once said, 'its water is blood, its air poison, you may live there a hundred years without making one true friend . . .'

'She is here?' Zara said, frowning at the guard. 'Hani al-Mansur?'

The soldier to whom Zara spoke was thickset, with cropped hair more salt than pepper. He'd been having one of those weeks.

'I'm not sure, My Lady . . .' The man made a show of unclipping a mobile from his belt, wondering as he did so, why the young woman's face suddenly tightened. 'I'll make a call.'

'*Zara Quitrimala,*' Zara said, '*Ms* Zara Quitrimala.' The way she said it made her name begin with a hiss. 'And you don't use honorifics when talking to me. I'm perfectly ordinary.'

The look the guard gave her begged leave to differ.

Moncef Hauara was unmarried which was rare for a middle-aged man in Tozeur, unmarried and about to retire from active duty. Living with his mother, a woman who'd spent her life repairing clothes for notables, he recognised both shot silk and the French way of cutting on the bias. Although, if asked, he'd have said the jet buttons were what he noticed. Most manufacturers used black plastic while a few of the flashier labels chose machine-cut obsidian. Only Dior and Chanel still used buttons hand-carved from Italian jet, the way they'd always done.

He knew, the way he knew a storm was brewing, exactly how long it would taken someone to sew that jacket. How long it took to double-stitch the hems and edge each buttonhole. There were a dozen differing grades of silk, variable in their wear and lasting qualities as well as their ease of cutting and ability to hold dye.

There was nothing ordinary about that dress or the cut. And Corporal Hauara doubted strongly that there was anything remotely ordinary about the woman who wore it. At least not in any sense that a soon-to-retire soldier who still lived with his mother would understand.

'Yes, sir. I'll do that.'

The corporal clicked off his radio and promptly dialled a fresh number. Sweat was beginning to show beneath his arms. A short conversation followed. Of which Zara heard only one half.

'A young lady.'

'Zara Quitrimala.'

'Quitrimala.'

'Yes, sir. Quite possibly.'

'Yes, sir. I'll ask.'

'Forgive me,' said the guard, 'but Major Jalal would like to know if Hana al-Mansur is expecting you? Also, why you think she is here . . .'

For someone so determined Zara did a good imitation of not having foreseen that question. 'My father's . . .'

Corporal Hauara knew who her father was. At least he did now.

'He's guardian to . . .' Stumbling over the sense as much as the words, Zara tried to work out exactly what her father was to Hani, other than extremely fond. A fact replete with problems for someone whose own childhood memories were of a loud, occasionally threatening figure; a version of himself Hamzah Effendi seemed to have left behind.

'She told me she'd be here,' said Zara finally, waving a piece of headed paper, signed by her father and the Khedive of El Iskandryia. This announced that they were the child's trustees and Zara acted with full authority. It slid over the fact they were trustees only where the child's money was concerned. Zara's furious request to her father that he let her go save Hani from imminent civil war had seen to that.

As for the Khedive, Zara had no doubts that he counter-signed Hamzah's letter because she had tears in her eyes when she asked.

'What time does curfew begin?' Zara demanded.

Corporal Hauara looked at her. 'Curfew?'

'It was on C3N. What time do Kashif Pasha's troops lock down the streets at night . . .'

'There is no curfew,' the guard said carefully. 'At least not in Tozeur. Perhaps in Tunis.' He wanted to add something else, but the years had taught him to swallow such thoughts. That was the secret of surviving. To stay silent while seeming to do nothing but talk.

The small ante-room into which Zara was shown looked vast, largely because all four walls were mirror. Each mirror was framed within an elaborate double arch, each arch supported on stick-thin pillars topped by gilded capitals that displayed endless repetitions of a simplified, stylised acanthus.

It was in the worst possible taste.

The left-hand arch of one wall hid a door. Zara thought she knew which mirror it was but had a feeling that, if she so wished, it would be easy to forget. Forgetting about her reflection was more difficult.

An intense, neatly dressed Arab woman with scraped-back hair, still not yet out of her teens and with perfect, almost American teeth. Thinner than she used to be if not as slim as she wanted. Unmarriageable, way richer than could be justified and very much alone. Zara swept tears out of her eyes with a furious hand, only to wince as a thousand doubles made the identical movement.

First Raf had gone, then Hani. So she was here to take Hani back, while there was still time. As for Raf . . .

'My Lady.'

'I'm not . . .' She turned to where a man in major's uniform stood by the open door, his sudden appearance and the opening of the door having rendered the room small again.

'His Highness is busy welcoming his mother, Lady Maryam. So he sends his apologies. When this is done, His Highness requires a word.'

'About what?' Zara demanded. Only too aware that her eyes were red.

Major Jalal shrugged. 'I'm only Kashif Pasha's *aide-de-camp*,' he said modestly. 'But these are difficult times so I imagine His Highness is worried for your safety.'

Chapter Forty

Tuesday 8th March

'Okay, let's try that again.'

Eduardo spun the knife in his hand and tossed it at a door scarred by more cuts than it was possible to count. At least, impossible to count without taking the offending object off its hinges, having the thing carried to police HQ and getting someone to shoot it, resize the photographs and cross off the cuts one at a time.

A lifetime's worth of staff at Maison Hafsid had stood in a short corridor outside the cellar kitchens and honed their throwing skills or taken out their frustration on that cupboard door.

'You know what's really interesting,' Eduardo said.

No one answered, but then that wasn't surprising. He'd recognised them all. Not the names and not even the faces, but the types. Loners and misfits. The usual scum found working in kitchens. And they'd recognised him. As one of them.

Besides, the knife he threw was the one found plunged into the heart of Pascal Boulart. In the alley behind Maison Hafsid.

'What's really interesting is that the killer left no fingerprints on his blade . . .' There were, in fact, dozens of fingerprints on the blade, but all of them belonged to the coroner, his assistant or members of the police who'd processed the knife later, when it was being bagged for evidence.

'Why do you think that is?' Eduardo asked.

A boy shrugged.

'Because he wore gloves?' The man who spoke was tall and dark faced, his hair grey with age. A heavy bruise ripened over one high cheek and his mouth was split. According to a report recently filed by Kashif Pasha's *mubahith*, Chef Edvard could be a difficult and sometimes violent man. So far there had been nothing to suggest that either of those statements was true.

'Gloves? Possibly,' Eduardo admitted. 'But then there are none of the victim's fingerprints on the blade either. Which is very odd, because Pascal was stabbed five times . . .' He paused and was disappointed to realise they didn't all immediately see the implication. 'Have you ever been stabbed?'

Only Chef Edvard nodded.

'Show me your hands,' Eduardo demanded.

There were faded slash marks across one palm and a long cicatrix that vanished beneath his sleeve. In return Eduardo showed the chef his own hands with their wounds from days Eduardo did his best not to remember.

'There were no defensive cuts on the hands of Pascal Boulart. His fingerprints were missing from both blade and handle. Do you know what this suggests to me?'

Ripping the knife from battered wood, Eduardo walked ten paces to the far end of the corridor and threw again. Another bull's eye. Straight into the middle of the door, where it joined a hundred other cuts.

Behind him, where the corridor gave way to the kitchens someone clapped, probably mockingly but maybe for real. That was Eduardo's tenth throw and the tenth time he'd put the knife in the door exactly where he wanted it.

A misspent childhood had its uses.

'You try.' He pointed to the boy who'd been clapping. A thin youth with a rash on his chin hidden beneath what looked like blusher. 'Come on . . .'

Reluctantly Idries stepped forward. Well aware that he had no choice.

The first thing Eduardo had done on entering the cellar was flash his shield. This was gold, maybe real gold, in a crocodile-skin case with a top that flipped up, like one of those little vidphones. It had been left for him at Police HQ, in his office, along with a matt-black .45 paraOrdnance and a scribble pad of notes covered with Ashraf Bey's writing.

Eduardo hadn't even known he had an office until a fat man with sweat stains under his arms, a man who wouldn't meet his eye, silently offered him the key.

It took Eduardo until the next morning to realise his scowling deputy with the striped shirts and perspiration problem was the old Chief, time during which Eduardo had been more concerned with trying to make sense of His Excellency's terrible writing.

In the end, unable to translate Ashraf Bey's notes into any language he understood, Eduardo stored them for safety into the top drawer of his new desk and turned to the files he'd asked Alexandre to bring him. Sometimes in life it was just easier to start over.

And he was right, the files were much more interesting.

'Find me the man with stripy shirts,' Eduardo demanded. He had a box on his desk that let him talk to a serious-looking woman in the office outside without having to get up and open the door.

'You wanted me?'

Eduardo indicated a seat without looking up from his files. 'You used to run this place?'

The man's nod was sullen. Although he added, 'Yes, sir,' when Eduardo raised his head from a folder.

'You can have it back once I'm done,' Eduardo said. 'I don't imagine I'll be staying. In fact,' he stared at the unhappy man, 'assume you have total autonomy in everything except the Maison Hafsid case, but first find me . . .' Eduardo glanced down at a crime report. 'Ahmed, cousin of Idries, who worked at the Maison Hafsid.'

At first Chef Edvard felt sure Eduardo was there to shut down his restaurant. Given the disaster at Domus Aurea and the fact he'd put an Egyptian deserter on the staff list as Hassan, because that was the only way to get the man through security clearance, Chef Edvard could hardly have been surprised if this was true.

Mind you, if the *mubahith* had even suspected that second fact he'd already be dead. Chef Edvard's position, held to under questioning, was that he'd assumed the thin-faced blond waiter was just another undercover police officer providing protection.

Neither he nor his staff had ever seen the man before.

'Throw it,' Eduardo told the boy.

'What about prints?' Idries glanced back at the others, looking for support. At least that's what Eduardo assumed he was looking for.

'I don't want to trick you,' Eduardo said. 'I just want to see you throw the knife.' Pulling a pair of cheap evidence gloves from his suit pocket, he tossed them across. 'Wear these.'

The boy threw as expertly as Eduardo had expected. Without even bothering to heft the knife to find its balance.

'Now you,' he told a girl hovering silently near the back.

She struggled with the gloves, finally throwing with the latex fingers only half over her own so they flopped like a coxcomb. The knife bounced off the door.

'Try again,' said Eduardo as he handed Isabeau the knife and a clean tissue, something Rose insisted he carry. 'Get rid of the gloves,' he said, 'then wipe down blade and handle when you've finished, I don't mind.'

She stared at him.

'Throw,' said Eduardo.

Without the gloves to hamper her, Isabeau put the blade straight into the door.

'I don't understand,' Chef Edvard said into the silence that followed the thud of the blade. 'Are you saying Ahmed flung this knife at my pastry cook? That was how Pascal was killed?'

'Of course not,' said Eduardo. His tone of voice made it clear he'd never heard anything quite so ridiculous. 'Wipe the blade,' Eduardo told the girl, 'and give it to someone else.'

They all threw after that. Taking the handkerchief and carefully wiping clean the knife before passing it to the next person. Even Chef Edvard, his throw little more than a dismissive flick of the wrist that buried the blade in the door at throat height.

'Right,' said Eduardo. 'Only two more questions and we're done.' Plucking the blade from the door one final time, he wiped it on his own shirt and dropped it back into its evidence bag. The stain on its steel blade was rust not blood and its edge was blunt. The only thing this knife had ever been good for was throwing at a door.

'Where's the fat boy?'

Eduardo had read the files, seen the photographs and memorised the names. But just to be safe he'd had the serious-faced assistant at his office type out a list of everyone working at Maison Hafsid and then he'd read them off at the beginning, like doing a roll call at school. He knew who was missing. Ahmed, obviously. Also Hassan.

'Gone,' Chef Edvard said flatly.

'Where?' Eduardo demanded.

'We don't know. He just didn't show up today. And he missed his shift at Café Antonio last Friday.'

'Let me know if he appears,' said Eduardo. 'Okay, final question. Where *exactly* in the alley was Pascal Boulet's body found? I want each of you to show me in turn.'

Back at his office desk, a plate of *droits de Fatima* lifted from Maison Hafsid already reduced to a blizzard of pastry flakes, the new Chief of Police drew up his own list of clues, using a fountain pen he'd found in the drawer.

Blunt knife, broken handle, rusty blade; no fingerprints; damaged door; empty corridor; clean steps. A body that changed position. And finally, most bizarrely, one misplaced murderer.

Eduardo drew circles around each and then joined them together as he'd once seen Ashraf Bey do, but because his clues were written in a list one under the other, the links just sank, like lead weights on a fishing line. So Eduardo wrote his clues out again, arranging them in a circle and joining them with new lines. And then, because it looked so good, he wrote it out a third time, folding one copy to put in his pocket and leaving the other on his desk for everyone else to see.

It was only when Eduardo reached the end of the street, still surreptitiously brushing flakes from his pastry-stained fingers that he realised his detective work would go unappreciated. He was the boss. The only person remotely likely to go near his desk was Marie, who stood up every time he came into her outer office. She seemed far too nervous to take such liberties.

He'd just have to show his clues to Rose instead. Then he'd tell her the answer, maybe. Licking his fingers, Eduardo wiped them afresh on his trousers and went to buy Rose some chocolates. Somehow eating always made him hungry.

Chapter Forty-one

Friday 11th March

'Your Excellency.'

Given that someone had stolen all three door knockers, the barefoot Nubian in the white silk robe had little option but to hammer ever louder on the door of Dar Welham. As a method of attracting Ashraf Bey's attention it proved surprisingly unsuccessful. All but the final knocks being drowned by the thud of ancient and unserviced fans inside.

Until he made his stop at Kairouan the previous week, Raf hadn't even realised he owned a house in Tozeur, let alone one in the oldest district; but the tall dar with its ochre, geometrically laid brickwork and dark interior had been a wedding present from the Emir to his mother, apparently.

Un présent de mariage.

Isaac & Son's files were dust-buried on the shelves of their deserted walk-up when Raf and three uniformed officers cut the padlock on the rear and kicked in a door at the top of the stairs.

All it took was Raf presenting himself at Kairouan's Police HQ and demanding the loan of three good officers, bolt cutters and a hydraulic battering ram, one of the small hand-held versions. His name alone had been enough to turn his wish list into reality. The officers being uniformed, respectful and obviously experienced. And the really terrifying thing, at least the thing that Raf found really terrifying was that at no point did anyone ask him for any form of identity.

He went looking for a wedding certificate and came back with copies of a deed of ownership which did just as well. The date he wanted was at the top. While his mother's signature and that of Moncef were at the bottom. Fifty years earlier, on the day after they were married, Moncef had presented his mother with a house in Tozeur and another in Tunis. Fifty years . . .

Lady Nafisa, his aunt, had known this because it was for her that the copies were made by notario Ibrihim Ishaq. Thanking the police officers, Raf had taken one copy of the deed and ordered the men to remove all other documents from the office and have them shredded, then burnt. He made the most senior officer repeat that order, all documents, all shredded, all burnt.

When Raf left to find Hani, Murad and the Bugatti, the officer was already radioing for backup while the other two had begun to arrange the files into dusty piles on the floor.

Dar Welham, his new house, stood behind the main road from the Palm Groves to Zaouia Ishmailia, on the right, halfway down an alley too old and narrow to merit a name. One side of his street had already been partly rebuilt using traditional yellow brick. Raf's side remained a mess of crumbling façades and locked doorways, with most of the houses obviously empty. Almost all of the triple door knockers which allowed long-gone inhabitants to know if the person calling was a man, woman or child had been stolen. As had a number of the old iron locks and the door handles themselves.

The private courtyard of Dar Welham still stank of cat's piss and sewage, although Raf had slopped it down at least three times and tipped buckets of rusty water through the open grilles of the drains. Hani and Murad had concentrated on the inside of the dar. Sweeping floors and scrubbing at mineral deposits that had leached up through the floor tiles.

That the dar had electricity to drive its fans at all was a miracle. One involving twisted flex glued direct to rough walls and fed through a large hole into next door's cellar, where Raf jammed open the trip switch of a junction box with half a clothes peg. Air-conditioning would obviously have helped. Although being somewhere other than Tozeur at the start of a *khamsin* wind might have been better.

Sand fall was expected. And Murad kept referring to a

chili, alternating that word with *khamsin*. It had to do with a depression moving into the Gulf of Gebes. One that had kicked the afternoon temperature up to 98° F and threatened to drop sand as far north as Madrid. The local radio station talked about little else.

'Door,' Hani said, looking up from a game of chess. She was winning five games to zero and the only way Murad had been persuaded to play again was her promise that this would be his last for the day: and her assurance that he'd soon be good enough to beat her. But then, as Murad pointed out, she'd said that the day before as well.

At Hani's feet stretched Ifritah. Panting in the heat.

'What?' Raf put down the deeds to Dar Welham.

'Someone's at the door,' said Hani. 'I'd go but it's probably for you.'

And it was. Apparently Kashif Pasha's messenger saw nothing odd in presenting an envelope featuring an ersatz version of a European coat of arms, one bearing a Western interpretation of an Othman turban on a silver salver in the style of Napoleon III, overlaid around the edge with Qur'anic script in beaten gold, bronze and copper.

'Will there be a reply?'

Having read Kashif's message, Raf put it carefully in his pocket.

'No,' he said, 'I think not.'

The Nubian might have come to the door of Dar Welham bare footed and dressed in a white robe but he drove off in a black 4X4 with smoked windows and roo bars big enough to knock down a buffalo.

'Who was that?' said Hani. She stood on the stairs with Murad behind her. A wind-up radio was in the boy's hand.

'Just one of Kashif Pasha's friends.'

'My brother Kashif doesn't have friends,' Murad said firmly, then paused, worried that he might have sounded rude. 'I mean,' he said more politely, 'he has only allies or enemies.' The boy's voice made no secret of which camp he'd found himself in. 'What does the message say?'

'That's private.'

Two heads turned to face Raf. Hani's frown now a full-on scowl. 'No secrets,' she reminded Raf. 'Remember? That's what you told me when Aunt Nafisa died. Anything I asked you would answer.'

It had been a simple enough promise, made to a crying child who wanted to know why life was so unfair. One that Raf would have liked an adult, any adult, to have made to him. And it was proving impossibly difficult to keep.

'Hani, I'm really sorry . . .'

'You promised.'

So he had. 'It's from Kashif Pasha,' Raf said.

'But that's the Emir's coat of arms,' Murad insisted.

'I know,' said Raf, 'but it's not his message. Kashif and I need to meet.'

'You're not going to go . . .' Murad sounded appalled that Raf might even consider it. 'Have you listened to the latest news?'

Raf hadn't.

Apparently C3N had been told by St Cloud that Ashraf Bey was behind the attack on Emir Moncef. Colonel Abad, that well-known war criminal, was mentioned. As was Raf's part in helping Abad avoid being brought to justice. The Marquis even managed to suggest that the bey might be behind last autumn's attacks on the Midas Refinery, jointly owned by St Cloud, and Hamzah Effendi.

'If you go, Kashif will hurt you,' Murad said flatly. 'I know him.'

'All the same,' said Raf, 'I think I must.' Skimming the note, he ran through words he already knew by heart. The message was short. 'It seems Kashif's captured the missing waiter,' Raf told them both. 'He'd like me to be present at the questioning.'

Hani opened her mouth and then shut it again. 'Something else,' she said finally. 'What else?'

'Because of the *current danger*,' said Raf, failing to extract the bleakness from his voice, 'my brother has extended his offer of protective custody to include Zara.'

'She's here?'

'Apparently . . .'

'So what do you want Murad and me to do?' Hani asked.

'Stay here,' said Raf. 'And keep out of trouble. If that's remotely possible.'

Hani's look was doubtful.

Chapter Forty-two

Friday 11th March

Three hours after Raf left, men in black jellabas locked off the unnamed alley using Jeeps which they swung across both ends, isolating the stretch in between.

Once again the Jeeps had smoked glass, fat roo bars and whip aerials. The man who seemed in charge had dyed hair combed forward like a Roman emperor, a heavy moustache and a black *mubahith* blouson without insignia of any kind. Only a slight bald patch and the fact his choice of top accentuated his paunch took the edge off an effect that was, Hani had to admit, still quietly threatening.

'You take a look,' she said, handing Murad an old pair of opera glasses. The boy did what she suggested. Staring down at the alley entrance.

'Soldiers,' he said.

Hani nodded.

'In disguise,' she said. 'Who's the man?'

Murad took a second look at the *mubahith* with the weird hair. 'No one I recognise,' he said, like he wasn't sure if that was good or bad.

'Are they from the Emir's guard?'

'Of course not.' Murad shook his head. 'All Eugenie's troops are women.' He spoke as if Eugenie were still alive. 'Those are not women . . .'

Only fear let Hani restrain herself. Some people shouted when they got afraid, others closed down, went silent. That was her. 'Look,' Hani said, 'you think they support Kashif Pasha?'

'You heard the radio,' said Murad. 'All the soldiers support my brother Kashif.'

'Now there's a surprise.' Hani sounded like Zara at her most cross. The way the older girl had been those last few days at the madersa before Raf vanished, sharp and snotty but nothing like as cruel as Raf had been with his dark silences and exile inside his own head.

'Kashif,' Murad said. 'He won't hurt you.'

'Yes, he will. And he'll hurt you. And it won't be the first time, will it?'

'He's still my brother.' Murad's voice was quiet.

'And the Emir is his father,' said Hani flatly. 'But he still ordered that attack.' She didn't know this, of course, but she knew her uncle and it was obvious he thought so.

'I don't believe it.'

'You don't want to,' Hani told him. They were sat together on the flat roof of Dar Welham, peering over the parapet. Behind them, sheets dried on a line and drifting sand wrote patterns across cracked tiles and gathered into tiny dunes.

Picking herself up, Hani stepped back from the edge. And four floors below, now unseen by Hani or Murad, the man without insignia ordered one of the jellaba-clad men to knock on the door. After that, the soldier tried the door without being told and found it locked. So he hammered again, harder.

Faces appeared from the roofs of houses opposite and disappeared just as rapidly when their owners realised what was happening.

'Open in the name of the NR.'

When this unnaturally loud cry went unanswered, the man tried the handle himself. Finding it still securely locked, Poul Fischer nodded to a young Berber. 'Plastique,' he ordered.

The flexible breaching charge the corporal pulled from under his disguise wasn't strictly plastique. At least not in any sense he understood. It was a short length of 300-grain-an-inch cutting charge with a soft rubber body that could be bent into any shape needed and a sticky foam that glued it to the door and helped reduce the danger of back fragmentation. Correcting a *mubahith* officer, however, was not in the corporal's career plan.

Fixing one length around the lock, the corporal positioned two more around the hinges and then did top and bottom where bolts might be, just to play safe. The FBC series also came in 600 grain and 1200 grain densities but for hinges of this age 300 grain was probably already overkill.

'It might be best, sir, if everyone stood back.' Quickly, so he didn't have to see Poul Fischer's answering expression, the corporal fixed an electronic match to each charge and began to enter his identity code into a firing box.

'Ready when you are, sir.'

Raf had never explained to Hani how he'd managed to break Zara's brother out of the basement of a locked house in Kharmous and she'd been careful never to ask. But with her screen, a satellite shot of El Isk and some serious intuition she'd been able to work it out.

Intuition was part inherent and part learnt. The percentages were open to debate. As they always were with anything involving socialisation versus heredity. Hani, however, was pretty sure she'd been born with heightened levels.

Hyper-sensitivity was one description. Hani knew this because she'd done a quiz on a medical website. It suggested childhood stress might have made changes to an area of her brain called the *cingulated gyrus*. Or rather, her time with Aunt Nafisa had ensured changes were *not* made: reducing Hani's ability to filter out life's raw mixture of competing noise and demands.

Persistent stress-response state was a term she got fed by the site in Santa Fe. And Hani had all the symptoms; stomach ache and sleepless nights, a tendency to focus on non-verbal clues rather than speech. A preference for animals over humans.

'Ifritah,' Hani said suddenly.

'What about Ifritah?'

'I've got to find her . . .' Hani was heading towards the stairs down into the house before Murad had time to move.

'Wait,' he said, louder than he intended. 'Let me see what's going on.' Putting his head above the parapet Murad watched a man far below glue something to the front door. 'I don't think it's safe,' he said.

'We can't leave her behind.' Tears had started in Hani's eyes and her face was set. Her cheeks pulled back as if battling through a wind tunnel of misery. 'She'll be in danger.'

Murad sighed. 'I'll go,' he said.

The cat wasn't on the top floor or the floor below. Just to be sure, Murad looked under beds and inside cupboards, fighting with the rickety shutter of a mashrabiya to check that Hani's kitten hadn't some how got inside, even though the mashrabiya's bolt were rusted almost solid and there was no way this was possible.

She wasn't on the floor below that either, where Raf, Hani and Murad had made camp in a huge room containing two sofas woven from rattan and a drinks cabinet still full of half-empty bottles of liqueur. Old copies of *New Scientist* and *The Ecologist* sat in a magazine rack. Someone had left a paperback face down and open under a stool so long ago that most of the pages had rotted away or been eaten by beetle, but there was no Ifritah.

'Any sign?' The question came from above.

'No. Not yet.'

Murad was half way down the last flight of stairs when the door blew in. A pressure wave throwing him back so he landed in a ragged heap. One of the steps caught his spine as he landed and it hurt.

The first soldier through the door shot the cat.

Get up, Murad told himself and was relieved to discover that he could. Taking the steps two at a time, he raced away from the black shadows tumbling through smoke, their weapons at the ready. At the very top of the house, at the foot of the stairs leading to the roof, Murad removed the key from the bottom door and used it to double click the lock from the other side. Then he did the same for the top door, the one that lead out onto the roof and took that key as well.

'Ifritah . . .'

'Not there,' he told Hani. 'I'm sorry.'

'You're bleeding.' It sounded as if she'd only just noticed the fact.

'What?'

Hani touched her nose and Murad touched his own, fingers coming away sticky. 'And your ear,' she said. That turned out to be sticky too.

'We'll be in worse trouble,' Murad said, 'if we don't hide.' Which proved to be easier to say than do, as there was only one exit to the flat roof of the dar and this was already locked.

'Down there,' suggested Hani, pointing over the rear parapet to a dusty garden which obviously belonged to a neighbour. 'We use that.'

Below them, built so that its nearest end joined the back wall of Dar Welham was the tiled roof of a fourth-floor balcony. The drop from where they stood to the tiles was maybe twice Hani's height.

'Unless you're afraid?'

Instinctively Murad's chin went up. 'Of course I'm not,' he started to say and then met Hani's dark eyes and stopped. 'Okay,' he said, 'I admit it. I've been scared ever since we left Tunis.'

'Me too.' Hani reached out to wipe dirt from his face. As if that was just a natural thing to do. Maybe it was, Hani didn't know and probably wasn't the person to ask about stuff like that. Until six months ago she'd believed that keeping a toy dog in her room deserved the slaps it invariably earned her, because Ali Din was male and her Aunt Nafisa had rules about such things.

Only now Hani lived with Raf whose rules were less strict. Which made life easier but doing-the-right-thing more difficult, because most of the time Hani just had to guess what that was . . .

'Like now.' Hani said to herself.

'Like now what?' demanded Murad.

'We need to move.'

She nodded to the sloping roof of next door's mashrabiya. 'You first,' she said.

'Wait . . .'

'No time.'

'But I'm not ready,' Murad protested. And that was when Hani realised both his ears must be damaged. Someone was trying the handle of the door at the bottom of the roof stairs. A fact that seemed to escaped Murad.

'Do you want Kashif's men to catch us?'

Sliding over the edge, the boy twisted round until he hung by his fingers and then she heard a clatter below as Murad flailed for a grip to stop himself tumbling over the edge.

Hani's landing was rather better, although less cat-like than she'd have liked; her knees coming up to hit her chest as she met the tiles. Something else to add to the list of bits that hurt.

'This way,' Hani said, dropping to her belly so she could peer over the edge of the mashrabiya. Its original carved screen was stolen and whoever had ripped it out had tacked a rotted tarpaulin in place to hide what they'd done. There was a market for architectural salvage, particularly at the top end. Back in El Isk, Hamzah Effendi had a house full of the stuff. Hani was about to explain this to Murad but decided to save her words. He looked a bit preoccupied.

'I'll go,' Hani said, 'you went first last time.'

The difficult bit turned out to be lowering herself over the edge, what with tiles scraping against knees, legs and tummy until the pull of gravity left her hanging. And that was before Hani edged rapidly along the drop looking for a tear she'd seen in the tarpaulin. Swinging once for luck, Hani flipped through the gap to land inside the mashrabiya.

It was all she could not to miaow.

'Now you,' Hani hissed, ripping aside some of the rotted canvas. 'That should make it easier.'

She saw his shoes first, scuffed Oxfords followed rapidly by socks, turn-ups from his flannel trousers and then the length of his body up to the waist. She thought for a second Murad was about to freeze but he kept coming until he hung, eyes shut high above the courtyard.

'Do it,' Hani said.

So Murad swung once, jack-knifing like a gymnast and when he landed it was on his toes.

'That was okay,' Hani admitted and Murad almost smiled. Together they refixed the rotten canvas as best they could. Hanging the tarpaulin from the holes that Hani had made when she ripped some of it down.

The empty house had two exits, a main one onto an alley and a small door, cupboard like, that opened into a cul de sac so tight it was little more than the gap between two barely separate walls, one obviously much newer than the other. They chose the narrow way and finally exited on a street called Rue des Jardins, walking quickly with their heads down until they passed through a car park behind a hotel.

Walking slowly would have made more sense. Only neither one quite had the nerve so they hurried instead, trying hard not to run. And when they finally reached the market on Rue Ibn Chabbat, Hani made Murad stop in the shadow of a lorry.

'Let me,' she said. Her handkerchief was unused and still held creases from where it had been ironed by Donna. Just looking at it made Hani want to cry. Licking a corner, she steadied Murad's chin with one hand and wiped crusted blood from the side of his mouth with the other. When she tried to wash blood from his left ear Murad began to cry as well.

'We *are* running away, right?' Murad asked, once his face was clean again.

'Not exactly,' said Hani. She smiled at the boy's exasperated expression. 'We're staying out of trouble . . .'

It was Murad who first saw the bus. And Hani who pointed out that the vehicle was actually a coach. A brief argument about the difference then followed before Murad eventually bowed to Hani's insistence that coaches had smoked-glass windows, air-conditioning and their own loos.

This one even had on-board newsfeed, computer games and four private cabins. A fact advertised in large gold letters along both sides. Right below a line that read *Haute Travel: Tripoli* and above the URL for a site few locals could get, because web connections without licence were banned by law in Ifriqiya. Not to mention most other parts of North Africa.

'We need a disguise,' said Hani.

Murad stared at her.

'Think about it,' said Hani. 'Those soldiers were after Murad Pasha and Lady Hana al-Mansur.' That Hani admitted her own first name was unusual in itself.

'If they *are* actually after us,' Murad said. He'd been thinking about that.

'Who else would they be after?'

'Ashraf Bey?'

'They waited until he was gone,' Hani said firmly. She turned to Murad, face serious. 'You're certain they were Kashif's men?'

'I'm sure,' said Murad.

'Even though they said they were the Army of the Naked?'

'Yes,' Murad said. 'That's why I'm sure.'

'Okay,' said Hani. Peeling $5 from her roll she gave it to Murad. 'You got this as a tip from an American journalist,' she told the boy.

'Why?'

Hani sighed. 'It doesn't matter . . . For showing her the way. For fetching her a glass of water. Make it up.'

'What do you want me to get?' Murad demanded.

He bought a white tee-shirt, made in Morocco, size XXL and a pair of plastic sandals with *sputnik* in red across the strap. Murad also bought a Dynamo's hat, which he wrecked by ripping off the brim so that from the front it looked like a skull cap.

'What do you buy that for?' Hani asked.

'The cap?'

'No silly, that . . .' She pointed at the tee-shirt still draped over his arm.

'Watch,' said Murad and stripped off his soiled aertex shirt and scrunched it into a ball. Slipping the new shirt over his head, Murad turned his back on Hani and unbuttoned his trousers, stepping out of those as well. With a tee-shirt down around his knees, his socks gone and cheap sandals Murad looked like most other kids in the market, his new shirt making do for a robe.

When he turned back Hani was pointedly staring into the distance.

'Your turn,' said Murad.

Chapter Forty-three

Friday 11th March

'You came,' said Major Jalal, as if he'd been waiting hours for Raf to appear. Hawk eyes glittered above a sharp nose and heavy moustache. And the smile that accompanied his comment hovered on the edge of contempt.

'How could I refuse my brother?' Raf said lightly. A single glance was enough to swallow the scene. Major Jalal in full uniform, a lieutenant and standing behind him the inevitable black Jeep.

Two soldiers stood by the Jeep trying to look casual.

'Well, now you're here,' said Major Jalal, 'where would Your Excellency like to sit, front or the back . . . ?'

'Zara?' Raf asked, not moving.

'Your mistress is safe,' Major Jalal assured him. 'And you can see her soon. But, before that, I've got orders to take you to Kashif Pasha. He would like a word.'

Raf smiled. 'You know how it is,' he said. 'Family comes first.'

'I understand that's one of the things His Highness wants to talk about.' Major Jalal's voice was dry. 'The fact you seem to believe he's your brother.'

Kashif hadn't always been manipulative. So people said. Mostly those who'd never met him. As a small boy he'd been loved and loving, open and happy to consider the feelings of others. That was how Kashif Pasha's official biography reported it anyway.

One day, maybe thirty years ago when he was first made a general, so sometime around seventeen, Kashif had demanded sight of his early school reports. Harrying some minor archivist into finding the file and doing whatever was necessary to get it released.

This was during one of Emir Moncef's periodic bouts of madness. With the man camped out under a summer sky somewhere south of Wadi al B'ir, speaking to no one and sleeping between two of Eugenie's troop for warmth. Wearing nothing, apparently. Although the girls were allowed to retain their pants. It was all extremely adolescent.

Of course, only Lady Maryam dared call it madness. Everybody else spoke of the Emir's retreats and his need to remain in touch with the land. But it was madness all the same. A howling depression that had Moncef claiming (literally) to be someone else. At these times only Eugenie could help. Wherever she was and whatever she might be doing, Eugenie stopped doing it and came, elegant and stern-faced. He was quieter after her visits. Sometime for months and once for the period of a whole year.

The school Kashif attended was at the rear of the Bardo Palace next to a mosque. School and mosque were not connected. It was, however, reasonable to assume they were and many people did, both in Tunis and abroad. There were eighteen and a half pupils in Kashif's class, this being the national average. And his year was taught the national syllabus, which included French, gymnastics, mathematics and poetry. The half pupil was achieved by allowing one boy to attend every other lesson.

If one left out the fact the other seventeen and a half pupils in Kashif's class were either his cousins or chosen from the sons of government ministers then Bardo High was a typical local school of the kind found all over Ifriqiya. What most news reports forgot to mention was that Kashif's school had only one class, his own. The school opened when he reached five and shut when he reached fifteen; there never was a year below Kashif or a year above. The pupil to staff ratio was two to one.

His reports had been as exemplary as his marks. Each master describing a warm and outgoing child. A boy who'd unquestionably have had a great future ahead of him irrespective of birth.

Having re-read these, Kashif Pasha demanded the real reports – on the basis that these must exist. A request which sent the already nervous archivist into near terminal decline. Faced with arranging the forbidden, the archivist tried to explain to Kashif about *secret bags*, inadvertently offering the seventeen-year-old boy a whole new source of information and income.

Secret bags were kept in a vault below the Bardo, that much the archivist knew. Once sealed they could only be opened in the presence of a witness, provided . . . There'd followed a long list of stipulations to which the young Kashif hadn't bothered to listen.

Practically dragging the archivist to where the man believed the secret bags were stored, Kashif demanded they both be given entry. With the Emir gone and that wing otherwise empty, the chamberlain had done the obvious; opened the front door and saluted smartly. It had taken Kashif ten minutes to identify the vault and another five to bully someone into unlocking the door. A problem never to arise again after Kashif relieved the porter of his key.

Goat skin, Kashif decided, maybe sheep, nothing too fancy. Cured in a way which was almost-intentionally perfunctory and stitched crudely with gut. Impressive signatures covered each bag, mostly from his father and occasionally Eugenie. One from the Soviet ambassador and even one from the Marquis de St Cloud. Any person wanting to open a bag to examine its contents had to sign the outside before the seal was cut. Some of the newer seals were almost silver, others oxidised down to a dull black.

Kashif was inordinately proud to discover that he had a whole rack to himself. Seven leather bags in total. Starting with the first, Kashif cut its seal and began to read an account of his life that he recognised.

He was surly, bad at games and prone to violence. His unbroken run of goals, his easy knock-downs in boxing and rapid fencing victories owed more to who he was than to any innate physical talent.

His marks suffered an automatic twenty-five percent inflation.

The French mistress he liked most had been paid off after complaining that he'd molested her in a corridor.

The summer Kashif turned seventeen was the year he got his reputation for working hard. He'd appear every morning at the relevant wing of the Bardo, notebook in hand and a nervous young archivist two steps behind. And each evening he'd make his way back to his mother's dar with another courtier's life pinned to the board of his memory.

He made friends fast that summer and was given three cars, including his first Porsche and a speed boat he used to take Russian girls water-skiing, until he hit a sunken rock and an attaché's daughter ended up in casualty. The high point was when he acquired his own villa on Iles de Kerkeah, from an elderly general whose devotion to his childless, long-suffering wife was apparently exceeded only by his devotion to a long string of pretty Moroccan houseboys.

Every bag he chose Kashif dutifully signed, leaving it to the archivist to repack the contents and affix a new seal. The one for his mother was especially interesting. Particularly in relation to a visit made to Gurda Schulte three weeks before she married his father. A surgeon briefly famous for patenting the only medically undetectable, biologically-foolproof method of restoring virginity. A technique surprisingly popular among the middle classes of North Africa and the source of her heir's considerable wealth.

It was a snippet of information Kashif parlayed with his mother into a new apartment in the Bardo, one with its own entrance. His other knowledge Kashif kept close as an enemy, deadly as a friend; using it only as necessary once that first flush of power was gone. Murad wasn't even born when Kashif discovered the bags and by the time he was the bags had gone. Exactly when they vanished Kashif never discovered. He'd gone to Monte Carlo one Monday and come back two years later to find the room empty and repainted, awaiting delivery of an apparently valuable collection of late-nineteenth-century tax returns.

One thing Kashif knew for certain though. No bag had made

reference to his father having married again. At least not until that American girl to whom Eugenie introduced him, Murad's mother. The one who went off a cliff. And the bag that dealt with Moncef's bastards made no reference to an Ashraf al-Mansur or Ashraf anything else come to that . . . Whatever the late Eugenie de la Croix or his father might claim.

'Afternoon,' Raf said to a guard by the side of the path. The man looked at Major Jalal, trying to work out if he was meant to salute Ashraf Bey or not. Just to be safe, he saluted anyway.

Up ahead stood Kashif Pasha, with no one else in sight. At least not obviously; although one sniper hid in a clump of palms to Raf's left. *Phoenix dactylifera*, tree of the Phoenicians with finger-resembling fruit. Raf had Hani to thank for that snippet of information.

Another sniper was behind him. The smell of tobacco as Raf entered the amphitheatre had been too strong not to whisper its warning. That Kashif Pasha felt such protection was necessary almost made Raf feel better.

'Brother.' Raf drawled the word. No greeting and no title, zero hostility either. Let the other man make the running on this. Kashif Pasha was supposed to be a poker player, famous for it apparently . . .

Raf smiled.

'Feeling happy about something?' asked Kashif.

'Always glad to see you,' Raf said. 'You know how it is.'

'No,' said Kashif, 'I can't say I do.'

Raf's grin was bleak as he adjusted his Armani shades and smelt the hot wind. Sweat, fear, anger and triumph. Beneath the distant tobacco and Kashif's cologne there was a veritable symphony of olfactory molecules being ripped apart by a breeze that filtered between salt-stunted thorns.

'Oh well,' he said.

They stood in the ruins of a small Roman amphitheatre with fifteen circles of seating cut direct into crumbling pink rock. The central circle was half buried in dust and a cheap kiosk near the entrance had signs that read *closed* in seven languages.

Its filthy window and padlocked door suggested the site had been shut since autumn.

There was undoubtedly a lesson there if only Raf had the mind for it, because according to Khartoum there was a lesson in everything; in appearance and the reality behind appearance and in the reality behind the first appearance of reality. In Khartoum's opinion to hunt knowledge was to lose it.

'You seem amused . . .' Kashif's voice was cold. 'Am I missing something?'

'We all are,' said Raf. 'That's the very essence of being human.'

Two of Major Jalal's soldiers looked at each other. One of them mouthing to the other and Raf caught the silent word. *Moncef* . . . His father, that was what they were saying. He was like his father.

Mad.

Even Kashif Pasha nodded. As if willing, for the moment, to admit that the one might be son of the other.

'This missing waiter . . .' said Raf. And got no further.

'He's confessed.'

Behind his shades, Raf blinked. 'To what?'

'Disguising himself to infiltrate the Domus Aurea with the express intent of killing the Emir.' Kashif's face burned with anger. Or maybe triumph. 'He was working for the French. As an *agent provocateur* in a revolutionary cell which also included the dead Sufi. He's admitted everything.'

'And you know his confession is true, how?' A reasonable-enough comment one would have thought.

'Because he wrote it himself.' So close to Raf was Kashif Pasha that Raf could identify at least three of the things Kashif had eaten for lunch. 'Ask the criminal if you don't believe me . . . And then we can shoot him.' A minor tic at the edge of Kashif's mouth pulled it out of shape. His pupils were large and his gaze direct.

Kashif Pasha meant it.

This was when Raf realised the pasha was serious. He'd summoned Raf to watch the execution of a man Kashif Pasha genuinely believed had tried to kill his father. All because of a throwaway line from Raf about suspecting Kashif. A barb which had dug deep into the pasha's flesh, dragging him to a point of intensity that owed far more to indignation than fear or guilt. That worried Raf.

Bluster, threats, fake fury, those Raf could handle. But a demand for approval, this expectation that he would immediately withdraw all accusations when faced with evidence . . . There was a sour note to this that rang like a cracked bell.

If not Kashif, then who . . . Berlin/the *Thiergarten*? It seemed unlikely.

'Your waiter,' said Raf. 'Where is he?'

In reply, Kashif jerked his head towards yet another black Jeep, parked beside the ticket kiosk. Smoked windows, roo bars and a radiator grille like the baleen of a loose-lipped whale. One could only assume the *mubahith* imported them in job lots.

'Get him,' Kashif demanded.

Major Jalal nodded and seconds later, as two guards tossed a naked figure at Raf's feet his heart sank. He should never, ever have let Chef Edvard register him with Domus Aurea security using someone else's name.

Hassan stank of fear and bled from a split mouth. His nose was broken, three front teeth were gone and his face was a veritable rainbow of pain. Whip marks scored his heavy shoulders. A dozen cigarette burns speckled his soft belly. There had been nothing subtle about the questioning.

'This is your waiter?'

Major Jalal nodded.

'According to my niece,' said Raf, 'the missing waiter was tallish and thin. This man is short and fat.'

'Lady Hana is mistaken.' Major Jalal's voice was firm. 'But then the dining room was lit by chandeliers and somewhat dark so it would be an easy error for a frightened child to make. Besides, Your Excellency has his brother's word that this is the man.'

'Let me guess,' said Raf. 'He protested his innocence for a couple of days and then decided to tell you the truth . . .'

'Is there a point to this?' Kashif's voice was hard.

'Of course there's a point,' said Raf with a sigh.

The three-day rule had been explained to him by two people he admired. One of them, as mother of Seattle's famous Five Winds Friendship Society had inherited an administration which kept *surgeons* on its payroll. And it had taken using their undoubted skills on two soon-to-retire elder brothers to get that anomaly changed, or so Hu San had said. The other person was Felix.

The rule of three was simple. And in a list of five it came just before the one that said blustering men broke faster than quiet women . . . No matter how brave or well-trained, even a saint was ready to confess to devil worship by the third day, there were no exceptions. Keep death away and rack up the pain and by day three all anybody wanted to know was where to sign.

Chef Edvard's sous-chef had been no different. Poor sod.

'Hassan,' said Raf and watched as the fat boy raised his head, eyes widening as he saw the man in front of him.

'You're . . .'

'Ashraf Bey,' said Raf, kicking Hassan in the stomach. 'Well done.' He kicked again and when Hassan finally looked up with imploring eyes, Raf went for the kidneys. It was this blow that knocked Hassan unconscious.

'You know the man?' Kashif's voice was thoughtful.

'Of course I know him,' Raf said. 'I'm Chief of Police. He's the main witness to the Maison Hafsid killing and on the precinct payroll as an informer. One of my lieutenants was wondering what had happened.'

'You recognised by sight a man who tried to shoot my father . . .' Kashif seemed to be trying the sentence for size, considering its usefulness.

On either side of the pasha his guards had gone very still. Maybe it was Kashif's tone of voice or perhaps he had some signal like a finger tapping against his nose, a shift of his weight or a certain nod of his head. Most people in his position had special signs and ways of giving instructions.

One of them must have said club this impostor to the ground.

*   *   *

'Well done,' said the voice. Raf ignored it. He had more important things to do than talk to the fox.

Twisting steadily, Raf pulled against his shackles until he felt one arm dislocate. It hurt no more than many other things in his life and far less than waking after the operation that replaced his kidneys as a child. About as much as a beating he once took in Seattle from a street punk called Wild Boy, back when they both worked for Hu San.

Raf hadn't seem the blow coming. Hadn't even felt the pistol butt that brought oblivion, the state to which his life seemed eternally drawn. One minute Raf was standing facing Kashif Pasha and then darkness came.

When Raf woke the first time he was in a waiter's uniform. The white blindness in his eyes the after-glow of a camera flash; and for a moment, floating on pain and watching camera burn on the inside of his eyelids, Raf believed he was young again.

And then he knew he wasn't and hadn't been for a very long time.

Chapter Forty-four

Friday 11th March

Opening the door was easy. Hani just pushed a button that read *emergency release* and a swirl of blissfully cool air exploded onto Ibn Chabbat Square. To close the door behind her she hit a button marked *shut*. This button was on the inside, obviously enough. And then they were in the coach, examining its hydraulic seats and checking the spiral stairs that led to a glass observation bubble.

'Too obvious,' said Hani.

At the very rear of the coach was a wall of showers and toilets (two of each, divided into male and female). Between these and the seating area further forward was a short corridor featuring a couple of sliding doors on each side. So the bus went seats/narrow corridor/wall of loos where a back window should be. The sliding doors were marked *stateroom 1, 2, 3* and *4 . . .*

'I don't get it,' Murad complained, not for the first time.

'Good,' Hani told him. 'Stick with that.'

She pushed him through one of the sliding doors, having first flipped up its lock with a penknife, an act of breaking and entry made much easier than she expected by the coachmakers' fear of litigation, which guaranteed that every door was simplicity itself to open from the outside should the need arise. Which, in Hani's opinion, it had.

A man's room, Russian to judge from the phrase book and an open magazine left on the side. 'Try the next one,' said Hani and bundled Murad back through the sliding door, re-locking it behind her.

A woman, travelling alone. The upper bunk unmade, blankets

still folded, the lower one exhibiting neatly turned back covers and a perfectly straight pillow. Also Soviet. Too neat by half. 'We'll try the other side,' Hani said.

Both bunks in the next cabin had been used. The cover on the bottom one hung neatly, the cover to the top bunk was still crumpled. A Bible in English, translated by someone called St James. Hani didn't want to be prejudiced, but . . .

Actually that could be good.

On a bedside locker, open and face down, lay a Discovery Channel guide to Ifriqiya, its spine cracked in half a dozen places. A handful of foreign change filled a saucer.

'*e pluribus unum . . .*' From one, many. Or was it, from many, one? Hani's Latin was too rusty for her to be certain which it was, if either. So she put down the coin and picked up a flowery dressing gown draped over a peg on the door.

'Nylon,' she told Murad.

The garment was surprisingly short, albeit still long enough to drag on the carpet when Hani tried it on without sandals. It was the gown's width which impressed her. She and Murad could have hidden inside the thing three times over.

'This'll do,' Hani said with the certainty of someone who distrusted thin people even if she was one. Years of living with Aunt Nafisa had seen to that. 'We hide here.'

'Hide?'

'Okay, then,' said Hani, settling herself on the floor. 'We wait.'

Around dusk, Hani heard the tourists finally clamber aboard and felt the coach settle on its dampers. Or maybe it was springs? Mechanical things weren't really her area. Computers now . . . But hard as it was to believe, the *e pluribus unum* couple making this trip were doing so without a single computer, PDA or screen. Unless they'd taken the lot with them and Hani found that hard to believe.

'We're moving,' said Murad, his expression worried.

'That's what we want to happen,' Hani told him. She indicated a spot next to her on the carpet and Murad looked doubtful. He was still slightly afraid of her, Hani realised. And of everything else. Beneath that buttoned-down manner her cousin was as raw to the world as she was, maybe more so, because she knew how to adapt while Murad was still learning.

Meanwhile he just looked bemused.

'Uncle Ashraf will be fine,' Hani promised, realising as soon as she spoke that this was not what worried the boy. She might worry about her uncle but Murad had his own problems, ones unknown to her.

'Do you think getting older makes you weaker?' Murad demanded suddenly.

Hani thought about it. 'I thought it made you stronger.'

'That's what they tell you,' said Murad, 'but is it true? I feel like I know less every day. Everything always used to be clear but now . . .'

'What was clear?' Hani asked.

'Knowing what to do . . .'

'And were you allowed to do it?'

They sat together until Murad was so desperate for a pee that he could sit still no longer. Hani didn't tell him she also needed the loo. Some things were still private for girls.

'Use the basin,' Hani said . . . 'Now rinse it out,' she suggested afterwards.

Murad and Hani then had a brief discussion about whether or not to bolt their door from inside. Hani won and the bolt was left open. Darkness arriving long before someone finally slid a key into the lock.

'We have to get them in here,' Hani said.

'What? We're not going to . . .'

'No,' said Hani. 'I've already told you, I just need them to myself for a few minutes. We . . .' she amended. 'We need them.'

'Why?'

'Because we do,' Hani announced firmly and together they crawled into a narrow space previously occupied by a suitcase.

'Who moved that?' The voice was Midwestern American and female, puzzled rather than angry. Hani didn't care who the voice belonged to, she liked them already. 'Carl, Carl . . .' The admonition was addressed to thin air. It had to be, because only one pair of legs could be seen in the room.

White plastic sandals shuffled over to the wall, the case rose from the floor and then it was being tipped on its side and pushed towards Murad.

He grunted.

That was what they'd agreed on, a simple grunt. Now came the dangerous bit when the cabin's owner might shout or rush out into the coach and demand help. They'd decided how to handle this too.

Hani whimpered.

'Who's there?'

The case pulled back, tipped upright.

'Come out,' the woman demanded. 'Come out right now.'

Murad crawled from under the bunk and scrambled to his feet. His eyes were lowered and his shoulders slumped. Inside his head he was trying to remember how Hani had suggested he should shuffle his shoes.

'Oh great. A thief.' The woman sounded exasperated. 'I suppose you've already pocketed all our stuff.' Her glance took in the whole cabin, all five paces of it and found nothing missing. 'Maybe not,' she admitted, 'but then what are you doing here? And what happened to your face?' She took Murad's chin in her fingers and turned his head to the light, tutting as she did so. 'Someone hit you?'

When the boy stayed silent, Micki Vanhoffer sighed. She was a large, home-loving woman very far from Ohio. Doing what her husband thought she should be doing, taking a break from comfortable cruises around the Caribbean. A month in North Africa was his idea. Well, and her eldest son's, Carl Junior. An anniversary present supposedly. So here she was on a glorified bus in the middle of a heatwave, in March for heaven's sakes.

'I'd better tell the driver,' Micki said mostly to herself, reaching for the door handle. 'And then we can call your parents.'

'He doesn't have any,' said Hani, rolling out from under the bunk in a tumble of arms and legs. After scrambling upright, she took Murad's hand and gripped hard when he tried to pull away. 'We're orphans,' she added quickly. 'From an orphanage. A cruel place.'

Huge black eyes looked up at Micki Vanhoffer from beneath a rather dirty scarf. Eyes that swam so deep with tears they appeared larger than was humanly possible. Below those eyes jutted a nose too prominent to fit any Western idea of beauty and under this a mouth that positively quivered with anguish.

'You speak English . . .' Micki meant it as a statement rather than a question, but her words were inflected, rising towards the end so Hani found herself answering.

'Yes,' Hani said. 'I learnt it from tourists. When I was working in a café with my mother.'

Micki looked puzzled. 'I thought you said you lived in an orphanage?'

'This was before my mother died,' Hani said firmly. 'When I was little.'

'When you were . . .' The large woman looked at the small girl and sighed. 'Things like this never happen on cruises,' she said. 'I'll get Carl Senior down from the bubble. You wait here.'

'You say he's your brother . . .'

Hani looked at Murad, then nodded. 'My brother,' she agreed. 'Unfortunately he's not very bright.'

The man asking Hani questions was big in a different way. His shoulders so broad that they seemed to stretch against his very skin. On his tee-shirt was a simple fish made from a single line that curled back over itself at the tail, Hani had a feeling she'd seen the sign before.

'You have the fish.'

The man nodded. 'You know what it means?'

Hani nodded. 'Of course I know,' she said. 'Everyone knows.'

'*Carl* . . .' The word was a warning. 'I know you want to do good in this heathen place but remember what our brochure said about preaching.'

'I'm not preaching,' said the man. 'She mentioned it first.' He dropped to a crouch in front of Hani. 'What's this about an orphanage?' The words were soft, unlike his eyes which were pale, watchful and just a touch angry. Mentioning his shirt had obviously been a bad move.

'We're running away,' said Hani.

'I can see that.'

'From an orphanage.'

'What's its name? Come on,' he said when Hani hesitated. 'Spit it out.'

Hani looked puzzled. 'Spit what out?' she said.

'*Carl!*'

'It's a fair question,' Carl Vanhoffer said to his wife. 'If she can't instantly name the orphanage then it probably doesn't exist. And that boy isn't her brother. Not full brother anyway. The skin colours are way different.'

'You'll have to excuse Carl Senior,' said the woman with a tight smile. 'He used to be a police officer. He gets like this sometimes. You should have seen him with Carl Junior when he was growing up . . .'

'That's okay,' said Hani. 'My uncle used to be a policeman. He gets like that too and your husband's right. We're not really running away from an orphanage.'

'Told you,' Carl Vanhoffer said. 'What are you running away from?'

'Marriage,' said Hani and slowly pulled the shawl tight round her face, shrinking inside it. With her hunched shoulders and narrow back she looked frighteningly young. 'And you're right about the other thing too, Muri's not my brother, he's my cousin.'

'How old are you?' That was the woman.

Hani thought about it.

'Well?' The man's eyes were less hard than they had been. Slightly mistrustful to be true enough but not out-and-out disbelieving.

'Twelve,' said Hani, adding a year to her age. Assuming Khartoum was right and she really had just turned eleven.

'You don't look it.'

'Carl!' Again that outrage, almost maternal. Like there were things men couldn't be relied on to understand. Hani glanced at the both of them, the American man and woman. Most husbands and wives she'd met had harder edges to their lives and stricter boundaries. However, Hani had to admit to not having met many.

Hamzah Effendi and Madame Rahina were not a good model. Aunt Jalila and Uncle Mushin even worse. One now dead, the other apparently in a sanatorium. Uncle Ashraf and Zara? They weren't even a couple, not properly.

'It's all to do with food,' Hani told the woman. 'The less you get to eat the smaller you look . . . A doctor told me,' she added, before Carl Senior had a chance to ask her how she knew.

'And the poor get married younger,' said the woman.

Hani wasn't convinced this was true because, the way Zara told it, the really poor people in Iskandryia couldn't afford to get married until their twenties, which might be why they got so cross. And that fact probably applied to Ifriqiya as well.

But Hani kept her silence.

Despite what Uncle Ashraf, Zara and everyone else thought, she always had known when to keep her opinions to herself.

'Have you met the boy you're meant to marry?'

'Oh yes.' Hani nodded.

'What's he like?' The woman sounded interested. Appalled, but still interested.

'Okay, I guess,' said Hani, jerking her narrow chin towards Murad. 'As boys go . . .'

'This is him?'

Hani nodded again.

'And he's running away with you?' Carl Senior sounded doubtful.

'Of course,' said Hani, 'Muri doesn't mind getting married but he doesn't want to leave school.'

'Why would he leave school?' It was Micki's turn to look muddled.

'Because he'll need a job for when I have a baby . . .'

'*When you* . . .' Their voices were so loud that Hani was afraid the Russian in the next cabin might start to wonder what was wrong.

'What exactly are you telling them?' Murad hissed, his Arabic so flawless he could have been reciting poetry at the court of a long-dead caliph. Needless to say Micki and Carl Senior understood not a word.

'That we're running away,' said Hani. 'Because our parents want us to get married.'

'*Married?*' Murad stood open mouthed in outrage. 'You're eleven,' he said. 'I'm twelve. Fourteen is the earliest a girl can get married in Ifriqiya. Sixteen for boys.'

'But they don't know that, do they?' said Hani.

'What are you telling him?' Carl Senior demanded.

'That Muri shoudn't be afraid of you,' said Hani. 'That you won't hand us over.' She was glancing at the man but she was talking to Micki.

Chapter Forty-five

Friday 11th – Sunday 13th March

He stank and there was little doubt that he'd just pissed himself again. Liquid his body could ill afford to lose. Raf had also started to think of himself as *he* and that was never a good sign.

Maybe it was this that allowed the fox to return. Alternatively, Raf had just got bored with trying to hold himself together.

'*Now dislocate your other shoulder,*' ordered the fox.

Raf shook his head. His teeth gritted not from bravery or pain but because he was trying to stop one of his upper left canines from falling out and keeping his mouth closed was all he could come up with, given both his hands were shackled behind his back and fixed to a wall.

Impossible.

'*Not impossible,*' said the fox, '*just painful. Work on the difference.*' And then Raf stopped letting the different bits of himself talk to each other and started to listen to the sound of a sea that had vanished millions of years before, after the Chott el Jerrid finally separated from the Mediterranean to become first an inland sea, then a lake and ultimately the flood-prone salt flats it finally became.

Except that the waves like the voices, came from within him and there was nothing supernatural about them.

What Raf could hear was the sound of his own blood echoing off the stone walls of an azib, a domed shelter built for goats and now his prison. At first the noise had been slight as meltwater over pebbles, growing louder, until now it splashed like a fosse falling into a cool meltwater pool far below. He was listening to what was left of his own life. In the darkness that looked like becoming his tomb.

'Do it,' Raf told himself. 'Dislocate.'

His first idea after Major Jalal had bolted the heavy azib door was to somersault out of his predicament by rolling forward to hang upside down from his shackled wrists, then twist sideways to land on his feet, facing the wall, with the shackles now in front of him. All he needed to do then was free his wrists and dig himself out.

Two failed attempts had convinced Raf this was impossible. So now he was going with the fox's suggestion, that Raf begin by convincing himself he was really merely testing the strength of the chains shackling him to the wall.

As ever, when facing something unpleasant, the trick was to remove oneself from the pain. A trick he'd previously spent many months unlearning. Although back then he'd been somebody else. Or rather, Bayer Rochelle had made him somebody else and done a good job of it too; much better than any of his schools had managed.

Removing oneself from pain wasn't a trick everybody could master. For a start, it required a certain working knowledge of the subject, preferably one built up over many years. Unless, of course, it was possible to go for a single cataclysmic thunderburst that shocked the flesh into learning something it never forgot.

Raf didn't know, that wasn't the route he'd taken.

The secret was to be somewhere else. Answering questions other than those asked. While hunting for the fracture behind reality.

Breathe through nose or mouth . . .

Saturday or Sunday . . .

Live or die . . .

'Just one collection of questions after the next, isn't it?' said the fox. *'Life I mean. Or what passes for it . . .'*

How long he'd been in the azib Raf wasn't sure. Being knocked unconscious did that to you. At least it always did to him. And his back history was punctuated, at significant points, by such bouts of darkness, although often differently induced.

Actually, it was probably more accurate to say his life, back history, call it what one would, was a string of cold darkness punctuated by sharp, occasionally contradictory memories of being awake. What Raf had taken to calling the *sick room conundrum* and what the fox insisted on calling Schrödinger's paint pot.

If he went to sleep in a ward that was green and woke in the same room but it was grey, what had changed? Reality, the room or Raf? There was something very primitive about that question. Almost classic. A puzzle replete with a dozen resonances Raf undoubtedly failed to appreciate.

There was, of course, an even more primitive conundrum slumped against the wall opposite, quietly decomposing in note after note of sweet decay. At what point did Hassan cease to be human? And what exactly did death remove from that original mix of 65 per cent oxygen, 18 per cent carbon, 9.5 per cent hydrogen and all those other elements neither Raf nor the fox could be bothered to remember?

Dying seemed simple, decomposing less so, if Hassan was representative. A veritable matrix of influences constraining or facilitating the metamorphosis: beginning with attack by insects, originally flies and then beetles, finally millipedes; amount of clothing intact, in this case none; level of physical trauma, considerable; ambient heat, sweltering . . .

The fox and Raf also agreed on the probability that soil type made some impact.

Felix would have known. Having wiped his finger on the floor of the azib he'd have announced a high saline content was hindering decomposition or saltpetre was causing mummification. Of course, the fat man was quite capable of wiping his finger straight on the body.

When Raf first woke, Hassan had been coming out of rigor, locked muscles slowly relaxing, starting with his eyelids, lower jaw and the soft jowls of his neck. And Raf didn't need voices in his head to tell him this was decomposition of muscle fibre.

By evening the boy's face had turned a weird greenish red, with a veritable tie-dye of corruption brightening his flabby chest and blotching his naked thighs. It was around this time that Hassan began to smell. At least that was what Raf thought then. Now, reassessing, he understood that corruption had barely started.

After the face began to melt, millipedes arrived to eat mites busy feeding on flesh, the blowflies having already gone. And gas-filled blisters began to appear under the skin as liquor leached from anus, nostril, mouth and ears. In all probability, Raf realised, he was taking more interest than was wise in the intricacies of what was happening. But it was hard to avoid when shackled in a stone azib, five paces from one's very own *memento mori*.

'Enough with the thinking,' said the fox, its voice completely present for the first time in weeks. *'You can dislocate your way out of this or stay here and die. Make a choice.'*

It looked out through Raf's eyes. The bit of him that had never been entirely human.

'You want this to end,' it said, *'then end it. But ask yourself this . . . How many more times can you afford to die?'*

Chapter Forty-six

Saturday 12th March

Sometime after the lights went down in the main part of the coach and those who had couchettes let back their seats and the loos and showers occupied by tourists preparing for sleep finally emptied, Micki took Hani to the loo, using the width of her hips to shield the child from anyone who might glance round.

Although Micki was pretty sure everyone was safely dozing, because she'd already made three visits, earning herself pitying glances from a middle-aged, pudding-faced Soviet woman in the back row who'd finally fallen asleep with a crumpled copy of the previous day's *Pravda* on her lap.

'I'll keep guard,' Micki told the child, ushering Hani through a door. 'Don't worry,' she added, when Hani looked anxious, 'I'll be here when you come out.'

'Micki,' Hani's voice was little more than a whisper.

'What now?'

'Um . . .'

The child had the face of an angel. A foreign angel obviously but an angel all the same. Men were going to fall into those dark eyes and never find their way back. Not for years though, Micki told herself hastily. When the girl was properly grown up.

'What is it?' asked Micki and when Hani still didn't answer, she dropped to her knees the way she used to do when something was worrying Carl Junior. Carl Senior never got the importance of this, although she'd tried to explain it more than once. He always towered over the boy and then wondered why he got frightened.

'You can tell me, honey . . .'

Something fleeting and sad passed over the face of the child as she bent close and whispered in Micki's ear.

'You know,' Micki hissed to her husband, when Hani and Murad were safely dozing on the floor, wrapped in separate blankets that they both managed to kick off in their sleep. 'She hadn't even heard about Kotex. It was a miracle the child even knew what was happening to her . . . Can you imagine it?'

Carl had less than no interest in imagining any such thing but had long since learnt not to say as much, so he muttered something he hoped sounded suitably shocked and had another go at drifting off to sleep.

'That must be how their parents decide they're ready to marry,' Micki announced. 'The first time they . . . You know.'

That was one *you know* and a couple more *theys* than Carl could follow but he didn't mention this either. 'Could be,' he said and drifted off to sleep, leaving his wife to the comfort of outrage.

'We've got problems,' Carl Senior said.

'Nothing we can't fix,' Micki insisted hastily, when she saw the anguish in Hani's face. The road block was waiting at Dehiba, thirty klicks after the blacktop shrank from two lanes to one. Right before Ifriqiya's border with Tripolitana.

Jebel Dahar's stark red spine with its low fringe of thorn and scrub was mostly behind them and ahead was a sixteen-hour trip to take in the hill-top town of Yafran. A double-page spread in Micki's *Insight Guide* revealed an area of olive groves and good red soil; while a box-out of traditional Yafrani architecture revealed squat buildings with heavy doors, intricate wrought iron and what looked like plaster helicopters, jets and butter-flies fixed to the side of Berber houses.

'Stay in here,' Micki told the children. 'They'll probably just count us.'

Carl Senior stayed silent.

'We could hide under the bed,' Hani suggested.

'Good idea,' said Carl. 'No one would ever think of looking for you there.' He grabbed his passport and camera. 'I might as well get a shot of the frontier. If they'll allow me,' he added crossly, sliding back the door.

'Ignore him,' Micki said. 'He's nervous.'

'About what?'

Micki smiled. 'Some people don't like breaking the law. Carl Senior's one of them.'

'But you don't mind?' While watching the large woman from the corner of her eye, Hani thought about that. The American was very pink and very big. With wavy blonde hair made fat by too much brushing.

'Honey,' said Micki, 'how do you think Carl Senior and I first met? It was in a line up. I was standing there and he was the one walking a elderly man down the line.'

'What happened?'

Micki shrugged. 'Old Amos had bad eyesight. So after the civilians had gone I told Carl Senior he owed me a coffee for my inconvenience. We went on from there.'

'You're not Carl Junior's mother, are you?' Hani was surprised she hadn't realised that before. 'Not really . . .'

'Honey,' Micki looked at her. 'You can be one weird kid.'

'But I'm telling the truth?'

'Yeah, you are that. He needed looking after and Carl Senior was useless. So he got me.' Micki shrugged. 'Whatever good that was. Now, you stay here and we'll soon be safely across that border.'

'If only,' said Hani. She could feel a decision coming on. The kind Uncle Ashraf might make. *When in doubt, change the rules.* She was pretty sure he'd said that to her sometime or other and if he hadn't then he'd probably meant to . . . Unless it was Hamzah Effendi.

'We're going to hide, all right' said Hani, 'right in front of the cameras.'

'You're . . .' For the first time since Hani had met her, Micki was lost.

'In front of the cameras.' Pulling back the cabin's curtain, Hani nodded to sand-filled barrels blocking off one half of the narrow road. 'That isn't a border post,' she told the large woman. 'That's a road block and those men with guns belong to Kashif Pasha. His half-brother,' Hani added, taking Murad's hand

Micki Vanhoffer looked as bemused as she felt.

'This is His Excellency Murad Pasha,' said Hani. She took off her scarf and tried to comb out her hair with her fingers. Then she straightened her shoulders and raised her chin. 'And I'm Lady Hana al-Mansur. Those soldiers out there have orders to find us.'

'To make you marry?'

'No,' said Hani. 'So Kashif Pasha can have us killed. Although he'll try to blame it on terrorists or my Uncle Ashraf . . .' She shrugged away the thought. 'You do have a mobile?' Hani said, pointing to Micki's handbag.

The American woman nodded.

'Good.' Hani up-ended the bag and began to sort through tissues, tampons, a shop load of loose make-up and what Hamzah would called a boasting book, a plastic wallet full of family photographs. The mobile was near the bottom, switched off.

'What's your code?' asked Hani.

Micki gave her a six digit number.

'Don't tell me,' said Hani, 'that's your date of birth . . .' She sighed at Micki's embarrassed nod. 'Think about changing it,' Hani suggested, fingers flicking through menus. When she reached the option she wanted, Hani punched in a number, remembering to make allowances for international dialling.

Then she took a deep breath.

'This is the truth,' Hani said. 'I promise you . . . I'm not an orphan,' she stopped dead. 'Well actually I am,' she said, 'but I'm not running away from an orphanage. And we're not engaged. But someone is trying to kill me. Well,' Hani thought about that one too. 'I guess they're really trying to kill Murad.'

'It was a lie about the marriage too?' Micki seemed to be one twist behind Hani, understandable really. . . Most of the adults Hani had met hadn't been too bright.

'No one is forcing us to get married,' Hani said.

'So you're not going to marry your cousin?'

Hani smiled. 'That wasn't what I said at all.'

'Micki.' The voice came from Carl Senior and, by the sound of things, he was either yelling from outside or was stood in the doorway. 'They got guns,' he said. 'And they want everyone out because they intend to search the coach.'

'God give me strength,' said Micki loud enough to be heard. 'Tell them I'm coming.' She banged her hip against the door and slammed a tiny drawer. 'Just as soon as I get this damn skirt on.'

'Take this,' Hani said, shovelling everything back into Micki's bag. 'As soon as you get across the border turn on the mobile and it'll remind you that you need to make a call.'

'I do?'

'Yes,' said Hani, 'definitely. Call the number that appears and demand to speak to Effendi.'

'What if Mr Effendi doesn't want to speak to me?'

'He will,' promised Hani, wondering if the American realised she'd just agreed to make the call. 'And if he doesn't, tell whoever answers that Hani says, *If Effendi doesn't come to the phone she'll stop letting him play with her money* . . . He keeps investing it in his own companies,' Hani added, as if that explained everything.

The words were Hamzah Effendi's guarantee that the message was real. What he did would have nothing to do with money. It would be done for Raf. A debt repaid.

'What do I tell him?' Micki asked anxiously. 'When Effendi does come to the phone?'

'Tell him that Murad and Hani have been murdered by Kashif Pasha . . . Tell him to tell everyone he knows.' Catching the American woman's appalled expression, Hani held up one hand as the first tears started to trickle down Micki's face, cutting tracks in her heavy make-up.

'It might not happen,' Hani said.

Chapter Forty-seven

Monday 14th March

The call from the minaret came harsh as a crow. Only there was no minaret and when Raf kicked at a shadow it squawked into life and sliced the night in a spread of serrated black blades.

'Very pretty,' said Felix, nodding at Raf's shackles. So Raf swung them at him and missed, earning himself a smile. A real fat man grin.

'Ignore him,' the fox said. *'He's just like all the others.'*

Tiri was talking about the ghosts who walked out of the salt wilderness towards Raf, their carcasses destroyed, their faces twisted in the final moments of death or smoothed free of all memory.

'I know,' said Raf and forced one foot in front of the other, extracting another step from his shaking body. They were dead and so was he. At least that was what it felt like. This razor state between existences, flash-filled with waterfalls of exaltation that appeared one minute to run down his spine and then vanished the next, leaving him spent as an hourglass.

Behind Raf stretched footprints speckled with blood from where he'd slashed his feet on rose petals. *Rose de sable,* crystallised gypsum. He'd come across a field of the things, stone flowers sharp as knife blades, and had walked through being too tired to walk around.

Raf thought they grew there naturally. But the fox insisted they'd been dumped as second grade goods, unsuitable even for tourists like him. It claimed to have been there when the dumping was done.

'I'm not a tourist,' said Raf, but the fox had to disagree. Informing Raf that he was a tourist in his own life. A hit-and-run recidivist who fixed himself on occasional moments of clarity. Their argument lasted so long that Raf forgot to feel pain and when he next looked around, he'd walked two, maybe three miles without ever seeing anyone he'd killed.

Felix came round twice and looked happier the next time he appeared, face shredded and egg yolk running from one eye but definitely more smiley. 'You're fragmenting,' he told Raf.

'You can talk.' The retort just came and Raf was still wondering how to apologise for his tactlessness when the fat man gave a shrug like he agreed and blew apart in the night wind. Without shades, minus clothes, his hands chained. And now rudeness. The fox was right. Raf was excelling himself.

Sharp edges cut his ankles every time Raf's feet broke though salt to hit one of the many puddles of brine beneath. Smears of what looked like rust threaded the chott's drying surface, marbling its saline whiteness. Blood on snow, his mother's favourite shot. Only the saline sting to tell Raf that what he walked on wasn't ice or snow.

Somewhere up ahead should be a road. A strip of tarmac floating on treated polystyrene blocks, linked together and slung across the chott, Raf seemed to remember that was how it went. Polystyrene blocks so the weight of the road didn't sink it into the chott's soft surface.

Raf couldn't have used the road even if it had been heading north towards Camp Moncef rather than west towards Tozeur. But Raf needed to cross it and until he did, he was, by definition, more than half a day away from killing Kashif Pasha.

'You know what?' said a voice.

Raf didn't.

'You look shit.' The drawl was skin-crawlingly familiar, the lips from which it issued tinted with a shade of Shu Uemura too deep to class as ironic. A turned-up collar framed a face sharp enough to break hearts. 'Life not treating you too well?'

'I'm fine,' snapped Raf.

'Of course you are,' said Wild Boy. 'Anyone can see that.' He touched pale fingers to his brow in a mocking salute, swept dark hair back from his eyes and vanished.

'I don't remember killing Wild Boy,' Raf muttered.

'You don't remember much at all, do you?' said the fox. *'And what you do remember changes each day. I've never met anyone like it for avoiding the obvious.'* The animal paused, took a look through Raf's eyes at the night wilderness of the chott and sighed. *'What do you think happened to him after you went missing?'*

'He came looking for me?'

'And did he find you?' asked the fox.

Raf shook his head.

'Did anyone?'

There wasn't an answer to that. At least not one that made real sense. Although maybe that wasn't surprising given his mind was full of ghosts and memories and things that might have happened but probably didn't or were about to happen, but only . . .

'Only what?' The fox demanded.

But Raf was already asleep. When he woke the walls had changed colour again. His bed was the same but the windows were different, wood not rusting metal. The oak outside was bare where it had been green. Only the firs on the far slopes looked the same. Like lazy smoke frozen in the act of rolling uphill.

'You can sleep again now,' someone said.

He'd had days like that at Roslyn. Dozens of them. And before Roslyn, days in a white room with flowered curtains across the window. Steel bars painted in childish reds and greens and blues because some expert decided bright colours made window bars look less intentional. As if the security measures had been put up by accident and no one could be bothered to take them down again.

For maybe a year Raf had believed the bars were there to keep him in. Only towards the end did he realise they existed to keep others out. Evil people, one nurse told him. Misguided protestors. She was Swiss, much younger than he realised and she vanished the morning after he took a bar of chocolate from her. Neither had realised they planned to do double blood tests that day.

One morning, shortly after that, Raf woke feeling stiff and cold with an ache in his ribs and new scars on his wrists. And his mother was sat in a chair in the far corner of his room. She was crying, which wasn't unusual and carrying primroses, which was . . .

'You look older.' He said it without thinking.

When she'd finished drying her eyes she came over and stood by his bed. Her fingers reaching out to touch his face. 'You don't,' she said. The coat she wore was new and her shoes were different, shiny at the toes and unscuffed on the heels. She'd also changed the colour of her hair.

As always, Raf forgot how angry he was about everything and agreed to come home. Although it was difficult to remember where home was at that point. Not New York for the second time, that came later.

He'd been . . . Raf found it impossible to remember how old. Somehow birthdays and candles and parties with presents had always seemed to pass him by.

'*That's what this is about?*' said the fox. '*Massive sulks that Mummy never gave you a proper birthday party?*' The voice was sardonic, darker than Raf remembered it having been for a years. '*You're going to die in the wilderness because no one let you blow candles?*'

'*I'm* not going to die,' said Raf.

Chapter Forty-eight

Tuesday 15th March

'Count them,' said the fox. So Raf did. A handful of *mubahith*, teenage girls in khaki jumpsuits, jellaba-clad orderlies and two visiting Berber elders wrapped respectively in lengths of blue and black. Awaiting a day that threatened to be as impossibly hot as the day before.

Eleven in all.

And then there was Raf watching from the chott, flayed by UV that already filtered through scummy cloud to tighten his skin.

Sweat shivering down his spine in anticipation.

He stank of shit and piss and blood, the smell assailing him every time he halted long enough for his own body heat to reach his nostrils. Evidence of his own humanity.

St John the Baptist. Minus the loin cloth.

Now that a road existed between Kibili and El Hamma du Jerid, carefully skirting the edge of the wilderness before slanting off from the chott's edge to cross at the narrowest point, few people except 'packers and Soviet tourists in fat-tyred UAZ 4X4s tried to cross the salt lake any other way.

The camel trains were gone, along with the slave markets and spice routes. And while it was true that an annual Sand Yacht Championship was held on the chott, this was only ever attended by Soviets and, in any case, was not due for another three months.

So the khaki-clad teenager sweating out her early shift on the southern perimeter of Camp Moncef watched the arrival of a naked apparition with disbelief. At first she assumed the tiny speck was an animal either lost or abandoned. Dogs escaped from cars, half-dead donkeys were cast loose when the amount they could carry stopped being worth what they cost in feed.

Not yet worried enough to find herself a pair of binoculars, Corporal Habib kept an eye on the approaching animal. But sometime between tucking a cigarette inside her hand because one of Kashif Pasha's men had suddenly roared up in his open Jeep and saluting the departing sergeant without getting caught, the speck vanished.

'Shit.'

Corporal Habib blinked into the chott's acid glare, ground the butt of her cigarette underfoot and reached into her pocket for a pair of shades; circumstances demanded it even if wearing them on duty was almost as bad as smoking, being the preserve of officers.

Her shades cut down haze and cancelled out most refraction but the figure was still gone, leaving only early-morning shimmer and diminishing slivers of what had to be surface water left over from the winter rains.

Fifteen minutes later, Corporal Habib was still squinting into the distance when the emptiness beside her suddenly took her feet from under her and followed the corporal down, slamming itself into her rib cage. Bone splintered, on the wrong side: but Corporal Habib's heart kept pounding and by the time she realised her aorta wasn't pierced and both lungs still drew breath the emptiness sat back on its heels, waiting, with the corporal's own machine gun to her throat.

Only the camouflage of her jumpsuit had kept Corporal Habib alive. Had her uniform been bottle green, the colour of Kashif's own guard, or the black of the *mubahith* she would have been dead. Something that might still happen to judge from the blue eyes that stared down at her, pale as cracked ice.

'Single shot,' said a crow's voice, raw and bitter. 'All you'll get at this distance is a gas star and no chance to cry for help. You ever seen a gas star?'

The corporal nodded. A *gas star* happened when muzzle flash entered flesh, for guns almost touching you got *burn rings*, and then *powder tattoos:* part of the corporal was certain gas stars only occurred on upper limbs or torso but she kept that to herself. Something about the apparition staring down at her suggested he might have a more intimate knowledge of the phenomenon.

'You want my clothes?' The corporal's strangled question did exactly what she meant it to, told the apparition she wasn't about to put up a fight.

'Water,' Raf demanded. Watching as the corporal silently unclipped her flask and held it out. She did a very impressive job of not looking at his nakedness or chains.

He drank.

'And those,' said Raf, 'I want these.' Lifting the shades off her nose, he nodded to the two spare magazines on her belt. 'And those.' The weapon he held in shaking fingers was an old-model MP-5i 9mm Heckler and Koch, the one issued with a 30-round mag.

'Now get up.'

Corporal Habib did what she was told.

Conditioning, Raf told himself, worked every time. He should know.

'Is Kashif Pasha here?'

The corporal nodded, only to freeze when she saw Raf's scowl. Very slowly, probably unconsciously, she began to shake her head, as if that might change the answer.

'And the Emir?'

A frightened nod. And with it a look that suggested she wanted to say more but wasn't sure whether to risk it.

'What?' Raf demanded.

'He's dying. So if you've come to kill him there's no point.'

'I haven't,' said Raf. 'I wouldn't . . . One last question. What's that over there?'

Corporal Habib never saw the blow that dropped her into a heap. Or realised, until long afterwards, that when Raf went through her ammo pouch he took only her bar of chocolate. Everything else he left . . .

'Fuck, no.'

Not that.

Jammed into a pocket on the passenger side of an open-top Jeep, Raf found a copy of the previous evening's *La Presse*, final edition.

He found it shortly after swinging his shackles into the face of the NCO driving, wrapping them around the man's fat throat, bringing his screams to an abrupt halt. The NCO was still alive but his jaw hung crooked, his moustache was thick with blood and his face sported bruises which would last for a month. His arm was also broken. But some of that was self-inflicted. The NCO had run his Jeep straight into a rock.

Having read the headlines Raf wished he'd just killed him.

'You're crying,' said the fox.

'Of course I'm fucking crying.' Talking to the fox avoided thinking and thought was the last thing Raf wanted. He wanted emptiness. The dislocation of mind from body and body from action; not so much cognitive as psychic dissonance, blood music. The sound of glass spheres as they ground against each other.

Behind reality emptiness. Behind emptiness . . .

This.

'You want me to take it from here?' asked the fox. If Raf hadn't known otherwise he'd have said Tiri was worried. Smart move. Raf watched himself watching the fox. Stood naked on a dirt track below Jebel Morra, scanning a headline he already knew.

Kashif Pasha accused of killing half-brother and cousin.

A photograph of Murad showed him staring into the lens with childish seriousness. The picture of Hani was an old papp shot, grabbed outside Le Trianon. A fact made obvious by a section of café canopy and writing on the ice-cream glass on the table in front of her. *Lady Hana al-Mansur.*

All the picture did for Raf was reinforce how fast Hani had changed in those last few months. In the picture she looked as he still thought of her. Would always think of her. Small and thin, with a wry smile and more imagination than was good for any child.

Rolling the NCO over with his foot, Raf bent to take his pistol and found it attached by lanyard to a leather holster, along with three spare magazines.

'You plan to do this for yourself, don't you?' said the fox.

Raf nodded.

Unbuckling the sergeant's broad belt, Raf ripped it through a handful of trouser loops to free the holster. And once he'd got the belt off, Raf decided to keep it anyway. His only problem being that, even on its tightest setting, the belt threatened to slide over his hips, so he slung it across his right shoulder instead. An action made difficult by the fact his hands were still linked by their length of rusting shackle.

One H&K with 3x30 rounds. One Browning, plus a total of four magazines. That made . . . Raf ran his eye down the edge of a black-metal clip, counting rounds, two at a time. Twelve to each, made forty-eight, add ninety from the sub-machine gun . . . How many guards could Kashif Pasha have?

There was only one track into Moncef's latest camp and at its entrance stood a temporary barrier; one of those striped aluminium poles, counter-balanced by a square weight at the pivot end. A single soldier stood guard, shaded by an open-fronted hut.

Possibly she should have been watching the track but most of her time was taken up wiping perspiration from her face or pulling at the armpits of her uniform where sweat had stained the camouflage almost black.

When she did look up the djinn was almost upon her.

'I've got a question,' it said.

Staring in disbelief, uncertain whether to be most shocked by the shackles, the brandished weapons or the apparition's sheer nakedness Leila de Loria broke every rule she'd ever been taught and took two steps backwards, ending up against the wall of her hut.

'Eugenie still dead?' the apparition demanded. It stank of battlefields and corpses, words as hot as any *khamsin* flowing across her face.

A shocked nod.

'Major Gide?' Raf dragged Eugenie's replacement from his memory. Her face and voice, even her weapons becoming visible to the fragment of his mind still interested in those things. 'Well?'

'She's been arrested.'

A bark of laughter greeted these words.

'By Moncef?'

Sergeant de Loria, who at twenty-seven had killed five men (all but the first in battle) dared a glance at this djinn who used the Emir's name so freely. He was too emaciated, too feral to be human. And yet his elemental fury was hidden behind cheap shades of a kind found in the local market and the sores around his wrists bled lymph.

'Who . . .'

'Lilith, son of,' said Raf. 'Busy failing to make the seven years' anonymity necessary to become like you.' His words were clear and stark, the meaning behind them less so; but then Sergeant de Loria had never met Hani or had her life told as a fairy tale.

'Who arrested Major Gide?' said the figure. 'Answer me . . .'

A kiss of warm steel convinced the sergeant that this really was happening. She stood helpless in front of an apparition which held an automatic to her head. The apparition was naked, shackled and stank of rotting flesh but the gun was a standard-issue Browning and its knuckle was turning white on the trigger.

'Kashif Pasha or the Emir?'

'Kashif Pasha,' the sergeant said, voice sticking in her throat. 'Kashif Pasha arrested Major Gide . . . The Emir is dying. They say he was poisoned.'

'Who by?' Raf demanded.

'It happened at a feast Kashif Pasha gave in Tunis. There was a waiter . . .'

Raf stepped around her sentry box and swung up the road barrier as he went through. Allowance for the faint possibility he might have to exit in a hurry.

'Leave it like that,' he told the sergeant over his shoulder.

Leila de Loria looked from the raised barrier to the Browning she'd just wrenched from her own holster. Then she stared at the buttocks of the naked djinn as it stamped its way up the path, a gun in either hand and rusted chain swinging noisily.

Returning her revolver to its holster, the sergeant shrugged. Her mother was from the Nefzaoua and followed the Ibadite branch of the One True Faith. She knew better than to interfere with the games of princes, madmen and djinn. All the same, she thought she'd better see if she could find Major Gide, arrested or not. This was something the major would want to know about.

Arrested or not? Leila de Loria thought through that bit again and unbuckled her gun for the second time.

'Not,' she decided. 'Make that not . . .'

On his way through the outskirts of Camp Moncef, Raf saw three more of the Emir's bodyguard. Although not one of the girls seemed to notice him. Serving boys stopped to gape, old women made fists against the evil eye or clutched pendants but the guard kept doing whatever it was they did while Raf stamped passed.

It was Moncef's camp and they were Moncef's bodyguard but Eugenie was dead, Major Gide was currently under arrest and their Emir was dying. They all knew the opinion of Kashif Pasha's mother, Lady Maryam, where Eugenie's guard were concerned.

Once Raf passed so close that he saw a jumpsuited girl hold her breath against the stink that clung instead of clothing to his body. All the same, her eyes slid over him and when he was gone she tapped a button transmitter attached to her lapel, muttering what sounded like an evocation.

Up ahead two other jumpsuited guards stopped moving towards Raf and turned to walk away.

'You.' Raf grabbed an elderly falconer by the sleeve and let go when hard eyes turned to face him. The man was old, with small tattoos like crude tears on both cheeks and a neat beard gone completely white, his teeth were so perfect they had to be false. 'Show me the Emir's tent.'

'No,' said the elderly Berber. 'That I will not.' Reaching for a curved knife in his belt, the man held it in front of him in fingers that shook with more than age. All the same, he dropped into a fighting crouch. 'No one can escape death,' he said. 'But I refuse to help you take the Emir.'

'The Emir?'

Raf's sour smile trickled blood from lips so cracked they'd begun to peel and when he whispered there were no words, just breath. Removing his shades for a moment, Raf tried again, pale eyes locking on the man's face; the curved blade that shook in front of his naked belly already forgotten.

'I haven't come for the Emir,' he said. 'I want Kashif Pasha.'

'This could be a trick.'

'It isn't,' said Raf, knowing that really the old man had addressed the question to himself.

Raf would have found Moncef's tent anyway even without help. It was huge, stood right in the centre of the camp and its ropes were made from palm fibre, something ancient and traditional anyway, unlike the nylon guys holding up the military tents in the distance. The tent was old, rotten in places and heavily patched with black goats' hair; rugs were spread round its edge to enable the Emir to circumnavigate his tent without once touching sand or gravel.

'Wait,' said the old man and Raf waited in the shadow of a generator truck. 'Don't move from here.' When the falconer returned it was with rusty bolt cutters which he struggled to use, further lacerating Raf's wrist as he snipped the padlocks fastening the shackles.

'The entrance is round the other side,' said the Berber.

Raf nodded.

'There are soldiers,' the old man added. And when Raf made no reply he sighed. As if he'd always suspected death was stupid. 'Kashif Pasha's soldiers. Two on the door, an officer inside, the small one . . .'

'Major Jalal . . .'

The man shrugged.

'Who else?' demanded Raf and held the old man's gaze. 'The more I know,' he said, 'the fewer I kill. That makes sense, surely . . . ? Lady Maryam?'

The man spat.

'Lady Maryam,' Raf told him firmly, 'was not responsible for the attack at the Domus Aurea.'

'She is Kashif Pasha's mother,' said the old man. As if that was crime enough.

'No one else?'

'Not really,' said the old man, bending to pick up the discarded chain. 'Apart from a *nasrani* television crew . . .'

Chapter Forty-nine

Tuesday 15th March

'So we now know that the kids are unharmed. The reports of their death undoubtedly NR black propaganda. This is Clair duBois for Television5 . . .'

Flanked by Hani and Murad, TV5's most famous reporter was talking direct to camera when Raf spun into the huge tent, leaving two dying soldiers in the dust behind him, windpipes crushed.

One was the corporal who killed Hassan, the other had just gone for a gun.

'Yeah,' said Raf, eyes locked on Major Jalal, 'it's us.' Behind him stood an impossibly beautiful Japanese boy and a fat man with half his head missing. Although when Clair blinked, looked again, those two were gone.

'I've brought you a present.'

Over by the door, Major Jalal continued scrambling for his own weapon. A pearl-handled Colt which had belonged to his father. It was elegant and valuable, came with the original buckle-down holster and was an incredibly stupid choice.

Clair duBois's backup camera was still trying to pull focus when the major finally freed his Colt and the feed went live on a naked man in shades, framed by the tent's doorway, an old-fashioned H&K in one hand and a Browning automatic in the other.

Backlit by daylight/filmed without lights from shade. One of the world's worst options.

'Drop your toy.' The words were in French, the whisper dry as dust. A change of angle caught the apparition's gun come up. 'One chance,' it said. 'More than you ever gave Hassan.'

Despite herself, or maybe because Clair duBois was who she was, she glanced at her notebook and made two minor adjustments for sound. One for volume, the other an echo on the apparition's voice, too slight to be noticed by anyone not in the business.

'Do as he says . . .' The command was soft, sickly sibilant, the words not much louder than those Raf had used; but it carried total authority, a complete awareness of the futility of the situation. 'That's an order.'

And there it might have finished, with Raf turning to the Emir and Major Jalal returning his Colt to its holster if only Kashif Pasha hadn't stepped forward. 'This is the assassin,' he told his father, voice furious. To his *aide-de-camp*, he said nothing, just nodded.

Major Jalal raised his gun, a young girl who was meant to be dead howled out a warning and Raf's head flicked sideways.

The major died on camera. Wounds pixilated in some countries, not shown at all in England, Sweden and Korea and featured widely everywhere else. Looped, in one case, into ultra slow-motion that let the major's brains crawl like sticky rice after Raf's casually fired slug, flowering into a fat cherry blossom that tumbled apart in a mass of bone, jelly and blood. So close to chaos in appearance and so utterly removed in reality.

Clair duBois screamed.

As genuine a response as she'd ever made and one, her unkinder critics later claimed, that went a long way towards explaining the clean sweep she made of most of the coming year's press awards.

As Clair watched, the naked apparition's searching eyes finally found the two children, still stood behind her.

'You,' it said to the boy, 'are not me.' Then it turned to the girl who gripped Murad's hand, her knuckles white with tension. *'I thought you were dead.'*

Picking up a mic, Clair duBois thrust it towards Raf.

'Who are you?' The mic was totally unnecessary, given the TV5 camera was already wired for sound but it made for a great image. Elegant reporter in light-weight silk suit (black obviously, with Clair duBois it was always black), interviewing a naked, stinking man in shades, carrying a still-smoking gun. 'Tell me,' she insisted. 'The world wants to know.'

'Ashraf al-Mansur,' said Raf. 'Guardian to Lady Hana and half-brother to Murad.' He stared at Kashif. 'Also to him.'

'I refuse to believe it,' said the pasha, 'without proof.'

Raf shrugged. 'What you believe is unimportant,' he said, adjusting the H&K so its first burst would take out several lengths of Kashif's intestines. 'I'm arresting you for murder.'

'I don't think so.' Kashif's voice was silky. 'Given they're obviously still here.' He nodded dismissively towards Hani and Murad. 'Their death was a lie. I wouldn't be surprised if you spread the rumour yourself.'

Nothing happened. It's a lie.

Away, to one side of the huge tent, Zara shivered and stepped back until she was pressed against an outer wall, which was still too close.

Really, nothing happened.

Shortly after Zara mentioned her uncle to her nanny, the man disappeared. There'd been more shouting, twenty-four hours of plate throwing by her mother. Zara had gone into Al Qahirah hospital for her *operation* a few days later, delivered personally by Madame Rahina while her father was on business in Sicily. The Monday following, when Zara got home was the only time she ever saw her mother with a black eye.

'I'm not talking about Murad or Hani,' said Raf. 'If you'd hurt either in any way you'd already be dead . . .' So intent was Raf on Kashif Pasha that he missed Hani's wide-eyed shock; missed too a softening in Zara's expression.

'You had a sixteen-year-old boy tortured,' Raf said flatly. 'And then gave the order for his death.'

'He was an NR terrorist,' Kashif Pasha announced to the camera. Neither of them wanted TV5 there. Neither could afford to be the one to tell Clair duBois to get out. 'Who tried to assassinate my father.'

'Crap,' said Raf. 'By the time your *aide de-camp* had finished Hassan would have signed anything.' He scowled at the body on the tent floor for as long as it took for the camera to follow his gaze. 'How do I know? Because *I* was the waiter. Acting for Eugenie de la Croix.'

Clair duBois turned so fast that the tiny Aeriospecialle camsat locked on her face went out of focus, something the manufacturers claimed was impossible.

'The missing waiter I can understand,' said Clair duBois, 'but how can Your Excellency talk of charging Kashif Pasha with murdering the Emir, when His Highness is not dead?' Even to Clair, her voice sounded childish.

'If not dead,' said Raf, 'then dying.' Wrapped in his borrowed kaftan and with his face sticky from analgesic barrier cream, Raf looked more ghoul-like than ever. 'Ask him.'

'That depends,' said Moncef, 'on your definition of *dead* and *emir*.'

Clair duBois sighed. Kashif was under guard courtesy of one very angry Major Gide, Murad was introducing Hani to the racing camels and Clair had just been handed the opportunity of a lifetime.

Since this was, so far as Clair knew, the only interview Emir Moncef had ever given she was sure TV5 would forgive her for agreeing to record the interview rather than have it go out live. As for handing over copy approval, they gave that to half-bit actors with only a fraction of the charisma.

'I'm not sure I understand,' she said to Raf. 'His Highness has Asiatic flu. I've talked to his doctor.' This last was only half true. She'd talked, briefly, to a Soviet nurse who'd pocketed a 1000F note with rather too much ease before confirming that a long-lasting flu variant was indeed the most likely possibility.

'Ask,' Raf told her.

She swallowed. 'Your Highness . . .'

The only way Clair duBois could force herself to ask was to pretend someone outside her did the asking. The same way that many years before, as a sixteen-year-old, she'd turned up on the doorstep of a haunted-looking soap actress and forced herself to ask the woman about a miscarriage, vomiting in a flowerbed the moment the actress slammed the door in her face, having first called Clair every name under the sun. All the confirmation her editor had needed.

'You have a question for me?' Moncef's voice dragged Clair back from her memories and shrivelled the snakes knotting inside her stomach. The very fact Emir Moncef prompted her meant he intended to answer.

Briefly the woman toyed with asking whether he had flu. What Major Gide, as his doctor, had diagnosed. How he was feeling . . . But then she asked the single best question of her career.

'Are you dying?'

'It's probably safe to say,' said the man, his voice amused, 'that we're all dying . . .' He sat up straighter in his bed, rug still tight around him and spoke direct to his interviewer rather than the camera, his hooded eyes never leaving her face. 'Except, of course, those already dead. And those who are immortal.'

And then he smiled that smile seen in stills around the world. The one that was either ineffably wise or completely insane. Verdicts differed, with Berlin willing to consider the first and Paris and Washington definite that it was the last.

'Is that your only question?'

If the Emir found it odd to be answering questions while blood glazed like sugar icing on a carpet he'd refused to allow be removed, then Moncef didn't let it show, but then . . .

Clair duBois shrugged, mostly inside her head. Who knew what the Emir found odd?

'Ask if he's immortal . . .'

Jumping, Clair looked round. It took her a moment to realise that Antoine, her back-up cameraman had activated his throat mic and was hissing the suggestion through her Sony earbead.

She asked it.

'No,' said the Emir, 'not since I ate the mushrooms.'

Chapter Fifty

Thursday 17th March

Bells rang from the twin towers of St Vincent de Paul, that Gothic monstrosity with all its pews removed and a Persian carpet covering the altar. Flags hung from office windows or whipped in the slipstream of car aerials. Drifting on the wind came the stink of cordite, bastard cousin to the endless firecrackers let off all morning, if too close to gunfire for the peace of everyone.

Martial law had been lifted, the act signed by Ashraf Pasha, newly created heir to the Emir. He'd signed the edict on behalf of his father, a man now too weak to hold a pen, even to write his own signature.

The return to normal law came the day after Raf had questioned his half-brother in the presence of their father. This took place in the al Andalus-inspired HQ of Dar el Bey, overlooking Place du Gouvernement.

Raf sat at a desk with Kashif on the other side, the Emir had a motorized wheelchair and only Major Gide stood.

It was a very polite questioning. There wasn't a blowtorch in sight and no one in the room, from the Emir to the major even suggested tying anyone else to a table.

'The snake,' Raf said to Kashif. 'That was your first mistake. A simple enquiry could have revealed that all venomous snakes at Tunis Zoo have their poison sacs removed. Only Major Jalal couldn't risk asking that question, could he? So you made an assumption, the Emir got bitten and Ifriqiya got its very own miracle . . .'

'I know nothing about a snake.'

'Of course you don't. How about the death of two guards,

326

bribed or blackmailed into releasing the snake in the Emir's tent . . . ?'

'I know nothing about any guards.'

'They got shot,' said Raf, 'at the banquet you threw for your father. Remember? The one where Eugenie died.'

Kashif was blaming it all on his dead *aide-de-camp*. In fact, he was horrified to discover some of the things Major Jalal had done in his name.

'I take it,' said the Emir, 'that you have proof for this accusation against your brother?' His words were thin and took longer to say than they should, but there was amusement in them and something close to admiration lit his lined and leathery face.

'If Kashif is my brother . . .'

Moncef looked at him then. 'Meaning?'

'I just wondered.'

'You are Ashraf al-Mansur,' said Moncef, almost firmly. 'And I am Emir of Tunis. Your mother was the love of my life.' Sad eyes swept the small office, barely noticing Kashif as they passed over Raf, a selection of police files in front of him. One of which contained the results on DNA testing that Raf had yet to mention to anyone.

When the Emir's gaze finally alighted it was on the young girl half perched on an office chair and the boy who gripped her hand, rather tightly. 'You have your responsibilities and I have mine.'

'Obviously,' said Raf. And when the Emir smiled, Raf was waiting with the only question that really mattered. 'What do you want done with Kashif Pasha?'

'And if I say kill him . . .'

'Then he dies,' said Raf and took a gun from its holster under his arm. Placing it on the desk at which he sat.

'If I say let him go . . . Which is what I'm minded to say?'

Raf paused, all too aware that Hani was watching him, just as Murad watched the Emir, both holding their breath.

'If you say let him go,' said Raf, 'then that's what happens. But it places this family above the law. And gives victory to

everyone who thinks Ifriqiya is corrupt beyond redemption.'
He added the second consequence as an afterthought. Not quite
realising how much weight it would carry with the Emir.

'So what would you suggest?'

'Let him stand trial . . .'

The Emir nodded and struggled with the control pad of
his wheel chair. Waving Murad away, Emir Moncef rolled
slowly towards the door and stopped, one hand reaching for
the doorknob, his other edging the chair into reverse. 'You're
right about everything,' he told Raf in a voice little more than
a whisper, 'except for Alex and Nicolai. The decision to have
them shot was mine. My only regret is not warning Eugenie, but
then,' Moncef shrugged, 'she'd only have tried to stop me.'

Chapter Fifty-one

Thursday 17th March

Eduardo sat on the edge of a metal table swinging his feet. Every time his shoe scuffed the floor it produced that unmistakable mouse-like squeak of leather against ceramic.

A noise that was driving everybody else in the room insane. And the really great part was that none of them could do a thing about it. He was the most senior officer present at the briefing, a thought so bizarre that Eduardo shut his eyes just to savour it.

'I'm sorry, boss.' Alexandre looked worried. Under the misapprehension his question had been stupid enough to drive the Chief to anger.

'No,' said Eduardo, 'it's a good point. Just not one I can answer.'

This truth elicited a frown from a thickset sergeant at the back. A man with a bald patch, common enough, and a Kashif-like moustache, which now made him something of a rarity in the Tunis PD. It was truly staggering the number of officers who'd decided in the last twenty-four hours to shave off their moustaches, reshape them or else begin to grow a beard.

'Got a problem?' Eduardo asked the man.

'Yeah,' a bull neck raised an even heavier chin. 'With all due respect, sir, I don't see how a case involving a dead pastry chef can be so secret that the master file has to be shredded in front of two witnesses.'

It was obvious from his tone that respect was the last thing the sergeant felt for the small *morisco* in the leather coat sat on the old Chief's table.

'I can understand that,' said Eduardo, 'to you it looks like a simple open-and-shut murder, hardly worth bothering about.

To me it had all the marks of a *cause célèbre* from which Ifriqiya needs to be protected. Maybe that's why I'm kicking my heels up here and you're kicking yours at the back.'

Several officers smiled and Eduardo resisted the temptation to take a brief bow. He was in the operations room; a large space of cheap desks and dirty grey chairs, wall charts, holiday rotas and a small kitchen, which might have been slightly too grand a name to describe a corner partitioned off with hessian boards and containing a sink, two ancient kettles and a cheap microwave.

Eduardo had called his officers together to make an announcement and the announcement was simple, the Maison Hafsid case was closed and, for internal security reasons, the files would be shredded and all evidence sealed in sterile bags and remain so for the next hundred years. The reason was actually very simple but Eduardo had explained this only to Rose.

She'd been lying there on a big double bed in their room at the Dar Ben Abdallah. And as she'd rolled over, a frown on her face, Eduardo had smiled as a breast popped out of her dressing-gown and he'd almost forgotten what he intended to say, the way he did some mornings when he looked over the foot of the bed and saw Rose, with her back to him in the early dawn, wearing nothing but a g-string and black tights.

'So what happened to cousin Ahmed?' She'd read the files and knew the names.

'There was no cousin.'

'So who did the *mubahith* arrest?'

'No one,' said Eduardo with a satisfied smile. 'That's the whole point. No one vanished in police custody. I've had every file checked. Even the ones that don't exist.'

'So who killed Isabeau's brother?'

'I think that's got to remain a secret,' said Eduardo. It seemed odd to be making those kind of decisions but no one else was available and someone had to . . . Well, Eduardo assumed that was true. His Excellency couldn't have dragged him from El Isk just to unravel who did what, that would be far too simple.

There was unquestionably more to the equation than could at first be seen.

It had taken Eduardo a while to work out the unseen integer but he'd got it the moment he saw the knife supposedly used for the murder. Once, long before, Eduardo had worked in a kitchen, although there was nothing very special about this, everyone worked a kitchen at some time in their lives. At least, everyone Eduardo ever knew.

The first rule of kitchen culture was that no one, repeat no one, touched anyone else's knives. Spit in their face, mock them and, if you must, insult their football team, that was fine, but no one messed with another person's steel.

Knives were sacred. *Touch my arse before you touch my knife. Mess with my arse and die* . . . Eduardo knew the sayings. Three months grilling *merguez* in a working-men's café in Karmous had been enough to guarantee that.

So what was anyone meant to think when presented with a blade that was blunt, bent at the tip and stained? Well, Eduardo couldn't actually say what anyone else might think. To him, however, it suggested no one really owned that knife. And if no one owned it . . .

The more Eduardo thought about it the more he was convinced he was right.

Notes said the mysteriously arrested Ahmed owned the knife when it was obvious that no one owned it or it wouldn't have been such a mess. Someone was lying. Actually, he told Rose, several people were lying.

She'd been dressing when he said this. After she'd undressed at his insistence and then gone to take a shower while he lay in bed getting back his breath, Eduardo had returned to his thoughts.

They ate breakfast in a café. Rose choosing coffee and croissant and Eduardo eating rough flatbread cooked on a clay griddle by a middle-aged woman who sat on a stool by the door. With the unleavened bead he ate slivers of some meat that obviously wasn't pork, with a helping of menakher dates, as befitted a man making the most of being in a different country.

Then he left Rose to her shopping and jumped a cab to the Police HQ without bothering to wait for his official car. A decision made easier by his discovery, right at the start, that naming the Police HQ as his destination was enough to ensure that no driver ever asked him to pay the fare. Their surprise on the few occasions he did was worth double the handful of change his journey actually cost.

So now he was sat on a table in the operations room, trying to explain without really doing so that there was no murderer; at least not one who could be arrested by the police. Eduardo knew exactly who killed Pascal Boulart and he was certain (as certain as he ever was about anything), that His Excellency knew too. Why else would he have brought in Eduardo but to tidy up such loose ends?

Chapter Fifty-two

Saturday 19th March

Isabeau checked her rail ticket and recounted the notes. No writing appeared anywhere on the envelope and she was willing to bet there'd be no fingerprints either. In her memory, she had it that the small man with the black coat kept his gloves on throughout his entire visit.

She was bathed and dressed, stood on the platform of Gare de Tunis beside a cardboard suitcase that looked like leather until one got close. She wore new shoes and black Levis, a shirt and a shawl as befitted the cooler weather. Her hair was covered in a waterfall of blue silk; not quite a *hijab*, not exactly a scarf; something elegantly in between. And though Gare de Tunis was less than a klick south of St Vincent de Paul and the air was clear enough for sound to travel, Isabeau ignored the bells. Despite the small cross she wore, politics not religion had been her life. All seventeen years of it.

The *MediTerre* ticket in her pocket was an open one. A month's rail travel anywhere in North Africa and Southern Europe. With the ticket came a student ID, an Ifriqiyan passport and glowing references from Café Antonio. So far as Isabeau could see all of these looked real: except they couldn't be, for a start she'd never passed her baccalaureat and no university would take her.

Isabeau had no illusions about what was happening. She was being bought off, which was, she realised, preferable to being jailed or killed. The small man who'd limped into her life with a simple telephone call had more or less said as much.

All he wanted was a meeting. It seemed not to have occurred to him that Isabeau might refuse and it was only afterwards, once she'd meekly agreed, that Isabeau realised it had never occurred to her either. And no, he didn't need an address.

He seemed scarily knowledgeable on most aspects of her life.

Four o'clock would do. He expected her to meet him in the hallway and to let him in. She would recognise him by . . . His voice had paused at that point. She would recognise him by a copy of that afternoon's *Il Giornale di Tunisi*, which he would carry under his left arm, folded in three.

And so a small man limped up the tired steps to her apartment block, his black leather coat bigger than it should be, a fedora pushed down over his eyes. The paper he held had a black border round the whole of the front page and was folded to reveal a headline:

L'emiro morto . . .

And below the news a picture of someone Isabeau had been telling herself for at least a day she didn't recognise. Only half of his face was showing because of the way Eduardo had the paper folded, but it was that double worry line like a knife flick which gave him away, where the top of his nose met his eyebrows. They'd thought Ashraf Pasha was *mubahith*. An infiltrator. And then Domus Aurea happened.

'Mademoiselle Isabeau Boulart?'

Respectably dressed in a blue jersey and denim skirt, sneakers without socks. Her lack of make-up made her seem younger than he expected, but then she was younger. All the same, Eduardo wondered if that look was intentional.

'I'm . . .' Eduardo paused, thought about it. 'You don't really need to know my name,' he said and glanced round the entrance hall. 'Where's the lift?'

Isabeau smiled. 'We have stairs,' she said. Whoever the man was, he lived somewhere other than Tunis. The only places Isabeau knew with their own lifts were big hotels and those huge stores in Nouvelle Ville, the ones with canvas awnings over street-front windows and French names.

'Show the way then.'

She looked at him and he stared back, indicating the stairs

with a slight wave of his hand; nothing impolite, just impatient like a man unused to being kept waiting.

'After you,' he said.

Isabeau walked ahead, all five flights, and at the second she stopped worrying about him staring at her bottom and concentrated on climbing, each turn of the stairs widening the gap between them. By the time she reached the third floor's half landing Isabeau was a whole quarter turn ahead and he'd lost sight of her anyway.

'Can I get you anything?' Isabeau asked when Eduardo reached the door she'd left open.

'Water,' he said. And then said nothing for a whole five minutes.

On the street below, workmen were busy stringing green and red bunting from one lamp-post to another and adjusting crowd barriers under the bored gaze of traffic policemen. One of the many street parties would be held there. Enthusiasm fuelled by Ashraf Pasha's announcement that all the food would be free. *Bread and circuses.* Eduardo was still trying to work out exactly when His Excellency meant.

'You own this?'

'I rent it from the city,' Isabeau said. 'My brother also used to live here.'

'You have a bedroom?'

'Obviously.'

'Show me,' Eduardo said.

The sex was perfunctory, almost matter-of-fact. And Eduardo thanked her when it was done. Not daring to show her contempt, Isabeau shrugged. Sat up from where she'd been tipped backwards onto her bed and adjusted her denim skirt, smoothing it down over her legs and his smell. She'd known what was coming. Expected it.

For his part, he hadn't bothered to use a condom or remove her shoes.

'Now what?' Isabeau asked.

'We talk . . .' Zipping his flies, Eduardo reached for his

notebook and tapped it to make it open. 'I know you killed Pascal. That's not the issue.'

Eduardo paused, giving the girl an opportunity to deny it but she just looked at him.

'You want to tell me why it happened?'

Isabeau shook her head. 'You don't want to know.'

'But the others knew? The rest of your group . . . ?'

She spread her hands, neither denying nor agreeing.

'And so when you killed Pascal they covered for you,' Eduardo said. 'In itself, that is significant. The way I see it.' He was proud of that phrase. 'You stabbed your brother in the kitchen and had someone help you drag his body up to the alley . . . All those clean stairs,' Eduardo explained. 'But first you swapped knives. Probably put your own through the industrial washer.'

Isabeau smiled.

'So what did you do with the real one?'

'There was no real knife,' said Isabeau. 'And he died in the corridor outside the chill room. The stab wounds came later. Someone else did those.'

'So how did you kill him?'

'With a leg of lamb,' she said flatly.

Eduardo looked at her.

'It was frozen.'

'Ah . . .' Eduardo thought about the coroner's report. A perfunctory half page with a throw-away line noting the victim had obviously smashed his skull on the cobbles of the alley when falling. 'And what happened to the leg of lamb?' asked Eduardo.

'We ate it. One night when a shift was finished. Me, the others, even that Egyptian waiter, the one who looked so very much like . . .'

Eduardo held up his hand, consulted his notebook. 'I believe the waiter's dead,' he said.

Isabeau nodded. 'A bit like my brother.'

As she waited for her *turbani* at Gare de Tunis, the first

Fez-Iskandryia express to stop there in thirty years and a sign of the West's sudden faith in the new regime, Isabeau told herself to be realistic. Everything in life had a price, including freedom. And if two perfunctory bouts of unwilling sex with a stranger were it, then there were worse ways to stay out of jail. As well as worse people to have such sex with, much worse.

When he was done questioning, Eduardo had tipped Isabeau onto her back again, pushed up her skirt until it reached her hips and, almost apologetically, grabbed the sides of her new knickers and pulled those down. Unzipping, he'd given himself a few jerks to strengthen his resolve and pushed into her, the toes of his shoes sliding on the tiles . . .

'I'm pregnant,' Isabeau said, her words enough to startle Eduardo into stopping mid-stroke. 'Did you know that?'

For a second he almost shook his head but the temptation to be seen to know everything was too great, so he nodded instead. All the same, he retreated to the edge of her bed and tucked himself inside his trousers. A manoeuvre made simple by the fact he never wore underwear. Too much extra washing.

'What do you intend to do about it?'

'About what?'

'The baby?'

'I don't know,' Isabeau said, bending forward to retrieve her knickers. 'What do you suggest?'

'I suggest a holiday.' Dipping his hand inside his coat, Eduardo produced a envelope. 'I was going to give you this when I went,' he said, looking shame faced. It contained a fat and tattered wad of Ottoman dollars. Almost no one used Ottoman dollars anymore, except in the suqs and most of those could manage credit cards. Only the very old still insisted on keeping their lives in boxes under the bed.

'Call it severance pay from Maison Hafsid.'

At least they were high denomination notes. Higher than Isabeau had seen before and in one case higher than she knew existed. To this man though, used as he must be to such things, they were probably small change.

'And this,' said Eduardo, 'is also for you.' As the exchange rate stood, the second, far smaller wad of US dollars was worth about twice all the other notes put together. On the black market the dollars were worth maybe five times that.

'You want me to leave,' said Isabeau. Although it wasn't until later that she realised she was only putting into words what she already knew.

'Wait, Madame DuPuis . . . You have to wait.'

A railway porter glanced round and saw a young police lieutenant in brand new uniform stride towards a woman about to clamber through the door of a 2nd class carriage. Alexandre scowled at the porter and the elderly man decided he had business elsewhere.

'Madame Isabeau?'

Isabeau nodded. No one had ever called her *madame* before. And DuPuis definitely wasn't her surname.

'These are for you,' Alexandre said as he handed her an envelope. 'The Chief told me to deliver them.' Jagged as a tidal pull between rocks, an undercurrent to the young man's politeness suggested he was less than happy to be hand-delivering notes on the morning the old Emir was buried.

'Thank you.' Isabeau flashed her sweetest smile and watched Alexandre melt. It wasn't their surliness or even the fact they often seemed to smell that put Isabeau off men, it was the fact they could be so childish, so unbelievably easily led.

'Oh,' said Alexandre, 'and I'm sorry . . .'

Isabeau raised her eyebrows.

'About . . .' He shuffled his feet, apparently unable to get beyond that word. 'About your husband. It was a messy campaign. A just one, obviously, but messy and I'm glad it's over.' He clicked his heels and gave her a salute, the smartness of which was utterly at odds with the state of his fingernails, which were bitten to the quick.

Once sat, with her case pushed into the space behind her seat and a capuchin from a cart that had passed by on the platform outside, Isabeau ripped the flap on her new envelope, then glanced round. The carriage was almost empty despite this being the first *turbani de luxe* to run for years. Outside, the concourse was crowded, but with people arriving not departing. *Nasrani* tourists, Nefzaoua up from Kebili to visit recently remembered family, farmers from the High Tell, pickpockets. Few wanted to leave a city when so much was about to happen.

Twenty-four hours of mourning for the old Emir and then seven days of celebration for the new. Isabeau supposed that made sense if she didn't think about it too hard.

Shaking out her envelope's contents, she saw two rings slide out and clatter across the table, along with something on a dull-metal chain. The small, official-looking booklet which followed landed without a sound and Isabeau wouldn't have known the envelope contained a letter of condolence if habit hadn't made her check inside.

It seemed her husband had died in a police operation, somewhere unspecified, south of Garaa Tebourt while rescuing his superior officer. Isabeau liked that touch. As if any man she married wouldn't frag all the officers and NCOs first opportunity he got, then head off down some wadi for Tripoletana. As if she'd marry any man . . .

They were returning his ring, his police tags and a photograph they'd found in his wallet of her wedding day. The face was Isabeau's although the body belonged to someone else; someone marginally thinner than she'd ever been with less full breasts. The man could have been anyone.

Isabeau was impressed to see they'd had a modern ceremony. She wore white and her husband was in uniform, their priest had a simple jellaba, his beard recently barbered and not at all wild. The room in which they stood was panelled in dark oak and had a photograph of the old Emir on the wall behind. It might have been more useful if someone had thought to write the exact location on the back.

The official-looking leaflet was a pension book made out to Madame DuPuis. At the bottom of the first page a space had been left blank for her signature. A footnote told her she could collect money monthly from any branch of the Imperial

Ottoman Bank or arrange to have her widow's pension paid direct by filling in a form on the last page.

As for the letter, this offered Isabeau the condolences of the state, commiserated with her over all she'd lost and hoped that her future from henceforth would be happier. It was signed with an illegible scribble, although the first letter looked like an A . . .

Chapter Fifty-three

Saturday 26th March

'Well,' said Raf, breath jagged and a grin on his face.

'Well what?'

Outside Zara's bedroom window, crowds were already gathering beyond the gates of the Bardo and Raf could hear the growl of early traffic and clattering as impromptu market stalls were erected.

The police would be along later to take them down but trade would continue all day, stalls going up as soon as the old ones were broken down. Food sellers, hawkers of rice-paper rose petals and purveyors of cheap plastic flags, Raf had even seen his face on the side of a balloon.

The woman lying beside him had already made her opinion plain on all of that. As indeed she had on many other things. It had been the kind of discussion that, in later years, would raise smiles and get described, only half ironically, as full and frank. At the moment they both still felt slightly vulnerable.

'Come on then,' Zara demanded. '*Well what?*'

'Oh, I don't know . . .' Raf wrapped one arm round Zara's shoulders and pulled her on top of him. 'How about, *Well, what do you plan to do with your day?*'

She laughed, kissed him back.

So Raf slid down slightly on the bed and took Zara's nipple in his mouth, sucking comfort from her breast. She watched him as he did so, seeing only the top of his head and feeling his uncertainty.

'Are you all right?'

When Raf didn't answer, Zara stayed where she was and closed her eyes. They had another hour before they needed to leave and if that wasn't long enough then the wretched ceremony could wait.

Last night had been difficult. Difficult and different. Zara so nervous her whole body shook. And Raf . . . ? She took him to her room, something she'd done with no other man and stripped to her thong in front of him, only losing her nerve at the last minute. Having sent him to the bathroom, she killed the light and hid under the covers.

Except that when he came back, all Raf seemed to want to do was lie in the darkness and let the moment wash over him. Something impossible for Zara.

'*This is not fair,*' she'd said suddenly.

And thinking he knew what Zara meant, Raf nodded agreement and in that second's movement shut down his night vision until everything in her room became outlines and shadow.

'It is now.'

'No, I mean *this.*'

And he knew then that Zara meant their lying in the dark, so much unspoken between them.

'There's something I need to tell you . . .' Raf said tentatively.

'Let me guess,' she said. 'I'm not the first. In fact you've fucked your way through an entire phone book of my friends. You have three children, well, that you know about . . . You're only after my millions . . .'

'This is serious,' said Raf.

'So was I,' Zara answered. And pulled Raf to her and kissed him as her hand slid under his rib cage and then both her hands locked behind his back, so that Raf's full weight rested on her trapped arm.

She felt him go hard.

'You're naked,' said Raf, the fingers of his right hand tracing the crease of her buttocks, just to make sure he hadn't got that wrong.

He hadn't known, Zara realised. She'd been safely tucked under a quilt by the time he returned to the room.

There'd been one night, months before, when she'd talked

and he'd listened, although she couldn't remember it and he could; but then, if Raf was to be believed, he remembered everything, which was maybe not a good place to be.

'It's important,' said Raf, holding her face between his hands. 'And it concerns who I am. What I am . . .'

'You're you,' said Zara. 'That's enough.'

'No,' said Raf sadly, 'it isn't. It's not anything like enough.'

Zara wanted to know why, so Raf told her. Or rather he didn't. He told her a fairy story instead. 'Once,' said Raf, his fingers caressing the side of her face, 'there was a son of Lilith . . .'

Raf took it as read that Zara knew Lilith's story. Adam's first wife, mother to vampyres and djinn. A woman expelled from Eden for fucking the snake.

'He was older than he looked because, although his days were as your days, his nights were often longer, one of them so long that fir trees grew and houses were built while he slept. Someone who loved him grew old and stopped loving him, seeing her own life and increasing age reflected in the puzzlement in his eyes every time he woke from the cold sleep . . .'

If Zara thought it was odd that Raf told her a folktale she kept this thought to herself. Remembering stories Hani had told her. Small girl's stories. Of the kind easily dismissed.

'He slept the cold sleep because that was the easiest way not to die. Until one day he awoke and Lilith had died and her friends had forgotten him or no longer cared if he escaped. So he did what sons of Lilith do, moved to a strange country to live undetected as a human for seven years. For if a vampyre or djinn can live undetected for seven years he will become as human.'

'So Hani told me,' said Zara.

'She did?'

'She's told everybody,' Zara said. 'It's in a book, the original story. About how a son of Lilith can become as human. But the children will be born sons of Lilith.'

'Sons of Lilith, daughters of Lilith,' said Raf. 'In my case it's called germ line manipulation. Whatever I am my children will become.'

'And what are you?'

Raf thought about it. 'I'm not sure,' he said finally. 'I get voices. I see in the dark. There are three extra ribs on either side of my rib cage. My eyes hurt in the daylight. My memory is too distressingly perfect for my mind to manage . . .'

'All of this is your mother's responsibility?'

'Or Emir Moncef's,' said Raf, 'but it gets messier.' He felt the girl go still and shifted gently away from her, giving Zara space. 'I've opened the bags . . . Secret files,' he added, when he realised she didn't quite understand. 'It's like reading the technical specifications for a new type of car. One that might not work.'

'What's the worst?'

'Immortality. Or if not immortality, then longevity. How long I don't know but longer than is now normal.'

'You knew this when you refused to marry me?'

'Some of it,' said Raf. He stopped himself. 'More than some,' he said but the anger was directed at himself. 'What I wasn't told as a child I overheard. It's relatively easy to code for heightened hearing. Less easy to understand the implications if one's own hearing is normal and the subject is three rooms away.'

'I'm sorry,' Zara said. Her hand moved up to touch his face and came away wet. She believed him implicitly.

'So am I,' said Raf.

Later, when he hung over her in the darkness, both of them drunk with longing, Raf bent forward and kissed Zara lightly on the forehead. There was something else he hadn't mentioned. If he understood it right, then immortality was sexually transmitted; the act of being pregnant infected both mother and embryo.

The second time they made love began slow and ended up hard and fast. It started with Zara swinging herself on top of Raf and straddling his hips, her face only inches from his. Outside their window, the city was expectant for what would come next day. Guards stood at the gates of the Bardo and patrolled the streets around the palace complex. Major Gide and Raf having agreed this as a matter of protocol only. Done because it was expected.

'Remember the boat?' Zara said.

As if he could forget. Water so blue it was almost purple. The scent of rosemary and thyme carried on a warm wind across a bay. And then the return trip. Hani safely asleep and Zara bringing him a beer as he sulked outside and time and the ocean slid past.

'What boat?' Raf demanded.

Leaning forward, Zara put her mouth over his and bit, hard enough to draw blood. 'That boat,' she said.

They kissed and, slowly and rather clumsily, Zara reached down to position Raf against her. To Zara he was a shadow against white sheets, a watchful silent silhouette; for Raf she was lit clear as daylight . . . He could see her mouth twisting, eyes open and fixed on nothing, her breasts swaying forward with each rock of her hips, impossibly beautiful.

Reaching up with open hands, Raf felt warm flesh overflow his fingers and tried not to be offended when Zara absent-mindedly lifted his hands away and went back to her rocking. After she'd ridden him in silence long enough for Raf to fade out his vision and lose himself in the rhythm, Zara took his hand and positioned it on her abdomen so that Raf's thumb reached between swollen lips.

'There,' she said, 'keep it there.' And went back to her darkness and a burst of half cries and swallowed words. There was no sharing this time. And angry was the only way to describe the abruptness with which Zara shuddered to a halt, her hand still holding his own hard against her smooth mons.

Smooth, because she lacked all body hair.

Zara had given him the list once. One night in another palace; the time she'd cried herself to sleep and woken to swallow him as she knelt on white marble tiles in the middle of a sunlit floor, three days before he prosecuted her father for murder. A fact neither one had ever mentioned. The list was relatively short and went no body hair, no labia minor or hood or tip to her clitoris . . . But, as she'd pointed out, a full pharonic would have been infinitely worse.

According to a doctor in New York (the one Zara saw at

seventeen, the week after she arrived at Columbia), a rewarding sex life was perfectly possible. It might just take more effort than for some other women. And she stood, the doctor said, a better chance than many of those whose scar tissue was mental rather than physical.

The tiny vibrator the woman gave Zara went unused. Ditto a collection of glass dilators from small to medium. Zara found one article on female genital mutilation, attended one meeting at which she said nothing and then went back to writing law essays. And lying in the darkness as she said this, that time in El Iskandryia, Raf had been unable to work out from the flatness of Zara's voice if she regarded this as common sense or cowardice . . .

'My turn.' Raf rolled the two of them over, so Zara lay underneath and he was between her legs. Widening her knees, Raf withdrew until the tightness at the entrance to her sex was about to release him, only to slam back, watching Zara's chin go up in shock or surrender.

Her hands rose and fell, arms crooked at the elbow as fingers fluttered bat-like in darkness. Tied to some plea forever unsaid. On her breath were white wine, hashish and the faintest trace of capers. Tastes that Raf took from her lips. And then her legs locked over his and her hips began to grind against him.

They came together with that blinding luck those new to each other sometimes get and slept, still locked in each other's arms.

Chapter Fifty-four

Saturday 26th March

'Take a guess,' said Hani, nudging Murad Pasha and nodding to where Zara and Raf stood beside a wall, holding hands. A half dozen of Major Gide's hand-picked guards stood impassive against the opposite wall of the decorated alcove, carefully not noticing. 'Go on, guess what they've been doing . . .'

Murad blushed.

'How do I look?' said Hani. She twirled on marble tiles, her silk dress spinning out like the cloak of a dervish. The dress was meant to go with knee-length socks but Hani had refused. Not just refused but refused totally. Sitting naked and dripping on the edge of her bath, unwilling even to let Donna dry her until the old woman agreed that white socks were out.

And Donna, still furious at being dragged from El Iskandryia to Tunis, had threatened to fetch Khartoum but even that failed to move Hani. In the end they settled on pop socks rather than the black tights Hani had wanted.

'How do you look?' Murad considered the question. She was dressed in white silk. Around her neck was a single row of black pearls, fastened at the back with a clasp made from jade and gold. Her ears were now properly pierced and a tiny drop-pearl hung from each lobe. On her feet were silver pumps.

'Anachronistic,' he said finally.

Hani punched him.

Not hard. Just enough to deaden his arm.

'The correct answer,' she said, 'is like a princess.'

They were waiting near the entrance to a salon de comeras, hidden from the crowd by an elegant carved screen. Admission to the ceremony was by order of precedence and some people,

347

mostly *nasrani* lucky to be there at all, had been sitting for over an hour as more upscale arrivals filed in to be shown their places.

It had given the new Emir great pleasure to make sure that the Marquis de St Cloud was one of those forced to wait in the cheap seats. Sat much closer to the front, looking slightly bemused, were Micki Vanhoffer and Carl Senior, dressed for what could only be a night in Las Vegas.

Outside, Rue Jardin Bardo was lined ten deep with people waiting for the Emir's Bugatti coupé Napoleon to sweep past, only to be hidden on arrival by veils of silk as it disgorged its occupants, a colonel from the engineers, his young wife and their two children. Decoys insisted upon by Major Gide, who'd gratefully accepted the new Emir's suggestion that she remain his head of security.

The actual players in the spectacle about to unfold in front of TV5, C3N and one other, randomly selected, camera crew had been the first to arrive, spirited into the salon via a back route.

'You ready?' Raf asked Zara.

She nodded. Not entirely convincingly.

Outside in the audience were Hamzah Effendi, Madame Rahina and the brother she'd tracked down to a squat on the edge of Karmous, half-brother really. Hamzah's bastard. Once a factory and later an illegal club, he'd sound-proofed his squat with cardboard and spraygunned that gun-metal grey. The floor had been earth, friable and damp but he'd doped it with liquid plastic, tipping the can straight onto the ground.

'What are you thinking?'

'About Avatar. You know, back when he was a kid, was it right to take him home with me – or was I just being a spoilt brat . . . ?'

'Ah,' Raf smiled. 'The *what-if* factor.'

Zara stared.

'For every action we take,' said Raf, 'there's probably a better one.'

'Does that apply to this?'

'Which this?' Raf demanded. '*Us this or this this*?' The sweep of his hand took in the coughing and restless shuffle of feet beyond the screen.

'Both,' said Zara.

In a different world Raf might have answered that there was nothing he'd do differently where Zara was concerned, not even his jilting her which put Zara across the front of *Iskandryia Today* and nearly cost him his life; because he loved her and had no certainty that any other course of action would have led him to where he stood; but Murad turned and caught Raf's eye and the words went unsaid.

Checking his watch, Raf listened to something in his earbead and nodded.

Three, two, one . . .

On cue, an unaccompanied voice rose in the salon outside. *Maaloof al andalusi*, the music Ifriqiya made famous. Frail and strong, haunted and ancient. The words a lament for those who had gone before and a greeting for those who were to come after.

Near the far end of the suddenly-silenced room, Khartoum raised his head and hung a note on the air so unearthly that Hani shivered. The poem that echoed off the salon's high roof came from Rumi, the great Sufi sage but the intonation was Khartoum's own.

Slowly, one note at a time an *'aoued* filled the spaces around the words. Then an instrument that Raf thought might be a *nai*, only deeper than any flute he'd ever heard.

'Time to move,' Hani whispered.

'Yep. Everybody's waiting.' This was, Zara knew, a stupid thing for her to say. Unfortunately it was also true: five hundred carefully chosen people were waiting on the far side of that screen to see the proclamation of the new Emir. A ritual intentionally designed to mix Western with North African traditions.

For religious reasons the proclamation needed to happen in the salon de comeras, the hall of ambassadors, rather than the

Zitouna mosque, because women and men could not be allowed to mix in the mosque and, anyway, letting *nasrani* into the prayer hall would outrage the mullahs.

Officially the beards were no longer a problem, Kashif's arrest and subsequent suicide had seen to that. Major Gide's interim report suggested reality was different. The fundamentalist tendency would remain quiet only for as long as their embarrassment lasted at having backed a man given to treachery and wicked living.

'Come on . . .' Zara was shaking Raf's arm.

And as Khartoum's voice rose to a note as ethereal as waves against rock and then ended abruptly, leaving only silence, Murad said, 'We can't do this.'

'What?'

'We just can't.' There was a sadness in Murad's voice, a maturity at odds with the anxious smile on his thin face. This was a boy who'd sat holding his father's hand while the old man died: a boy who'd insisted on attending not just the funeral of his father, as was expected but also of his brother, after Kashif shot himself through the head. Three times. The funeral of Lady Maryam, who succumbed to the same flu that killed the Emir, he refused outright to attend. And that took a different kind of strength.

'Look at us,' Murad said.

Age was more than a simple sum of years. Into the load went experience and modes of survival. Strength could be learnt and adopted or developed through necessity and nothing tempered it faster than learning to stay alive.

Murad nodded towards the hidden crowd. Then swept his gaze across Hani, Zara and Raf, finally ending with a glance at a mirror which showed a twelve-year-old boy in a tight uniform, stars of gold and enamel across his narrow chest.

'Look at what I'm wearing . . .'

Murad's new uniform, identical to one worn by Raf, was based around an Egyptian version of the old British cavalry tunic, borrowed by an earlier Emir and introduced as court dress. No North African or Ottoman regiment had ever gone into battle wearing such clothes. Its use was strictly ceremonial. The only difference was Murad's lack of shades.

'I don't support this,' said Murad. 'I didn't think you did.' He looked sadly at Hani reflected in the mirror. 'And I don't want to be part of it. I refuse to become Emir.' Lifting a felt tarboosh from his head, the boy nodded to a guard. The hat Murad held was inlaid with gold thread and seeded around its base with tiny fresh-water pearls. Pinned to the front was a priceless diamond spray of feathers. The *chelengk* a recent sign of favour from the Sultan in Stambul.

The guard who reached out to take it retreated at a scowl from Raf.

'You have it then,' Murad said and Raf shook his head.

'Wrong size,' said Raf. 'And anyway it belongs to you.'

'Why?' Murad asked, and everyone looked at Raf.

That was the real question. All of Raf's life had been leading up to this, it seemed to him. Standing in an alcove off a crowded salon de cameras, off-loading his responsibilities onto a child. Which was one way to look at it. The other was that Raf was trying desperately to do the right thing in a situation where there was no right thing to do.

'This is difficult,' he said.

'Really,' said Hani. And when Raf nodded she sighed. 'That was irony,' she said.

Beyond the screen, Khartoum's voice edged into the silence and soared away, stilling the crowd again. '*Ya bay.*' Raf caught the word in a refrain and lost the meaning as he looked down and saw Murad still waiting for his answer.

'You think it should be me,' Raf said, not bothering to make it a question. They'd been through this. None of them believed there should be an Emir to start with, but that wasn't really the point. A coup had been averted.

A new era had arrived.

The last of the UN sanctions had been lifted that morning.

Five hundred people were waiting within the salon for sight of Ifriqiya's child ruler. A hundred thousand filled the streets. Camera crews wandered the Medina recording anything

and everything for worldwide syndication. There were two
members of the German Imperial Family, a first cousin to
the Sublime Porte, the President of the United States, both
Presidents of Russia and the Prince Imperial of France, despite
his recent disgrace. All gathered to welcome Ifriqiya back into
the family of nations.

As squabbling, incestuous and venal a group as ever existed.

In thirty years the country hadn't seen half that number of
VIPs. Hell, even one VIP would have been more than Ifriqiya
had seen in thirty years. The ice age was over and the state's
political and diplomatic purdah had been quietly brought to
an end.

At a high cost, a fact not doubted by any of those who stood
in the alcove; although they differed in their understanding as
to how high and what they now discussed was, if one were
honest, who should be the first to pay.

'The problem,' said Raf, crouching until his face was level
with Murad's own, 'is that your father was not my father.'

That got their attention.

'Yes he was,' Murad insisted.

'No.' Raf shook his head. 'I've known this for days. One of us
had Emir Moncef as a father. The other didn't.' From his pocket,
Raf pulled a sheet of paper folded into three and Hani, being
Hani, recognised it for what it was. A sanguinity report.

'This is your father's DNA,' Raf said to Murad as he pointed
to a column down one side of the slip. 'And this is your own,'
he pointed to the next. 'And this third one is mine. You can see
there is no relationship between the first two and the third. My
mother was not your mother and my father was not your father,
we are not even cousins.'

'I don't understand,' said Murad, face crumpling. 'Who are
you then?'

'My mother once told me my father was a Swedish hiker.
That's probably as true as anything else she ever told me.'

The boy nodded, a movement so small as to be almost
imperceptible. And then, meeting Raf's eyes, he nodded again,
his second nod firmer, more confident.

'Give me that printout,' he ordered.

Without a word Raf handed Murad the DNA results. Instead of looking at them, the boy ripped them in two, did it again and then one more time, struggling in his final attempt.

'You're my cousin,' he said in a voice that allowed no room for argument. Only Murad's eyes, made larger than ever by sadness, betrayed him.

'And your bodyguard,' added Raf. 'Should you need one.'

Hani raised her eyebrows.

'I thought you might enjoy living in Tunis,' Raf said. He didn't quite glance at Murad as he said this but Hani scowled anyway. And he got the feeling she might have stuck out her tongue, if Murad hadn't been watching. 'Or we could commute between here and El Isk,' added Raf, 'if that works better for everyone . . .'

Zara's face was unreadable.

Beyond the screen, Khartoum fell into expectant silence and the guards around the edges of the alcove strained forward as if they might toss Murad's group into the waiting hall themselves so worried was Major Gide's expression.

Hani, Zara and Raf began to move. Only to stop when Murad held up his hand.

'I go up there alone,' he announced. That wasn't how it had been planned or practised in dry run after dry run, but Murad's voice was firm as he stepped through a gap between wall and marble screen. 'It's my responsibility.'

'And us?' Hani asked. 'What are we expected to do?' There was hurt in her eyes and her chin was up. Had Murad not been on the point of walking out in front of the world he'd have had a serious fight on his hands. One look at the boy's face showed he understood that.

They were children, Raf reminded himself; balanced on the cliff edge of puberty, behaving as adults because that was what politics required of them. In a different world there might be other answers and other systems that worked better. But they were here, in the salon de cameras in Tunis. And this was all the world they had.

'Well?' said Hani.

'You come with me,' Murad said, compromising. 'When we get to the two steps you stop and I'll stand at the top.'

Hani considered this.

'No,' she said, 'You walk ahead when we go out but I climb the steps and stand just behind you.'

Murad sighed.

'And us?' Zara asked.

Hani and Murad looked at each other.

Raf and Zara went first. Walking through the silence beneath infinitely repeating muqarnas vaulting, inset with imported roundels of flying babies. Although the cherubim had the wooden rounds to themselves, an elegant script edged the space where ceiling and tiled wall joined. It said what the *Fatiha* always said, words which had echoed across the sands of North Africa for centuries.

Bringing war, civilisation, coffee and the veil. Poetry and bloodshed. Algebra, an understanding of the physical working of the human body and civil war. No worse or better, in Raf's opinion, than the beliefs it replaced or competed against.

Although maybe the words were more beautiful.

'In the name of God, the merciful, the compassionate . . .'

They walked in silence. Zara staring straight ahead.

Her parents were sat near the front but by a side wall. A position chosen to reflect Hamzah Effendi's vast fortune whilst not ignoring the occasionally dubious nature of its gathering.

Hamzah smiled, proud and slightly disbelieving.

Zara stalked by without noticing.

Two rows ahead, Koenig Pasha, whom Raf still thought of as the General, sat beside Tewfik Pasha, whose ghost of a beard and moustache were now almost manifest. The Khedive and the General had been busy ignoring each other ever since His Highness decided to dispense with the General's position as Iskandryia's Governor. Suggesting they sit side by side had been Raf's way of breaking the ice. Just ahead of them, assorted uberViPs squatted the front two rows, except for three seats left blank on the right; one should have been Hani's but obviously she wouldn't be needing it.

Raf stood back to let Zara go first and the look she gave him was hurt and slightly disbelieving. There were tears in her eyes. Although once she realised he'd noticed, she started to scowl.

'What have I done now?' Raf whispered.

'How could you say that to Murad?' she said. 'And how long before Hani realises that if you're not Murad's half-brother then you can't be . . .'

'Her uncle?' Raf asked.

Zara's nod was abrupt.

'What will you tell her?' she demanded.

A smile just wide enough to create laughter lines lit Raf's face. 'I'll tell her the truth,' he said, leaning close. 'And then swear her to secrecy.' Behind him Raf could hear a double shuffle of footsteps where the aisle started at huge double doors neither Murad or Hani had actually passed through.

'The truth being what?'

'That I *am* her uncle,' whispered Raf, 'but Murad is not her cousin.' He took Zara's hand and though it lay slightly unwilling in his own she didn't try to remove it.

Who had gone to whom with what, Raf had found impossible to discover from the secret files. Somewhere in the mix was the Emir, his mother and Bayer Rochelle who'd been working on cerebral transplants, the operation that killed Emir Moncef and left Eugenie de la Croix with a dead commander, international pressure to open labs that could not possibly be revealed to the world and a frightened Swedish hitchhiker as his replacement.

Obvious really, when one thought about it.

And Lady Maryam hadn't been the only woman Eugenie had refused to let see the ersatz Emir. Raf's mother had been the other.

He spoke quickly and very quietly, always aware of the footsteps getting closer. Khartoum, who still stood at the front, both silent and watchful in a simple woollen robe, watched Raf and Zara with interest; when he saw Raf had noticed, the old man flicked one hand in quick greeting and smiled.

'Eugenie knew this?'

'Of course.'

As Murad and Hani reached Micki Vanhoffer, the large American burst into tears and wrung Carl Senior's fingers until he almost joined in. 'They're going to get married,' she told the Japanese ambassador sitting next to her, who only stopped being appalled when Carl Senior leaned over his wife's ample lap to explain that this wasn't likely to happen for some years yet, if at all.

'Okay?' Hani demanded.

Murad nodded.

She could hear her cousin humming softly as he climbed first one marble step and then another, stopping at the point where his proclamation could begin. It took Hani a second or two to recognise the tune.

Emir Murad al-Mansur, Ifriqiya's ruler and bey of Tunis was humming the chant from *Revolt into Nakedness*, street song of North Africa's disposed. The new Cheb Rai/Ragged Republic version obviously.

He'd managed to find it that morning on his radio.

Acknowledgements

Thanks to the Pathology Guy for information on human decomposition. Hassan in Tunis for taking me up onto the roof of the souk to look at the Great Mosque of Zitouna. Aziza and Hafida, cooks from the Maison Arabe (Marrakech) for not laughing too much at my attempt to make chicken tagine. Antony Bourdain for writing the best insider book on kitchens ever written (plus some seriously sick/slick crime novels). The Yugoslav girl with no knickers in the kitchens at Oslo airport for giving me the idea of the knife. And the soldier on the train outside Palermo who insisted on showing the backpacker opposite his scars.

A tip of the hat to the usual lunchtime crowd, including Kim Newman, Paul McAuley, China Mieville, M John Harrison and Pat Cadigan (all of whom I'd happily buy in hardback). New Scientist again, obviously enough, for the usual reasons. Farah Mendlesohn, for providing supper everytime I finish a script. JJ for commissioning the Ashraf Bey novels in the first place. Jane Holland for editorial skills. Darren Nash for marketing brilliance and Jess Gulliver for getting them out to reviewers.

Finally, thanks to Moritz, for letting me steal his name on a couple of occasions. (The deaths were nothing personal . . .)